THE ARCHER QUEEN

HOUSE OF ROMANTASY

E. P. Bali's
House of Romantasy

This first edition published in 2023 by
Blue Moon Rising Publishing
www.ektaabali.com

ISBN ebook: 978-0-6455686-8-4
Paperback: 978-0-6456909-6-5
Hardcover: 978-0-6456909-7-2
Paperback (Pastel Edition): 978-0-6456909-8-9
Hardcover (Pastel Edition): 978-0-6457846-6-4

Illustrated Cover design by Carly Diep
Naked Hardcover by Etheric Designs
Map artwork by Najlakay
Chapter Art by Etheric Designs
Book Formatting by E.P. Bali with Vellum

The author acknowledges the Traditional Custodians of the land where this book was written. We acknowledge their connections to land, sea and community. We pay our respects to their Elders past and present and extend that respect to all Aboriginal and Torres Strait Islander Peoples today.

A NOTE ON THE CONTENT

I care about the mental health of my readers.
This book contains some themes you might want to know
about before you read.
They are listed at www.ektaabali.com / themes

E.P. BALI

THE ARCHER QUEEN

BOOK 3
OF
THE ARCHER PRINCESS
TRILOGY

THE ELLYTHIAN ISLES

THE GREAT
WESTERN OCEAN

LOTA CITY

LOTA ISLAND

TIGER ISLAND

LEVU VILLAGE

GULAB VILLAGE

JUNGLE
SCHOOL   TARAKA TOWN

THE LOTUS

SEA

BONEWEAVER ISLAND

HUMAN REALM

OBSIDIAN COURT

MIDNIGHT COURT

REALM OF THE DARK FAE

BLACK COURT

FARLOUGH CITY

SERUS

PEACH TREE CITY

KAALON

LUMINOUS QUARTZ QUARRY

LOBRATHIA

QUARTZ

THE TEMARI FOREST

TEMPLE RUINS

THE SILENT MOUNTAINS

ECLIPSE COURT

SAMPATI CITY

KUSHA

TRAENARA

SHOBNA CITY

WAELAN

BALNOR CITY

THE LOTUS SEA

ELLYTHIA

LOTA

THE JUNGLE ACADEMY

Pronouncination Guide

—❖—❖◦❖◦❖◦❖—❖—

Agnolthi: *Agg noll thee*: The Goddess of beasts and birds. Altara's patron Goddess.

Altara: *Al Taa ruh:* The second-born Voltanius princess

Atax: *Ay tacks*: one of Zale's brothers-in-arms. His Commander

Bhairavi: *Bhay rah vee:* Ellythia's General, high priestess of Xalya

Camar Lafaro: *Cum ar*: Pia's ex-bethrothed. Maimed with excessive power sharing

Cherimani: *Cherry mah nee*: The maiden/trickster Goddess

Cheshni: *Chesh nee*: Queen of Ellythia, Yasani's mother

Cholnayak: *Choll nai ukh*: The crone Goddess

Daanav: *Daah nuv*: Blue-skinned marine demons from under the Lotus Sea

Ellythia: *Ill ith ee uh:* An magical tropical Island Queendom west of The Continent

Falja: *Fal juh*: High Priestess of Lisanthi

Geravie: *Jer ah vi*: Altara and Saraya's elderly Ellythian nursemaid

Gulaab: *Gul aahb*: A coastal village on Boneweaver Island

Harranpul: *Har ann pull*: Geravie's house

Jaya: *Jay uh*: High Priestess of Cherimani

Jessine: *Jess eene*: Headmistress of the exile school

Kai: *K eye*: Zale's brother-in-arms with white hair

Keshmi: *K air sh mee*: A priestess of Agnolthi's temple on Boneweaver Island

Kraasputin: *Krasss piu tin:* A fae monster

Levu: *Lair voo:* An northern village on Boneweaver Island

Lisanthi: *Liss ahn thee:* The Mother Goddess

Lobrathia: *Lo brath ee uh:* The south-eastern most human kingdom of the Continent

PRONOUNCINATION GUIDE

Malika Yashra: *Maah lick uh Yaash ruh*: A student of the exile school

Naina: *Nay nuh*: The name Altara gives to her mating mark

Odeelia: *Oh dee lee uh*: Queen of the Carnal Fae Court

Othar Dhumvar: *Oath uh Dhoom varr*: High Priestess of Cholnayak

Pia Lota: *Pee uh Loh tuh*: The exiled Lota princess

Rahana: *Raa ha na*: Pia's mother, the Crown Princess of Ellythia

Rassul: *Ra sool*: One of Camar's friends, nobility

Reshmi: *Resh mee:* One of the priestess twins of Agnolthi's temple at Boneweaver Island

Rani Umasri: *Raah nee Umar sree*: An student at the exile school

Raen: *Ray en*: Zale's brother-in-arms. His mage

Saraya: *Sar eye uh:* The eldest Voltanius princess

Taraka: *Tar uh ka*: Southern most town on Boneweaver Island. The "capital".

Trisane: *Tris ayne*: Nobility. Etiquette Teacher at the exile school

Ulanna: *Ul ah nah:* Female leader of the Old Ones in the Eternal Forest

Ulfas: Ull fuss: Male leader of the Old Ones in the Eternal Forest

Umali: *Oo mah lee:* Goddess of Chaos and Rage

Vayashi: *Vay ah shee*: A person who holds magic for another

Xalya: *Zal ya:* Goddess of war and weapons

Yasani: *Yuss ah nee*: ex-queen of Ellythia. Altara's mother

Zale:(rhymes with gale): The Crown Prince of the Old Ones

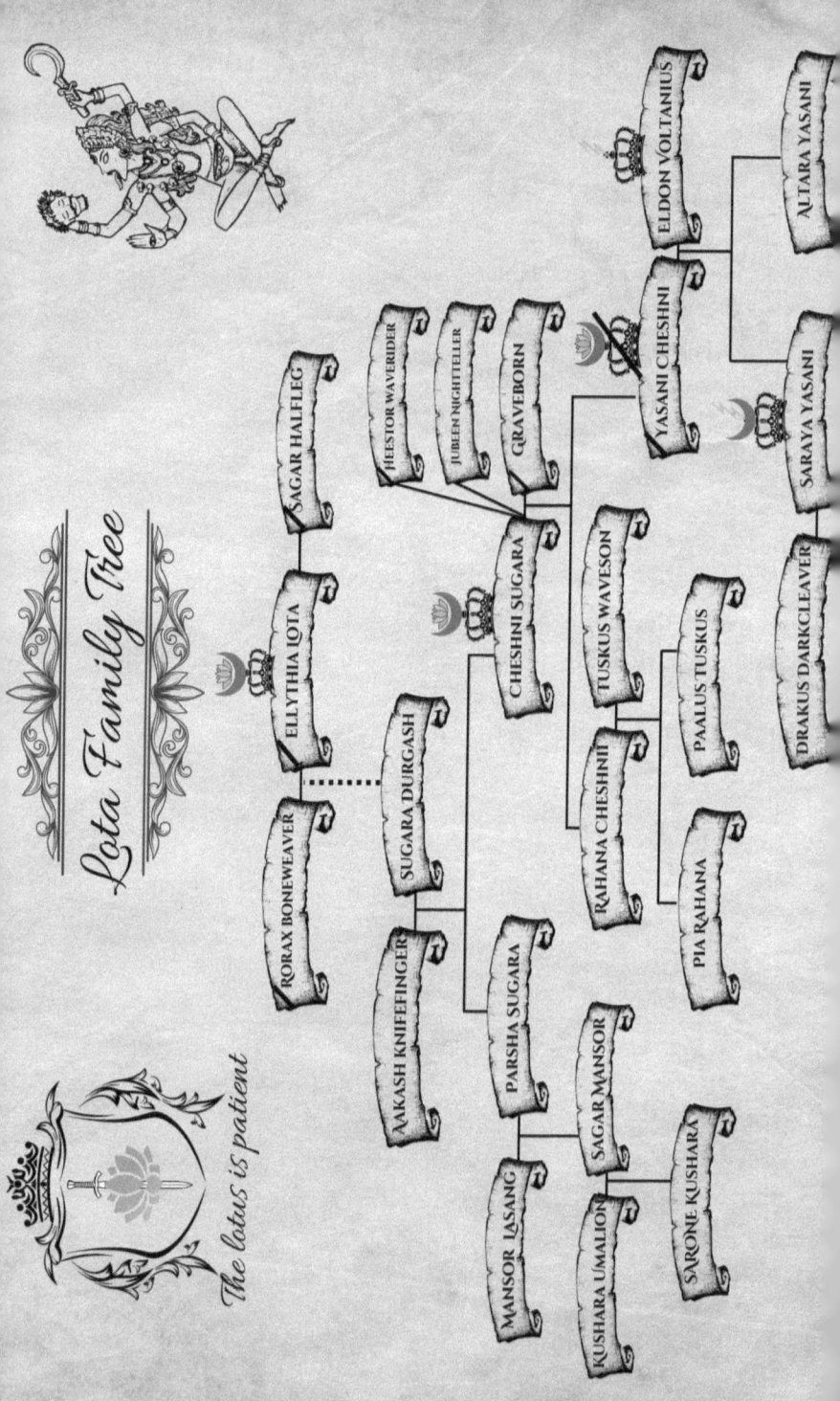

Lota Family Tree

The lotus is patient

Bonewearer Family Tree

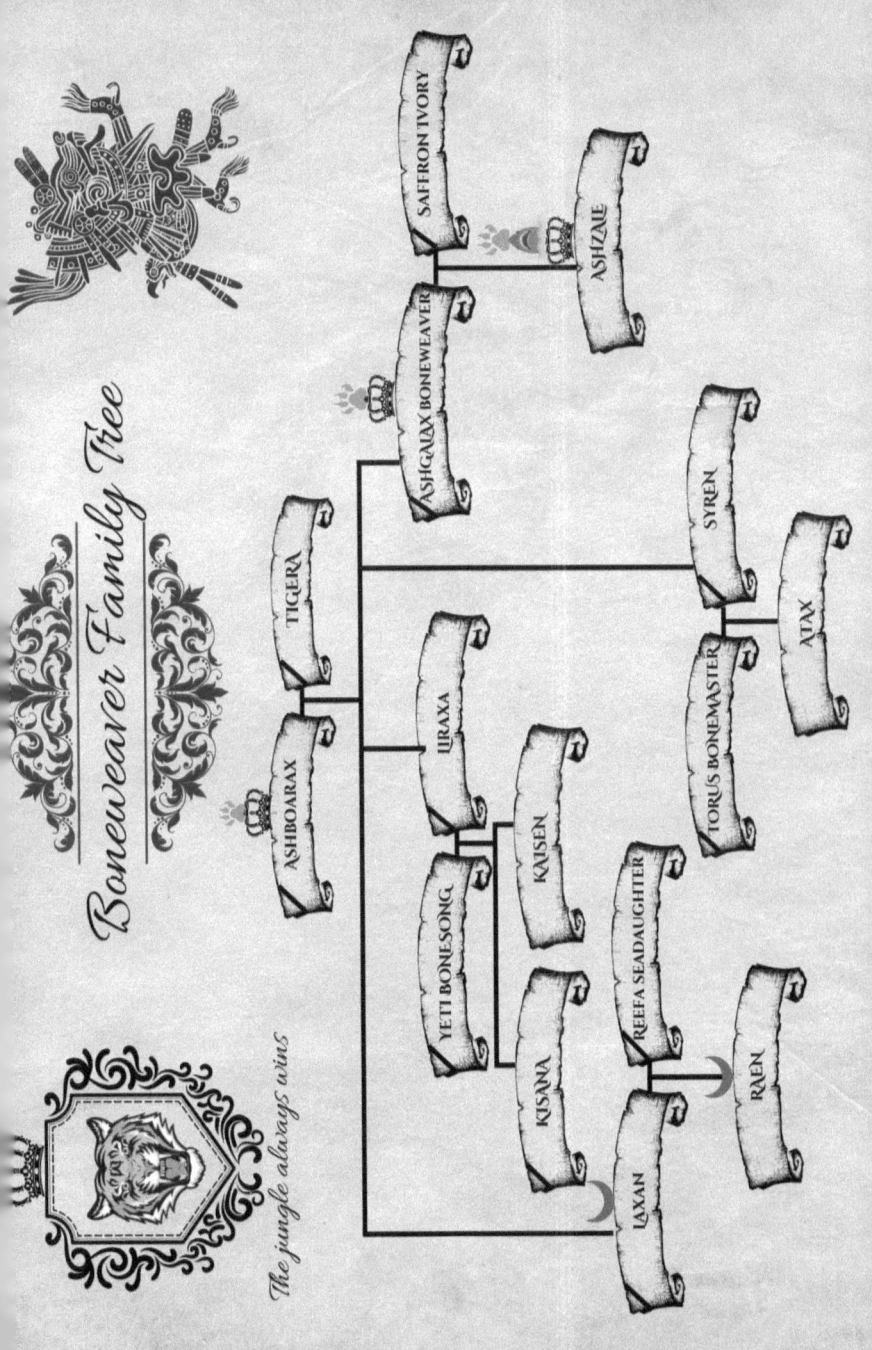

The jungle always wins

SAFFRON IVORY

ASHGALAX BONEWEAVER

ASHZALE

ASHBOARAX

TIGERA

URAXA

SYREN

TORUS BONEMASTER

ATAX

YETI BONESONG

KAUSEN

KISANA

REEFA SEADAUGHTER

LAXAN

RAEN

For those of us who yearn for happy endings.

ALTARA

He sat on a throne of twisted black metal, the armrests made of the skulls of old demonic kings with curled horns. Alabaster hands rested atop the skulls, his body hidden by a robe of midnight shadow. Six blood-red eyes set in that cadaverous face looked out over the sea of demons, fallen to their knees in submission.

Sometimes they called him the Reaper. Other times, the Green General or Emperor. More recently, God.

The entire hall was silent, and that was the worst thing of all because demons were *never* silent, not in the time that I had observed them in the week we'd spent in the demon realm. I stood at the base of the high steps with Zale by my side. He was always by my side now, always angled towards me, snarling at anyone who got too close, always aware of my every movement, my every breath. Tonight, his tattooed, muscled torso was splattered with demon blood, the black of it melding with the black ink on his skin, making him look like a whole new sort of monster. On the other side of the throne steps stood Atax and Raen, the former similarly splattered with blood and the latter ever-clean, despite the fact they'd both killed tonight.

Before us, Kai knelt over the newly dead demon king. It was lucky I'd had the forethought to braid his hair back because his entire face and body was smeared with black splashes. Where Raen was a clean killer and Atax a brutal one, Kai was a messy, chaotic whirlwind of death. And carving out a demon's heart was no clean task.

Determinedly, I kept my eyes forward and away from my youngest brother-in-law, my hand clasped in front of me in an effort to stop the trembling.

My father would have called it the veteran's tremble. It was memory, biting and aching and severed of all reason. It was not me on that floor, after all. Not me being cut open by the Butcher. It was just Kai. It was just Kai. It was just Kai.

The shadows surrounded me, a layer of spider silk clinging to my body like a second skin. Before, those shadows protected me from the world, pulling me down into the abyss of my own doom until I could barely function. I'd let them control me. Let them take me over.

Now, I commanded them. Now, I was the one in control.

And I let them surround me like a weapon.

The air was thick with sour demon odour and sweat, but luckily for me, my shadows muffled my smelling ability too. I was a wraith, once again, and my husband, a monster of the night; cruel, vicious and cold. Cold most of all.

Zale stood as a king did, for nothing could ever take away the kingly grace from that warrior's body, but he somehow managed to move discreetly closer to me. A tiny change in the angle of his torso and I suddenly felt safe. Here, in this hall of hundreds of demons, that should have been impossible, and yet my hands stopped trembling and my heart slowed to a steady thump.

Kai leapt to his feet with a small giggle and held the whole bloody heart of the demon king for all to see. A prize. The cost of not falling in line. The demons all looked up at him, thrust their fists in the air, and roared.

The ground beneath my feet vibrated as Kai turned around and ran up the steps to the black throne and bent on one knee, presenting the Reaper with the still warm black heart.

Zale and I turned to look as the crowd behind us snarled and roared in their guttural demon voices. The Reaper inclined his head to Kai and patted his cheek with a sort of fondness that grated at my insides. Kai's cheeks were round with his grin before the Reaper took the heart in one hand and set it alight with vibrant green flames.

"All hail the Reaper!" Raen cried.

"Reaper. Reaper. Reaper."

The message it sent was clear. To disobey meant something worse than death. It meant annihilation.

The Reaper stood and Kai scampered back down the steps to come and stand next to Zale and I. Unable to look at Kai, somehow still sweet as a child, I watched the Reaper raise his arms to signal quiet.

The crowd obeyed like obedient dogs.

Without a visible mouth, the Reaper's voice appeared inside our minds. *"The demon realm is mine."* It was rasping, cold and quiet, like a chilled knife against the brain. *"The Dark Fae Realm is mine. And soon, the Human Realm will fall to me."* I tried not to stiffen against this information. Tried not to remember that my sister had been there, in Black Court with her new husband, Drakus Silverhand. *"He who holds the*

3

Quartz Quarry holds the power of the continent. Together, we will unite human, demon and fae in a new utopia under my name. My power will be infinite. My empire will reign supreme." He pointed to Zale with one long finger and my husband turned around to face the demons. I followed suit.

"Ashzale Boneweaver will lead the forces to take the Ellythian Isles. With human mages as our slaves, I will be unstoppable."

Sounds of surprise and excitement tittered amongst the demons. They had not expected this, I realised. Demons had been trying to take Ellythia for two thousand years and had been unsuccessful. Once, it had been a fanciful dream for them. But now, with Zale?

Zale's voice rung out deep and commanding. "Under my command, the Reaper will take Ellythia!"

The roar was deafening and all I could do was sink further into my shadows.

WE DEPARTED THAT DEMON PALACE, FOLLOWING THE REAPER outside into the forever-dark of the Demon Realm. The sky glowed a dull rust red through the smoky wisps of my shadows, as if the very sky were bleeding along with the old, rebel king of this court.

My husband and his brothers were silent, lethal warriors who now obeyed every command their black hearts and the Reaper gave them. There was murder in their hearts and violence in their veins and the power they bore was unlike anything I'd ever felt. It made me want to flee, but at the same time, it drew me closer to them.

The Reaper headed towards the chariot he travelled in,

stationed just outside the black palace. It was a golden-green flying vehicle made for war, thick metal twisted into demonic and fae patterns, impervious to assault. Tied to it were tied two winged zekar mounts, cousins to the horse, only monstrous, and with an acute intelligence that allowed them to talk to those who could understand.

Zale and Raen had flown in next to him, with me on Zale's back and Atax and Kai on Raen's massive black raven form. Zale refused to have anyone except me seated upon him, and despite what was no doubt a heavy load to carry, Raen never showed any sign of strain during flight.

As Zale and Raen prepared to shift, the Reaper's voice rung out in our heads. *"Princess Altara will ride with me."*

I tensed at the same time Zale did. But his response was not out of retaliation. As his mate, a primitive part of him wanted me to always be at his side. But he now defected to the Reaper as his personal god. Every order the Reaper gave, Zale was only happy to obey, that black bond sharp and strong between them. Zale reached down and pressed his lips to my neck—a silent reminder of his claim to me.

Suppressing a sigh, I followed the Reaper to his chariot and climbed in to stand by him. The smell of burnt flesh singed my nose, and I allowed a tendril of smoke to hover over my upper lip. The smell receded, but the Reaper's heavy, malevolent force weighed me down like a foreign, suffocating blanket.

He flicked the reins of his chariot and the two monstrous zekar stallions lurched into a rabid gallop, their wings angled behind them. I gripped onto the gilded edge of the chariot with fierce knuckles to avoid keeling over while my witch's boots kept my legs in place.

With powerful downward beats of their wings and the

zing of the Reaper's sour magic, we ascended into the air, the demons below cheering and stomping their feet. Nausea roiled in my stomach, but I determinedly held firm, focusing on the mating mark on the back of my right hand, Zale's blue-eyed tiger.

I'd come to discover that it liked to change and move. To my delight, and much like Zale, the tiger turned on my hand and bounded up my wrist and onto my arm. Sometimes, I had to search for it on my body, but she would come into view like she knew I was looking and settle back down upon my hand. I wondered if Zale knew, but no doubt he would find it satisfying that his mark was roaming my body, just as possessive as he.

The real Zale flew close behind us in his eagle form, and I felt his eyes burning on my back as we flew, the golden thread between us humming with irritation at our distance.

It was unnatural, how the sky here was always dark and starless, and I could almost understand why the demons wanted to leave this place and colonise above ground. They might not be able to survive the daylight, but at least the stars might have been a comfort.

"What can you tell me about Saraya Voltanius?" The Reaper asked in a husky voice that hit my eardrums with a *very real* scrape.

My head snapped towards him, and not even my extensive court training could stop my mouth from gaping.

In place of the six-eyed monstrosity was a strikingly handsome fae prince, six and a half feet tall, with green swirling eyes, a perfect aquiline nose, and a smirking, masculine mouth. He really was a fae prince, I realised. Had been once, anyway.

The malefic, predatory feeling remained, however, and

any person with sense enough would never miss the evil presence behind those eyes. I gulped, reminding myself that if he wore a mask for me now, it was only because he was trying to appeal to my womanly instincts.

Tough luck on that one; no man had ever come close to Zale's lethal masculine beauty.

I cleared my throat to answer his question and turned to look out at the flying zekar. So, he wanted information on my sister, *that* was interesting. "My sister is like me, I suppose. A warrior born and bred."

"She is *not* like you." His voice bore a cold sort of melody that chilled my insides. "Though you are both like me in your own way."

I stopped myself from raising my brows. And gagging. "How so?"

"Her husband is a being made to be a fulcrum upon which the time shifts. Upon which destiny shifts."

It was almost poetry, and this news was very surprising. "Her husband?"

"Drakus Silverhand is a creature of destiny. Saraya Voltanius is his mate. His equal. The other half of the coin. She is essential."

The way he spoke about her made my neck prickle. My older sister had always seemed like the sort of person who was... well, invincible. She took the pain of our stepmother for so long. Endured and yet still remained strong. I supposed it made sense that she was *mate* to a creature like Drakus.

"That makes sense," I admitted. "She always had an air of power to her."

"And then there is you."

My stomach fell at his tone, and then he turned to look at me and I felt as if my very organs had been put out on a table

7

for his inspection. I remained so still that I thought I might disappear into nothing.

"You and I are the same because you have the same seed of darkness I was born with. You know pain, Altara Yasani Boneweaver."

My mother's name in his voice made me want to retch. A sacred name made into a curse. But I abated my anger.

"Even now, you fight it. There is a darkness in you that will never be destroyed. I must thank the Butcher for it. Without him, you would not be here with me, fighting for our freedom."

A sharp pain in my palm was the only thing that told me my fingernails were cutting into it.

"You want to kill him." A low chuckle. "In my new world, Altara, the weak get eaten by the strong. If you can kill him, I will bless it."

A shiver crawled down my spine, and not in a good way. He thanked the Butcher, and yet he would approve of my revenge. The thought made bile rise in my throat at the pure evil in that. The Reaper approved of me. Tears burned the back of my eyes, but I would die before I let them fall, here in the Reaper's fucking chariot.

"Turn from your Goddess to me," he continued. "And you will have more power than she could ever give you."

Not in one million fucking years.

2

RANI

If Umali, the raging Goddess, was the chaos that came before the end, Cholnayak, the crone, *was* the end. She was the great eternal force that existed before everything began and the latent power who lies in silent repose after everything ends. It is she who stands at the Gates of Death with her mighty scythe, ready to welcome souls into eternity.

I found my solace in the arms of her temple and the White Widows who ruled it, with their quiet strength, dedication to the dead, and understanding eyes. But no matter how diligently I cleaned, how hard I meditated, or how carefully I tended to the bodies of the dead, my nightmare remained the same.

Worse still, the High Priestess of Cholnayak demanded I sit in her temple office and tell her about it.

"What is it that you see?" asked the high priestess, Othar Dhumvar, her grey eyes fixing me to the spot like Cholnayak's own scythe where I sat in her bare bones office. There was nothing much in it, as was the way of the renunciate. A plain wooden table and two chairs with a single framed sketch of Cholnayak on the wall behind her, silver eyes always assessing.

"It's always the pure green field of my parent's estate," I said dully. "It was dotted with daisies by the river. Sometimes Yulara and I would dangle our feet in there." I wouldn't normally go into so much detail, but the high priestess insisted upon hearing it all. And I found in the telling of it, a little of the wound inside of me softened. "And then it was as it happened. I was walking along the riverbank as the sun set. Some of the village boys were sailing little boats on the river, but they were collecting them up to start making their way home. Vasi remained behind when he saw me. He had one of those big smiles that showed all of his little teeth. A sweet boy." I sighed, rubbing my eyes. Making me repeat this over and over again was, in truth, also getting a little tiring. "And then we were alone. It was getting dark, so, in the dream, I said something like, 'Let's get home. Your mother will have my head if you are home after dark.' But he just looked up at me like I was... I don't know, like I'm everything he wanted to be, and he says, 'But if I'm with you, I won't ever be in danger.' That's the worst of it, because before I know it, I'm on my knees, and Vasi is all floppy in my arms, one of my own metal spikes spearing him right through the middle." I swallowed the lump in my throat and met the high priestess' eyes.

"What else?" she pressed.

"That's it." I shrugged.

She made an annoyed sound. "But there is something that comes between the smiling and the death."

I grimaced as that slicing pain entered my heart. "The dream never shows me what happened in between. But there were three demons who'd swum ashore and snuck onto the estate. I'd never seen them, not up close like that; their blue skin, their fangs. I reacted on instinct and the spikes appeared. They were all dead within seconds."

Othar was silently nodding, her knobbly hands clasped on her desk. "Including little Vasi."

I swallowed and stared into my lap. "When will the pain go away?" I whispered. "When will I... be able to... live with it?"

"You are living now, Rani. You will always remember it, until you are as old as me. I believe that if it wasn't him, it would have been someone else."

I stared at her, because that's all I could do.

"And you've never lost control of your power since?"

"I did, in the weeks after, but at Taraka School, Armsmistress Vari worked with me daily to learn to control my emotions. The only time it happened was when Pia, Altara, Malika and I were attacked by Daanavs and Malika got shot. The arrows appeared in a close circle around me, but no one got hurt by them."

"The vision of your friend being shot with a demon arrow did it," she mused.

I glared at her for her flippant attitude. "I took an innocent life, High Priestess." My voice was low and cold.

"You have a dangerous gift," she said, all trace of amusement gone from her voice though her eyes glittered, "but a gift nonetheless. Cholnayak given, no doubt. A heavy weight that you will carry with you forever. Such is your power. Such is your responsibility."

My sigh was long and laboured. "I'm coming to understand that."

"And here we are. You will continue with the task I have set out for you. You will continue to learn the weight of responsibility. You may mourn as you wish, as long as you do not shirk your duty."

"I will." My hands curled into determined fists.

She waved her hand at me to leave. I stood, bowed, and left the room as fast as I could.

This entire time, I'd thought my power was metal working. To manipulate the metallic elements. But I'd been wrong. My power had been made for *weapons*. Because everything that I created could be used to kill.

IN THE DARK, I HURRIED ACROSS THE COURTYARD BETWEEN THE huge white marble temple and the long double storey building that made up the female dormitories. It had been peaceful here once, I imagined. A place of quiet contemplation. But now was not a time of peace. It was a time of war.

The air now permanently hummed with magic as every citizen of Ellythia, right from the youngest children to the most experienced mages, prepared to protect our Queendom. Xalya's general and the senior priestesses of Agnolthi had their sectors running attack and defence drills all day and all night.

It stung the skin, just a little, as if the very atmosphere were primed and ready for attack. Somewhere out on the Continent, I thought, Umali's high priestess was also preparing for war. Somewhere, Altara's sister was working to save her own kingdom. We needed Umali even more than we needed the other six, and Ellythia had never, in its history, seen war without the Goddess of rage and chaos.

This is a lot of what I'd been thinking about this past week since Altara had left with the Old Ones and the Reaper.

Kai's face haunted me most of all.

In my whitewashed room with a single window, on my hard, narrow bed, I spent my nights tossing and turning, my heart swathed in a sort of mad turmoil, my dreams making everything worse.

That night, yet again, I dreamed the second dream plaguing my mind. A crimson pool stretched towards me, and in it I saw my own lanky reflection. As I gazed into my own horrified eyes, a high-pitched scream sent me reeling. On and on it went until I was sure my heart would shatter into a hundred pieces, sending piercing shards into my spine. Shards that I would never be able to put back together.

After the screaming came the silence.

The clanging bell of dawn hurtled through the air and I woke with a start, drenched with sweat, a crumpled parchment clutched in my fist as if I'd grabbed it to fight off the nightmares.

Dawn light spilled through the open shutters. The Ellythian sun was always a pleasant glow, but today's sunrise held a strange crimson tint. I cringed and rolled to sitting at the edge of my bed and smoothed open the parchment.

Kai's deft charcoal strokes made an image that struck me in the heart every time I looked upon it. And every time I asked myself the same question.

Why?

He'd drawn Yulara and me, hand in hand, laughing with a type of happiness that was impossible. Yulara was happily married, our betrothal wreath sliced open and kicked to the dirt alongside my heart. She'd replaced me, and I had no reason to blame her. I was to blame for the single most awful

13

thing to happen to her family. She had never spoken to me after the incident, never responded to my letters.

I rubbed my bald head, feeling the prickly surface along the callouses of my palm. I had always hated my hair. It had been unruly and difficult to tame, but a small part of me missed it. I stood in my loincloth and breast band and assumed the sequence of prescribed morning stretches. I was glad I was here as an acolyte in Cholnayak's temple, away from everyone else.

At Taraka school of exile on Boneweaver Island, my uniform had been brown pants and a pink overdress. Here, I got ready each day by wrapping a long robe about my legs in a way that made loose pants called a dhoti, then I specially draped it over my shoulders to make a cowl.

I needed my hands and legs free to move for my work. When the high priestess had asked me why I wanted to be an acolyte, I said I deserved to be punished. That she should give me the worst work. The work no one else wanted to do, that everyone dreaded, for amongst the worst of the world, that was the place that was acceptable for me to be.

She had observed me with those sharp, grey eyes and nodded. She then sent me to the place the acolytes lovingly called the Swamp. It was a place where Ellythia's most unwell criminals came to be tended. There were steel bars on the doors, and the smell of the dying and cleaning spirits permeated the air.

If they were animals, we would have put them down already. But because they had done bad, immoral things, they needed to suffer, and we needed to care for their basic needs while they did. I was not permitted to show my face or body here, and it was just as well my nose and mouth were covered. Only male monks worked here, and because of my tall and strong build, the inmates assumed I was a male too.

The death rattle of lungs was Cholnayak's song, and we heard it here every other day. It would take me a while to get used to the sounds and smells of human waste and illness and the desperate, groping hands of the forsaken. But the cleaning and caring kept my mind and body busy while my soul sought its redemption.

Once I'd attended to my main chores, I discreetly went underground to attend to my other chores as instructed by the high priestess. A secret task, she'd called it. When she explained it to me down in the bowels of the Earth, I'd had a sudden realisation that Cholnayak's high priestess was the most brilliant and morbid of the seven. That only a mind twisted and dark and yet imbued with selfless light could have come up with this.

It was that day that I also realised that fate had put me here. That I had a purpose.

3
ALTARA

Foul smells I couldn't identify filled the air as we travelled in this direction. Though, I couldn't tell *which* direction because of the lack of a sun or stars in this cursed place. The emperor of demons navigated by some magical means, because after an hour of flight, he quite obviously tugged on the reins and the two zekar angled their noses downward and we began our descent. The Reaper's presence next to me was an astronomically awful weight, his power pressing on me, as if trying to dominate the very cells of my body. He just stood there, the entire flight, still and silent; the picture of an emperor looking over his land. I couldn't imagine what he was thinking, didn't even want to know.

Zale and Raen followed us closely, the sound of their wings beating a steady, reassuring current in my ears as, just on the horizon, the obvious sight of thick black smoke billowed. Something large was on fire, and it wasn't long before I could make out what it was.

Demons of all sizes loped about amongst the torn bodies of the fallen. Kai let out a mad cackle at the sight, and I contained the urge to look back disapprovingly at him. I would have to put up with their lack of conscience and inhibition now. For warriors like them, it only meant they were more bloodthirsty than ever. Reminding myself that this crazed version of Kai wasn't really the true him was a task, and the fact that Atax egged him on and Raen and Zale were apathetic towards everything made it all the more difficult.

We flew over what looked like a military compound—a collection of low set buildings where armoured demon warriors swarmed—and headed towards the site of the burning, a mighty black palace, sprawling across the land to rival the Ellythian Lotus Palace, except for the fact that it looked like someone had tried to tear the thing apart.

As we touched down on the blackened dust, Zale shifted back into his human form and waited impatiently for me at the edge of the carriage. The Reaper stepped out first, placing a hand on Zale's shoulder. My husband's eyes slid to the Reaper's now fae ones, and he nodded solemnly in response to some silent order. The Reaper strode away and Zale all but grabbed me from the chariot, putting a heavy arm around my shoulder, possessively keeping me close as we followed after our liege lord, the other Old Ones flanking us.

A strange, sharp smell permeated the air. It was familiar in its almost ethereal scent and the realisation hit me at the same time as it did for Kai, skipping along beside me.

"It smells like Lobrathian lightning!" he said excitedly, wiggling his eyebrows at me. "From a few weeks ago, maybe."

If it weren't for Zale's firm arm around me, I would've stumbled. My shadows stuttered in awareness.

Lightning could only be produced by the Lobrathian royal line, and so far, I was the only one who'd done it in generations. The only other living Voltanius' were Saraya and our Uncle Ansel, who'd never really been present in Quartz, forever off voyaging at sea. But my mind rapidly thought of this, the demons on the compound were eyeing us and I caught their guttural mutters as we passed.

"The Lobrathian lightning princess," they said, *"destroyed Havrok's Court."*

My breath caught in my throat as the last image I had of my sister swam before my eyes. Her kind green eyes had looked upon me, telling me that she loved me and to remember our mother.

They couldn't mean... oh, but they did. My sister's power. My sister had been here, had torn down this court with *lightning*. The wing-brothers had told Zale and I this very thing. That she and her mate had been captured by demons, imprisoned and then escaped, apparently tearing the place down while they were at it. Pride shone through me as I surveyed the devastation of the place. My kind, sweet Saraya, midwife, princess, and now... she would be the lightning queen Lobrathia deserved. If she could do *this*... what else was she capable of? My shadows seemed to dissolve around me as the positive emotions whirled through my chest, but I let them go immediately, careful to keep my shadowy cloak about myself. Pia had told us that Saraya was also High Priestess for Umali, chosen by the raging Goddess as her representative and leader on Earth. Lightning in its nature was chaotic, the very essence of a storm, and it just made so much sense that she would wield that power. Not having seen her in this long made an old part of me ache. There would be a Saraya-shaped emptiness inside my chest until I could see her again.

Smaller demons were scavenging from the little that remained of the fallen demons and strange, leathery bird demons were poking through the bones. Whatever had happened here, Kai was right. It had been weeks ago. As they caught sight of the Reaper walking past them, they all stopped what they were doing to fall prostrate.

"All hail the Reaper!" one of the warrior demons roared, stabbing the air with his broadsword. Cheers followed, but the Reaper ignored them. He bent down to gather a bit of dirt between his fingers, lifting it up to his nose to inhale deeply before standing. His aura pulsed, and I somehow got the feeling that he was pleased and displeased at the same time.

A hulking demon, seven feet tall, crimson and black-skinned, with huge black ram's horns, strode down the steps of the castle with purpose. He strode right up to the Reaper and bent on one knee. "All hail the Reaper!" he said in a calm voice. "The strongest demons battled for days, Your Imperial Highness. And now, in your name, I claim this court."

I suddenly realised that his skin wasn't just crimson and black. He was covered in old blood, streaks of it staining his skin.

"What is your name?" the Reaper asked.

"Potag Yarox, Your Imperial Highness."

"Havrok Scorpax was a gullible fool. But you will not disappoint me."

"No, Great Reaper. My forces are yours to command."

While they were talking, demons of all sizes and shapes had gathered around us and muttered excitedly. Some were a sickly yellow colour, their stomachs hollowed out, their eyes bulging; others were shades of red, their eyes bloodshot, professional grade weapons in hand. They had the look of mercenaries, eager to kill. A crawling feeling covered my skin like the caress of a dirty hand. I had thought the marine demons were awful, but they were positively civilised compared to these barely clothed monsters.

They smelled like old blood and decaying flesh and suddenly there was a thump and an *oof* behind me. When I turned, a demon crumpled to the ground and Atax was wiping his obsidian blade against his pants. He grinned and shrugged at me as the demons hastily shuffled back to give us space. Zale let out a soft growl and pulled me in front of his body, encircling my waist with both arms like he owned me.

I mean, he *did* own me. I was glad to be considered his, but *I* also owned *him*. Zale leaned down through my smoke, pushed my hood aside and slowly scraped his teeth down the soft skin of my neck. I shivered under the feel of his hard body pressed behind me and his lips on me, but in this place of death, it was hard to be aroused. I realised then that there were only male demons around us and his open, claiming behaviour suddenly made sense.

There was movement ahead and the apparent new king of this demon court, Yarox, was barking orders to his surviving warriors. Within minutes, a throne was carried out, a creepy black and white twisted wood affair, upon which the Reaper sat down. Other seats were set next to his, and we sat on them. Well, Zale sat on his and roughly pulled me to sit on his lap.

The last time he'd been without a conscience, he'd not had a mate. Now that he did, the effect was at once confronting and satisfying.

With his inhibitions removed, he now brought out every possessive, obsessive and animalistic mate-bond instinct Boneweavers had, and I suspect the star-bond exacerbated it further.

He buried his nose in my neck and kept it there as if my

scent was his oxygen. His muscled arms roped around me, keeping my ass planted on his groin as if my weight on him was essential.

These things, I had learned rather quickly in the past few days, were non-negotiable. The bond between us hummed and preened under our physical closeness. I couldn't lie, I did enjoy his touch on me, but he chose the worst times to show everyone I was his—which was *all* the time.

Perhaps a tiny part of him, deep in the depths of his mind, needed my presence to keep from going completely rabid. And I could see that without me, he might become a blood-thirsty, vicious creature. He felt incredibly tense under my body, like coiled metal. As if he were a second away from committing some great act of violence and only my presence could keep him from doing that.

To me, sitting in my wraith form, it was as intoxicating as it was hair-raising.

As King Yarox assembled his army for the Reaper's inspection, rattling off the numbers of soldiers they now had, demons inched forward on their bellies and kissed the ground in front of the Reaper. Kai sniggered at the sight of the line of them, waiting to meet their god and saviour. Acid churned in my belly at the obvious fact that the Reaper was preparing and assessing his forces on *this* large scale. That Zale, his brothers and I were supposed to fight alongside him against the humans of the Continent. This was what they wanted for the rest of the world, a place of demons where brutality and malice ruled.

Yarox said, "The human slaves are all gone, taken in the uprising through the portal to Lobrathia. We tried to chase them down, but by the time we got there, it was too late."

My head snapped to Yarox at that. *Human slaves.* If the

Reaper would make slaves of the humans, it would become a literal prison world. Goosebumps puckered over my skin and Zale growled as he no doubt felt them, caressing his thumbs over my arms.

The Reaper's head gave a quarter-turn towards me and I made sure my mental defences were up before sinking into my shadows once again. It was not lost on me that I was the only human here, in the midst of monsters. If the Reaper thought I was not sympathetic to him, he would see me as his enemy. He had the power to kill me, and yet he seemed to think that we had *similarities*. That idea made me shudder and, for a moment, I was back in the Eternal Forest, in a dark castle full of goblins covered in misery.

I'd been a malevolent creature then, or close to it. Capable of killing. Capable of shooting the goblins because I felt the need. But I'd quickly realised that was not who I was. In my core, I was a healer. In my heart there was fire, not ice.

"Very well," the Reaper said in his audible fae voice. "Prepare your army. We will gather here, at the quartz portal, with the rest of the forces. Mine as much quartz as possible. Forge more weapons."

Whoever holds the Quartz Quarry holds the power, was what the Reaper had said. In Lobrathia, where humans couldn't use magic, quartz was only something we used for decoration and light. But in Ellythia, quartz was a part of daily life, and that included weapons. Against hundreds of quartz-forged weapons, the Lobrathians would be powerless. Our military had no power at all. Clenching my teeth, I slid off Zale's lap.

Yarox bowed and muttered his thanks before the Reaper abruptly stood and made for the ruined palace behind us. We hastened to follow, but my step stuttered as my very world came crashing down around me.

I was not the only human here, after all.

Sitting on the stairs, like a polished queen of the demons in a simple dress of black and green, was a person I'd never actually thought I'd see again. A woman who had been the cause of me and my sister's nightmares. My stepmother.

4

ALTARA

"I t's been weeks since the battle at Black Court," Glacine Voltanius huffed as she stood. "Where have you been?"

I was not prepared for what happened next. The Reaper stepped forward and backhanded her so hard she slammed into the dust with a cry.

Zale turned and pressed his nose to my hair, inhaling for a brief moment, otherwise unbothered by this display. Without a word, the Reaper stepped over her and continued on.

Glacine spat dirt out of her mouth as Kai bounced forward and enthusiastically lifted her off the ground and set her roughly on her feet as if she were a doll, then pranced around her in a haste to follow the Reaper.

So, she'd been hiding out here while the demons took Quartz City?

The rest of us remained still and Glacine raised her chin and stared us down with narrowed black eyes. Her skin was even paler than her usual alabaster, no doubt from her time down here without sunlight. With her black hair, the fine features of her face, and grooming, she was an objective beauty, and I felt Raen and Atax's assessing eyes upon her face and body.

But all I saw was a wretched, vile woman who relished the pain of others.

This woman had physically abused my sister for years. She might have been responsible for my torture at the hand of the Butcher, but that had been one awful occasion. My sister had suffered regularly for *years*. My fingers twitched for a weapon, the pure, violent need to have her life's blood on my hands. I'd joked about her death many times with Saraya. But now, the idea of murdering her was very, very real. But the Reaper's words from the chariot stalled me.

We are alike.

I let out a puff of air in dismay. We couldn't be alike. I would not let myself be a cold-blooded killer like him. I would not do something that *he* would approve of.

There was something else that stayed my hand. Something primitive told me that her death belonged to my sister. Glacine's hands had never hurt my skin. She was not my mark and I would not deny my sister the satisfaction.

I had never thought of Saraya as a killer. A murderer. But both our parents were dead now, and Glacine was still here, right as rain, familiar enough with the Reaper that she'd spoken to him casually. This was war. And this… woman was our enemy.

But as my stepmother surveyed us, her red lips twisted. Fancy her being arrogant while she'd just been struck by the Reaper? While she stood at the ruins of this castle at the hand of my sister?

With the Reaper here, I could not act upon her in any form, lest I give myself away. Our vengeance would have to wait.

Her eyes looked Zale up and down, a lascivious smirk growing on her lips as she admired his perfect face. I could have cut her eyes out then and there for looking at my husband in that way, but suddenly her eyes flickered to me, and with some realisation, she went still.

"Altara," she murmured, the surprise tinting her voice only a little.

She'd always been a smart woman. Cunning and incredibly intelligent. But my name on her tongue sent me into a sudden untethered rage. The shadow around me darkened until I was in a skin of solid black that sparked with lightning and I stepped up to her until we were toe to toe. The smile faded from her face as she looked down at me. But our height disparity didn't matter because I knew right then that I was more powerful than her. That I had the power to kill her, destroy her; cut her into tiny, pathetic pieces.

Her voice was a python's hiss. "I heard my Butcher found you again."

My hand snapped around her throat and squeezed.

Glacine's eyes went wide, trying to drag in air with a wild, choking sound. Her hands flew up to claw at mine, but I dug my fingernails into her soft skin until she bled.

"*Enough.*" The Reaper's voice shattered through my body. A power like I'd never known before weighed down on me like a thousand grimy, groping hands and at the flick of his fingers, I was thrown backwards into Zale's arms.

A kind of shock settled into me. I had known the Reaper was powerful, but this was the first time I'd felt his power on me. How easily he'd torn me open. It was such colossal power that I suddenly understood why Zale's father and these demons had taken him as their god.

Zale's big, calloused hand wrapped around my neck and a

low, rumbling growl of disapproval sounded in my ear. "Do not touch the Reaper's consort."

I nearly choked on my own spit. *His consort?* By Agnolthi.

"Your father's body lies behind the arena," Glacine spat, rubbing at her throat, her eyes burning with vengeance. "Go and see what is left of the *dead* Lobrathian king."

If it were not for the Reaper standing there, towering with malice, I would have lunged at her with a killing blow, damn everything. Damn being *good*. From the tone of her voice, from the gleam in her eyes, I just *knew* she'd contributed to his death.

The Reaper's head snapped to the left as if he'd heard something. The abrupt and uncharacteristic movement had us all staring.

He said, "Come, Glacine, I have need to speak with the dark fae kings in Obsidian Court. Ashzale, you know your orders."

My stepmother gave me one last narrow-eyed look before she took the Reaper's hand and together they headed back towards his chariot.

"Obsidian Court?" I murmured, getting to my feet.

"The Reaper has taken over the Dark Fae Realm," Raen said, studying his fingernails as we all watched the Reaper leave. "Once he has Ellythia, we will prepare to invade the rest of the human continent. The demons already hold Lobrathia."

"Isn't that where you were born?" Kai said, blinking at me. "Now you can return to tear it apart!"

He grinned at me in that silly, happy way of his, though his smiles never reached his eyes anymore. No warmth glowed in his face, only cold, sinister mirth. But I couldn't dwell on that for long because my homeland, Lobrathia, was the closest to the fae realms, sharing the Silent Mountains as a border. In her last message to me, Saraya had declared she was going to take back Lobrathia as queen. I don't know if the Reaper knew that information or not, but it would seriously deter his plan if she were successful. And with this new power of ours, our lightning, perhaps she...

Could she even do it? With what forces? I swallowed my rising panic, bringing my shadows about me further as Zale tightened his grip around my waist.

"Your sire," he said in my ear, "what type of man was he?"

I broke out of his grip to turn and look at him. The others cocked their heads as if wondering how much they should care about my father having been killed. A small crease formed between Zale's dark brows as I saw him try and calculate what this could mean for him. There was no emotion there, only assessment, and once again, I was glad for my own emotion muting protection keeping the sudden fire whirling around my body, at arm's length.

But Raen stepped forward, gesturing to where Glacine had indicated. "We must cremate him, to prevent his spirit from wandering."

Zale nodded in agreement as I stared at them. Finally, I managed to swallow the lump in my throat. "Good thinking, brother." Zale made an approving noise before grabbing me once again and pinning me to his side as he led us through the palace to whatever arena Glacine had mentioned.

The inside of the building was scorched, black marks on the ceiling and walls. *I hope my sister is responsible for this*, I thought with clenched fists. I hoped she'd killed and maimed the demons that had enslaved her, and I hoped she was somehow building an army to take back Lobrathia with her husband. A part of me wanted to go and find her, hunt her down so we could do it together. But I couldn't leave Zale and the beasts I now called my brothers. They were not of sane mind and I needed to be here to prevent them from causing *real* harm that they would never be able to forgive themselves for.

My tactical tutors would have called me a double agent.

We worked our way through the carnage and out the back of the palace, where a huge arena made of white stone was set.

"How fun!" Kai shouted. "Look, my queen, they had gladiator tournaments there!"

I refrained from gaping because I had no doubt they used the human slaves to fight for entertainment. Barbaric. Luckily, the new king had mentioned they'd all escaped, and if my sister had been a part of that, I was proud of her.

It was quieter inside the stadium and a hush overcame the place as if the remnants of a particularly sinister magic was left behind. Dark residue clung to my skin, along with the feeling of quiet doom. Zale's presence by my side was cold but steady, and despite his lack of showing any feelings at all, he was still a stabilising presence.

My heart remained steady in my chest, and when Kai trotted ahead of us into the stadium grounds, my eyes found my father.

His supine body was a thing of madness drawing me in on a silent, vicious song, and I followed the call like a ghost on feet I couldn't even feel touching the ground.

They had left him a wide berth, his body decapitated by a perfect, bloody line that could not have been performed by any blade.

For the first time, my shadows evaporated against my will

and the world became visible to me in stark, horrible clarity. I couldn't feel my body at all, only a dark, mutilated feeling clawing at my mind.

I fell to my knees with a heavy, crunching thump that I heard but didn't feel. The cry that emerged from my throat was little more than a whimper of, "No!" A hoarse mimicry of my usual voice.

Hot, broken tears spilled, and I let them, because they blurred my vision and I needed a reprieve from the sight of my decapitated father lying in an old sticky pool of his lifes-blood, his head nowhere in sight. With his wheeled-chair still angled just behind him, he must've fallen straight out.

Kai thumped down next to me, his giddy energy telling me he thought we were playing some game. Without thinking, I grabbed his hand as if it were a life rope. Kai's large hand gripped mine back, and he began swinging our arms before Zale growled and Kai disentangled my fingers from his.

My head spun with a tidal wave of thoughts that threatened to drown me. I clutched my stomach with my other hand, begging myself not to heave. They'd taken his head. Someone had taken his head.

Had my father known what was happening at the time of his death? Had his mind been too far gone to register the terror? I hoped so, for his sake. Had Saraya been here, watching?

My husband crouched next to me, frowning deeply.

"I never did see my father die," he said thoughtfully. "I wonder how it happened."

"I doubt it was like this," I whispered.

"You didn't know my father. He was not loved by all."

"My father was a good man. Kind. He raised me well, taught me archery."

"He did not know you found your mate, I think."

My heart threatened to cleave in two.

"Raen," I said.

"Yes, my queen?" I felt his presence behind me.

"Do you know the last rites?"

"Of course."

"Help me do them? Kai?" I cleared my throat and tried to put a more commanding voice on. "Bring his body here, and be gentle with him."

Raen had Atax and Kai find kindling while he and Zale prepared my father's body. They wouldn't let me help, so I sort of just stood there, useless, watching as they first arranged a pyre and then laid my father's body atop it with the brisk, no-nonsense efficiency of warriors who'd done it many times before, and I didn't even have the energy to be disturbed by that. Kai had sniffed out lard from somewhere and we doused the wood in it.

Raen then beckoned me forward, beginning a slow, deep funeral chant in the Old Language of the Boneweavers—strange, guttural sounds that came from the throat woven into a slow psalm. While I didn't know the meaning of the words, Raen's power thrummed through the air, making my body vibrate in response. He'd spoken this language at my wedding to Zale and Fangar, binding us in marriage. The air then felt the same as it did now, like something with gravity was happening. Something important that made the air itself still.

So it should be, when we couldn't be at home where he would have been given a funeral worthy of a king, with the people who had loved him, watching over him. Crying at his memory. But today, there would only be me and my four Old Ones.

We had no head to burn and so Zale, by some sense of logic, put a large stone in its place, so that from afar, perhaps between the flames, my father's body would have the pretence of being whole.

"I wonder what they've done with it," said Zale, frowning at the stadium around us. Despite trying to hunt for it by scent, none of them had been able to find it.

"Probably doing some ritual with it," Atax muttered.

I shivered and pretended I hadn't heard him as Raen placed two gold coins on top of the rock as if those were my father's eyes. Atax set a flat black sword into the crook of my father's arm and nodded to me. "No one should go into the afterlife without a weapon."

Nodding my thanks, I reached out and took Zale's hand, and he used my grip to pull me into his side. "It is proper," he said simply, and his brothers came to stand beside us.

After a few minutes, Raen finished his song and gave me a nod. Taking a deep breath, I moved to the other side of the pyre, opposite the men, and summoned my bow. Gold and black wood sat heavy in my hand.

"You gave me my first bow," I said to my father, "when I was two. It's probably still in Quartz Palace in my room, gathering dust. But I kept it because I wanted to see how far I'd come. How big I'd grown." Emotion filled my throat, and I exhaled through my lips. Slightly embarrassed, I looked up at the four beasts. Zale was looking at me with remote curiosity, Raen and Atax bore deep frowns as they stared at the tracks my tears made, but... Kai surprised me. A shining tear strayed from one eye, and as if he were confused by it, he wiped it away and stared at the fluid on his fingers.

I swallowed and continued on, tears filling my eyes once again. "You told me that as long as I listened to my gut, my aim would be true. And I did that, Father. I did that every day since. I rarely missed, you know that. But somewhere between then and now, we lost everything. I'm sorry that I left you for Ellythia. I'm sorry that you died without your court by your side. But if you're with Mother and Grandmother Cheshni now, I'm glad for that one thing."

I took a shaky breath. "Lightning never misses its mark, Father. The Lobrathian lightning princesses are here and *lightning does not yield*. It never yielded to darkness back in the old days, and Saraya and I won't yield now."

Knocking an arrow onto my bow, I drew my crackling blue-white power through it. I aimed at the pyre and, with a breath, loosed my arrow. It hit the greased-up wood with a low thud and sparks went flying as the pyre erupted into flames.

Somewhere out there, my grandmother's funeral was also being arranged. I tore my eyes away from the flames and up to the Old Ones. Every single one of them was staring at me. I searched for some connection, some emotion in their eyes. But I was no more than a thirsty woman in the deserts of Kusha for all that I found. I was met by ice chips, frozen and glazed irises. These beasts were not my husband and his brothers. They were buried somewhere beneath all of that.

The Reaper had taken away everything from me. I'd known it from the moment I'd seen that perfect red line around my father's neck. I decided then that I had a lethal arrow for him in my astral quiver—that I had an arrow for every fucking one of his six bloody eyes.

"Whatever it takes, Father," I whispered. "By whatever, even treacherous means, Saraya and I will see it done."

The flames roared up into the sky, burning hot enough to turn my father's bones to ash. My eyes found the back of Zale's hand where he'd looped his thumb into his pants. There, made of celestial black ink, I swore the wings of his butterfly mating mark gave a little flutter.

5

PIA

I t was just after midday when the waking bell went off in the soldier's barracks. Because demons were nocturnal creatures that were damaged by the sun, we expected any attack to happen at night. Therefore, our training schedule had been shifted to make it so we trained at night as well. I rolled out of the top bunk of my bed and landed on the floor in a crouch.

"How the fuck do you always do that?" muttered Teesha, who bunked under me. I wasn't going to say it was because I had already been awake for a while now, my muscles tense, my heart pounding.

As if my body knew something big was coming. As if sleep was no longer a luxury I could afford. Even without my own magic, I felt it in the air. The anticipation. The blood to come. Every cell in my body was alert, had been alert, since the night the Reaper had appeared and Altara had left us. Something sour in me roiled at the loss of my cousin. We'd only just gotten her back from the Eternal Forest, only just got our High Priestess of Agnolthi back, before she'd stolen away.

Now, our enemy.

Or so the city muttered.

It was another betrayal in the long line of betrayals and unexpected occurrences of the last few weeks. Everyone thought it was all of those things that had finally driven me to the brink.

I knew better. My madness had been stewing long before I'd ever met Altara.

We filed out of our barracks, dressed in our Xalya blacks. Short-sleeved black shirts, and stretchy long black pants with space for hiding weapons. We wore our city appointed swords all the time now, most of us with a baldric of knives.

An Ellythian midday was hot, the sun beating down relentlessly, the air smelling of soldiers, sweat and the metal of our weapons. There was also the ineffable scent of magic in the air; a powerful hum that came from Agnolthi's and Chol-nayak's sector as they made their own preparations. It also came from the four giant quartz cauldrons sitting in the centre of Xalya's sector, where everyone, except me and the other magic-less were now headed.

I parted from the main group, keeping my head down against the shame of it—for being unable to fill the city's caul-drons of power when we needed it the most. Those cauldrons were being used to power weapons, and they would be used in the battle itself by the mages covering large scale, tactical assaults. Every day, the soldiers gave a little tithe of their magic to contribute, waiting dutifully in long lines to deposit their gift.

Every day of watching my comrades do this was another reminder I didn't have my magic. In my three years at Boneweaver Island, I'd tried not to think about it too much. I'd put it to the back of my mind so I could just get by, day by day. But now, it was a slap to the face each time we left our barracks.

The way to the mess hall was desolate, my heavy boots crunching against the gravel of the path. It was just me and my dark thoughts until a prickle at the back of my neck gave me pause.

Voices, low and gravelly, speaking as if they didn't want to be heard and a higher-pitched soft voice, pleading.

As if my body had been waiting for it, I was darting down the small branching path between barracks within seconds, a fire burning through my chest at the pleading in that small voice. I found them, three male soldiers—two low ranking, one a lieutenant—cornering a smaller male against a wall.

"You'll pay up," said a familiar voice, "or we'll see to it that your sister doesn't get that position she wants at Lisan-thi's temple."

"I've already paid!" said the cadet. "I told you—"

"You haven't paid the interest, you idiot," growled the lieutenant.

"No one said anything about interest!"

It was a voice I recognised right away. Because my ex-betrothed, Camar, had never been seen without him.

"Still a bastard then, Rassul," I drawled, crossing my arms and leaning against the side of the building.

The three men with their backs to me whirled around. Idiots. They hadn't even noticed me sneak up on them. In the battle to come, they'd be dead quickly with those piss poor instincts. The other two had been a part of Camar's wider friendship group. The lanky Bimla and the heavyset, muscular Hisspan.

Rassul's handsome face was little more than an ugly sneer as he raked his eyes up and down my relaxed form. "I wondered when I'd see you around here," he said, crossing his arms as he assessed me, the picture of arrogance. "Sneaking around like a whore, Pia? Nothing new there."

His voice grated at my nerves, and I laughed through my nose. At one time, I would have crumpled under those words. But, three years later, I only felt a cold, lethal calm. "You always were a vapid cunt, Rassul. I'm just happy I get to tell you to your face now."

That handsome face twisted. "Oh, I'm sure you're happy now. You get to fuck who you want now, right?"

His continued sexual jabs were starting to bore me. Men really didn't know how to throw a good insult around without bringing in sex somehow.

"Doesn't your family have any money left?" I said, nodding at the frightened cadet behind him. The boy had been looking between us with wide, startled eyes, his dark hair askew. A rabbit caught between two predators.

Rassul's fists tightened, and he took a further step towards me. "You can't talk. You don't even have a family anymore."

The cadet chose that moment to dart around his assailants and, quick as a mouse, bolted around them and rushed past me to freedom. Bimla let out a cry and made to chase after him, but I stepped forward and slammed my foot right into his groin. He flew two feet backwards with a cry, courtesy of the quartz I'd stuffed into the ends of my boots, powering my kicks to be stronger than any man's.

"Bitch!" Hisspan unsheathed his sword, but Rassul merely narrowed his eyes at me. I raised my brows at Hisspan's weapon.

"I'm going to give you one chance to run, little girl," Rassul said, stepping sideways to set more ground between him and Hisspan.

My smile was cold but my insides *burned*. "I'm not going anywhere." My back leg shifted subtly, putting me in a fighting stance.

"She's mad," Hisspan said. Behind him, Bimla didn't stir from the ground. He'd managed to land on his head and knocked himself out. Idiot.

"Put that away," Rassul snapped at his friend. "If she wants to fight with the men, let her fight."

He flew at me, but I was ready. I ducked under his first punch, and thanks to the quartz bracelets I wore, newly charged, I landed a heavy blow to his jaw. His head snapped back, but Rassul had been trained to fight from a young age, just like me. He recovered quickly, aiming a blow at my side. I skipped backwards, and he pursued me. I aimed a strike for his ribs, but he blocked, grabbing my wrist and yanking hard. Allowing him to think he had me, I struck with my left fist right in his sternum, hard enough to break bone.

He cried out, and we both dropped to the ground, his grip on my wrist crushing the bone. I sunk into the pain with a laugh, flipping my legs around to pin them around his neck into a chokehold. But like Malika, Rassul had fire magic and his fingers found my shins, burning spots right through my pants and into my skin. I held on for a moment, but Hisspan rushed forward and I saw him too late. He landed a punch on my temple, knocking me back. Stars burst in my vision as I crumpled.

Rassul was back up in seconds, lunging for me, pinning me with his hips and grabbing my wrists in a grip that singed my skin.

He leaned closer, his sour breath on my face. "I know you did it on purpose."

My entire body stilled. I had thought no one knew what

Camar was like, but of course his friends knew the type of man he'd been. I hadn't told anyone. Hadn't told anyone their princess was a trained warrior who hadn't been able to fight off a single man from taking advantage of her, even if he was her fiancé.

In a place where we worshipped the female form as Goddess, a crime like that warranted immediate execution. We took it so seriously as a population that it hardly ever happened at all. It was why, when it had happened to me, I'd reacted in perhaps the most visceral way. I'd taken my revenge instantaneously, ferociously, and ruined him for it. But it had been so violent that I scarred my own magic in the process.

I didn't even know where his family kept him, probably deep in their estate opposite Harranpul house, where he was cared for by servants. I didn't care, but clearly his friends still did.

I raised my head, even as I smelled my own skin burning. "He deserved what he got."

Rassul frowned, not at what I said, but at the fact I wasn't reacting to his burning of me. My skin was bubbling, melting off the bone, but I laughed again. A high-pitched keen that didn't even sound like my own voice.

He swore and let my wrists go. Rearing back, he slammed his fist into my jaw. I allowed it, only because I wanted to see how hard he could punch. How much it would hurt. If it would break bone. Hisspan swore from somewhere on my left and I was vaguely aware of voices entering the square. They wouldn't stop a fight, though. Not a one-on-one fight between two soldiers. We were allowed to fight out grievances.

Rassul bent down again, his face contorted in confusion

and anger. "You're not a princess anymore. You're no one. I could do anything I wanted to you and no one would care. For Camar, I could kill you."

I laughed in his face.

My anger was not feral like Malika's, nor wild like Altara's. It was cold and calculated. Every movement I judged extensively, but rapidly, before I made it. Armsmistress Vari had taught me to think and think quickly. In the jungle school, I had become a woman capable of damage that I never got the chance to inflict.

Thanks to the quartz around my waist, I flexed my hips, and he went careening. I might not have my magic, but I wasn't stupid enough to go walking around without my entire body laced in quartz. I wasted no time as the crowd gathered around us and began my rapid and deliberate assault upon Rassul; I struck him right on the nose and the bone shattered under my fist, blood spurting. He reached for my throat, but I struck with my right elbow into his ribs, feeling the bone splinter, then with my left to the ribs on the opposite side. He doubled over, wheezing, clutching his side. Without thinking, I grabbed his head and slammed my knee back into his nose. Blood warmed my leg as Rassul fell to the ground.

Only then did I look at my wrists, where the skin was red and twisted. My jaw was also broken and my head pounded, but I didn't care. The crowd around us had grown silent.

From the side of my eye, I saw *her*. Huge armoured boots, muscular legs, the lethal edge of her mighty axe, black as night, cold steel glinting in the sun. The air around me felt light, as if I might fly into the air at any moment.

I grinned knowing that Xalya was watching me, blood dripping from my teeth.

"You crazy bitch," Hisspan said, his jaw slack.

I grinned at him. "And don't you fucking forget it."

"Pia." The new voice was resigned, but not cold.

Turning around, I now saw why the crowd of soldiers around us had gone quiet. There, with the cadet Rassul had been bullying, was the old general of the Ellythian Forces, Reeta Castram, in her wheeled chair. She'd been a formidable woman in her time, the youngest High Priestess of Xalya on record, but due to injuries sustained in a Daanav assault that could not be healed, she'd been stuck without the use of her legs and honourably discharged from her position. She'd returned to the corps to assist in battle preparation.

Suddenly, I saw the similarity between her and the young man next to her. A relative then.

I bowed. "Lady Reeta."

The crowd shifted as Hisspan and other lieutenants carried an unconscious Rassul and Bimla away.

"Come with me, girl," Reeta said and promptly turned her chair and rolled away. I cut a glance at the crowd, but people avoided my gaze and left in haste. I followed Reeta, who was headed to the main walkway, and then turned left, away from the mess hall. I sighed. Looked like I wasn't going to get breakfast any time soon.

Silently, I came up to walk beside her and her young relative. "You didn't have to knee him again in the nose," she said mildly. "He was already done."

"Yes, my lady," I said obediently.

"Then why did you do it?"

I glanced down at her, rolling along beside me at a swift pace. Though her legs had become skinny with lack of use, her arms were strong and muscled, her hands still calloused. She still trained, then. I admired that. But I did wonder how to answer her question without looking like a complete madwoman. But gone were the days of my saving face and speaking in a court-trained voice. I was free now. And with my freedom came a sort of radical honesty I was only too happy to provide.

"He needed to be punished," I said simply. "And I was angry."

"Punished for what crime?" Reeta didn't glance at her young cousin.

"Rassul is a man of multiple crimes," I said mildly. "Today's crime was just another."

Reeta made a sound that was neither agreement nor disagreement. But now, I saw where we were headed. Xalya's high priestess and Ellythia's current general strode out of her rooms on powerful legs, with her face like stone and her brown eyes trained right for me.

I sighed again and Reeta looked at me sharply. "Did you see her?" she asked as we came to a stop to await the high priestess. I didn't need to ask who she meant. So, she had seen Xalya there as well.

"Yes."

"Hm."

Ellythia's General reached us and we all bowed low.

"Pia," she said. "Reeta, what happened?"

"This cadet took it too far in her fight against Rassul Gulgan," Reeta said matter-of-factly. "An extra knee to the nose that was already broken."

All three turned to look at me, but I had nothing to say. All I could do was nod. "Her ladyship is correct."

"Fifty hours in the kitchen," the general said. "We're short, anyway."

"Is that all?" I asked stiffly, as my jaw refused to open all the way. Last week, when I'd gotten into a tussle with a soldier in the mess hall, it had been twenty hours in the armoury, sharpening daggers. Hardly the brutal punishments I'd been used to at the palace.

The general gave me a droll look. "Your damages are also punishment. Go to the healing building."

I bowed low, twice, feeling the swelling rising hard and angry under my cheek. "My lady. My lady Reeta."

As I walked away, their eyes were like tiny burning embers on the skin of my back.

THE HEALING BUILDING WAS BUSY AS MY HEALER, A STRESSED, older gentleman, handed me a flat block of ice-cold blue quartz wrapped in a cloth. He'd healed the fracture in my jaw and the burns on my skin, but he wasn't going to waste his energy on the residual swelling in my face. More training in the corps meant more injuries, and the healers needed to manage their power use carefully. I sat there for a moment, letting the cold seep into my aching bone. It could've been worse. I wasn't permanently disfigured, after all. And I'm not sure I would have cared if I had been.

"Pia?"

That quiet, familiar voice had me on my feet within seconds, the ice pack forgotten on the bed. I wrenched open the curtains to find warm brown eyes set in a rounded face that was slowly losing its boyishness.

"What are you doing here, Paalus?" I asked sharply, looking behind him.

My brother drew his shoulders straight. Like this, he was almost my height. "I'm a prince. No one dared stop me."

A smile curved my lips as I grabbed him and pulled him in for a rough hug. He'd grown more muscle in the three years since I'd seen him sadly waving at me through the palace windows as I was carted off for my exile. After I'd arrived back in the palace, I'd not had a chance to talk to either him or my father. It stung that my father hadn't come here too, but I'm sure my mother would have forbidden him. Even being a prince-husband, he was still under her control.

"Here, I bought this," Paalus said excitedly. He pulled out a folded banana leaf and held it out to me.

When I just stared at it in a sort of daze, he unwrapped the banana leaf. Inside was my favourite sugary sweet delicacy, made out of coconut and tapioca.

"You remembered baclolo was my favourite," I said quietly.

"Yes," he whispered. "I remember a lot, gigi."

The Ellythian word for sister made my heart swell to the size of the sun. "So you haven't disowned me as the queen apparent wishes?"

A fire suddenly burned in his eyes, so bright that I stared at him in shock. "*Never.*" Gone was the little boy I'd played armies with. Here was a budding young man who knew what he wanted. Who wanted to make his place in the world.

"I want to know," Paalus said, "what do they look like? The Goddesses?"

I froze, staring at the sweets in his hands.

"I know you see them. What is she like? Xalya?"

Grinning despite everything, I closed my eyes, remembering when she'd appeared to me after the Reaper arrived in the city that night. "She's like a weapon made into a human. Her power is like a mortal blow."

"And her axe?" he asked eagerly. "Grandmother wouldn't tell me. I didn't think she appeared to her in a long time."

I opened my eyes. I didn't think any of the Goddesses had appeared to my grandmother in a while at all, except perhaps Cholnayak, a herald of her end.

"It was massive. Obviously made of some divine metal, but it was like a living thing. Like it was sentient, you know?"

"Wow."

He came to sit on the bed, and reluctantly, I joined him. Three years had passed, but it seemed like no time at all with my brother. It healed something inside of me.

Paalus took a deep breath as if he was steeling himself and I instantly poised to listen carefully. "I want to know, Pia. That what you did to Camar—you did for a reason?"

I swallowed the lump in my throat. How many people knew, suspected, that it hadn't been an accident? My voice was so quiet, my lips barely moved. "How many people know?"

"Once he'd had word of your return, he started talking. Babbling, more like. Talking about being sorry for something. It's not clear though. Only rumours from the servants who help to look after him."

"Shit."

I honestly didn't know what was worse. The entire world thinking that I was a weak princess, or the entire world thinking of me as a vicious snake who'd ruined a man on purpose.

Paalus gently took my hand in both of his. "I'm glad, Pia. I'm glad you did it. I'm glad you're back. And…" I turned to look at him, though my vision was slightly blurry. "Despite

46

everything—Mother, Father, all of it—I'm glad you're my sister. You… You handled this in a way that would have made our ancestors proud."

The honesty shining in his eyes almost broke me all over again. Because I didn't think I was handling this very well at all.

6

ALTARA

After watching my father's body burn into ash and taking some time to sleep, we left that demon court for the next one.

I was, in truth, getting a little homesick. After I'd run from Lobrathia, I'd done nothing but travel, never really settling down in one place for an extended period of time. I was tired of it and wished I could get the imagined image of the demons ransacking Lobrathia out of my head. I knew what these creatures were capable of now, and to think they'd taken over my home city made my stomach turn.

All I could do was huddle into my shadows and wait it out. The knowledge that Saraya was out there, also planning something, gave me a seed of hope, and I clung to that golden promise with all my heart.

This time, we travelled without the Reaper and in his stead, Raen procured a giant, glowing green skull with six makeshift eye holes just like the Reaper's. On top of Raen's raven's back, Kai held the thing up on a pole in the air and through the endless dark of the demon realm, it could be seen from far away.

It was a call to arms, and the demons responded.

A slow, silent crowd of all different types of demons began gathering, following us to the next court. Entities made of shadow, rotting flesh and bone felt the call of the Reaper and slithered out of their black holes and dark caves to join us, kicking up an eerie red mist behind them.

Within a few hours of flying, ahead of us loomed our next demon court. A monster all of its own, made of black and grey stone, covered in a dark haze of smog and filth. It was built in a spiral, like a serpent, and at its centre sat the remains of a giant's skull, its eyes burning with a blazing red fire, the heat of which I could feel from this distance. It looked like a *real* giant's skull, and by now, with all the mythical things I'd seen, I could very well believe it was.

When they saw us flying up, winged demons sailing over the city cried out warnings, their rasping caws making me want to cringe.

"Reaper!" they cried. "The Reaper is come!"

The cries got louder as we landed before the city gates, and the horde behind us clacked their jaws, shook their weapons, and hummed in their foul languages. Though I could not understand the words they spoke, their energy bore the universal signs of a rabid sort of excitement and eagerness.

Rusted black city gates, like teeth in the mouth of a monster, swung open as Zale flicked his hand and two guards, seven feet tall with long, straight black horns, strode out.

Their skin was the colour of blood, their veins inked black, and their all-black predatory eyes narrowed as they took us in.

"All hail the Reaper!" they cried in husky, booming voices.

"Take me to your king," Zale commanded.

"Where is the Reaper?" the first guard said, looking about as if he would appear from behind us.

"We represent him," Zale said.

On cue, Kai shook the glowing skull he still held on the pole.

The demons both snorted as if they found this funny. "Prove it."

Atax laughed without humour before lunging past Zale and me to slice the neck of the first demon. Raen took the second, snarling, two long black daggers in his hands. Both demons fell heavily to the ground, blood spurting.

Atax turned to grin with all his teeth at me before dramatically sweeping onto one knee. "I dedicate this kill to my king and queen."

Zale patted Atax's bent head as Raen rolled his eyes and strolled back behind us. I didn't have to tell them I wasn't officially their queen yet, but they were insistent my defection from the Ellythians to Zale's side had made me so.

Atax remained on his knee, and I realised he was waiting for me.

"Very good, my lion warrior," I rasped through my smoky cloak. "I accept your sacrifice."

He stood, flecks of blood splattered on his face. Pleased with himself, he returned to flank us.

As we entered the city and became surrounded by the blood-skinned, horned demons that inhabited it, Zale shifted closer to me.

The King Boneweaver's walk had changed.

I noticed with vague interest, and more than a little arousal, that it was less the walk of a man and more the slow, languid, confident walk of an untamed beast. His head was lowered like a feral predator, his glistening skin stretched over sculpted muscles that were coiled as if ready to spring at a second's notice. It was a walk that warned of danger and promised violence.

As we made our way up to the giant skull, the crowd around us growing louder, Zale noticed me glancing at him and his head swivelled to me, his gaze heated and intense.

The thread between us quivered and there came a caress down my cheek. I preened under his invisible touch and a slow smirk lifted his lips. His eyes suddenly flicked down my body and, under some thought, his power enveloped me in a cold tickle. My witch's robe and simple priestess gown were lifted off me, and quite suddenly, I was wrapped in purple silk so dark it was almost black. It fell across my skin like liquid, plunging low to show the inner curves of my breasts, hugging my hips, then falling to the stone floor. High slits came up both thighs, and as I walked into the domain of these demons, I felt as light as air. Zale returned my witch's cloak and boots to my astral repository with confident ease and put black slippers on my feet. Behind me, Kai laughed and clapped his hands as if it were a great trick, and I cast our white-haired savage warrior an indulgent smile over my shoulder.

Zale was showing his mate off. Apparently, losing his conscience had not taken away any showmanship. I didn't mind, something primitive in me preened at his care. Despite the Reaper's dark magic making him cold, he still saw me as his mate and responsibility. A deep part of him felt the glittering bond that linked us as readily as the black bond that linked him to the Reaper.

The giant skull castle finally towered above us, and as we watched, the red flames blasting in the eye sockets turned green in a violent *whoosh*.

The crowd around us cheered, high-pitched shrieks mixed with deep racketing booms, their eyes on the smaller six-eyed skull on the pole Kai hoisted high behind us.

Demons loitering around the steps leading up to the castle's mouth fell to their knees upon our approach. Shouts of, "All hail the Reaper," surrounded us as we walked into the skull, and it was then that I noticed some of these demons were blue.

The Daanav marine demons who had detained us on Boneweaver Island were blue, just like my demon husband, Fangar Sharksbane.

He had betrayed us, worked with these crimson skinned demons, and brought me for torture to my personal devil, the Butcher.

I had plans for both of them. Sharp-eyed, I surveyed the demons falling to their feet around us to see if Fangar was also here. He usually lived in the Daanav Kingdom beneath the Lotus Sea, but it was telling that these marines were spending time here. They were still collaborating. Plotting against the Ellythians.

We came to a stop just inside the mouth of the building and our group spread out on either side of us.

"All hail the Reaper!" a new voice boomed. "All hail the Green General!" The voice came from a creature who was clearly the leader of this demon court. He had to be seven feet tall, his skin that sickly blood colour, his black horns huge and curling, and white teeth bared in a snarl. The biggest sword I'd ever seen, silver and black with a serrated edge, rested upon his shoulder. In my subdued wraith state, the only thing I felt was impressed. He shouted, "Hiraxos Court welcomes the Reaper!" He held his arms wide. "But where is our Emperor?"

"Demons muster at the Reaper's command!" Zale boomed. "The war that was promised is here. We fight for the Reaper's empire above. And I"—Zale placed a palm over his own bare chest, where his black cloaked heart lay—"will be his General of War."

All eyes turned to look at my husband. Zale, who wore only pants, the rippling muscles of his tattooed torso glistening with the finest sheen of sweat, grinned with all of his teeth. His voice became low and rough in the way it was when he let his beast-self take over. It rang out through the crowd like a war drum. "And we take the Ellythian Isles on the half moon."

I suppressed a dry heave as my stomach churned. That was two weeks away.

D emons were strange creatures with even stranger tastes. Many preferred to eat rotting or spoiled meat, and their music played on flesh and bone instruments scratched at the ears. It was no matter to me, however, as our purpose was being fulfilled, and with my mate by my side, I could want for nothing.

Inside the skull castle, the demon king gestured to a throne of freshly severed heads and roared that it was to be the Reaper's honorary throne. My brothers and I flanked the flesh seat and set the glowing green skull atop it. Next to me, my mate was cloaked in writhing shadows so dark I could no longer see any part of her skin or face. I could smell the fear and arousal in the air as the demons stared at her magnificent, terrifying form in wonder.

The demon king threw a minor demon at the base of the throne before slashing his black nails across the demon's throat in sacrifice. Blood sprayed upon the throne and on my legs. I inclined my head as the demons roared with glee and warriors proceeded to take the corpse and put him on a permanent spit they had set in the middle of the hall.

Demons were often cannibals, happily eating their own kind. It was one of the reasons they were so eager to invade other realms. It was hard for livestock to live here, as they often withered away without sunlight.

As I stood there, getting a little bored as the debauchery continued, a hulking demon male, on his hands and knees, crawled towards my mate, dragging something along with him.

My mate shifted, the smoke around her whispering as if it were displeased. On my other side, the Reaper appeared in his astral form on the throne, glowing a translucent red in his cloaked six eyed form. I knew he'd turn up from time to time to check on the preparations as he liked to keep an eye, or six, on things. I bowed my head in acknowledgement as he turned his hooded head to watch the demon put something at my mate's feet. No one else except Raen reacted to the Reaper's presence, and I knew then that only we could see him.

Before my mate was placed the bloody severed leg of some creature that lived down here; green, leathery and clawed. The demon blinked up at Altara, lust and fear in his eyes, but his intention was clear to me.

"Leave before I end you," I growled to him.

But the demon either did not hear me or did not want to, for his eyes were fixed on my mate and her feral shadows. While I appreciated the offering, because my mate deserved gifts and respect from all creatures, I would not tolerate his abject lust. With a snarl, I lunged forward, my obsidian blade slicing through the tendons and muscles of his neck as if it were butter, and honestly, there was no more satisfying feeling—save for the feeling of being inside my mate. His head toppled to the floor, followed by his body with a satisfying thump.

"Another offering, my mate," I said quietly as together, we watched his blood spill across the black floor.

She hummed in either approval or disgust, I couldn't tell. She would take my gift, anyway. The little creature that used to sit on my shoulder was no more and was not here to tell me about emotions. Though I didn't have positive emotions anymore, I could have used him to tell me about my mate's.

The demons enjoyed violence just as much as my brothers and I, and quite quickly, we were accepted as males of their own. A table was brought out, and we sat alongside their king and ate some type of rare dark meat from an animal I could not identify. The Reaper sat on his honorary throne next to me and silently observed his people.

The cool darkness of my mind was a welcome reprieve from emotions. I remember that emotions had been useful, but I could not remember why. This way, I could achieve whatever task I wanted as quickly as possible. There were no boundaries, no inhibitions, and that was real freedom.

The Reaper turned to me. Three sets of blood-red eyes stared, penetrated, into my mind. His magic whirled, assessing, checking, violating. But in the abyss of my cold dark, I did not care. *"Would you kill her if I commanded it?"* he asked. *"You would be more powerful without her."*

I replied without hesitation and told him the truth, though I couldn't have lied if I had wanted. *"That heart."* I pointed at my mate sitting still and silent next to me. *"Is my heart. If I kill it, I will be killing myself."*

The Reaper stared at my mate, his three red eyes never blinking, only staring, as he no doubt looked into her mind, too. Had any other creature attempted this, they would've been dead already, but my allegiance was to the Reaper now. His preference was also my preference. His magic surged around me towards her, probing around shadows and skin and... hesitated. As if he couldn't breach her protections and had come up against stone.

With a faint, unimportant thrum, I realised he could not see into her mind like he could the rest of us.

I could also tell that he was not happy with my answer, but that was not my problem. I was more concerned about how much more he could see with two extra pairs of eyes. Did it make him hunt better? Would it make *me* hunt better if I had that many eyes? I made a mental note to ask Raen about it later. When he finally spoke, cold amusement laced the dry menace. *"She is the opposite of her sister in almost every way. In the battles to come, it may serve me."*

Goosebumps erupted all over my skin, but I did not know its meaning and let it be. He approved of my mate's power. Good. *"My father would be proud of me,"* I said, setting down the bone I'd been gnawing at. *"All our fathers would be. We will speak of it in the afterlife, no doubt."*

"Indeed, Ashzale. Your father was a good servant, but his love for his wife got in the way. You will not make that mistake."

I frowned at that. *"I did not think my father loved my mother. He loved only power and violence."* It suddenly occurred to me, that like my cold self, love may be a thing he could not really understand, nor detect properly.

Though the Reaper sat still unmoving on his throne, fingers colder than ice wrapped around my throat and squeezed. The veins and arteries in my neck throbbed, and I froze in my seat. Cold seeped down into my chest and every vessel leading through my heart chilled. Pain was an old friend of mine and I considered it carefully. The implication was obvious. He would kill me if I defied him in any way. The Reaper's punishments were like none other and even as his mental fingers left my throat, the icy burn in my chest remained.

"His emotions made him weak. Ties of any kind make you weak. I am the only being strong enough to hold dominance over a mate. You, on the other hand, will find a way to break your mating bond without killing her. She will be of no use to me dead."

The golden thread inside me shrieked in protest as the order was given. Every cell in my body cried out as an ineffable, primordial darkness gripped me. But that black bond between me and the Reaper twanged painfully. *"Your word is my god,"* I murmured, inclining my head.

With that, the Reaper left, leaving only a cursed wind in his wake.

THE ONLY REASON WE STAYED IN THE LARGE BARN THEY GAVE US was because of my mate. Female mates needed private spaces to rest and groom, whereas if it were just my brothers and me, I would have preferred to stay where I could see the demons in an open space. As it was, Raen and Atax automatically set watch, and we could hear them heckling the demons and cutting down a few for good measure. The demon king had proudly shown me his warriors, and there were only two deaths in the process, making it a success. Their army was strong and their weapons sound, but these demons were the stupid sort and needed direct and frequent orders to stay their course. Once the fighting started, however, it wouldn't matter; war was war and it would be a bloody mess, regardless. We couldn't *just* use this court to take Ellythia. We'd need cleverer demons for that, and a part of my job would be to choose which ones would be appropriate to take down the greatest island nation on the planet.

My mate lay on soft blankets, dozing under weariness from travel. I rubbed her bare feet, checking them for blisters and grazes. I needed to bathe her, but we would have to wait until I could find clean water. The fetid water the demons bathed in and drank down here would likely make her ill.

Kai lay curled by her other foot, gently rubbing the arch with practised fingers. He'd done the same for his twin sister when she'd become unwell after my father's experimentation on them both. While Kai had survived the illness that had made his hair white, Kisana had not, and over the course of days, we'd all watched her skin turn as white as the colour of the hair she and Kai shared. She'd died slowly, and every night—even after Kisana stopped responding—Kai would hold her in his arms, crying himself to sleep. He'd kept crying, desperate, shrieking sobs when I'd torn him away from her after her death. No one else had had the heart to remove him from her corpse, and I'd been the one with a cold heart at the time. He'd demanded to be buried with her, but I wouldn't allow it.

Kai tickled Altara's feet and she let out a sleepy giggle that made my cock twitch.

"Enough," I barked. "She needs to sleep."

Kai pouted, but released my mate's foot and set about putting tiny black flowers he'd summoned between each of her toes. Once he was happy with his work, he threw himself back on his bed and took to carving up a bone he'd found. It looked like he was making a flute. The Bonesongs had long used the breath from their lungs for magic for generations, and now Kai was the last of his kind. I would enjoy it immensely when he sang for me next.

I inspected the rest of my mate's skin, shooing away the smoke as I ran my fingers up her smooth thighs, then up the plane of her stomach.

Raen and Atax returned, and I sighed in annoyance because I had been ready to bury myself inside her. A king fucked his mate in private. I was not a common animal.

So instead, I checked the skin of her face as she asked sleepily, "Where do we go tomorrow?"

"The Guild of the Pentarax."

Her body went stiff as a tree trunk as I checked her ears.

I frowned as I let her ear flip back in place. "Did I hurt you?"

She blew out a slow breath, and the shadows seemed to darken around her. Her voice was mouse quiet. "No."

I stroked my mate's hair, silken under my fingers, removing tangles until she squirmed in annoyance.

"Stop it, Zale."

"No. I am grooming you. There could be insects in your hair, feeding on your blood. Sleep."

She sighed, and when her breathing became even again, I looked at my brothers, their athletic bodies lounging. We were beasts in our prime. Beasts who had been created and nurtured for the sole purpose of serving the Reaper in his destruction.

And we would do our job well.

Taking Ellythia would be easy. But as I looked at the bond of gold that lay between me and my mate, we had a few things to do first. I glanced at Raen, who was inspecting a sample of obsidian powder in a glass vial. Those black granules alone were a powerful weapon.

"I must break this bond without killing my mate," I spoke into his mind. *"The Reaper commanded it."*

"Very well, brother," Raen said, his iceberg eyes flicking to her supine, smoky form. *"We will find a way."*

8

PIA

The entire city gathered in the dark of pre-dawn before the Lotus Palace. Today, the woman I had once called 'mother' was to become queen. A bead of sweat trickled down my back, absorbed at once by my black fighting tunic. The air was already warm, perfumed with smoke of the many sandalwood incense sticks stuck into the ground around the crown princess where she sat in the middle of the square.

An Ellythian coronation was the event of a lifetime. Ellythian queens usually lived long lives, well past one hundred, and when the next queen was called forth, it was often when the current queen was sixty or seventy.

As a result, an Ellythian only ever saw a coronation once or twice at most, so it was customary for everyone to bear witness. Plus, the ritual was a fascinating thing to watch. All seven Goddesses were to arrive to crown her.

Until yesterday, Crown Princess Rahana had worn white mourning robes. Once the funeral for my grandmother was complete and her body turned to ash, the city had been instructed to stop wearing white. Today, the queen-to-be sat in the middle of the square by herself. She wore a magnificent deep pink gown, embroidered with gold, her head bowed in meditation, Matrika's sword in its golden scabbard at her hip. Her hair was in a glossy bun at the nape of her neck, and she was incredibly beautiful in a severe sort of way. My heart gave a little sigh at the vision of her.

If I had still been a princess with all my titles, I would have stood closest to her, right beside the high priestesses. Instead, my father and brother were no doubt nearby some-where, watching, maybe trying to see where *I* was, but hidden amongst the masses of my new black-swathed sisters, there was no way I'd be noticed.

Except for a wide berth of twenty paces on all sides around the crown princess, the square was packed. The senior priestesses of each temple made a circle closest to Rahana, and behind them, the remaining acolytes mixed with the rest of the citizens of the city. The high priestesses themselves stood magnificent in their ceremonial gowns at the east corner in a row, with a spot of honour—or perhaps dishonour—for Agnolthi's high priestess, Altara, and for Umali's priest-ess, my other cousin, Saraya.

I had never met Saraya, but if she'd been chosen by Umali, she was no doubt a formidable young woman.

As the sky turned orange, the murmuring crowd hushed.

Heavy, divine power reverberated around us and I stilled to see where it was coming from.

In the clear space around the princess, Cherimari, the maiden Goddess, appeared out of nowhere, dressed in pretty pink traditional dancing pants of many folds and a white blouse, merrily dancing around Rahana. Cholnayak, the crone, watched on in her white robe that covered her silver hair, clapping along to some maniacal divine beat I couldn't hear. I knew only I could see them because no one, including Rahana, gasped or dropped to their knees. It meant the Goddesses were only appearing for *me*, as some type of warning or message.

My skin crawled because Cherimani was also the trickster and her dance was... taunting. The last time she'd appeared, Altara had defected to the Reaper's side and abandoned us. Great joke.

A hysterical giggle bubbled up in my throat and I swallowed it down with seasoned practice. I didn't think I was mad. Completely. Not yet, anyway. Perhaps on my way there. But until then, I had some control. I cleared my throat, but no one paid me any attention, all eyes on the square.

Behind my back, the other soldiers now called me the Mad Lotus. I understood why. Rassul had been one of many opponents. Every few days, I got sent to the healers with something broken, administered by a much bigger and senior warrior. Male or female, I didn't care. I *wanted* to fight, and I didn't care if I got beaten up in the process. No one held back with me anymore, and it was the best sort of freedom. I had no bonds now, nothing holding me back.

In Xalya's army, I found my freedom, and took it wherever I could get it; in the gruel they fed us in Xalya's mess hall, in the hard, narrow bed I had to sleep on.

It would make sense for the novelty to wear off, but it hadn't.

Xalya's acolytes had taken their time in accepting me. Honour was their currency, and I had arrived at Ellythia's military compound dishonourably discharged from the royal line. But day by day, I'd earned my honour back, in the military fashion, with my fists. Any words spoken about me now were hushed and far away from my hearing.

It meant that I could stand here, in the crowd of Xalya's followers, without being stared at, despite everyone knowing who I was. No one dared to make snide comments under their breath anymore, nor did anyone dare to look at me directly. No, instead they watched me from the sides of their eyes like a wild animal that could pounce at any minute.

They wanted to see my reaction to Rahana's coronation, but I would give them none.

Because as we watched the dawn arrive and the square filled with the golden light of a new era, none of the Goddesses appeared to the masses as they should have.

Worse still, Cherimani paused her dance and both she and Cholnayak swivelled their divine, perfect heads to pin me with severe stares.

My heart leapt into my throat, and a vise formed around my chest as they stared at me without kindness. I gulped as the weight of it almost made my knees buckle.

This was a bad, bad sign.

At the dawn of a new queen's coronation, all seven Goddesses should have appeared to give their approval.

My eyes flicked to my mother, and I saw at once that she looked like she was going to explode. Her cheeks were red, her breathing shaky. This was embarrassing. This had never happened before.

She raised her head and glared at the five priestesses standing in a row. Lisanthi's priestess beckoned behind her and an acolyte rushed forward with a red pillow. On it sat a simple crown of gold and quartz, likely the fastest thing they could have made as a backup.

The high priestesses had suspected this as a possibility, then. My grandmother had told me the story of her own coronation—the Goddesses had made her crown themselves.

The crowd was shifting uncomfortably now, and I heard someone behind me swear. The high priestesses all strode forward, their expressions grim.

They surrounded the crown princess, Lisanthi, at the front with the pillow, the gold crown catching the dawn sun.

There was a collective gasp as Rahana snatched up the crown and placed it on her own head. I refrained from swearing myself, as I stared at the woman who looked so much like me, slamming the filigree and diamond crown upon her midnight curls.

Wrong. Wrong. Wrong.

My blood screamed it, wanted to tear through this crowd and rip the thing off her head and smash it to pieces. Rahana didn't deserve the throne of Ellythia. She'd taken it out of spite. Not out of love and duty, as was proper. Not out of the need in her blood to make the world a better place. All I could do was clench my fists so hard my tendons groaned in protest. This woman would lead us in war. This woman with the blank stare in her eyes would *lead* Ellythia.

The wrongness of it bit at my insides like the scrape of a bone knife. A part of me was surprised, I had not expected such a visceral reaction.

When the Goddesses were quiet, chaos would reign. I didn't know why they were doing this, choosing to send Cherimani to dance and taunt me. Whatever their message was, I couldn't read it.

But I understood why the high priestesses were doing this without their Goddesses' blessings. They basically had no choice. War was coming and Ellythia needed a queen to lead us, to bless the troops. We needed stability. But no one in the two-thousand-year history of Ellythia had anointed *themselves* as queen. She wouldn't be able to handle the power. It was a curse of the worst type.

The five priestesses simply stared on. As helpless as I was.

"All hail the queen," droned Xalya's high priestess.

All of us obediently dropped to our knees. "All hail the queen," we murmured back.

Rahana stood, a determined gleam in her dark eyes. She clutched her sword in white-knuckled fists, a mirror to my own.

We were all well and truly fucked.

9
MALIKA

I n the royal throne room of Ellythia, sat atop the Lotus throne like a goblin in a gown, sat the cunt-queen, sneering down her nose at a long roll of parchment as if it said "fuck you" on there. Geravie, Keshmi and I had been summoned by her royal highness, among a long line of other courtiers and palace dwellers, so she could tell us what she wanted to do with us.

"New queen, new court," Geravie huffed in my direction.

I held onto her arm with my nose in the air as we shuffled down the queue to the throne. Some people had left the room sniffing back tears—clearly people Rahana had a grudge against and wanted gone. And some people left tight lipped with their nostrils flaring—those whom Rahana had given some sort of insult to, via the clerk.

Oh no, *she* wasn't giving the orders to us directly—*that* would be beneath her. The line of pink and black swathed clerks sitting on a long table before the throne steps had the lists and designations Rahana had clearly put together before her coronation. It was they who were to tell us where to go while Rahana read off papers given to her by her husband or the other court officials. As I observed her, as a hawk did another hawk, I tried to see how it was that she had become such an all-round awful person.

I bet the Goddesses not turning up to her coronation *stung* like a bull ant on the ass. If only the humiliation could have humbled her. But a person like Rahana was only made more terrible by something like that.

So what if her sister left her to pursue her destiny?

So what if her mother didn't think she was suited to be queen?

That wasn't near enough to make a person turn rotten to the bone, was it?

"Keshmi," I murmured. The elderly priestess looked at me with alarm, her face already damp with nerves. I knew she was worried about her twin, Reshmi, stuck at her temple on Boneweaver Island, which was now under the Reaper's rule.

"What happened?"

"I was just wondering if we ever found out how Queen Cheshni got a hold of the Reaper's evil magic in the first place? Did"—I had to mouth the word 'Altara' in case anyone was eavesdropping—"ever mention how?"

Keshmi gave me a disturbed look, her eyes flicking to Rahana. "No, dove, she didn't."

It was cute that she called me dove. I didn't mind being considered something soft, sweet and gentle once in a while. It made for a good change. But this idea sparked a dark sort of feeling in my belly. Surely they were investigating that at the high priestess level? Except... the high priestess whose job it was to do such a thing was gone.

We got to the head of the line and I patted both ladies on the back, bracing ourselves for what was to come.

As the clerks shuffled through their papers, finding our names, I glanced at the throne. Rahana's husband and son stood by her. Her husband, a lovely and genteel man of noble bearing and stature, was clearly the parent Pia got her traits from. And there was Paalus, a boy of twelve, who kept scratching the back of his neck as if his new clothes were too tight around his throat. No doubt it was just the feeling of his mother, breathing down his neck and making snide comments at the poor boy. I wanted to take Paalus into my arms and tell him it was alright if his mother was shit. My mother would happily adopt him and feed him sweets.

And there it was. My parents and sister were stuck on Boneweaver Island, now under Reaper rule. Fuck this queen and the one before her, who'd never stepped in to help their people stuck there. They were all dead for all I knew. And if they *were*, there would be hell to pay. I'd make sure of that.

"Geravie and Keshmi Harranpul," the clerk announced, "due to your advanced age and lack of battle ability, you are to return to Harranpul estate immediately. All elderly residents are to return home for the war."

Both women sighed, their shoulders slumping. I'd expected as much.

I gave my name and there was more parchment shuffling.

"Malika Yashra you've been appointed into the care of Lisanthi's temple."

Lisanthi's temple? As if I was an orphan or homeless, what an insult. I waited for Geravie to make a snide comment. I waited for Keshmi to say something reasonable. Neither said anything at all. Without another word, I took both silent elderly women by the elbows and escorted them briskly out of the throne room.

"For Goddesses' sake, Geravie, eat!" I snapped.

The older lady simply blinked at her plate and the roti and potato curry I'd put in it. I sighed, leaning back in my chair.

It would be our final night in our suite at the palace. *Those of us who are left*, that is. As far as I'd seen it, Keshmi, Geravie and I had been abandoned by our friends, our family. Keshmi eyed Geravie with worry.

Both women appeared to present a strong front to the outside world. Every day that they'd been at court, and even at the queen's funeral, their hair had been carefully braided and coiled, their gowns or saris immaculate. I'd followed their lead, knowing it to be the smart thing to do after Altara and the Old Ones' defection, after Pia's title got stripped and Rani pledged herself to the white temple. But it was all a facade, because I saw what everyone else overlooked. Both women, who were already small to begin with, had lost weight, and there were now deep bags under their eyes they tried to conceal with powder. Whenever we got back to our rooms, their eyes became glazed, their thoughts elsewhere, their bodies hunched like small turtles.

They were worried. They were grieving. They were tired.

As for me? I *burned*. Revenge was a wildfire in my mind and it would rage until I got what I wanted. Fuck them all.

Geravie didn't reply to me, her hand poised over her roti. It was shock, I think. She was still trying to register what the hell had happened to us.

I supposed that's what happened when you got old. Processing these things took time. Both women would return to their natal home, Harranpul estate, far on the other side of

Lotus Island. Rahana's message was clear: war was coming, and the elderly had no place in it.

They'd not taken the news well, hence Geravie's rapid blinking into her plate. I eyed her, a little worried because Geravie was more like me than she'd care to admit. She was prone to violent outbursts and raging for hours, as I'd been known to do. I thought she would flay the clerk alive for daring to call her a person of *advanced age*. But she'd taken to silence and I'd had to haul them back to our suite to pack.

"Where is your backbone!" I slammed my fist on the table. The glasses and plates rattled, but to my dismay, neither woman gave me so much as a flinch.

Either they were getting too used to me, or they were at the end of their tether.

"Shit," I muttered, pinching my nose. "I'm sorry."

"We can do nothing," Keshmi said, her voice cracking. "About any of this. The queen gave us a direct command."

"She's not the queen and we all know it!" I hissed.

"Malika." Geravie's voice was terse, and she didn't even look at me as she spoke. "Queen Rahana will hang you if word gets out about how you *regularly speak about her*."

My mouth snapped shut because I sort of, kind of, knew that, but it hadn't really become a reality until now. Shit in a woven basket. Geravie was right. I might actually have to watch my mouth these days.

I sat back in my chair and pinched my nose again.

Ugh. The Mother's temple was the worst temple for me, because that was where lone women my age were put to figure their lives out. I'd much rather Luana's temple, where I'd get to dance and seduce men and women, if I so chose. Everyone knew that when war came, Luana's temple was needed more than ever. But I had more fire than Luana's priestesses knew what to do with.

Squaring my shoulders, I tapped Geravie on the shoulder to get her attention. She looked at me, her eyes a little red. "I'm going to join Pia in Xalya's sector. I want to be a soldier sorcerer."

Geravie closed her eyes as if she'd guessed as such, while Keshmi pursed her lips. "I want to ask you to come back with us, to Harranpul estate. Once Reshmi can be freed, we will bring her there, too."

I didn't say that it was unlikely for Boneweaver Island to be freed any time soon.

"And leave my friends to fight Altara, Zale, and the Reaper alone?" And Atax, though I wouldn't say his name out loud unless it was in a curse. His betrayal had stung, and I kept the obsidian dagger earring like a talisman in my pocket.

A talisman of my revenge.

Did Atax actually think I wouldn't have something to say about his defection? That weak, fuck-faced asshole. I had a blade with his heart's name written on it. And I would find him on the battlefield at the end of all this.

"Thank you, Keshmi," I said quietly. "But my place is in this war. I want to fight for Pia, for my friends and family."

"Are you sure we can't talk you out of it?" Keshmi asked, even as Geravie shook her head at her.

"She's got her mind set," Geravie huffed. "You're more like my two girls than you know. You'd like Saraya." Her face went tight again as she mentioned her old charge, Altara's sister, apparently trying to take back Lobrathia from the demons.

Colour me inspired.

"I hope I can meet her one day." I nodded. "If she's going to slaughter as many demons as will be required to take back her throne, she and I will be good friends."

GERAVIE AND KESHMI LEFT BEFORE DAWN THE NEXT DAY, SHAWLS drawn over their heads, faces downcast. I hugged both of them, but said little. In truth, I could hardly be annoyed at them for their sub-par reactions. Both were nearing seventy and the battle on Boneweaver Island had taken more from them than I'd thought. They would probably be safe on Harranpul estate, bordered by mountains where the demons were unlikely to dock any ships.

As I watched them leave in the horse-less carriage, trundling down the palace road, I determinedly shouldered my own bag and stomped in their wake right to the recruit-ment building in Xalya's sector.

If they wanted soldiers, they were about to get a mighty fine one.

10

ALTARA

The next morning, or whatever the demons took for morning, since it was always dark in this realm, we left the second demon court. Because Raen was a Boneweaver from his father's side, he could also change into any beast he wished, while Atax and Kai were Boneweavers on their mother's side, so they could not. Something about how the magic worked through males made it so, though I thought it was unfair.

Apparently, Rorax Boneweaver, Ellythia's second husband, had sired a daughter who'd passed down the Boneweaver power. Her line had left Lota Island but could not be traced to the present day. Raen seemed to think those females had left this realm for another.

Today, I flew on Zale's back in his eagle form with Raen flying next to us in the ever-dark sky. But now Kai ran in his black cheetah form and Atax in his lion form on the ground because they wanted to stretch their legs. I got the feeling they needed their beastly forms to burn off some of the blood-lust they carried.

But with every beat of Zale's wings, my stomach grew tighter.

We were headed to the Guild of the Pentarax Assassins, and there was *no* way I was going to step foot in that place.

During our travels around Boneweaver Island, Pia had educated me on the various types of demon species. While the Daanav marine demons under the Lotus Sea bore blue skin, the land demons were typically red, green, grey or yellow-skinned, and within that, there were strange and corrupted varieties. But the most dangerous kind, the species of the Butcher—with his corpse white skin, low cheekbones and heavy warrior's body—were called the Pentarax demons. They were elite, lethal assassins who usually worked alone and were able to wield magic.

My stepmother had sent one to punish me when I was thirteen years old. The Butcher had strapped me down, cut into me, and inhaled my golden magic like a drug. Once the torture was over, she'd promised that if I ever disrespected her or went against her, she'd call him back. She'd kept her promise when I'd run away to Ellythia, and the Butcher had banded together with subterranean and marine demons to come after me and Zale.

Once again, I'd lain strapped to a table. With each cut of his blade into my flesh and then bones, he'd drunk my magic, and it had made him strong. So strong, that even though I'd filled his body with arrows, he'd remained standing, staring at me in a sort of disbelief. I was glad for my wraith form in that moment because, without it, I might have been a mess of panic. I no longer considered myself *tainted* by what happened to me. Zale's love and my own self-acceptance had given me that much. But he was still a threatening enemy who would be difficult to defeat, even with my three brothers-in-law. Worse still, we were going to their guild to parlay. How many of these elite assassins would be there, just waiting for us?

I tried to broach Zale's mind through our celestial connection, but whether it was my form or the Reaper's magic on him, something was blocking me from getting into his mind. This should have disturbed me, but under the shadows, my brain was numb. It was a dangerous place for my mind to be in, but more dangerous still for those around me. I had killed the master of fear in the Forests of Eternity with this mindset, and I wondered who would succumb to my raw power next.

But the Pentaraxdemons were something else.

It would take us three days to get to their guild, according to our instructions. They lived away from everyone else, on their own, in dangerous lands, and no others—apart from their servants—were permitted there. They were elite demons, proud and lethal, and held a lofty sort of disdain for other demons, hence why they usually worked alone.

Time was passing and I was losing track of how much. There was a contract in my blood, between me and the carnal fae queen. I had promised to deliver my husband to her, tricking her into thinking I meant Zale. She hadn't known that I was also married to a second male. But I'd not seen Fangar Sharksbane with the other Daanavs in the demon courts here. I needed to find him and get him to Odeelia soon.

We landed to rest for my benefit because I knew the men could have travelled for a lot longer. None of them showed any signs of tiring, and in fact, Kai was bounding around the area they'd chosen, enthusiastically checking for threats, his white hair flying behind him like a kite.

Raen put up a massive shield of shadows that would hide

us from sight, scent, and hearing while Zale summoned a comfortable blanket for me to sleep on.

As Kai and Atax set about skinning the strange bull-like creature they'd found to eat and Raen sat down to shave his scruff with his obsidian blade, I confronted Zale.

Drawing my shadows around me like a shield of solid night, I said, "I'm not going to the Pentarax Guild."

Zale stood from where he was crouching by our blankets, his face blank as marble as he surveyed me. Even in this state, his face was devastating in its harsh beauty. He always made my heart beat a little faster, and what he said next made my heart skip two whole beats.

"You have no choice, my mate." He grabbed my wrist with the intent to tug me towards the blanket, but I snatched my hand away.

"*How dare you,*" I hissed. Behind me, my brothers-in-law went preternaturally still.

"Why." The question was flat and emotionless, less of a question and more of a command to explain myself.

Because one of them had tied me to a table and cut me open? Because my power was laced through his very bones, and in some heinous way, it felt like he owned me? Because one of them might very well do it again? Zale knew this. At least, I think a part of him knew it.

"You know *why*, husband. You were all there when *it* happened."

"The Reaper has commanded us to go. And so, we will go."

I crossed my arms, my anger rising at his ruthless tone. "You can go, then. I will wait here."

His voice was a low growl of warning. "No. I will not be

separated from you. You are mine to keep. You are *mine* in all ways. Where I go, so will you."

His possessiveness was suddenly like nails scraping on glass. "Why can't the Reaper go there himself? Why do we need to go for a *few* warriors?"

Zale stepped towards me and I took a wide step back, lightning sparking down my arms in warning. His head cocked as he noted them and he paused in place. I suddenly missed Wobbles, who always seemed to help Zale in these situations. "Because," he said slowly, "we cannot defeat the Ellythians on their islands without them. We will not win by force. The Ellythians are too smart, and their magic is too powerful. We need the intelligence and power of the Pentarax, and there are more than fifty of them in their guild. With them, we can easily take the remaining two islands."

My entire body, including the smoke around me, froze in space. *Easily.* Zale was moving to take Ellythia, and he thought it would be *easy*. I blinked rapidly at him as he monitored my every breath and movement with his ever-observant eyes.

He knew exactly what he was doing, and he would achieve it. I turned to look at Raen, who'd also been monitoring our exchange carefully.

"Is this true, Raen?"

The mage's eyes flicked between me and Zale, but he did not reply.

Zale bristled where he stood, his hands clenched into fists. "You do not ask *him*. My word is your god, my mate."

Goddess, rage struck through my veins, hot and fast. I had become a *thing* to him. He saw me as his property and nothing more.

With a rabid snarl, I viciously lunged at my husband, and

Zale—allowed himself, I think—to fall back onto the ground with a thump. Wrapping my hands around his throat, I squeezed hard, letting a little lightning skitter over him.

Zale's body was anything but submissive. He was rock hard and taut beneath me, but his eyes drooped to half-lidded. He was aroused by this? Enraged, my voice was low and dangerous when I bent my face to his and hissed, "A monster you may be, Ashzale, but you are *my* monster. You might think you own me, but *I* also own *you*. You listen to my command. Do you understand?"

Zale let out a puff of air and arousal came down the bond like mellow wine. "Yes, queen of my black heart."

Our bond vibrated so hard our bodies shook under its force.

"You will *never* disrespect me like that ever again. You do *not* tell me what I will and will not do."

Kai leapt forward with an enthusiastic chuckle and dropped to both knees, his hand pressed over his heart. "You own me too, my queen!"

Turning my head, I cupped his cheek with one hand. "Yes, my darling boy." His sky-blue eyes glistened over his wild grin. "You are also mine."

He rubbed his face against my palm until Zale snapped his teeth at him. Raen hastily came forward to haul Kai away, and Zale grabbed me by the waist, angrily swinging me onto the dirt and pinning me with his hips.

"I will execute anyone who hurts you," he growled. He grabbed my chin and turned it to the side, proceeding to lick me up the side of my neck, and I was so shocked that my anger stalled. "If you wish me to kill the Pentarax who hurt you, I will. You are *my* responsibility." He turned my chin to the other side, licked up that side of my neck, and I shivered.

"You are *mine* to protect."

His words claimed something deep inside of me. Scraping his teeth along my jaw, he muttered, "You smell of this fucking realm. I must mark you to get rid of it." The bond between us thrummed happily and I couldn't help but let out a small sigh at the feel of the hard length of his body on top of me. My anger sizzled a little less under my skin just as the space between my legs longed to be filled by him. I was still furious, but it served to make my blood hot, making my senses even more aware of his masculine strength over me. It was intoxicating, almost like a drug, I imagined, but so much better. My breathing became ragged as I stared at his mouth, his lips, and became suddenly consumed with the need to taste him.

Zale's brothers were muttering to the side until Atax mumbled something I couldn't hear.

"Oh," came Kai's feeble reply, then heavy footfalls as they left us.

I frowned up at Zale, but he was busy shooing away the smoke over my skin. "Let me see you properly," he whispered, pushing up my black silk dress and running a palm over my abdomen. With the wave of a hand, we were covered in an opaque obsidian shield-dome, closed off from the entire world and my black dress was tossed to the side. He crawled down my length, gently rubbing his face and body against mine, marking my skin with his own scent. It was something I'd come to understand was the way of the Old Ones, a part of their beastly urges. No matter how irritated I was at his possessiveness, his body, his smell, stoked the embers within me, and in seconds, it was a raging fire and I writhed under his hands. He gripped my thighs and roughly spread them apart. Cool air hit my wet sex as I allowed my shadows to part for him. Open-mouthed kisses graced the inside of each thigh before, with great impatience, he pounced forward and covered my core with his mouth.

I cried out at the sudden sensation of his hot mouth against my core, my back arching of its own accord as he noisily devoured my pussy like he'd been waiting years to do it. He ran that delicious tongue up and down both lips, then plunged deep between them. He was a beast possessing his prey, and his hands roamed over my squirming body with hungry fervour. I dug my fingers into his scalp, tugging on the long strands of his black hair, groaning as he brought me higher and higher with his lapping and sucking. I ground my hips against his mouth, searching for release.

"Altara," he groaned, low and ragged.

I froze.

11

ALTARA

I t was the first time since our defection that Zale called me by my name instead of the animalistic 'mate'. As the real-isation hit me, I grabbed a bunch of his hair and yanked his head up, *hard*. His expression was furious as he looked at me, his mouth shiny with my slick. But there within his blue eyes was something hot, not cold. Something aware, not glazed. Before he could wrestle his way back into position, I lunged for him, shoving him roughly onto the ground by the shoul-ders and climbing on top of his body, shoving my witch's robe completely off and tugging his pants down. His manhood sprung free, hard and ready. Zale's face was only dark wonder as I straddled him, hovering over his bare, massive cock, already glistening with a bead of his desire. I pressed him against my wet opening, claiming him in the most dominating way I knew how.

I hissed at the burn of his large girth stretching my entrance. His hand, the one bearing his mating mark, a black butterfly in flight, came up to cup my cheek as a soft, sensual groan slipped from his lips. I gripped Zale's broad shoulder, murmuring his name as I eased him into me a bit at a time, pressing my cheek into his hand.

Finally, fully sheathed within me, I observed Zale's eyes again.

"Altara?" he said hoarsely. His thumb tenderly brushed my cheek in a sort of awe, his blue eyes wide. Somehow, in our most intimate place, the shadow of the Reaper eased off him.

"How do we stop this, Zale?" I whispered, grinding my hips in a slow, delicious circle. "How do we stop the R—"

He slapped a palm over my mouth, though it didn't hurt. "Do not, Tara. I…" he grunted as I began to ride him, terrified that whatever this was would slip away. Zale breathed, "He may hear his name being used by you in particular. He is able to access all of our thoughts, but for some reason, not yours, so he is watching you closely."

That was new information, and very good news.

My hips paused as I thought. "By the force of his power when he'd knocked me off Glacine, I'd assumed he was strong enough to do anything to me."

Zale flexed his hips into me and I let out a wanton sound, tilting my head back at the sheer stretch of him in me. It had been two weeks since we'd been joined, and I couldn't believe I'd forgotten how big he was. How… extraordinary he felt in me. "It might be Agnolthi's power," Zale said, his voice strained, the muscles in his neck visible and turning pink. "Your high priestess powers." He was likely right. "We are entwined, you and I," he continued. "Your magic is inside of me and I think that is why it is different this time, why I can come out of it when I am in you." He jerked his hips for emphasis, sending us both groaning, his fingers digging into my thighs.

"How do we break the connection to him?" I whispered. "The black bond between you and him?"

He encircled me in his arms and pulled me down to lay on top of him. With my breasts directly against his chest, I swore I could *feel* the Reaper's heavy malefic power stalking in there. But I also felt that part of me within him too, lurking beneath a trapdoor. Waiting. Deliberating.

I couldn't just go in there and get it out like I had done with my grandmother. With her, I'd pulled out the Reaper's magic from her body. She'd eventually died from that, but Zale was *bonded* to the Reaper. That was a deeper sort of tie.

Zale bucked his hips up, bringing me back from my thoughts. Against the side of my neck he whispered, "Raen was working on something, I think, though he cannot speak on it. Your magic in me is doing something too, but Tara, we must be clever about this."

Clever enough to thwart a god-like being who was hundreds of years old? I dared not say out loud what I was thinking.

"The Reaper ordered me to break the bond without killing you." I froze my grinding to stare at him, my heart sinking. "Tara, you need to find a way to stop me. In two weeks, I will be leading the charge to take Ellythia. He keeps mentioning your sister. I don't know what he plans for her, but it can't be good."

What *was* the Reaper thinking? I had to trust my sister could handle herself. But only death could break a star bond like ours. How did he expect Zale to break it?

Zale ran his large hands down my back in long comforting

strokes and, despite our precarious figurative position, I could not help but feel *safe* with him. Was I mad? Zale was more dangerous now than he'd ever been. Our bond felt stronger than ever, humming with happiness under our closeness.

"You must forgive me," he panted into my hair, holding me tight on top of him while fucking me slowly, "if I do vile things, I will be acting on cold instinct. I..." When he trailed off, I pressed my palms to his chest and lifted myself to look at him. His face contorted into something foreign; something dark and hollow.

"What is it?" I said softly.

"I'm so sorry, Tara," he whispered, pausing all movement, his blue eyes were suddenly lined with silver. Horrified, something dark wound its way around us and I gently cupped his cheek.

"What is it, Zale?" I breathed.

"I was the one who killed your grandmother."

The words hit me with the force of a maelstrom. All the blood drained from my face as I closed my eyes against the onslaught of everything. Every emotion, every ounce of pain, every bit of grief I'd felt these past few days. He'd not been in his right mind. He'd been under the influence of the Reaper.

"It's alright," I breathed.

"Look at me, Altara." His voice was soft, low, insistent. Laced with a grief I'd never heard in his voice.

I blinked my eyes open.

"I will never forgive myself," he whispered. "He gave me an order, and I followed through. She was dying already, but it does not change that it was through my hand that she met her end."

A lesser man might have tried to minimise what he'd done. But here was Zale, open and honest, as he stared into my eyes. Not pleading. Not even asking for my forgiveness, because he knew it was not fair to ask that of me. But I would give it to him anyway.

"This is war, Zale," I said firmly. "This is why we fight. Why I told my father on his funeral pyre that I would do whatever it took to end this."

His jaw clenched, and he nodded reluctantly.

"I forgive—"

"No," he said firmly, squeezing my hips. "Worse will happen between now and the end of this, Tara. *Worse.* Do you understand? I cannot have your forgiveness right now. I cannot. I will not be deserving. I am not deserving."

I bit my lip against my own fear, the idea that it was going to get worse than Zale killing my grandmother. I let out a shaky breath.

"I love you with every part of my being," he said. "I will do anything, *anything* to keep you safe. Do you understand what anything means?"

His blue eyes were fierce upon me, striking me with a rawness I'd never ever seen in another human being. Anything. And he meant that. He'd once told me he would burn down the Lotus Palace for me.

I knew he meant it. I knew he was capable, and that knowledge sunk into my bones like a heavy, savage blow.

Zale swallowed. "That is why I am telling you now. You must do what needs to be done. Whatever savagery you need to do against Raen, Atax, Kai and me to stop us from causing real harm. You *must* do it. They will not be able to live with themselves if they do something unforgivable."

My own vision blurred at the force of his words, at the sheer gravity in them. We both knew what had happened to Rani. How she fell into the grief of something she never meant to do. Of harm she never meant to cause. He ran his hands down my thighs as if memorising this moment, the feel of my body, my skin on his.

"I love you," I said firmly. Then I tossed my head and lifted my hips, sheathing myself roughly down again. He groaned. "And I know." The wet sound of our love created a swirl of desire through my lower stomach. "I am not afraid to use my powers on you or my three brothers."

His arms tightened around me, and his pace quickened. "Use them, my Altara. Cut me open if you must."

"Fine," I panted as his cock pounded into me with short strokes, spinning pleasure up through my spine. I exploded with a cry, stars exploding in my vision, pleasure surging up my back, digging my nails into the skin of his neck. Zale came in me with a low groan, his hot seed spurting and filling me up in the most satisfying way. I moaned with primal pleasure as I felt his power roaring into me, filling me with the sheer force of his magic. Panting, I fell back onto him, burying my nose in his neck and relishing in the burn of his wild power filling my veins.

It was then that a thought struck me like a bolt of Lobrathian lightning. Abruptly, I lifted myself to look into his eyes. He was panting, but with each breath, I could see the ice returning, glazing over his eyes like a film of frost. I had no time left. My options were running low.

We were on a direct path to bring the Pentarax to our side, and I had to stop that from happening. I also needed to find Fangar and perhaps I could kill two birds with one stone.

It occurred to me that, if I ran, Zale would follow me.

Everything in my being told me not to do this. Not to leave my star-born mate. But I *knew* in my very soul that Zale would divert whatever plans to hunt me down. Even without a conscience, with a cold black heart, his instincts would demand he follow his mate. We had to be smart to defeat the emperor of demons, and this was perhaps the only way.

"I'm sorry," I mumbled.

Lightning shot down my arm, and with a heavy dose of my magic behind it, I punched Zale right in the temple, hard enough to cause a minor concussion. His eyes widened in understanding before they fluttered shut, his head lolling to the side.

The healer in me urged me to stay and heal him, to bring him back to consciousness. But he was an Old One. He would heal, perhaps too quickly for my machinations.

So, biting hard on my lip, I leapt off him as his obsidian shield around us dissolved into nothing. Tugging on my silk dress and covering myself with my witch's robe, I allowed my magic to envelop me. Taking on the appearance of my surroundings, I sprinted into the dark away from him. It had been a long time since I'd had to use this particular skill of mine, but I was essentially invisible like this. Even so, the first time I'd met Zale, he'd been able to track me *easily* when I'd been invisible.

And without a conscience, he'd do literally anything to get me back.

"Magrin?" I called out into the ether. I needed help if I was going to get out of here. As much as I'd tried to pay attention to what was going on, there was no way for me to know how to get to a portal out of the demon realm. I also didn't know

how long the Reaper would be occupied with his dealings with the dark fae kings.

But as I sprinted into the dark, there came no answering reply in my mind. Swearing, I called out again. Perhaps from the Eternal Forest, Magrin and the Nine witches were not able to reach the demon realm? In my witch's cloak, I had concealed a magical ruby, straight from the snake's hood of Ulanna, a Boneweaver from Zale's court. She had told me to use it to call if I needed them.

But their allegiance was to Zale, their king. And the last thing we needed was a horde of powerful predators on the Reaper's side. No, they needed to be kept safe in the Eternal Forest for the moment.

The dark landscape of the demon realm was not a nice place to be. Howls sounded in the night along with strange shrieks. Demons were not the only beings in this realm, monsters were as well.

Panicking slightly, I desperately called out for Magrin again, sending a pulse of my power with it. *"Dear Goddess, help me. Magrin? Any of the Nine? If you can hear me, I need your knowledge! Shit!"*

I hadn't meant to swear at them, but I didn't know how long Zale would be out for.

Finally, like a raven in the dark of night, soft wings fluttered at the edge of my awareness. With a sigh of relief, I gave the presence permission to engage with me. Magrin's voice was a familiar husky, deep feminine sweep against the inside of my brain. *"Your voice is distant, High Priestess. What delightfully dark place do you haunt?"*

"I am in the Demon Realm. And I must lead my husband on a chase to my second husband. But I need a deft head start. Any idea how I can find the demon Fangar Sharksbane with haste?"

"You will need a portal. And speed. I sense you still have the boots on."

The witch's boots were a solid, beautiful, and strong piece of leather work that laced up to my thighs. They'd helped me stay on Zale's back when we were flying, but I grinned as Magrin's sly voice instructed me to zap them with my electricity.

With a flash of light, I was lurched forward by a new power, bounding in a wide leap across the dirt. I swore loudly, as with each step I took, I was propelled forward incredibly fast. Grinning like a madwoman, I adjusted my stride until I found a rhythm. Soon, I was zipping past the demonic countryside faster, even, than any of the beasts Zale and Raen could turn into.

"Magrin, you genius!"

"We made it with the Old Ones in mind, but I had never thought you would need to run away from them."

"You and me both. How on earth do I know which direction to go in?" Hair askew, I came to a jarring stop, frowning at my surroundings. It was desolate in all directions, no landmarks natural or otherwise to go by.

"You are a high priestess now, your majesty, as well as wife to the Boneweaver king. Do you feel those powers within you?"

Blinking sheepishly, I turned my awareness inward, to where my power lay hidden under all the layers of smoke and darkness. It had always appeared golden to my inner eye, an energy with its own sort of personality, though inherently a part of me. The one part of me, I supposed, that encompassed all of my rebellious traits.

But since Agnolthi ordained me as her high priestess, I'd not taken the time to look closely at my new powers. Too much had happened between then and now. The only way I could put it was that my power seemed *heavier*. Its light was a deeper, richer gold, denser than before. Its weight was welcome within me, and better still, twined around it with solid bands of deep blue light, was a power that smelled familiar.

I gasped softly, recognising Zale's magic. At the same time, the back of my hand tickled, and I opened my eyes to find my tiger mating mark, pawing at my skin.

It responded with an audible purr.

"I see it," I murmured.

"Enquire with it," Magrin said. *"Ask if it will do as you need."*

It wasn't with the talking sort of language exactly, but I posed my power a question. *Where is the closest portal?*

There was more tingling on my hand, followed by a burn.

Then the tiger disappeared off my hand entirely—and appeared glowing and translucent before me, as big and as feral as Zale himself. The tiger stalked towards me, rubbing its phantom face on my leg, its tail high in the air, the picture of a happy cat, before it bounded off into the distance as if leading me on a hunt.

I grinned. "Looks like we're off."

"Go. Then call upon us," Magrin said, amused. *"And we will come."*

I ran for upwards of an hour, following my tiger, who snuck looks at me from time to time. When I was happy I had some distance up my sleeve, I collapsed, panting, on a hill where I could see anyone coming from a distance. My furry guide nuzzled my neck, and I felt a velvety smooth face against my skin.

I sat up. *"Now, Magrin, how does one find a person?"*

"Let us scry," she replied happily. *"May we join you?"*

"If you can."

The Nine witches of the Eternal Forest were around me within seconds, tall black-cloaked women, their hoods drawn low. Pale white faces looked serenely down at me, long-fingered hands pressed together as they bowed.

"High Priestess," they said in unison, bowing low.

"Teach me," I commanded.

12

ZALE

I woke up with the side of my head burning.

No one had knocked me out since... well, *ever*. My father had given me beatings to the head, but I'd only ever blacked out for a heartbeat at most, those times. Slowly, I stood, prodding the ache on my left temple. The sting of residual magic skittered over my entire skull.

My mate's power was a force I would recognise anywhere. I could be blind and deaf and still able to tell that it was her who'd knocked me out. Snarling, I whirled around to assess my surroundings.

The demon lands were desolate around me. Dirt below, dark, starless sky above. No creature, demon, monster, fae or human moved within hearing distance, only my three brothers, bickering over the last leg of meat.

And my mate is nowhere in sight.

Every negative emotion tore through my rotten heart. A pain I could only describe as serrating and crushing obliterated my mind. I snarled into the night, turning like a rabid animal, sniffing, my pupils blown, my body demanding to become a beast.

Some memory lingered in the back of my mind, but try as I might, I could not reach it. It only served to enrage me further.

The golden thread of our starlight bond shimmered from my navel, and on plucking it, there came no answer. I raised my head and sniffed at my surroundings. The only scent filling my head was her sweet, enticing, powerful fragrance, borne of our coupling. It made my mouth water and my cock ache for her body against mine.

Skin and bone exploded outward as I burst into my tiger's form with an audible snap. My vocal cords elongated, and I roared, tearing the darkness in two. It was both a warning and a summons.

For any beast nearby, except my brothers, to run.

For my mate to get her body back to me before I ripped this realm apart.

From over the land came an answering reply. Atax's lion's roar followed by Raen's.

I stood there, still within my own rage, simply breathing as I listened to my brothers storm back to me.

After a breath, unable to keep still, I charged at them.

We met in the middle, the four of us, hackles raised, snarling into each other's faces, rubbing our cheeks against one another as they silently questioned my rage.

I blasted back into my human form, and the snap resounded around us. My brothers changed back as well, their faces masks of feral alertness, their eyes darting around, noses sniffing.

"What is it, brother?" Raen snarled, pressing his forehead

against mine. It stilled the fire in my veins only for a second and I grabbed at his arms.

"She's gone. My mate is gone. By her scent, it's been an hour at least."

Atax let out a rabid sound and he and Kai aggressively prowled in a circle around us, sniffing the air, the dirt, our combined magic and agitation making the particles in the air thrum.

"I'll kill them!" Atax snapped, shoving at Kai to expel his own violent energy.

Kai used the momentum to twist and fall to the earth, pinching some dirt between his fingers and sniffing. "Who?" he purred softly.

"The cunts who took our queen!" Atax spat. "I'll fucking tear their throats out with my teeth!"

We all went still at that, and Raen caught my eye. No other scent marked this area except hers and mine. We could all scent that.

"She ran from here," Raen said, inspecting a footprint in the dirt. "Her witch's boots leave a distinct mark."

We all crowded around him, nothing more than four naked feral animals sniffing and grunting.

Her absence grated at me like a serrated knife across my soul. I wanted to obliterate the entire world and burn it to the ground until there was nothing left but me and her, panting under the ashes of a destroyed world, covered in the blood of our enemies.

"But... we do not need her tracks to follow her," Raen murmured, his eyes sparkling as he looked at me.

A slow, feral grin spread across my face.

She had forgotten one thing. She was still dripping my

cum from her sweet centre. I'd marked her as mine before she left, so every male would know who she belonged to. Even so, I would track her all the way to the ends of hell and drag her back kicking and screaming by our combined scent alone. My rage knew no bounds and she wouldn't be the first to learn that tonight. But of course, I didn't need her scent *either*.

We had been bound by a primordial power that superseded flesh and bone, scent and sound. Our souls were twined together like two rivers flowing into one another, becoming one. I did not end at the borders of my body. I ended at the borders of *hers*.

"We go on a hunt." My voice emerged so low, it was nothing more than monstrous.

Kai hooted and clapped, his white braids bouncing, his muscles rippling. "Hunt, hunt, hunt. Who is our prey?" he sang.

"My mate."

"My queen!" he cried, shoving his fist in the air and pointing at the sky. "She'll be sorry! So, so, so sorry! Because..." He cocked his head at me. "Because— Did she run away?" His mouth dropped open into a big 'O'. He covered it as if horrified.

The rumble in my chest was so deep it was barely audible.

Raen sucked air between his teeth, the tattoos across his cheekbones dancing in the low light. "Oh, little queen, what have you done?"

"Your king is going to be very angry," Atax snarled, rubbing his scruff.

I took a long, slow breath that should have calmed the pure hellfire burning through my arteries.

It didn't work.

With one glance from me, all four of us burst into our beastly forms and charged headfirst into the dark. My mate had just unleashed four very angry, savage monsters upon the world.

13

ALTARA

As I peered into my tiny cauldron of water—a cauldron I'd made with earth and water from a nearby stream, under Magrin's instruction, a slow smile spread across my face. Fangar Sharksbane, my second husband, sat at a camp-fire messily devouring a lamb shank. His blue skin looked navy in the firelight, the fire glinting off his armoured shoulders, yellow eyes darting around at his soldiers. An entire company of armoured Daanav marine demons sat and milled about the fire around him. Palm trees swayed about them and I recognised the jungle in which they sat immediately.

Boneweaver Island.

"This both complicates things and makes it easier," I murmured to the Nine. "On one hand, I'll be leading Zale right back to Ellythia. On the other hand, I can capture Fangar and get him to Odeelia before the month is up, thereby fulfilling my blood contract to return my husband to her."

"It was a clever plan." Magrin grinned with all her teeth as she peered over my shoulder.

"It's lucky Zale forced me to marry the both of them, I

suppose," I said wryly, remembering that he'd made that nasty choice when he'd been cold-hearted.

A sudden, ethereal *pluck* on the thread that bound me to Zale resounded through my body. I grunted, doubling over as the echo of a purely violent roar sounded in my ears.

I swore. *Looks like Zale is up.*

Magrin made a noise at the back of her throat, and I turned to give her a look. "I should—"

I grunted again as Zale pulled on the thread so hard it physically pulled me forward. A deep primal ache spread through my centre at the feeling of my mate pining for me.

"You must go before they catch up to you," Magrin warned. "Angry Boneweavers are fast Boneweavers. And an angry Boneweaver king…"

"Right." I stood up and hooked my little cauldron on my arm by its handle. It was a cute little thing, its base only as wide as my palm, but it would serve me well for all sorts of things, including making any drinking water clean, and even storing food.

My transparent tiger guide sat next to me so close I swore I could feel her heat. I turned to her—because the intelligent, reasonable gleam in its eyes could only mean it was a *she* —and asked it a silent question.

There *had* to be a portal that would lead towards Boneweaver Island, if there was such a thing. When we'd been attacked and taken by Fangar all that time ago, I figured they'd had a way to get the Butcher and the other subterranean demons directly onto the island.

My tiger growled and dipped her head before bounding forward and looking back at me expectantly.

As I stood, I glanced worriedly at my witches. "If there is such a portal, I should destroy it, shouldn't I?

We can't have the demons coming and going as they please."

But the Nine witches murmured and shook their heads. "Destroying and creating portals is colossal power-work," Magrin said seriously. "Portals are tears in reality, and often permanent in their nature. Even the ones that shift. That level of power is beyond any mortal."

Disappointing, but I couldn't dispute the laws of nature.

As I prepared to zap my boots again, Magrin's deep voice rung out behind me. "Be wary in these lands, Altara." There was a small frown on her face as she and the other witches suspiciously looked around. "There are other predators about, other than your king husband."

"Thank you," I said quietly. "All of you. I do not feel so alone right now."

They graced me with delighted smiles. "We serve you, High Priestess. It is our pleasure and honour for the queen who gave us our freedom."

I ran through the demon lands once again, following the streak of blue light that was my tiger, bounding over dirt, streaking past foul creatures that stalked the night. I never got a good look at them, nor them at me because I was but a shadowy blur on the wind, and in some ways, I was glad for it. I wanted to save my murderous energy for Fangar, after all.

The boots did most of the work for me, even then the muscles of my thighs and stomach burned with the hours of driving down through the dirt and catching myself. I rested regularly, but not for long each time, and more than once, an angry, ravenous hum came down the bond between Zale and I. There was a dominating energy to it now, a sort of thrill that I imagined predators got when they gave chase. My veins tingled with the realisation that I had made myself prey, and was no more than a deer, sprinting through the dark away from the hunger of a tiger.

I BOUNDED OVER THE LAND, FOLLOWING MY TRANSLUCENT GUIDE for upwards of an hour. Nervousness bubbled up, spiking every time Zale plucked on our bond or when his anger resonated through it. They would travel as fast as they could, so I dared not stop again, even if I had gotten a good head start.

Eventually, the ground sloped upwards, and I was sweating and panting up a rocky mountainside. My guide slowed down, and so did I, until I was barely more than crawling as I approached the crest of the small mountain. I hauled myself up and over a lip, and my jaw dropped open at what my guide was indicating.

It was a gaping maw in the earth itself, twenty paces long and wide. No light came from it and I couldn't see any bottom either, only shadows and a salty wind that pulled the loose strands of my hair forward. As if it wanted to suck me in.

I shivered.

"You're telling me we have to go in there?" I asked the tigress in disbelief.

In response, she changed. Much in the same way that Zale did, my guiding tiger's bones crunched. Ligaments snapped and her mouth turned into a beak, her front paws extended outward until they were wings. She shook out her feathers and turned around, looking over her shoulder at me.

"Goddess," I muttered, before carefully making my way

forward with an arm outstretched. My hand met her velvety soft feathers and the lithe, powerful body underneath. Tentatively, I climbed on her back, scooting up to grip the feathers at her neck.

Zale's magic thrummed beneath me and I felt as if I could almost smell his hot-blooded, masculine scent in her effervescent plumage. This was Zale's power, made manifest in me. I wondered if he knew who was helping me, if he had any awareness that I was using his power against him.

Then she dived right into the maw of the earth.

My own scream filled my ears, shrill and unexpected as we plummeted into the darkness. Within a few seconds, I shut my mouth and got control of myself, gripping my guide's velvety feathers with my fists. My witch's boots holding me firm around her body, we plunged into the shadows, my hair flying, face chafing in the harsh wind.

All at once, completely without warning, we slammed into icy water. My breath was knocked out of my lungs at the impact. Completely numb, I tried not to panic, trusting that Zale's power would guide me to where I needed to be. Under me, velvet feathers changed into something smooth and sleek, and I scrambled to maintain my hold as we surged upwards at break-neck speed.

I landed on a sandy shore with a smack, gasping for air, the sun glaring down upon me like an angry god. I blinked up and glared at my surroundings, because what type of portal tried to kill the people going through it?

"Well, pardon me!" I gasped through panting breaths, pushing myself up to sit as I looked around for my so-called guide.

Apparently, the joke was on me because Zale's magic had the same dark, stupid sense of humour. The tigress was sitting there, blinking at me innocently, her transparent skin hardly visible under the beaming sunlight. I fisted a bit of sand and flung it at her. She didn't move an inch while the sand sailed right through her body.

Huffing, I looked around to see a thankfully empty beach that looked nothing like any beach on Boneweaver Island.

"Wait a minute!" I cried, jumping to my feet. Water spilled off the witch's cloak and boots, thankfully water-resistant, but underneath, I was soaked. I couldn't find the strength to care about that when a distinct sign up on the beach read: Beware of Tigers.

I whirled around to glare at my guide. "*Tiger Island?* It's the wrong island!"

The transparent tiger jerked her chin towards the sea, and I looked out at the clear turquoise ocean.

"We didn't have a choice, I suppose?" I threw my hands up in the air. "Well, come on then. We need to cross this island and get to the next one. Unseen, mind you." I stomped up the beach, grumbling about how this was going to extend my trip by days, while I made sure I was still invisible.

My guide ignored me, and I had no choice but to follow her, bounding through the shadowy humidity of the jungle. But my reprieve from the harsh sunlight didn't last long as the jungle cleared, revealing grassy rolling hills and, in the distance, an estate with a creek that merrily trickled along.

I filled my cauldron with water from the creek and found it to be so crisp and fresh that I rested there amongst the daisies awhile, drying out the last of the dampness from my body. The grass was soft under me and I turned my face towards the sun for a moment, simply enjoying the light. Gods, how the demons spent their days in the dark was beyond me. The night sky was all the more beautiful for knowing that the dawn was going to come and replace it. Even the air of Ellythia smelled sweet and fresh, like a sip of cool water on a hot day.

I'd not quite appreciated that until now. And knowing that this freedom was under threat made me give my guide a dark look.

"I need to give you a name," I said thoughtfully. "Perhaps we should make it a male name, just to tease Zale and give him a rival, hey?" I laughed when she rubbed her face along my thigh and I tickled the top of her velvet head. "Naina, I think. For a pretty girl. I—" I frowned as a tickle in the centre of my chest made me look east, towards the distant estate. Something expectant brushed against my skin. Something important.

It was dark like a storm cloud, but small enough that it might have fit into the palm of my hand. Frowning, I jerked my head towards the estate. "I think we need a slight detour, Naina."

A low growl.

"I know, but it's calling me." I was already moving towards it, determined by this feeling on my skin. Naina growled softly, but prowled after me nonetheless.

Getting more and more curious as I approached the busy three-storey mansion, I observed the people bustling about.

The entrance gate was open, but above it in the cast iron was written:

Umasri Manor
Hail Lisanthi

This was Rani's family estate, I realised with dull shock. Well, I was going to have to have a look around, then, wasn't

I? A vicious smile crept over my lips as I lurked through the archway and up to the mansion.

These people had treated my friend without compassion for a mistake she made as a teenager. Adults should have had more sense than that, and by the sound of what had happened on my friend's way to the capital, things had taken a further turn for the worse. Rani's lady love was wed to others, her marriage silks thrown to the floor.

I skulked over the gravel stones as quietly as I could, because even invisible, my footfalls were still audible. The feeling in my chest was a guide that led me around the house and around to the back where the family crops were set out in neat, labelled rows upon dark tilled earth. It led me to the back door where the air was magically cool from the three green quartz gems above the wooden arch of the door.

There was a kitchen inside, but instead of food and cooking utensils on the worktable, before me was a long line of knives, daggers and swords, gleaming as if freshly polished. Smart people, preparing for the battle that was coming.

There was only one person inside, sitting on a stool with her side facing me, a heavy axe in her hand and a whetstone in the other. She was lean and tall, with corded muscles along her arms, her strength impressive considering the weight of the axe she wielded easily. Her brown face was narrow and flushed from her work. Long lashes fanned over her cheeks and a short braid was coiled into a knot at the top of her head.

The dark feeling was, without a doubt, coming from her, and I could now place what it was.

I'd felt such a thing twice before. The first time, around the neck of the Headmistress Jessine, and the second on two fae captives I'd released in the Eternal Forest.

There was nothing around this girl's neck. In fact, she wore no jewellery at all except for her wedding necklace, which was unusual for a girl whose family worshipped Lisanthi, who was wealth incarnate.

I glanced at Naina behind me and she nudged the door shut. With the click, the girl whipped around, her eyes wide, searching the air.

"What is your name?" I asked curiously.

"Goddess!" she hissed, holding her axe at the ready in a practised fighting stance that immediately told me she knew how to use it. "Reveal yourself!"

Obliging her, I allowed myself to reappear, letting the world around me slip off my shoulders like Ellythian silk.

The girl's eyes widened as she took me in, no doubt dishevelled from travel. But her dark eyes flicked to my forehead, and she abruptly sunk to her knees.

"High Priestess, please do not kill me." Her axe dropped with a clunk to the floor as Naina closed the door to the side of the kitchen that led to the rest of the house.

"What is your name?" I repeated, scanning her body.

She brought her palms together in front of her chest and it was then that I saw it. "Yulara, High Priestess. My name is Yulara Devdi."

Ice flooded my veins at the two things that I saw. One, Rani's childhood sweetheart, and two, the malefic tattoo on the inside of her wrist.

"Yulara," I repeated, testing the name out. "Rani's Yulara."

Her head snapped up, her eyes wide, pupils dilated as her chest took in shallow, frantic breaths. I would not have expected to see her here, but Umasri house was wealthy, no doubt they employed many from the families who lived here.

Perhaps the family felt responsibility for what had happened to Vasi.

"What is this?" I tapped the inside of my own wrist.

The older girl looked down at the tattoo and then covered it with her other hand, shaking her head.

"Who did that to you?" I took a step forward. "And do not lie to me. I know dark magic when I see it. I detected it all the way from the other side of the field."

She swallowed, her eyes glistening with restrained emotion, and I did not miss the tiny tremble in her hands. "I cannot speak of it." Her voice was barely a whisper.

Taking another step forward, I reached down and gently took her wrist. She never tried to resist, her limbs loose, her shoulders slumped.

My magic sprung forward, eager for a taste. Hungry, no doubt, as we'd not healed anyone or gobbled up magic in a while for all our traipsing around the demon realm.

Yulara gasped as my magic invaded her hand, claimed the magical tattoo—a series of triangular shapes in obsidian ink— and sucked it back into my body. I let go of her wrist and cocked my head, studying the nature of the magic I'd taken, as my own broke it apart into pieces and turned it into golden dust.

My eyes widened as I recognised Rani's name amongst the spell.

"A spell to stop you from going to Rani?" I asked the young woman for confirmation.

She nodded miserably, the corners of her mouth down- turned as she stared at her now red wrist. "I tried to run after her when she left for the exile school but they caught me, and paid a lot of money for a mage to keep me here." Her eyes turned fierce, her fists clenching. "I would have *killed* to get

Rani back, to follow her, and I almost did. It took five men to hold me down." A look of resentful pride shone in her eyes. "But once the spell took hold I couldn't leave the island, nor communicate with Rani."

"These people who did this to you…"

"My father. My brothers."

I felt sick to my stomach.

"They are no longer your family, Yulara. You realise that?"

She gritted her teeth and nodded. I observed her carefully, wondering at her nature. Rani had loved her, and I still remembered the wistful look of a woman in love during the brief times she'd spoken about her betrothed. Yulara, for her part, met my gaze with hesitancy at first, then to my surprise, she raised her chin.

"Thank you, High Priestess."

"What will you do now?" I asked, trying to keep my voice casual. What she would decide next would be telling.

She took a deep breath. "I want to find Rani."

It was a cool relief that washed over me. "Is that right?"

Her fists tightened around her axe as she nodded with determination.

"Well. You should go and find her."

Yulara gave me an uncertain grimace. "Do you think she will want to see me?"

I remembered a picture Kai had drawn and dropped in Rani's room. "Yes, Yulara. Rani will want to see you. Her heart is the purest I've ever met, perhaps even more than my sister's."

Her throat bobbed again. "Thank you."

I stepped away from her. Her fate was her own now, and she had much to do to prove herself to Rani. "I must go. Farewell, Yulara. Goddess be with you."

As Naina and I strode out of the Umasri kitchen, Yulara whispered, "Goddess be with you, too, Your Majesty."

NAINA CAST ME A LOOK AS WE HEADED SOUTH.

"I know, I know," I muttered.

If I was to complete my blood oath in time, I needed to keep moving over land. That evening, after a dark look from me, my guide paused her leading and allowed me to get onto her back. For the remainder of our trip, we alternated between me using my lightning boots and when I got tired, me on her back.

At the end of the second night, I came to the southernmost part of Tiger Island and walked right into an Ellythian military outpost.

I'd known to expect it. At the Priestess Moot, we'd all seen Xalya's high priestess send her troops here as soon as she'd heard tell of the demon attack on Boneweaver Island. This was Ellythia's first line of defence against the Reaper's forces that were already here, mostly made up of the Daanav marine demons that Fangar was supposedly leading. It was time for my second husband and I to reunite.

14

ZALE

We followed my mate's scent at a full sprint over the demonic countryside. Rage spurred us on; we never stopped, and no one even uttered so much of a complaint at the rough pace. I had no idea how she had crossed this land so fucking *fast*. Clearly there was some magic involved, because the scent of her lightning burned through my nose, proud and sure.

More impressive still was the fact that her scent led us straight to a portal built into the centre of an ancient, long-dead volcano. We changed into our human forms to more easily scale the mountain side.

"Scary," Atax remarked as we squatted on the narrow ledge at the top, sniffing into the dark.

"She really jumped in there," Raen said, impressed.

Kai let out a laugh, and before anyone could stop him, he leapt off the ledge with a perfect diver's form with his arms over his head. "I'm coming, my queeeeen!" His gleeful voice echoed all the way down until it faded into nothing.

Atax snorted and the rest of us, not willing to be outdone, followed suit.

The fall was a mad rush, and with as much delight as I was capable of feeling, I sensed the open ocean nearby, salted air filling my nose.

My lips twitched as we hit the water hard enough to knock a human out and a mild panic rose in me as I became concerned for how my mate had survived the fall. But she was still alive, I knew that in my heart, and also quite well, otherwise I would have felt something through our bond.

All I *had* felt through our bond was a smug detachment that made me growl. I changed into my shark form and, leaving my brothers to fend for themselves, gulped down fresh ocean water and it slid past my five gills in a satisfying way.

I registered that it was the middle of the night as I sped towards the shore, and with one grand leap, I shot into the night air and landed, crouched in my human form in the shallows of the brushing tide. The sound of the waves lapping on the shore of Tiger Island cooled the fire in my veins only a little. Overhead, a thousand stars sprawled above us and I scowled, knowing they could see my mate as she travelled away from me.

My brothers noisily splashed ashore, Raen with two large trout in his hand, and Atax with a huge turtle, gripping it by its shell—easily bigger than a human military shield.

"Ahhh, that's better," Atax huffed, shaking ocean water from his eyes. "I'd forgotten what normal air smelled like."

We all growled in agreement.

"It smells like ass down in the demon realm," Kai said.

"How would you know?" Atax shot at him.

"Let it go," I growled at Atax and nodded to the turtle.

"We don't have time to sit and eat."

Atax sighed, but returned the flapping turtle to the sea and accepted a trout from Raen. I crouched in the dark, trying to centre myself as my power and my beast readjusted to being back in our home realm. My blood sang in recognition of our land being close by, and after so long in the darkness and desolation of the heinous realm, I had not realised that I'd not been functioning at my optimal level. It hardly mattered down there, where my brothers and I were physically superior to any of those demons in a fight, but my body relished being back.

In truth, I could easily make it to Boneweaver Island by sea. But my mate had come over land, and there was a chance her mark was somewhere on this island. What was her mark? What was it she hunted?

Raen came up behind me, the moonlight reflecting off the water dripping from his body. "Eat, brother," he said softly. "We need the fresh meat." There was a limp fish in his hand and I didn't care what kind as, barely without thought, I bit into it.

Salt and flesh exploded in my mouth and I did not stop chewing and biting until the thing was bones in my hands. My brothers surrounded me, eating silently—well, in one case, noisily. Raen took my fish frame and selected a few bones, snapping them off and keeping them. He used them to tattoo us, and my brother never wasted an opportunity for good tools.

It reminded me of a time when we'd all sat on the beach as boys no older than five, bloody and bruised and our fathers had forced us into the water. The salt had stung on the many wounds our fathers had strategically placed upon our young bodies.

"To scare away the weakness in you," Raen's father had called it, laughing as we'd screamed in pain. As Boneweavers, we healed quickly and without much scarring, but it didn't mean it hurt any less, and the salt slowed the process down.

Raen's father had been right. The weakness had been scared away. In fact, everything and everyone had been scared away from us. It meant we'd only had each other. Bonds like that couldn't be broken, and even under the Reaper's command, here we were, together. I suddenly looked around at my brothers, who'd come with me, without question, to find my mate, their queen.

Kai was playing with the carcasses of two fish, making them battle each other in the surf. Atax sat, looking up at the waxing moon with a deep frown. Raen also had his face turned up to the night sky but with his eyes closed.

We were a force, the four of us. Ellythia, these isles, would be the Reaper's without much thought, and very soon.

I just had to get my star-born mate back.

We'd only been here for a matter of minutes, but I felt rested as I rose and made my way onto the beach and into the jungle, past the wooden sign warning: Beware of Tigers.

Sniffing the air, I growled as I realised that having come through the ocean, the water had washed away much of my mate's perfume. Most of what I smelled was jungle, animal, and traces of other humans.

I could also feel every one of the twenty tigers within a twenty-minute radius of our location in the jungle. My brothers also felt the presence of other predators, but not in such an acute fashion as me. Atax looked about, ready for a fight to prove his dominance at any second.

"None are close enough," I muttered to him.

He gave me a sharp nod back, but disappointment flashed across his eyes.

Kai came bounding out of the jungle, his knees springing upwards with each step, a mad grin on his face and—

A massive, writhing fucking king cobra in his hands, its mouth open in protest where Kai had his fingers jammed along its jaw.

I hissed reflexively as I measured the reptile. It was easily ten strides long, its muscular body as thick as my own bicep.

"More food!" Kai said happily.

"It's still alive," Atax said glumly. His mood was fouler than ever tonight. I vaguely registered that foreign, dark thoughts were swirling inside his commander's brain.

"Oh." Kai frowned as if he'd forgotten this fact and opened his mouth, long panther incisors elongating seconds before he ripped into the space behind the cobra's head.

"Collect the venom," Raen said, stepping forward and producing a glass vial from his repository. I turned away from my brothers as I surveyed the landscape.

"Oh, we need to stop here," Kai said.

I turned and arched a brow at him. "What for?"

"Trouble?" he said hopefully. "It's on the way, brother!" He pouted in response to my frown and pointed to distant lights. "They were bad to Rani. She was our friend, remember?" A mischievous glint came to his eye. "Let me *sing* for them."

Right now, I cared for nothing except my star. No one else. Kai's pleading eyes met mine in the night.

"She may have gone there," Raen said mildly. "Our queen may have wanted to see her friend's family."

It was this and *only* this idea that allowed me to follow Kai's white mop of hair speeding towards the lights.

I'd spent my day washing and peeling potatoes in the barracks kitchen until my fingers and thumbs were numb and wrinkly from the water.

Almost all Ellythians had magic, but the unfortunate few without any, or much, were relegated to the lowest division of whatever Order they pledged to. For Xalya's army, it meant that after combat training, we cleaned and cooked and not much more.

And at a time like this, where the battle for power was nigh, those with magic were further relegated to the sidelines, and the more power you had, the more you were prized. All that meant for me was that my numerous punishments for getting into fights *added* to the amount of cleaning and cooking I did.

Now Malika, on the other hand, I could easily see from the wide kitchen windows overlooking the protected training grounds. The new cadets trained within their various magical specialities, so anyone with a wisp of flame had Malika to contend with.

And she'd taken her division by fiery storm.

I couldn't help but suppress a grin as I watched my friend train with two fire lieutenants with years of training, positioning her in the front and centre of their line. On the other side of the grounds, ten practice mannequins zipped forward on their rig—but only three were marked with a red X for her mark.

Malika's hands moved and an orange whip of flame split into three and struck each marked mannequin, setting them ablaze, leaving the remaining ones unscorched. The other soldiers clapped as the commander of the fire division rubbed his chin, looking Malika up and down her curved body.

It was an exercise in control, and Malika had no match. Somehow, she'd managed to fine tune her anger and hone it into something precise and lethal. I'd never seen anything like it from anyone except Xalya's most senior fire priestesses. Most people ended up scorching the mannequins on either side of their targets, at the very least.

Malika blew a strand of hair off her face and shrugged with a nonchalance that made me laugh under my breath. She'd been much the same at our exile school, and this was the least of her powers. But I knew why she'd chosen today to bat her eyelashes at the commander. She'd put her name down to head off to Tiger Island's outpost tonight, and only a select number of new recruits were allowed to go. I'd put my name down under hers right away because I'd been thinking about our friends on Boneweaver Island for a while now. Like jagged nails scraping against my mind, I itched to help them, to *do* something for the girls at the school we'd left behind. Girls who, at one time, had respected me for being one of them.

My mother and grandmother might have forgotten about

our people on Boneweaver Island, but I *never* would. That had been my vow from the start.

"Girl." The head cook's sharp voice cut through my thoughts like the peeling knife in my hand. Something about using my name had everyone stumped. It was too personal for them. Too familiar. To call a member of the royal family by name was the height of disrespect. I guessed the compromise had been 'girl', which, to me, felt like a whole new title. I was *just* a girl now. Nothing more. Nothing less.

I turned to look at him, the round-faced middle-aged man I'd spent more time with than anyone else in my entire regiment. "Yes, Cook?" I replied, respectfully straightening my spine.

His eyes flicked to my latest injury, a freshly healed ice burn on my chin. The skin pink and shiny from healing after a fight with an arrogant soldier who'd zapped a girl's ass right in front of me. Cook jerked his head to the door. "You're off to the Tiger Island outpost tonight. Sunset ship. Collect your things."

I could barely hide my grin. "Yes, sir."

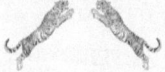

IT WAS A DAY'S TRIP OVER THE CHANNEL TO GET TO TIGER Island, and to our excitement, Malika and I got to watch Ellythia's naval forces running drills just off the south-eastern port as we left.

Three ice mages froze patches of sea water and, pushed by the water mages behind them, rode the boards of ice across the water between the ships, shooting ice spears into the targets set high on the masts of the practice boats—cheaply made wooden structures the water mages would practise capsizing later.

Each spear found its mark in the red bullseyes.

We clapped and cheered from the deck of our ship.

They'd run drills right through the night, each order of soldier-sorcerer practising their assault and defence techniques until they could run them on instinct alone. These groups were experts at what they did, and had trained together for decades.

The key to an effective force was bundling them into smaller groups who got to know each other's powers so intimately that they became a force on the battlefield; or, in this case, the sea.

Being new recruits only a few weeks into training, the commanders were still figuring out where best to put us—which combinations of personalities made best partners. Those of us without magic were paired with magic groups and became known as the 'runt' of the group. Malika's presence next to me was a comfort—no doubt they'd decided to throw me a bone and put me with someone I already knew with a sizeable power. Even being discarded by the royal family, their instincts told them to protect me. It was something I tried not to think about.

On the voyage, we wasted no time, and the commander had us training. Malika and I sparred on the deck along with the others. We knew each other well enough by now that it was always a brutal sort of battle. We made each other better fighters every time we fought, and it wasn't long before the soldiers and crew stopped their duties to watch us, a little slack-jawed.

I deflected a vicious punch to the jaw and ducked, kicking a foot out to sweep her legs from under her. Malika's feet were her weakness, so I always targeted them. But she knew my mind and jumped in time, hitting out with her elbow. I skipped back, and she only missed me by a hair.

"Is that how you'll fight Atax when you exact your revenge?" I jeered at her.

She scowled, her face flushed, and she aimed a kick to the side of my left knee. It landed, and my knee crumpled. But I knew she'd leap for me next, so I dived right, tucking my chin, grinning against the pain, and rolling smoothly back onto my feet.

"No, I'm going to stab him," Malika hissed, recovering from her fall and stalking me, her fists up. "Right in the eyeball."

"I'd like to see that." I chuckled. "And with his own sword, too. That's poetry."

She grinned until I lunged, tackling her to the ground with a heavy thump. Winded, Malika wheezed, and I slung back my fist.

"Not the face!" one of the male soldiers cried.

Malika grinned at me, her eyes flashing, and I brought my fist down on her brow.

"Oof!" Malika grunted as it landed, softened by a magical barrier. "Lucky I have a shield up, woman!" Malika choked.

"Yeah, I knew that." I laughed, rolling off her to crouch, panting and sweaty. "Killing blow, if you didn't." Because in an actual fight, I'd have charged quartz bracelets on, or be armed with a knife.

Malika jumped up and offered me a hand. I grabbed it and she pulled me up. We wiped the sweat off our faces as our crowd dissipated.

"You'll have to fight better than that if you want to beat up Atax," I said wryly.

Malika looked out over the turquoise ocean where Tiger Island could just be seen on the horizon, green and lush. "No man can withstand fire," she said darkly. "Not even an Old One."

She might have been able to convince herself that her grief was anger, but she'd never be able to trick me.

WE DOCKED AT TIGER ISLAND DEEP INTO THE NIGHT WITH ORDERS to stick close together. One of the air mages struck up a bubble shield around us in case of any stalking tigers. There were plenty here, and they were not the only predators in the dense jungles. Huge cobras and wild zekar stallions haunted the deepest parts, and it was no doubt the reason demons hadn't bothered to try and overtake it yet.

We trekked down the main path towards Rani's home-town for only an hour before our commander abruptly raised his fist and we halted.

Malika and I, directly behind our commander, exchanged a look because we'd been through this very path not that long ago, after a unfortuitous non-visit with Rani's family. But our group was to pick up a supply of silk from her family's farm which, spelled with protective charms, our soldiers used for cleaning and undergarments.

"You said you know the Umasri family?" Commander Charad turned to ask us. He was a hulking sorcerer, well-built and in his prime. He was a harsh taskmaster, but fair, and had a gentle hand with any injuries.

So I didn't hesitate when I said, "Rani's a good friend, but we don't know her family. We came through here on our way north."

He nodded. "There's a disturbance on the eastern side, but I can't pick up what it is, exactly. Come with me." He turned around, signalling to our lieutenant halfway back before we split into two groups and our smaller group continued forward.

A dark feeling twisted its way around my core as three other soldiers, Malika and I followed Charad into an open field. In the distance, the town quartzlights sparkled, and on a hill to our right was Umasri estate. But Charad led us left, to a huge building in the shadow of the jungle.

I remembered that it was a sort of barn they likely used for sheltering bigger farm animals against the rain, but we'd never gone near it. Malika shivered next to me as a low shout sounded, followed by a pathetic, sad moan.

Charad began running, and our group followed, our packs bouncing with each stride. Our commander raised a hand, and with a gust of air, the huge barn door swung open and when we found it dark inside, he summoned a massive yellow spotlight, his quartz bracelets glowing dark blue as he drew on its power.

We rushed in, but what I saw stopped me short. Malika and a few others barged into me, but I stood still as stone.

Somebody behind me swore.

In the centre of the barn, three men were strung up by their bleeding thumbs, their faces pale, drawn and bloody. Three familiar men. But it was none of these things that horrified me. It was the way all three of them had their legs twisted. As if the bones had been fractured in multiple places, prised apart and joined the wrong way making crude angles. The overall effect was nauseating.

I stepped forward to allow the others behind me to get through. Charad was at the men in a heartbeat, and with a slice of his hand, all three men came crashing to the ground, the ropes cut. They screamed as they fell, likely both in relief and pain.

"Two days!" Yulara's father screamed, unable to sit up. "Two days we've been strung up there! No one came. We thought we were going to die!"

"Who did this?" Charad said, holding up his canteen to the older man's mouth. He drank, spilling water everywhere as the younger men were helped by the other soldiers. Neither Malika nor I moved.

"The fucking *Old Ones*. The four of them! They came in like ghosts in the night."

"More like monsters," said a man who must've been one of Yulara's brothers. "They were ruthless, cold. Worse than any monster. The crazy one, the one with the white hair—" he trembled so violently that he could no longer speak.

We'd never seen any of the Old Ones use magic in this way. Perhaps they'd just never *let* us see it.

As Malika and I began edging out of the room, Yulara's father spat. "*You two.*" The entire room turned to look at us, frowning.

"What did they say?" Malika asked, crossing her arms. "When they did this to you?"

Narrowed eyed, Yulara's father shook his head. "Nothing. They said nothing."

Malika and I exchanged a look. Surely a lie. Kai loved to talk, he would have spoken the entire time, black heart or no. We knew exactly why the Old Ones had come here. It was just... surprising they'd done this at all. Surprising that they would want revenge for Rani's sake. But I wondered what it meant as Malika and I left the room in silence.

Somewhere in those black, Reaper-shrouded hearts, was there an ember of life?

16

ALTARA

Nothing made you more alert to the fact that war was coming than a contingent of Ellythian sorcerer-soldiers on guard at the edge of their territory. Goosebumps erupted over my skin as I followed Naina as she stalked through the human military camp.

Two off-duty soldiers smoked outside their tent, talking in low voices. They hadn't taken their weapons off, I noted, and their hands never strayed far from their hilts. There was a general air of tense quiet among the soldiers. Even at the beach, a place that had once, I'm sure, been nothing but serene beauty at night, a cold shadow of awareness hovered above and in between all things. Guards dotted the beach at intervals, and I marked them by their campfires. They stood talking softly with spears and swords, their eyes trained on the ocean and the whitecaps breaking on the shore.

Maybe they expected the demons to come by sea and take over Tiger Island in a sort of progressive conquering of the three islands. But Zale planned a direct attack on Lota Island by show of massive force. The capital was the heart of

Ellythia after all, and then Tiger Island would be theirs by default. The small numbers in this outpost told me that Xalya's general perhaps expected something of the sort, otherwise she'd have sent a larger force here. Defending three islands was tactically very difficult. It was why the fabled Blade of Temari, Umali's gift to Ellythia, had been such a precious thing. It had created a shield around all three islands for thousands of years until my mother came along and took it away with her to Lobrathia.

Naina chose a spot in the dark, between the fires, to lead me into the beach. It was then that I came to the shocking realisation that we were going to have to travel to Boneweaver Island by sea.

I swore under my breath because the idea of being out in the ocean in the dark was terrifying. There were sharks in these waters, plus Goddess knew what else. Naina was a competent swimmer, but I'd have to ride whatever form she chose to take and tolerate the damned cold and rolling swells. Sighing, I trudged after her, the crashing ocean waves masking the sound of my boots on the sand, though it did nothing for my tracks. I took off my cloak and dragged it behind me so my footprints wouldn't be so obvious, but I hoped that by the time morning came, the natural wind would have swept them away. Naina stalked right up into the water, softly lapping like a sweet caress on the sand.

But she halted and hissed, baring her white canines. I immediately saw why. A magical wall barred our way. It was a fine magical sheen, standing as an impressive sheet of magic that hummed against my skin. I got the distinct feeling that it grilled the demons like meat on a hot stove if they tried to swim through undetected.

I swore internally, looking around as if there'd be some

answer to this, but Naina shook her head and headed straight into the ocean, her body changing as she went, losing her legs, her fur becoming glossy smooth skin that shone under the moonlight.

It was a dolphin that turned to look at me, bobbing her smooth blue-grey head from the shallow water, fins flexing. I couldn't help but grin at the sweet face I'd only ever seen in illustrations and knew at once that I would have to demand Zale shift into one so we could swim together. I was sure he'd never done such a thing, always choosing a predator's body instead, but damn it, I would *make* him.

Reluctantly, I waded into the water, my boots keeping my feet dry and my tread stable as I followed Naina, who swum a little deeper into waves and then paused for me to get on.

This was going to be a long night if she expected me to hold on to her dorsal fin for the entirety of the trip. Grumbling, I placed my hands around her fin and straddled her body.

"Are you sure this is safe?" I asked, looking up at the magical shield.

All she did was bob her large head, and I had no choice but to hold back my scream, flatten my body onto hers and grip on for my life as she took off, like a battering ram, straight into the ocean and towards the sheet of magic.

I squeezed my eyes shut, gritting my teeth against the water moving swiftly past me and waiting for some magical sting or burn... but we sailed right through as if it weren't there at all, nothing more than a soft *whoosh* in my ears.

Until massive red sparks shot up in the air behind us and shouts rang out from the beach. A loud clanging bell boomed through the night so loudly that I almost, *almost*, let Naina go to clap my hands over my ears. But my guide continued on, speeding impossibly fast through the water and into the night, water spraying on my face.

The shield was one-way then, thank all seven Goddesses.

I was also surprised when I realised that the water was actually fairly warm, not chilly as I imagined. But I'd only ever seen and felt the water at Quartz Harbour and assumed all ocean was cold. Naïve on my part, I'm sure. So my only worry then was other predators swimming between the islands.

The trip between Tiger Island and Boneweaver Island was supposed to be half a day by boat, but Naina was preternaturally fast in the water. So fast that my face lost all sensation against the wind and sea spray, leaving me desperately clinging on in the dark.

My hands and body were well and truly numb by the time a dark mass along the horizon made me weep in relief.

But Naina kept swimming along the shore, instead of taking us up to land. I groaned, snuggling into my water-resistant witch's robe a little further against the constant deluge rushing past me. I had to trust whatever her instincts were telling her—perhaps it was unsafe up there. But with the island on my right-hand side, we were going south, and that meant we were headed down to Taraka village, where I'd landed with Geravie so many months ago.

I'd get to see what had become of the girls and teachers from the school. I cringed at the thought of the demons finally taking over this place and, with their tendency to make slaves of humans, perhaps they had done the same thing with the girls. Either way, I needed to find out and see if anything could be done to save them.

A little while later, Naina brought us to the shore, and I fell off her back with a splat and lay supine in the surf.

Catching my breath and massaging the feeling back into my cramped fingers, I looked up at the stars and scattered clouds in the night sky. It was a relief to look upon them, back here, in a place I'd once escaped to for my own safety. Now, it was enemy territory and anything but safe. Eventually, Naina's tigress nose impatiently nudged at my side hard enough that I got myself together and rolled to my feet with a groan.

But now, I was in a foul mood. Apparently, travelling for hours on the back of a mad dolphin would do that to a person.

I stalked the shores of Boneweaver Island just as the crescent moon rose above clouds. The night was warm on my skin, and as I made my way across the sand, as fine and soft as flour, I spied a crystal slab of rock large enough to be an altar. My body stilled in warm recognition.

Zale, Fangar and I had been married here in a time that seemed so very long ago. A time that seemed all at once hazy and clear. My thumb found Zale's pearl and obsidian ring on my finger and I pressed it as if I could feel my husband through it. He would be close to me by now, surely, and with each step, his possessive anger would become furore.

Or so I hoped, because what I was about to do was borderline insane.

But it was there, with my boots on the floury sand on Boneweaver Island, with the warm breeze cooling my wet skin, I felt *it*.

A power caressed up through the sand, through my boots and into my feet, swirling up in a warm, open welcome that sent my heart pounding. A soft gasp escaped my lips as I turned to look upon the dark, dense jungle that I knew teemed with life.

Knew it, because as that colossal power moved in me, I

could feel a hare rustling in the bushes ten paces away as if the leaves of those very bushes were my own skin. Palm trees swayed to their own song, just as the strands of my hair swayed to that same breeze.

I could feel every leaf, twig, and bird in my surroundings as I could feel my own fingers, my own toes.

Something ancient sang in my blood. Something deeper than the marrow of my bones whispered to me, *Welcome home, my queen.*

Unbidden, a sob left my throat, the backs of my eyes burning like night-time coals.

Is this what Zale felt on this island? Did his blood thrum to the breath of animals and birds as mine did?

Stunned, I stood there for some unknown amount of time, simply feeling the jungle and the waves, the deer, the mongoose, the rabbits. It was power like I'd never known. A power that did not belong to me as such, but was *of* me all the same.

With a vivid realisation, I finally knew what it meant to be High Priestess of Agnolthi, Queen of the Boneweavers.

I belonged to this island, and it, along with every living entity, belonged to me.

And just so, alongside the natural elements of the island, I felt a force spreading like a fungus under wet rock. A mould that was unwanted, dirty, overriding.

I know, I silently said to the force spreading through me. *We will be rid of them soon enough.*

My hands clenched into fists and determination spread through me like the rapid winds of a new tornado.

And so I went.

I made my way past the moon altar and headed for the jungle path that would lead me up to the exile school near

Taraka village. The place Pia, Malika, Rani and I had met at and then left, taken by Zale on his royal tour around the island after our marriage. But the girls here had been at the mercy of the headmistress, who'd been selling them to the Daanav marine demons for marriage. We might have put a stop to that with Zale's execution of Jessine, but now the Reaper had the entire island in his fist. No doubt demons were crawling everywhere, with Fangar at the helm.

As I passed through the first palm trees and into the humid dark of the jungle's womb, my surroundings slowly ceased their chatter.

A quiet jungle knew that a predator had arrived. *Its own* predator.

My grin was wide as I drew the world around me on top of the shadows. Hidden from sight, I felt like nothing but a ghoul in the dark, a prowling predator in-between things. Years from now, when old men sat around campfires and spoke of monsters that haunted the jungle, they would be speaking of *me*.

A sly sense of satisfaction rang through me at that, because now I would haunt these demons as they had haunted *us* all those months ago.

Skulking forward on soft feet that barely touched the earth, I made my way into the dark. When Agnolthi anointed me high priestess of her order, I had promised to dance under all full moons. To worship the deep dark of the jungle, of the night sky, and glittering promise of the stars. Tonight, I *would* dance, and if it was a dance of death, then so be it. If the demons had hurt the girls at the school, if they had done so much as touched a hair on their heads, they would die.

All I had to do was find them.

Within minutes, I came across a patrol of two Daanavs

swaggering along the path, swords at their hips, blue skin turned navy under night's cover. I shot them with three arrows drawn from my bow at the same time. Their throats bled, and they went down like boulders, hitting the earth with the dull thud of their metal armour. Stepping over their bodies, I moved on up the path that would lead to the school.

Let them know I was here. Let them know they were in danger. It would also make a nice little present for Zale when he arrived.

I heard the demons at the school before I saw them. A fire crackled, glasses clanked, and guttural voices barked and shouted. I knew what I would see before I cleared the jungle and stepped onto the school lawn.

An entire contingent of demons lounged on the grass before the school, sitting around multiple bonfires burning through the dark. Barrels of island alcohol were strewn about the area and half the demons crowded around them, filling cups and draining them in one go.

To the side, marine and other demons sparred each other with shiny new swords, their hilts sparkling with magic infused quartz. The blows they hit were heavy and backed by magic. The demons blocking with regular swords were blown backwards. When met with another magical blade, sparks flew under the force and at one point, a small grass fire began from the sparks of one fight. It was quickly stomped out, but I could see the damage those blades could do.

Behind them, the school was aglow with the yellow quartz-lights gleaming through the windows. People moved inside, but whether they were demon or human, I couldn't make out. Outside, no humans were in sight, male or female.

The back of my neck prickled as if I were being watched. I whirled around, scanning the night for some sign of activity.

The breeze made the palm fronds sway as if they beckoned to me. I stilled, allowing my senses full access to night and everything that was in it. The breeze swept over my skin like an old friend, gentle and warm. I felt no threat from within the jungle, only an excited hum stroked my insides.

Letting out a breath, I turned back to the demons. My enemies. Determined to find the human students, I beckoned to Naina, who shrunk in size and scrambled up my leg, where she became a black tattoo once again, settling down on my hand. I swept forward, headed for the entrance doors to the school, my heart pounding, worried at what I would find in there.

Did they have the girls caged and bound as they'd done to me? Did they have them tied to a slab of stone, knives cutting deep into soft skin as *he'd* done to me?

As I wove my way between them, hidden in the shadows of the night, more than once, the demons glanced over their shoulders, as if they knew something sinister lurked behind them. Their hands casually landed upon their sword hilts, their shoulders tense and alert.

If they had hurt these girls, they would *all* die. Scrap that, they would all die, anyway. I made it to the front doors without difficulty or accidentally stepping on anyone's foot. Slipping into the open doors, I cast my eyes around and made a plan to sweep the floors one at a time. The entrance hall was empty, so I headed to the kitchen, the next likely place.

As I came down the stairs and into the corridor leading to the single, large kitchen area, the sound of pots and pans banging around, as well as low female voices, sailed to me. Swearing under my breath, I rushed into the room.

Three girls in their early twenties stood by the stove. Two of them were chopping meat at the counter and the third stood over a huge bubbling pot. I took in their condition quickly. They were all lean, but not emaciated, so they weren't starved, and otherwise looked unharmed. They wore loose, plain dresses, but one of them had put on the black school overcoat, no doubt taken from a dormitory. All three had metal cuffs on one leg, with chains leading to a piece of wood staked into a bench top.

My blood fired up as I registered the chains. They were too old to be recent students from the school, and I didn't recognise them. It was more likely they had come from Daanav kingdom, previously sold to the demons by Headmistress Jessine.

I released the magic hiding my body and cleared my throat. All three girls jerked, a knife clattered onto the bench, and two of them gasped. Pushing back my hood so they could see my face better, I said, "Are you three alright? Have they hurt you?"

They glanced at each other, worry marring their ashen faces. The eldest, by the stove, stepped forward, peering at me. "Are you a Lota lady?" Her eyes flicked to the glowing symbol on my forehead.

"I am the High Priestess of Agnolthi," I said calmly. "And yes, also a Lota princess. Now, are you three alright? Did you come from Danaav Kingdom?"

Their eyes widened, and they curtseyed immediately. "We are alright," the eldest breathed. "And we came with the Daanavs from under the sea. We were sold to them three years ago, but there were no humans here when we arrived last week." She cast a nervous look at the other girls. "Please, you must not let them see you."

"Don't worry about me," I said, waving a hand. "I'm looking for the other girls of the school. Where are they?"

"They are hiding," whispered the girl who'd dropped her knife. "Armsmistress Vari sent pixies to see if they could free us, but we sent them away. It's too dangerous."

Hearing the armsmistress' name made relief wash over me. They were alive. "Hiding where?" I pressed.

"We don't know. Somewhere underground, I think. They wouldn't tell us. We... We said we would stay and be spies for them. We want to help Ellythia win this war!" She banged her fist on the table and nodded with determination. "We want these bastards to suffer for what they've done."

"That is noble of you," I said in admiration. "Were you all married off to the Daanavs?"

"Yes," the eldest sighed. "We have a *husband* each, but often they share. They've been trying to get us pregnant, but they didn't know that Sapna"—she gestured to the girl with short hair—"has healing powers and has been able to stop us from ovulating."

I cringed, wanting to flay these demons alive. This was going to stop. And now. Fury boiled through me at the sheer bravery of these girls in the face of these brutes. They deserved better, so much better than this. Clenching my jaw so hard it creaked, I whirled around and stormed out of the kitchen.

"High Priestess!" the girls hissed after me. "Oh Goddess, what is she going to do?"

They would see soon enough.

I stomped my way back outside, slapping on my invisibility once again, and headed for the cover of the tall trees that bordered the land of the school.

When I was happy with my position, I turned around and held my arm up in the air. My bow, black with gold jungle detail, landed in my hand with a crack that vibrated down my legs. The demons all froze.

And then I began shooting. The first arrow appeared in the neck of a demon sparring with a quartz blade, and I marked the rest of them with dangerous weapons to go first. The party quickly turned into a chaotic mess of blood, screams, and murderous shouts. Within seconds, they marked my position, so I leapt into the grounds and started running while I shot, never keeping still.

Lightning never misses its fucking mark.

Each arrow I shot found a neck, a heart, or an eye. It was quick and ruthless, and by the end, when all the Daanavs lay on the ground, their black blood glistening under the bonfires of my husband's land, of *my* land, I stood there for a moment, panting and sweaty, and simply looked at them.

Thirty-two, I counted.

That feeling I was being watched crept over my skin again and a thirty-third arrow was knocked and ready to fly as I whirled around to see what had crept up on me.

17

ALTARA

M y jaw slackened as I stared into what the night had brought me. What the *island* had brought me.

Three creatures made of bark and leaf and shell loomed over me, simply… staring. Well, they had no eyes, the same as I remembered them, from all that time ago when Zale had kidnapped us girls from our beds and stolen us away in the night.

Island monsters.

Their bodies were made from the broken trunks of palm trees and they bore gnarled arms and hands that could easily hold a person firm against them—as they'd done to us—or snap a man's neck, I'd bet, if given the chance. Old coconut shells bunched together at the top to make a sort of head and ferns sprouted from atop them as if to give them hair.

"Where did you come from?" I breathed, lowering my bow.

As one, all three dropped to their thick knees and *bowed* their heads. A voice that was not a voice whispered on the breeze and I understood them in that new, yet ancient way.

Our queen has returned.

The backs of my eyes burned as I stared down at them. Zale had told me that Wobbles had turned to ash when the Reaper took over the island. I had assumed that had meant Zale's magical hold over the island had dissipated, rendering his monsters dead.

"Please stand," I murmured, not even sure how much they understood.

But they obliged, groaning to their feet once again and looking around at the dead bodies as if they were trying to tell me something. Their ferns rustled in the night wind and I turned to look around at the massacre, frowning.

Perhaps because I had slayed these demons, I had reclaimed this part of the island?

"Have you seen Wobbles?" I asked tentatively. The three monsters said nothing, but turned their heads with a creak to stare out at the jungle.

"That's a no, I suppose. But... we can't stand here either. Can you see if you can find a set of keys? I need to free the girls inside the school."

They moved immediately, loping over with their long legs towards the dead, or dying, demons. I watched on as they yanked up the demons and shook them, tugging at their pockets until a chinking noise drew my attention to the smallest island monster, whose head was made of old hibiscus flowers bunched together in a sort of bouquet. He smelled sweet as I approached him and he held out a set of keys from flower-tipped fingers.

"Thank you." I beamed up at him and thoughtfully looked around. "Collect the quartz weapons. I want them for our use. We'll give them to Armsmistress Vari when we see her."

Without another word, I hurried back up to the kitchen, where the girls were hovering by the door as far as their chains would let them, their faces ashen but otherwise calm. To my surprise, when they saw me, they straightened their backs, their eyes eagle sharp. It was with a little dismay that I registered what this meant. These girls were used to violence. They'd spent years in the Daanav Kingdom, of course being around demons made them accustomed to brutish behaviour. As sad as that was, it would serve us in this war.

"You killed them," Sapna breathed.

I held up the set of keys. "What are your names?" I crouched before them to the metal cuffs around their ankles.

"I am Nala," said the eldest girl, bending down with me as I reached for her shackle first. "And this is Preethi." She pointed to a small girl with deep bags under her eyes and, I noticed with rage, the fading remnants of a black eye.

"Pretty names," I said, fumbling with the keys.

"Thank you," Preethi said.

I glanced at the three of them as I tried the first likely key, a large iron thing. "You're taking this very well."

Nala spoke darkly. "We've lived with demons for three years, High Priestess."

I paused, looking up at the girl, her face drawn. Her eyes met mine, not accusingly, but more in acceptance. For a moment, I felt responsible for this violence placed upon them. That the violence I'd committed was just another string in the long tapestry of blood and slaughter they'd been a part of for years. Was I any better than the demons by slaughtering them all?

"I'm sorry for what you've been through," I said quietly. Her shackle fell off. "Now you are free women. Or as free as any of us can be while the Reaper still threatens us with war."

139

Nala grabbed my wrist, her grip strong.

"This *is* war, High Priestess. We all do what we must to survive."

My jaw clenched before I gave her a nod and moved to the next shackle.

When we were done, the girls collected all the food they could carry into mesh bags. Wherever the Armsmistress Vari, her wife, Lady Trisana, and other teachers and students of the school were hiding, we needed to find them. And fast.

A small amount of awareness prickled at the edge of my mind, as I registered that Zale was inching closer to Boneweaver Island. I could feel his presence; near, but not near enough that he had reached the shores yet.

In any case, I needed to hurry. This had been a detour I had not anticipated.

We hurried into the night, the moon high above us watching our movements. The island monsters were still outside, waiting patiently. All three carried bundles of blades, glowing with quartz magic.

The girls gasped when they saw them, huddling around me in alarm.

"It's alright," I murmured. "They're friends." I gestured to one who'd found the key with the hibiscus bouquet head. "Do you know where the schoolgirls are hiding? We need to get to them quickly."

The three of them bowed and abruptly turned, striding down the gravel drive away from the school and forward on the main road.

"I'll take that as a yes." We hurried after them.

The girls and I panted loudly in the night as we jogged after the monsters. I was nervous that we were headed straight down the main road, which demons were likely using as a main thoroughfare. But it seemed I needn't have worried because as a patrol came up, far ahead of us, the sounds of screaming and bodies thumping in the ground filled the night, then subsided rather quickly. We rounded a corner to find the three monsters waiting for us, four Daanav soldiers lying at their feet.

"Goddess!" Nala panted. "Lucky we have these monsters."

The monsters, for their part, did not move any further when we came up to them. Looking around, I realised with a jolt where we were.

A familiar squat house on stilts loomed like a ghost in the dark before me, old banana mango trees crowding around its walls as if trying to protect it. This was the house of Reshmi and Keshmi Harranpul, the elderly twin priestesses of Agnolthi's temple.

I hoped Reshmi was okay. She'd stayed behind with Raen and our pixie friends to keep watch over the island.

What good that had done. As if they could have done more against the Reaper and this many demons? They should never have been left behind, but Zale and I had no say over that when we'd been taken by the Forests of Eternity. Pia and the others had moved northwards of their own accord to get help.

Now, our group had been disbanded. We'd all gone our separate ways.

A long sigh emerged scratchy from my throat as I tried not to think the worst.

"I think," Nala said quietly, "they mean for us to go to the temple."

As the keepers of Agnolthi's oldest temple, the twins' house lay before it as a sort of gatekeeper. I stared at Nala as she looked at it meaningfully, the other girls nervously looking around. The temple might have been protected against something like this. It might have some magic that stopped the demons from pillaging it. Was it too much of a fanciful hope?

"Well, let's find out, shall we?"

As we walked onto the stepping stones leading behind the house, a beam of yellow light shot up into the sky in the south —directly in the location of the school.

Sapna grabbed my arm. "High Priestess, that is how they have been alerting each other! A patrol must have come across the dead. A company will be headed this way!"

I swore softly. But as we made to hurry into the dark, a sound made my heart turn as cold as ice.

Demon voices, from behind the house.

"Come here!" I hissed.

The girls crowded around me as I gathered them up in my arms and let my magic swallow us all up. "Tree monsters!" I hissed. "Hide. Quickly!"

The monsters dutifully loped into the jungle, where the shadows quickly swallowed them up. Sighing in relief, I placed each of the girls' hands on my shoulders, just as the sound of heavy demon boots jogged up to us. "As long as you keep contact with me," I breathed, allowing my body to take on my surroundings. "You'll be invisible."

The girls' ragged breathing was all I could perceive of the girls as the demons came into view. There were four of them, and they ran right past us and turned up the road to head for the school.

"Let's head to the back," I whispered.

Together, we shuffled down the path, with me in the front

and girls with their hands firmly on my shoulders as if we were children playing a game.

A very dangerous game.

Because as we walked down the overgrown stepping stone path of the dark temple grounds, gruff voices came from up ahead. And when we came upon them, we saw that no less than ten armoured demons stood guard.

My walk became a prowl as I led us to the cast iron gates and glanced up at my mother's name written in the stone.

Yasani Temple

Demons muttered to each other before us, the light of their flaming torches reflected dully off their armour. That's what demons did; they made the profound, profane.

My fists clenched as I sucked air through my teeth, making a soft *hiss*. The demons stilled by the temple gates, peering about them to find the source of the noise. The girls' grips on me was almost painful, a dire warning, a plea. But covered by the night, I merely scowled at our enemy.

This was sacred ground I would not murder upon if I didn't need to. While that was looked down upon, it was not considered a heinous crime to protect the temple either. Agnolthi was a Goddess who represented both the dark and light. The Old Ones had sacrificed livestock in her honour on full moons. The only thing they wouldn't sacrifice was a lion or tiger.

By all rights, I should kill them.

It was then that I spotted the glint of metal lying at the temple entrance. Broken weapons littered the area, as if the demons had used them here, then cast them aside. I glanced up at the sandstone that made the temple, the pillars that led up to it, and the stone doors.

The stone was unmarred. A slow smile spread across my lips as I led the girls up to the gates and flung them open with a bang.

Demons jumped and cried out, drawing their weapons. But they could only see wind, their eyes never finding purchase on us.

Two of the girls were hanging onto my body and one of them half strangling me, but I merely readjusted their grips back onto my shoulders and continued forward.

Demons had tried to destroy my temple, and the temple had not let them. Some old magic must have laid upon this place that stopped damage being done. Grinning wildly now, I pushed open the heavy stone doors of the temple and led the girls inside. The demons roared in surprise outside and I turned just in time to see two of the guards hitting an invisible barrier as they tried to pass the gate. Purple light sparked to life, throwing them backwards.

Smirking, I turned my back to them and stepped inside.

Nala, I think, let out a soft cheer.

It was here, in the cool and dark of the temple, that I allowed my magic to fade away, and allowed myself to re-emerge from invisibility. This temple had been a sight the first time I'd laid eyes on it, and it was still a punch to the gut now.

The seven Goddesses surrounded us in larger-than-life quartz sculptures in their respective colours, their glow giving us light to see by. At their head, in a brilliant purple quartz that had never dulled with time, was Agnolthi, her eyes peering down sternly at me.

In Agnolthi's temple at Lota city, a huge cauldron lay at

the centre, but here at the home of the Old Ones, a petal-shaped ceramic sculpture lay like a divine flower, a tribute to the female core. It was easily as long as I was tall, two sets of folds meeting at the top and bottom, with a bulb at the top. I thought it was beautiful and could have sat there, staring at it, if not for the flicker of golden light that zipped past us.

Preethi gasped.

Something shifted to my left and high pitched voice squeaked, "Princess?"

I turned slowly, not because I hadn't been called 'princess' in what felt like an age, but because that tiny, musical voice was achingly familiar.

A golden light, just the size of my hand, bobbed and flickered with excitement. Her wings fluttered so fast I could barely see them, her brown face pointed and sweet. Wide, beautiful eyes stared at me in wonder.

My vision went blurry. "Leela?" I breathed.

My old friend let out a sob before launching herself at me, hitting me straight on my cheek, her arms spreading wide to hug my face.

"Tara!" her muffled voice came.

"Oh, Leela," I murmured, placing a gentle hand on her back. "It really is you."

"Princess, you got taken and Pia said we had to stay with Priestess Reshmi, but blue demons came, and Reaper, and— Oh, it was awful! — and took Lord Raen, and— How are you back? We have to go see everyone. They'll be wanting to hear all news—how did you get in here?"

Her pixie-rambling ceased as she made a shocked gasp, prying herself off my skin and landing on my raised palm. I tickled her face with my finger as she peered around me at the commotion still going on outside. The demons couldn't see us, but I knew I wouldn't have long before their backup arrived.

"I missed your voice, Leela. But where are the others?" I murmured. "Tell me they are here somewhere?"

She blinked up at me, confused. "Lord Raen hid us before the Reaper came!" She pointed to the tiled floor of the temple. "Secret passage that goes under the ground, and—"

I clamped a finger over her lips and Leela went silent with a squeak.

"Do not tell me anymore," I whispered. "The knowledge is best kept secret."

Zale may have been right about the Reaper being unable to read my mind, but there was always a risk.

Her bright eyes went wide with alarm. "It's true then!" she whispered.

"I don't have time to explain, but..." I took a deep breath. "Who can I speak to? Is Armsmistress Vari and Priestess Reshmi here?"

"Yes," came a deep voice from behind Agnolthi's statue.

Leela squeaked and leapt off my hand, zipping over to the incredibly tall, armoured woman stepping out of the shadows. The three young women exclaimed in familiarity and ran over to her. But I stayed where I was.

Vari nodded at the girls who huddled around her, expert eyes surveying them for injuries. The relief on her face smoothed over her harsh features before she looked back at me. She clasped her hands before her, legs spread wide in a pose I knew too well. A sword glinted on her hip and she looked down her nose at me, brown eyes wary. "So it's true that you've defected."

"She saved us!" Nala said. "The high priestess massacred the demons and saved us all!"

Vari looked from Nala and back to me with her brows raised.

"You need not fear me, Armsmistress," I said carefully. "I am glad to see you alive and well."

"Then?" she shot back. "Why are you here?"

Her aggressive tone made my heart clench in agony. This woman had been kind to me once, as teacher and weapons master at the school.

But now, I was the enemy.

I raised my chin. "My mark is a demon, Armsmistress. My second husband, Fangar Sharksbane."

Vari's face calculated as she took in my body from head to toe, from my witch's cloak to the high priestess arrow and moon mark ever-glowing on my forehead.

"Is it also true that you are High Priestess of Agnolthi now?"

"I am Goddess anointed, yes."

Vari looked to Leela hovering anxiously next to her. Leela nodded vigorously.

"I feel your power, High Priestess," Vari admitted, setting her chin. "But it does not change which side you are on, even if it was Lord Raen who hid us away."

"Tell me nothing then, except what the demons already know."

Vari nodded slowly. "We've been taking them out, one at a time, with the pixies scouting. I thought if we could make a difference, somehow, eventually their numbers will dwindle."

I did not have the heart to tell them of the thousands of demons in the realm below, ready to follow the Reaper. That, off the southern coast of Boneweaver Island sat multiple war ships just waiting to transport warriors. Killing two demons a day here would do nothing for our cause.

Vari frowned at me, as if sensing the truth. I nodded in return. "There will come a time where that will not be enough, Armsmistress. Be ready."

She clenched her teeth and grunted at me.

"I need to find Fangar Sharksbane, my demon husband," I repeated. "Have you seen him?"

"They call him the commander now. Leela tells us that there is an outpost in Gulab village. He's due to return from there tonight. His movements have been regular for the past few weeks."

Leela nodded. "Midnight!" she piped. "Sharksbane will be back by now—"

A commotion from outside told us more demons were arriving to inspect the disturbance I'd made.

A sharp pain in my navel suddenly made me gasp.

"What is it?" Leela rushed towards me, inspecting my abdomen

A loud, demanding pluck on the thread that bound me to Zale snapped my attention inwards.

"He's here," I breathed, a shiver crawling up my spine as I straightened.

"Who?" Vari snapped.

I met her eyes with what I was sure was an excited gleam. "My *other* husband."

18

ALTARA

Despite Vari's warnings, Leela refused to leave my side. She tangled herself in my loose hair, as she'd once done long ago, except tonight she combed through its messy length under my hood with her tiny fingers. The gentle movement was a balm to my pounding heart.

I'd get to wash my hair at some point, surely, though Zale had brushed through it often enough when he 'preened' me, as he called it.

The commotion outside grew and the three young women frantically gestured for me to join them.

"Sharksbane must be back," Vari hissed. "Can you hear them calling for the commander?"

We all listened to the shouts, and sure enough, demons were calling for Fangar by name and by title, their voices excited and bloodthirsty. I was familiar enough with the cadence of *that* sound to be sure.

"Then it is time I bid you farewell," I said carefully, eyeing the three young women. "Ladies, I'm sure we will meet again.

149

For now, you should get back to safety. Leela, stay with me for a little longer so you can relay what happens to the good Armsmistress afterwards."

Leela tittered excitedly, burying herself deep in my hood while I was met by three worried faces and one stern one.

The older woman stared at me, her gaze cold and assessing. Finally, she nodded once and led the girls away into the shadows behind the statues.

"Thank you, High Priestess," Nala said, lingering behind. "We'll never forget what you did for us."

I smiled at her and raised a hand, trying to appear more confident than I was. She disappeared behind Agnolthi's statue and I was alone in the temple.

That golden thread in my navel vibrated ferociously and I could feel Zale's anger tunnelling down to me. A bubbling excitement filled my stomach and I couldn't help but smile. I missed him, I realised, and even in his black, murderous state, I revelled in the thought of seeing him again.

As I went back outside the temple towards the shouts, I murmured to Leela. "I think it's high time my two husbands reunited, don't you?"

Leela squeaked under my hood, but I felt her tiny limbs trembling with fear. She'd already met both of them, of course, but had never known Zale as anything other than a villainous kidnapper who'd forced me to marry him. I didn't tell her that his demeanour was even worse now, along with his brothers this time.

The demons were all gathered at the gate to the temple, lined up, their blades unsheathed. When they saw me exiting, shouts of alarm rang through the grounds. The ones closest to me jeered and hissed.

"*Princess,*" they muttered amongst themselves.

"The whore princess!" one shouted.

My bow was in my hands, and an arrow flew before *that* particular demon could say another word. It hit him in the throat and he choked once before falling to the ground. The demons roared in anger.

"Come out here, little girl!" one shouted, showing me a row of yellowed incisors. "Don't be afraid."

"Yes, I think I will come out," I said, stalking down the path to the gate. "But I'm looking for Fangar Sharksbane."

A gravelly voice rang out over the din, silencing the rest. "I'm here."

I stilled. The demons at the front parted, revealing a tall blue demon striding down the paved stones towards the gate. Fangar was over six feet tall of Daanav marine demon, blue-skinned, yellow-eyed and hulking with muscle. He wore fighting leathers and plate armour on his shoulders to match his warriors, and held an axe in one hand, ready for battle.

I couldn't believe I'd kissed him once, even if he had been in a human disguise at the time. Sure, I'd stolen his penis right off his body shortly afterward, but he'd gotten it back easily enough. Hardly a fitting punishment for what he'd done—given me up to the Butcher who'd then cut me open.

"My wife," he spat, yellow eyes gleaming with pure venom through the night.

"Still got your cock, Fangar?" I asked lightly, though my fists were clenched. "Or are you keen to lose it again?"

He stiffened as the other demons went quiet.

"I'm going to kill you," he sneered.

The thread inside me went taut, and I hid my smirk. Without a word, I pulled the temple gate open and strode right out. I was promptly grabbed by two demons and both my arms were wrenched backwards.

"Watch out," Fangar warned his soldiers, stepping forward to study me. Cold obsidian shackles were bound to my wrists so I wouldn't be able to use my power. I tilted my chin upwards as Fangar bent a little. He smelled like sweat and metal as his eyes suspiciously searched my face. "What the fuck are you doing here?"

"I follow the Reaper now, didn't you know?" I said lightly. "And he told me to come and see my other husband while Zale is recruiting the Pentarax demons."

Fangar's face twitched at the mention of the Pentarax and I noted the other demons shifted uncomfortably. Apparently, they were wary of the elite assassins too.

His discomfort only lasted a moment before a cruel smile punctured his face. He stepped back and cracked his neck. "If my wife wants to attend to her wifely duties, who am I to stop her? Take her to the tombs. Let's string her up there. Maybe I'll let all my soldiers get a turn."

My stomach sank at the pure menace in his words as the demons laughed in excitement. They roughly dragged me around the side of the gate. I'd never been down the path that led behind the temple. It was where my four Old Ones had lain under the Reaper's tortured sleep for two hundred years. I'd *known* there was something down here even before I'd known about Zale's existence. I'd felt an urge to go down there before the twin priestesses had stopped me.

As the demons stomped down into the dark, the golden thread vibrated incessantly now, almost as if Zale knew I was close and was getting agitated.

That was good. The angrier he was, the better.

Demons with flaming torches ran past us to light the way

and, to be honest, I was glad for it. The darkness was thick and heavy, as if the dark magic that had spent two centuries keeping Zale and my brothers asleep had permanently cursed the very grass and stone.

Four hulking stone tombs sat side by side. It was an unnatural sight here in Ellythia, because neither the Old Ones nor the Ellythians buried their dead. It was always cremation for them. The presence of the stone structures seemed almost Lobrathian, if it were not for the demonic markings etched above each stone door.

Each set of doors were open.

"What does it say?" I asked out loud.

I half expected them not to reply, but to my surprise, the one on my left gruffed, "Here lies Ashzale Boneweaver. A monster who waits until he is called."

A shiver ran down my spine. The markings on the other tombs were almost identical, so I guessed it said the same of the other brothers.

We went into the biggest one in the middle and I got my first look at where Zale had spent two hundred years.

I'd expected to see a slab of stone upon which he'd rested, but there was none. Instead, four black shackles were welded into the back wall. Two up the top and two down the bottom. With small horror, I realised that Zale had been strung up in an X position for his 'sleep'.

"She's too short," Fangar barked. "Hang her up by her wrists and use chains for her legs."

I allowed them to manhandle me and do as Fangar instructed. I'd known they'd want to contain me somehow, and a part of me wanted to see if I was bothered by being tied up again. I'd had a sort of rebellion against the notion, in Odeelia's Court of carnal fae, when I'd arrived in nothing more than ribbons 'tied' all around my body. Zale had proceeded to cut them off one at a time and it had been a healing sort of thing. A way of telling myself I was not bothered by what the Butcher had done to me.

But my heart still beat wildly in the cage of my ribs as they fastened the shackles around my wrists and put me in a position of complete submission. Suddenly, the world appeared in acute clarity and I became aware of every sharp weapon in my vicinity. They had blades, both large swords and smaller knives, similar to what the Butcher had used. I had no magic, and couldn't use a bow or dagger with my hands like this. But there was one thing that I did have. And that was my trust in Zale. That he would always come for me, hunt me.

I allowed my anxiety to travel down my bond to Zale, let him feel the tremble in my fingers, the pounding of my heart, the shallow, bated breaths and the sweat now coating my body. Leela whispered something from inside my hood, but I did not hear what it was.

In the distant jungle, there came an ear-shattering, animalistic roar.

The demons jumped, unsheathing their swords as my heart beat frantically.

"There aren't supposed to be lions on this island," one of the demons said, his voice sharp with panic.

"That wasn't a lion's roar," Fangar said darkly, yellow eyes burning into mine.

"No, it wasn't." I couldn't help but smirk.

"Then what was it?" the demon looked between me and Fangar, but the commander just stared at me with the knowledge like a sharp blade between us.

Fangar said quietly, "It was a tiger's."

Demons screamed outside. I let out a laugh as the six

inside the tomb made to rush out, but Fangar called out something in their guttural demonic language. They all froze, then moved back into position to guard me with the ease of warriors who'd trained from childhood.

I stretched out my fingers in the shackles and tried to slow down my breathing. As the sounds of the battle drew closer to us, around the temple and down the path to the four tombs, my heart began to pound less from fear and more from excitement.

Barely a minute later, Fangar and the six guards stiffened as, from the shadows around the temple, the tall naked body of a monster made human emerged. Zale was a warrior whose every defined muscle was limned with violence so dark it made me shiver. His blue eyes, blown out in their tiger's form seemed to glow through the dark as they assessed their environment with lethal acuity. In this moment, as he stalked down the temple path, he was death incarnate.

Behind him were Atax and Kai, similarly naked, and even Raen, usually the vain one of our group, wore only an expression of icy agitation.

My heart skipped a beat at the furious sight of Zale, face and body splattered with demon blood, obsidian blade unsheathed, his face a mask of pure rage. His shoulders heaved with his anger and his predatory lope told me he was ready for more blood.

We locked eyes over the path and he went still. His eyes took in the tableau of me, chained up in his shackles, in his tomb, surrounded by leering demon guards. With each second that passed, everyone in that space could feel the visceral sheet of his power surging like a hurricane over the grass. Finally, his gaze narrowed on me, his head lowering into that dangerous position. "My mate," he growled.

I shivered as he stepped closer to the tomb, each movement constrained, feline violence.

Raen muttered something from behind him and Zale halted just before the tomb, cocking his head at what lay between us. Kai saw me and did a little happy jump, waving at me, black blood smeared on his cheeks like war paint.

It was then that Fangar gave a signal and the demon guards poured out of the tomb to fan it in a guard. The four Old Ones remained still and silent as they eyed the demons guarding me.

"Did you forget about him?" I called to my husband.

Kai cocked his head so far in his study of Fangar that it was almost sideways. Atax screwed his face up. "*I* did. But he was irrelevant before now."

Zale growled, but did not answer.

They'd had their orders from the Reaper. In the face of that, everyone else had paled in importance.

"Fangar is my second husband, Ashzale," I said mildly. "Did you forget that I am wife to another? That I am another man's woman?"

It was a goading, dangerous thing to say, considering we were already teetering on the edge of something dangerous.

Zale's eyes flashed, and I watched as that aura of rage coiled like a snake around his shoulders, settling like a moving weapon around him.

His voice was so guttural it was hard to understand. "You have no husband but me. No man, no animal, no *demon*, but *me*."

I couldn't help but tremble from the ice in his voice. At the promise in it. "Not according to Ellythian law *or* the blood debt I owe to Queen Odeelia of the Carnal Fae."

Zale made a sound in this throat that was half a thought,

half a rumble. I watched his face as thoughts moved through his mind. Fangar glanced back at me, his brows furrowed.

"What are you talking about?" the demon commander snapped.

"You will not kill him," I said firmly to Zale. "But... you may kill the others."

Kai laughed, and Atax grinned at me.

"As my queen commands!" Atax gallantly raised his sword as Zale glowered at my order. He probably realised this had been my plan all along, but he did not stop his brothers when they leapt forward to engage the demons in a bloody, messy battle. Kai used only his claws and teeth, ripping out his first demons' throat with the long incisors coming out of his human mouth. Raen sliced crucial arteries precisely, almost bored, not exerting any more energy than he thought they were worth.

Fangar and Zale stood still in the middle of it, staring daggers at each other as their men fought, as blood sprayed and male voices screamed. Fangar grew more and more agitated as each one of his demons fell heavily to the ground, never drawing breath again.

Within minutes, it was just Fangar left standing, with my Old Ones, barely sweating, staring at him as if they were ready to rip out his throat.

My husband took a step forward and Fangar took a step back into the tomb. I had to give him some credit for not cowering, because they had him cornered.

"Zale," I warned, a reminder that we needed him alive.

"You touched my mate with those hands, one time, did you not?" Zale asked quietly. "By all means, I should cut them off." He glanced around Fangar to me. "Odeelia won't be happy, but she will make do."

"Stay back, animal," Fangar growled. "The Reaper won't allow this. I'm commander of the Daanavs. He'll have your head."

Zale smirked. "He will not mind, I'm sure." Then, under the moonlight, the shadows cast his face into something from a nightmare. "Say you are sorry. Ask me for forgiveness. Beg me."

"Fuck you."

Kai let out a purely feline hiss, baring his bloody teeth at Fangar.

But Zale only smirked and raised his obsidian blade as if assessing it. "My mate and I shared power, did you know? She doesn't know it, but I learned something from her. Was *inspired* by her when she took your cock clean off your body." The smile slid off my face as I stared at Zale, wondering what he meant.

Raen suddenly grinned, full and wide, and it made me go cold. Zale's blue eyes flicked towards Fangar. The blue demon choked, hunching over as a wet splat sounded. I gaped in horror.

"What did you do?" Fangar wheezed, staring down at the organs lying in the dirt.

We all stared at the glistening stomach and bowel lying in a wet heap on the forest floor. But there was no wound on Fangar's abdomen, no blood seeping into his clothes.

"You should pray to me, for today I am your God. I wonder," Zale said, stalking forward, "how long you will last without your entrails?"

Raen snorted. "I give him three days."

My mind whirled to comprehend what Zale had just done. What he was now capable of. How he'd twisted my power into something actually horrific, and had done it with such *precision*. And yet a morbid part of me was fascinated.

It would be a slow, painful death. He would die of dehydration first, or perhaps nervous shock. Worse, this time, there was no Kraasputin here to give those organs back to him.

Fangar's voice was little more than a strained rasp, leaden with shock. "You are worse than any monster I've ever met."

The words were supposed to be an insult, but Zale paused, and over his shoulder, he threw his words like daggers. "And do not forget it. Make sure everyone knows it. Let them know that Ashzale Boneweaver does not take revenge lightly."

He stalked towards me, with a look of pure unadulterated out-of-this-world rage. Perhaps for the first time, I was scared. But not for myself.

"That is the least of what we will do to the creature they call the Butcher." It was a promise to me and made my heart swell.

Kai was rolling on the ground, clutching his stomach, gasping with laughter as Atax grabbed Fangar and tied him up with a rope Raen summoned.

Zale stepped into the tomb and cut through the metal of the shackles with his obsidian blade.

"My husband," I murmured, as he pulled me into his arms and I melted into his body with a sigh. He tipped my chin up to meet his face. Those tiger's eyes searching me for injury. I was trembling from adrenaline when he leaned down to press his lips against mine. Drawing back a hair, he murmured against my lips in a low growl, "If you do that again I'll—"

"Do what?" I arched my brow at him as he glowered at me.

I don't think I understood how dangerous my beasts were until just now. How dangerous and... insane. Perhaps I didn't realise just how much their consciences had *protected* the rest of the world from them.

19
ZALE

I stared at my mate after she interrupted me. I'd hunted her all the way across realms fed by only rage and violence, only to have her arch her brow and look upon me *defiantly*? That look confirmed my suspicion from the beginning—that she'd planned the capture of Fangar at my hand by using herself as bait.

Lowering my face to hers, I said with lethal softness, "If you ever run away from me again, if you ever think about using yourself as bait, or put yourself in danger, I will come inside you so deeply that your womb will never forget who you belong to."

She sucked in a surprised breath and the festering rage inside of me couldn't help but continue. "I will hunt you down until the end of time. Across space, across realms, and even after our death when our bodies are dust, I will chase you back to the star whence we were born and merge our spirits together until we are one and you can *never* escape me again."

Burning emeralds met me, igniting a flame in the coldness

161

of my chest. She touched my face and whispered. "You mean more than just these words, I think."

I didn't know what she meant, but her arousal stroked my nose and I closed my eyes to savour it. She pressed herself against me and, from the depths of my rage, lust burst forth. Lust and something else I could not decipher. Did not care to decipher.

My fingers reached into her witch's robe and I tore the dress I'd made her from neckline to hem.

She made a small feminine sound of surprise.

"I will have you here. I *must* have you here." I shoved her robe off and she eagerly leapt into my arms. A savage grin spread across my face at her need for me. Bare breasts pressed against my naked chest, her brown thighs wrapping around me. I gripped her throat in one hand and kissed my way down one side of her neck.

"Zale," she gasped, nails scraping down my back. The sting was sweet and urged me on as the golden thread between us hummed with approval and pleasure. It was as thick as a rope as we stood entwined, and I was vaguely aware of a golden orb zipping from her hair and flying outside. I turned to look at it, but Altara growled and leaned forward, biting my neck.

I grunted in surprise as I felt her draw blood with her tiny, blunt teeth. Slamming her against the wall of the tomb—my tomb—I pressed her head further against my neck, encouraging her.

"Bite me, my mate," I groaned. "Mark me."

She made a tiny, high-pitched noise of assent and bit harder, her nails dragging down my back. I held her tight against me, her pussy pressed against my groin. My cock jumped and twitched, desperate to kiss her wet warmth, and

I reached down to drag the head of it against her sex. She whimpered, and the need to claim her in the most beastly way took over.

I shoved my cock into the source of her wetness, that ever-sweet pool of her I spent my nights dreaming about. Altara's head snapped up, and she moaned. I rubbed my face along her neck, and her shoulders, spreading my scent to wash away the stink of the demons on her.

A stink that was slowly driving me mad with the need to remove it.

"Mine," I growled in an ear as I sheathed myself in her. "Fucking mine."

"Yes," she whispered, accepting my girth. "I'm yours, Zale."

A deep sense of satisfaction wormed its way into my very soul at hearing her words. At the sound of my name from her lips. Like the most primal part of me had needed to hear her say it, yearned for her to tell me she was mine, over and over again.

Like clouds parting for a dawn sun, a light spread inside my mind. But my need for her overpowered it—reduced me to a beast, and I pulled my length out and slammed into her again.

"This body," I rasped by her ear. "This pussy, this mind, this soul, is *mine*."

My thrusts evolved into a sheer, possessive, claiming rutting of my hips into the deepest part of her. She came with a cry and that sound—that fucking sound—tore something open in me in the sweetest way.

"Holy Mother!" Altara cried.

"Altara," I gasped desperately. "Altara." Her name was a hymn I clung onto for sanity.

"Zale?" she pushed at my shoulders and I growled reflexively, slowing my thrusts but not near ready to be without her.

"Let me look at you," she gasped.

I shifted my hold to grip her around her thighs and pulled back only enough to stare into the depths of those emeralds that plagued my brain. My hand found her soft cheek and both of hers found my face.

"Is it you?" she asked.

"Who else would it be?" I asked angrily.

She *rolled her eyes* at me, and though I frowned deeply, some dust was wiped from my consciousness and realisation struck me.

"Oh fuck, Altara," I whispered. "You hit me."

A giggle came from her throat and I kissed her furiously.

"It was smart," I panted. "My clever mate. When we fuck, my mind is clear."

"Will he know?" she asked, eyes wide.

I had to rein my mind in before I lost myself in them. So I closed my eyes and concentrated on thrusting into her tight centre. "It is possible."

"Raen saved the schoolgirls," Altara breathed. "And the townsfolk too, I think. But I did not want them to reveal more to me."

"Good. He is working on something, but I don't know what." Her eyes searched mine, and I placed my forehead against hers. I breathed, "Gods, I thought I was going to go mad. I can't handle you running away from me again."

Those plush lips curved into a smile as she pressed them to mine. "I will do whatever it takes to get you out of this bond with that monster, *Ashzale*."

Ashzale? My head whipped up and my hips paused mid-thrust. "Is that a threat, wife?"

I had never seen a grin more wicked on her face. "That is a promise, husband." She wriggled her hips, and I groaned at the rivulets of pleasure shooting up into my stomach. I grabbed her around her waist again and thrust into her. "You will listen to me," I whispered in her ear. "You need to find out what Raen was planning before we were taken over. There was something he was working on, but I cannot get it out of him, nor is it safe to do so." She swore, tilting her head back, her eyes glazing with pleasure. "Focus, my love. Use my magic you have in you, use everything, to break this bond. Do you understand?"

"This is going to be difficult, Zale. Maybe too difficult."

I shook my head. "There is always a way, Tara. If the three queens found a solution the last time, we can surely do the same."

"What, summon a second wife from the stars?"

The growl that came from me was little more than a dense rumble, and I gripped her ass from both sides and pummelled into her with punishing strokes, my balls heavy as they slapped against her core. Her cries hit me right in my gut, and when she screamed my name, I came with a roar, sending ribbons of my cum right into her cervix with short, deep thrusts. My power zipped right down my cock into her body, twining around hers.

"Take it, my love," I whispered. "Take all of me."

I fucked my power into her until she was trembling with it, full to the brim, practically glowing.

"Oh Goddess," she sighed. "I feel like I could turn into a beast right here and now."

I took her hand off my shoulder and kissed her knuckles.

"That would be fun, though I don't think it works that way, but..." I slipped my manhood out of her and felt my mind cloaking over once again. "I love you," I whispered, kissing her lips with a sigh.

Suddenly aware that my mate was naked with demons roaming about, I summoned a new dress for her. Black silk covered her from breast to toe, and I reached down to pull her witch's robe protectively over her shoulders and tugged her hood up. She tolerated the dressing, but scowled at me the entire time.

A wound inside of me knitted together being in her presence again. With her by my side, everything was right.

"I want britches or fighting leathers," she demanded, looking up at me fiercely. My head cocked as I looked down at her nipples puckered through the material. I wanted to suck them, but now was not the time.

"No," I said firmly. "The gown makes fucking and preening you easier."

She gave me a disgusted look that sent me growling, and pushed past me to walk out of the tomb. I followed close on her heels.

"Enough, Zale," she said imperiously, waving a hand like some ancient jungle queen. "We have business to attend to."

She strutted out into the temple grounds, where my brothers were poking at Sharksbane. A tiny orb of light zipped itself back under her hood—a pixie, I remembered. I would have to kill it later, but for now, she could have it, if it amused her.

She strode up to my brothers, who immediately jumped to their feet before her and bowed. Kai immediately bounded up to her and kissed her hands. I growled a warning at him, but my mate placed her hands on either side of his cheeks and kissed both of them. Kai beamed under her attention and procured a pink lotus out of nowhere, presenting it to her nestled between both palms as if it were the key to the moon.

The beast part of me appreciated her command over my brothers. Atax's eyes found my mate's bite mark on my neck, and he grinned like the savage beast he was. But, as if he'd remembered something, the grin fell off his face, and he frowned up at the night sky, rubbing absently at his ear.

"My queen," Raen said impatiently. "My king. Fangar is threatening the life of your uncle, Prince Ansel."

I narrowed my eyes on Fangar's ashen face, sitting slumped and sweating in front of Raen, but my mate got there first. Lightning skittered down her arm to her fingers as she crouched before Fangar and grabbed his face in one hand. The demon cried out as the tiny lightning struck over his skin. The smell of burning flesh filled the air, and I smiled adoringly at my mate.

"What have you done to him?" she snarled. "How did you capture him? Where is he?"

"He is alive," Fangar said, flinching. "But I will not tell you anything until you return my... stomach back."

"No," Raen said, hauling him up to his feet. I pulled my mate back and stepped before the demon, now panting with pain. "You will tell us, or I will take your cock and balls as well."

Fangar groaned, but said, "He is with my guards at Castle Ivory, working as a slave. We caught him on a return ship to Lobrathia, coming from the southern sea."

My mate was fuming. This was unexpected and mildly annoying. I hadn't even known there might be another living male in my mate's family. There was a possibility he might want to claim her back for the Voltanius line. It would also be something to consider when the Reaper took the war to Lobrathia—

"We don't have much time," she bit out. "It *has* to wait. The month will be up in two days. We need to go to Odeelia first. How do we get into the Eternal Forest?"

I was the only one who knew the answer, since it was me who'd frequently been visiting with Odeelia all those years ago.

"Then let us go," I said as Fangar glanced between us, trying to figure out what we were talking about as he looked like he was going to vomit. There'd be nothing to vomit, though. "The fae queen awaits."

20

ALTARA

Z ale took us deep into the forest with Fangar being towed by a gleeful Atax—well, as gleeful as one can be while murderous. A cold smirk was glued upon his lips and a malevolent chuckle burst from him every time Fangar tripped —because Kai, who brought up our rear, would periodically poke him with a stick.

I couldn't find it within myself to feel bad, seeing as he'd been responsible for the destruction of Malika's village and our subsequent kidnap. I might have completed the rituals required to marry him, but he'd never been worthy of it.

Leela obediently zipped away back into the temple after a quiet word from me. I would miss her, but the Carnal Fae Court was no place for the tiny pixie. At one point, I was sure Zale had spotted her, and a momentary murderous look had crossed his eye. I wasn't going to lose her. I'd lost too many already.

I was pouring with sweat within minutes of trekking through the heavy damp air of the jungle and had to return my witch's cloak to the ether. Zale threw a look of promise over his shoulder at me, but I was sated from our mad fucking against his tomb wall. A poetic justice, if I'd ever heard of one. But our brief conversation had been important. I looped my arm through Raen's muscled one, and our tattooed mage visibly straightened. I was feeling particularly endeared towards him after his saving of the schoolgirls using the temple.

"My queen," he murmured, the fine black tattoos across his nose and cheeks seeming to shift in the night.

"Raen," I said. "I fear I might fall upon this uneven ground."

He inclined his head, glancing at my boots, but said nothing. My witch's boots made me sturdy on my feet, and no doubt Raen had sensed the magic in them. Zale had seemed to think that Raen had been working on something before the Reaper arrived, and if that were true, I needed to appeal to his unconscious mind to figure out what it was. Perhaps by touching him, I might get some magical sense.

"I worry about my Uncle Ansel being taken by the demons," I said quietly. "You do not think they've maimed him, do you?"

"They probably have," he answered flatly. "Especially now that they know he is your relation. Both the Daanavs and subterraneans have long kept human slaves for entertainment and work, but he is now a high-profile prisoner."

"I wonder how they figured it out. He should have kept his mouth shut."

Raen frowned down at me. "He is valuable to the Reaper. We must use him as leverage over Lobrathia and the other human kingdoms."

My heart sank at the cold calculation in his words. Of course, they were going to think that way. Getting them to help me free him would be asking to go against the Reaper. They'd never do it. But if I could somehow make it look like he *wasn't* useful, and to do it just for me, perhaps they would. I just needed a good enough reason. Uncle Ansel had always been the party-going, responsibility-fleeing sort of prince, content to wander the world on his own terms. I'd respected that about him, and he'd always brought me back gifts from the strange lands he visited.

"Here," Zale's deep voice called out from the dark and Raen carefully led me to him, as I could barely see where my feet tread. In a small clearing, I could just make out Zale's large figure crouched in the grass. His obsidian blade flashed, and he cut his own finger. "Be quick. Hold on to me, and by the Reaper, do not let go."

I cringed at his choice of language, but it was then that Zale looked up and saw me clutching onto Raen's arm. With a growl, he lunged and grabbed me around the waist, pulling me into his lap. I shrieked in protest, but his teeth were at my neck immediately, pressing down in gentle warning—as if I were a pup that had misbehaved. My lightning zapped in protest, but he didn't even flinch and only held me tighter.

The others gathered around us, all placing a palm on Zale's back, with Atax forcing a panicking Fangar to do the same.

Zale held his bleeding hand over the grass before us, and it was then that I saw the wonky shape of a circle of black mushrooms hidden in between the long grass.

Zale's blood spilled onto the grass, and suddenly, the ground disappeared beneath us and we were falling. I let out a shrill scream before Zale grabbed the back of my head and shoved my face into his shoulder, stifling my sound. Instantly, I felt safe as he held me, remembering the last time I'd fallen through the portal into the Forests of Eternity, when I'd been cold and alone.

Kai's whoops of delight were inconceivable, but Atax and Raen wrestled with a protesting Fangar behind us, all the while trying to maintain their grip on Zale. Wind and light passed us, but I kept my eyes closed, my nose buried in Zale's hot scent. After what felt like minutes later, we landed with a thud onto soft, sweet-smelling grass.

As we climbed to our feet, I shivered at the change in temperature. It was no longer humid, but fresh and clear. Summoning my witch's robe, I bundled myself in it. The fresh pine and floral scent of the forest around me reminded me of the last time I was here, ready to kill the fae queen who'd taken Zale from me.

"Magrin?" I mentally called through the ether.

Raen looked at me sharply, and I stared at him. It was possible that he'd heard me, but how much dared I risk?

"The Nine are with you," said Magrin's deep, melodic voice. *"It is a joy to hear your voice so close to us."*

Despite everything, relief poured through me like a warm summer breeze. *"Dear Agnolthi, I've missed you. Enemies are about. You must tell me nothing unless I ask specifically,"* I warned.

After a pause, she said, *"Very well, High Priestess."*

I smiled despite myself. *"Be ready, old friend."*

"Always. The blood moon calls."

Cringing at the memory of the last so-called 'blood-moon', I shook my head and said, *"And the high priestess answers."*

A satisfied chuckle came into my mind before her presence faded into the night. While Magrin and the Nine witches' allegiance seemed to lay eternally to Agnolthi, and therefore me, I was wary of their particular skill set. The last time they'd done a ritual for me, they'd sacrificed a young wolf in my name and given me his power. It was an awful experience, and one I would never forget. Though I'd firmly told them 'never again', I knew their breed of magic was oftentimes darker than what I wanted.

Then again, these were dark times, and here we were, sacrificing a bowel-less Fangar to save Zale. I couldn't deny it was twisted in more ways than one. A dark sort of hate spread through me. Powerful beings like Odeelia and the Reaper cared little about the damage they caused others.

Behind me, Fangar had fainted and Atax was slapping at his face to wake him up. Fangar suddenly jerked awake, screaming into the night—all because Kai had jammed one of his long claws under one of Fangar's fingernails.

"Enough playing," Zale chastised. "Let us go." He gestured before us and under the light of two full moons, the curling golden gates of the Carnal Fae Court were revealed. Golden-clothed fae soldiers were striding towards us from the other side, white teeth glinting in the dark.

No doubt they were ecstatic to see Zale again.

Reminded by their lecherous treatment of my husband the last time, I stalked past Zale, standing protectively before him. Satisfaction lingered down the bond between us as he laid a hand on my shoulder. Amidst their finery, I suddenly felt underdressed.

"Give me pretty clothes," I demanded, without taking my eyes off the guard now at the gate, ogling my brothers-in-law.

I took off my witch's robe and returned it to my astral repository as Zale's fingers stroked my neck where he'd bitten me moments before. With a flutter of fabric, my black silk dress disappeared and was replaced by a dress of blood red silk that cupped my breasts and hugged my curves before falling straight down. A single slit came up one side, right up my thigh that would allow one leg to be visible as I walked. After a moment of thought, Zale touched my head and something heavy came to sit atop it.

Kai *oohed* behind me.

"What is it?" I said, touching it with my fingers and finding cool metal.

"A temporary diadem," he murmured, as if surprised by his own actions. "So Odeelia will know that you are *mine*. She will want to take you after what happened last time."

"Take *me*?" I said, aghast. "She had her interests set on *you*."

An intense look set in his eye, and he lowered his head to say. "You only wore ribbons the last time we were here, remember? It was *your* seduction that set her off, not mine."

Leaving me slack-jawed, he placed my hand on his forearm, clothed himself in black and gold tunic and led us forward, leaving Raen behind to dress the others.

A crowd was gathering on the other side of the gate, and as it swung open, the richly dressed fae parted to reveal their queen strutting towards us with a triumphant smile.

She was stunning in her immortal beauty, as usual, in a dress of white brocade, a tight corset, and a long lace veil trailing behind her. A bride, about to attend her own wedding.

Zale growled in annoyance so softly in his chest, perhaps I was the only one who'd heard it.

She held her arms dramatically akimbo. "So you have returned Ashzale to his rightful female?"

I had forgotten how enraged she could make me. Before I could summon a weapon, however, Zale spun me into him, crushing my mouth with his own in a rough, claiming kiss. I moaned as his tongue swept over mine and his grip around my waist tightened.

A few fae in the crowd sighed.

Zale released my mouth, though not his hold on me, and I had to turn my head to give Odeelia a gloating smile.

"Nope." I waved a hand behind me and Atax dragged Fangar forward. Only a lifetime of courtier's training stopped me from choking in surprise.

Raen, I'd forgotten, had a greater sense of style than any of us because Fangar was now naked, in nothing but his blue skin and a red bow, nearly as big as his head, fastened around the side of his neck. A leash of silk led from the bow to Kai's fist, and he tugged on it for emphasis. I tried not to look at the way his abdomen caved in now, but the carnal fae were experts in the bodies, and were quick to notice the distortion.

"What is this?" Odeelia spat, her face contorted into disgust.

"I kept my word," I said evenly. "I said I would return my husband to you. Fangar is my *second* husband. We were married the same day Zale and I were."

Her nostrils flared as she raked her eyes down his sagging, only just-conscious form. "He is barely alive!"

"I never specified what condition he would be brought in."

Odeelia stared at me, her amber eyes flashing. Her court could do nothing but look between the two of us. We were two queens in a standoff, and Odeelia seemed to realise that, her eyes flicking up to my new tiara. But as those immortal eyes slid down the length of my body, her face visibly softened, her body becoming languid. She sighed dramatically and shrugged.

"Well played," she said begrudgingly. "I enjoy a good

E.P. BALI

trick as well as the next person. I'm sure Cherimani is laughing somewhere in her celestial realm."

I did not let my relief show. "Over two hundred years ago, three queens called me forth to break the Reaper's curse upon Ashzale Boneweaver, here in this time. In this place. An Ellythian queen. A Boneweaver queen and a Pixie queen. There is no way in any reality that he could be anyone's other than mine."

Her eyes flicked to Zale and widened slightly as she clearly recognised his heart had returned to that cold and dead-as-ice state.

"Indeed," she said softly. "Your point is made. And well. I am old enough to be able to admit that." She inclined her head. "Your Majesty."

I raised my chin and nodded once.

"Stay for dinner, at least," she sighed dramatically. "Beings like you don't come around often in the life of an immortal. If you would allow us the benefit of your company for one evening, I would be grateful."

Zale went still for a long moment.

"Oh, can we, Zale? Please?" Kai pleaded.

"I think it's a good idea," Raen murmured.

I turned to frown at him in surprise because I wanted to get the hell out of here.

"This is acceptable," Zale announced. "My mate needs to eat properly."

As cheers erupted, my heart sank. I wanted to rescue Uncle Ansel as quickly as possible, but my brothers-in-law were now being enthusiastically accepted into the throng, with Fangar's leash getting taken by gleeful, jeering courtiers.

T he carnal fae were nothing if not the most indulgent, debaucherous creatures I'd ever met. As soon as Zale agreed to stay for a little while, we were immediately swept up into their madness of silk, chiffon, music, and wine.

Odeelia's dress changed into a transparent chiffon gold affair, and she led the throng as musicians struck up bois-terous music with flutes and a couple of lutes.

As they led us down to their dining hall, I realised Raen had become the ultimate lord of seduction—both fae males and females had taken a liking to him immediately, clinging onto his arms from both sides and fluttering their eyelashes up at his cold blue ones. An *almost* flirtatious smile twitched at his lips as he murmured compliments about their clothing. One of the females actually fainted when he touched the glitter on her cheek and inquired about it, to which everyone shouted and then laughed, two other females easily hoisting up their fallen comrade between them.

"I never realised how popular Raen was with women," I said to Zale.

He smirked at his cousin and the giggling crowd gathered behind him. "Women love the poetic priest. He used to be a romantic of sorts. His father was much the same, to the woe of his mother."

Kai was taken up by the younger fae, who giggled with delight when he produced colourful roses out of thin air.

Atax, to my surprise, glowered at anyone who came too close and flat out ignored those who tried to talk to him. Zale and I watched—him with cold, detached interest, and me with bemused wariness. There was a look in his eye that I recognised, and I wondered how our friends were doing in Lota City. If they missed us, or if they hated us for abandoning them.

"Your Majesty," a voice murmured by my shoulder. I turned to see two familiar pointed female faces with two males behind them, eyeing me with interest.

"Oh, well met!" I said, placing a hand on the shoulder of the female closest to me. "Thank you for your help last time." These two fae had been held captive in the dark castle I'd taken over, forced to be wives to the old master of the place. Once I arrived, I'd released them from the magic binding them there, and they'd been able to come back to their home.

They cast their eyes down in submissive politeness. "The thanks are still ours. Our debt is not yet fully paid."

"Ah, the fae and their debt ledger." I waved a hand. "You need not thank me further. I only did what was right."

"Indeed," said one of the males, glancing at Zale. "However, if you require anything, you need only ask us."

I inclined my head before my attention was swiftly taken away to a bejewelled dining hall made of glass standing. It was in the shape of a spectacular flower, the glass petals pink and purple that allowed you to see inside. The edges of the petals were limned in sparkling gold, giving the entire building an ethereal aura. The courtiers traipsed inside, with the band leading the way, Odeelia and Raen just behind them. The fae queen had batted the others away and claimed Raen for her own, sliding her hand up the bare skin of his tattooed arm and murmuring something into his neck I was sure I didn't want to hear.

Zale, with a possessive arm around my waist, and I entered behind them, only to be met by the smell of a roast feast. I'd been surviving on demonic meats and scraps for so long that my mouth watered immediately. The musicians took up their spot by the central dance floor—a delightful mosaic pattern of two lovers licking food off each other's bodies—and we followed Odeelia to the high table where the food was already set out.

The tables groaned with towers of garlic roasted potatoes, dozens of glistening, basted chickens and turkeys set beside solid gold goblets of wine and golden-crusted bread rolls.

After weeks of travelling through the demon realm, the sight could only be described as heavenly. What little reprieve I would get to eat now, I would take it all.

"Oh, do sit next to me, High Priestess," Odeelia cooed, patting the chair on the other side of her and Raen.

I would have wished to sit elsewhere. *Anywhere* but there, but now I couldn't avoid it, and was forced to oblige her, arranging my gown as Zale pushed my seat in. He sat down next to me, immediately placing an arm around my waist once more.

Atax refused to sit anywhere except between Zale and Kai, roughly shaking off one male's attempt at dragging him away to dance. I kept one eye on our commander as we sat, but couldn't hear what Zale murmured to him. Atax's shoulders relaxed immediately, and he picked up a goblet of wine and drained it in one go.

"Eat!" Odeelia commanded her people. "And be merry, for we are in the presence of the King and Queen Boneweaver and their court! Our guests are valued and we *will* feed them well!"

At the suggestion in their queen's voice, the crowd cheered from their tables, and immediately, couples took to the dance floor, striking up a slow, sensuous waltz.

I piled my plate high with crusted bread and meat, to which Zale grunted in satisfaction, until I noticed Odeelia delicately sniffing in my direction. My fork stopped halfway to my mouth as I realised that she no doubt smelled our love-making from earlier.

Her red lips stretched in a seductive grin and it was then that I noticed Raen's large hand stroking the inside of her fair thigh, the twin slits in her dress affording him perfect access to her flawless skin. But the mage was murmuring to someone else on his other side, as if he weren't paying attention to Odeelia at all. I quickly returned to my food, determined to eat my fill, which was far more important than anything else.

"Might I ask you one question, High Priestess?" Odeelia's voice was low and husky as Raen's hand wandered, though the fae queen's eyes were only for me.

Hiding my smirk, I said, "Of course, Your Majesty."

"Why didn't you kill me? I assumed you would when you returned next."

I raised my brows, the bread roll never going back to my lips. "I was told you are unable to be killed."

She raised her own delicate brows and waved her filigree goblet as she spoke. "But you are *high priestess*, with the

Boneweaver Bow, you could destroy the blood contract between us. Could have destroyed me too. Why didn't you? I know you have it in you."

I tried to hide my jaw going slack at this information. I obviously failed because Odeelia's eyes widened, her pupils dilating. "You didn't know."

Glancing at Zale, I realised he was busy murmuring to Atax, who laughed cruelly at some joke.

Turning back to Odeelia, I said, "I don't have it. I was told the Ellythian queens stole it long ago."

Ulanna, a serpent from Zale's court here in the Eternal Forest, had told me this very thing.

From the side of my eye, I saw Raen's hand disappear between Odeelia's thighs, though his fork went to his mouth with his left hand. Well, impressive. Odeelia sighed wantonly. "Stole it?" she said, her voice slurred, her arousal perfuming the air. "My dear high priestess. The only person who can string the bow is the High Priestess of Agnolthi herself. Only she and the Boneweaver King can even touch it! Of course, old Ashgalax Boneweaver *took it* from his wife. A weapon that could hurt him or his god? He'd never let her keep it. No, he took it to the deadliest guardians he knew. Probably spun some story about it being stolen."

A cold feeling of doom coiled my stomach.

"Who were the deadliest guardians he knew?" My voice was as dull and flat as Zale's.

Odeelia popped a grape into her mouth and sucked her finger. "Why, the Pentarax, of course. They have it in their guild tower."

The Pentarax. All the blood drained from my face and pooled in my feet. *The deadliest guardians Zale's father knew.*

"The entire place is booby trapped," she sighed,

completely oblivious to my lack of response. Raen's hand moved in and out between the queen's thighs and she spread her legs a little wider. "You'd need great skill to steal it from there."

"Steal it?" I repeated lamely.

If the bow could destroy a blood contract, it could destroy bonds. It could destroy the bond between Zale and the Reaper. Dear Goddess.

"Mmmm," Odeelia breathed, her head lolling back for a moment before it swung to look back at me. Her eyes wandered down my face to my chest. This close to her, I could plainly see her pupils were blown out, completely obliterating the amber irises. Her own breasts heaved as Raen's hand moved faster between her legs.

"You'll need all your power, of course," she panted, her head lolling back again. "It can't even be picked up otherwise, let alone drawn."

All this time, the Pentarax had it? The knowledge sent a lick of fire through my veins, and the intense need to retrieve it from their dirty clutches thrummed through me.

"The Reaper wouldn't like you having it," Odeelia murmured so only I could hear. "But do you know what? Fuck him. He's a horrible fuck, anyway."

I choked on my wine.

"Oh, it was a long time ago, when he was a handsome prince of Spring Court—that's what they called Blossom Court back then—and I used to go travelling around visiting cousins. Why ever would you cut off our lovely ears? They're so pretty and he's so ugly now. And for what?" She blew a raspberry. "Power over the humans?" Her back abruptly arched, and she gasped. I dared not look between her legs as her entire body spasmed and she let out a tiny cry.

"Ah, by the Gods!" she crumpled into her chair with a sigh. "No, I'm happy in my little heinous corner where I can do as I please." She smiled fondly over at Raen, who finally looked upon the queen, and she raised a hand to stroke a finger across the line of tattoos over his cheekbones. "Now here is a pretty creature who knows what he is doing. Oh, you must come and visit me again, Raen Boneweaver."

Raen leaned down to kiss her and Odeelia grabbed his face with both hands, their tongues twining around each other. I stared, fascinated.

Zale's grip around my waist tightened, and when I turned, he was looking at me. "Eat," he commanded.

And for once in my life, I obeyed, but *only* because I was still starving.

WHEN I NEXT LOOKED UP, RAEN AND ODEELIA WERE GONE, along with Atax and Kai. Before I could look for where they'd gone, Zale, who had just finished wiping his mouth on a napkin, threw it on the table and pulled me into his lap.

"Where is—"

"Are you full, my mate?" His breath tickled my ear and I couldn't help but feel every inch of his hard masculinity beneath me--likely aided by the fae wine and hedonistic fumes in the air. I turned to look at him with half lidded eyes. For a long moment, we simply stared at each other.

I drowned in those cold blues. Like a deep ocean pulling me right into an icy riptide that I could not free myself from. Would never free myself from. But freedom was in there, and there was nothing else in this world that I wanted more than to sink within those depths.

"I'm rethinking my rule on taking you before others. Let me claim you here," he growled, fingers digging into my ass. He pressed an open mouth kiss onto my neck, scraping his teeth down the length of my soft skin. "Let me put a cub in that womb of yours."

Licking my lips, I looked out at the crowd of fae, many of whom were engaging in their own lovemaking on the tables or on the floor—as was the way of these creatures. But more than a few had their eyes on us, sitting at the high table, set on its dais, their eyes glazed, light fingers trailing down their own bodies. I wondered what it would be like, having Zale take me here, on this table before them all as an audience.

But Kai and Atax and Raen were about, and I couldn't risk Kai of all people seeing me sprawled naked here, moaning wantonly.

"Another time, perhaps," I murmured. "And no cubs yet. There's a war, for Goddess' sake."

There was neither disappointment nor sadness in his eyes. Only calculation and lust, only the beast assessing his mate. His chest rumbled in reply.

An hour or so later, Odeelia returned, her hair unbound from its previous fancy-do, and with a satisfied glow, Raen trailing behind her, lacing up his pants. Atax and Kai reappeared with a few giggling girls blushing behind Kai.

"I will return you to Boneweaver Island," Odeelia said happily, her body gleaming with fine sweat that only served to make her look more beautiful. "You need not use those batty old owls this time."

"My thanks," Zale said, though his tone was harsh and impatient.

Odeelia rolled her eyes at me before striding off the dais, and I climbed off Zale's lap to follow after her.

Voices called out in goodbye to us, and more than a few promises were made for our next visit. Kai waved enthusiastically at them and Fangar, slinging his arm over a scowling Atax's shoulders. Raen and Zale continued on either side of me, sheer blocks of ice cold predatory instinct. None of us cast a parting glance at Fangar Sharksbane, who sat next to multiple fae, his eyes closed as if in pain.

I looked sidelong at Raen, but the look he returned to me was as devoid of emotion as ever. He'd not only insisted we stay for dinner, but had helped me get information from Odeelia. I wondered what was going on in the depths of his mind.

Odeelia strode out ahead of us through the golden gates, though there was a little kick in her step, no doubt thanks to Raen's apparent skill. We met her just outside, where she promptly twirled and offered her hand to Raen, who delicately kissed the back of it.

We obliged as she indicated we gather around her, and with a nick of one long red nail upon the pad of her thumb, a single drop of her blood fell to the ground.

"Fare thee well and do come again," she said coyly. "Do not make me wait, Old Ones."

The ground fell away from us once again, and against Zale's hard body, I felt like I might finally be able to get used to travelling between realms.

Wind and light whizzed past us, Kai's laughter hit my

ears, settling my stomach, and when we landed, Zale caught me so I didn't topple over.

He promptly fell onto his knees, as did the other Old Ones. Confused, I pushed back my loose hair and looked up into the night of the Boneweaver Island jungle.

Before us, standing tall with his six red eyes viciously trained on us and a horde of Daanavs at his back, was the Reaper.

22

MALIKA

"Here, take this," Pia said, handing me an open parchment packet of dark blue berries. "The bilberries help us to see better at night."

It was dusk on the final leg of our march to the southernmost part of Tiger Island. Naturally, we'd volunteered to be stationed at the most dangerous part of the war effort and had journeyed with twenty other soldiers on a three-day travel on foot to the military outpost there. Pia had also volunteered to come. This is why I knew she would make a good queen. Her dedication to the people on Boneweaver Island had never faltered. When everyone else in Ellythia had forgotten about its most southern island, Pia never had. The movement was also helping her be less jittery. I think a part of her was getting antsy sitting still in Lotus City, just *waiting* for the war to come to us.

There was only a narrow strip of sea between us and the islands the demons had fully claimed. The island of my family home, where my parents and my sister were. Being closer to them would help my mindset as well, though it didn't help my endless anger.

Tiny glowing dots in the distance told us we were, thankfully, almost there. My feet were sore and blistered in my new black boots, my lips chapped, and my temper even worse than normal.

Bad enough that everyone stayed away from the Mad Lotus and her new, rabid dog. Me. Pia's barracks had thought *she* was not right in the head. I scoffed at that because I held that status *first* and Pia was only catching up.

Why did this trip seem so much worse than when we'd travelled in the opposite direction just a few weeks ago? Part of it probably had to do with what we'd seen at the Umasri barn, where we'd gotten to see the Old One's handy work first hand. I was sure Atax would have been the one stringing up those men, and a tiny little part of me appreciated that effort to avenge Rani's poor treatment; the people who'd hurt her badly enough that she'd spiralled into pledging herself to the White Widows.

But Yulara's father and brothers had almost died. It had been too much. They'd already lost Vasi. More deaths weren't fair.

I scowled as I tipped the packet of berries into my mouth and swallowed it down with water from my flask, not bothering to chew.

There were rumours that Altara had returned to Ellythia from wherever it was the Reaper had taken her and the Old Ones. There'd been a breach in the shield around Boneweaver Island, and someone had recognised the feeling of Agnolthi's high priestess' magic in the air. A shiver ran down my spine as I considered how I felt about this.

To be honest, as pissed off as I was about the entire thing, a tiny part of me stood in awe of Altara. That she and Zale had a love so great that she would willingly follow him into the dark. Literally follow him to hell, just to be with him. To have a man worthy of such profound loyalty? It was almost unthinkable.

As if she knew the direction of my thoughts, my queen murmured, "Do you think she's alright?"

I gave her an incredulous look. "Probably having the time of her life. With those four Old Ones to protect her? She's living every woman's fucking dream."

Pia rolled her eyes. "You know what I mean. Did you not remember the way their eyes *turned* into something... colder than ice?"

If only I *could* forget. As we'd stood there, looking up at Matrika's Hill, when the Reaper had the four Old Ones by his side like his personal soldiers. Naturally, my eyes had been drawn to one of them. Atax's face had been created by the Goddess Luana and Xalya themselves, in the way it was a brutal, savage sort of perfect. But the pure, unadulterated cold fire in them was enough to turn me into a blithering mess. I'd not been able to move, to breathe, to think.

For Atax's type of violence to be now unrestrained?

Unfathomable. The Reaper had a true weapon at his side, and I shuddered to think of the type of heinous acts Atax would now have to commit in the Reaper's name.

Because while the four Old Ones had their hearts frozen, we were all in true danger. Ellythia herself was in true danger.

But Ellythia still had *us*. I'd seen the soldiers of my barracks fight. All the way from cadet to commander, these soldiers fought with a tenacity and intelligence that had me impressed. They were truly Xalya's devotees in the way they moved during a fight, in their dedication to their craft of killing.

And with Xalya's axe marking my uniform, I was now one of them. An agent of war.

BY THE TIME WE MADE IT TO THE OUTPOST, IT WAS WELL INTO THE night, and we set about putting up our tents and helping with dinner. Since Pia had been relegated to cook's assistant, she had her duties to attend to while I had mine, so it wasn't until the moon was low in the western sky when we met again to take our watch.

"The demons are getting bolder," the soldiers said at the hand-over. "There are attacks every night now. Sometimes they're scouting missions, sometimes they're here to kill. Either way, they'll be looking to invade within days, I'm sure of it."

I should have been frightened. Instead, the fast beating of my heart was the excitement at the anticipation of getting revenge through blood. My first taste for fighting demons had come when my village had been attacked. We'd fought well and hard against those blue-skinned bastards, and the entire time, a fire had roared within my veins. But we'd had losses too. Levu had been ruined, Altara had been taken for torture, my father wounded. What had become of them and my little sister now, I could only imagine.

If those demons had done any damage to them, I'd burn the skin off their balls one by one. Death wouldn't be enough. I'd had half a mind to travel right over there and see for myself.

"Mal." Pia elbowed me in the gut and I realised I'd been grinding my teeth and the group was all staring at me.

"I'm just worried about my family," I said. "I come from Levu village."

The lieutenant, a bald, stocky man, eyed me with new interest, but not in a positive way. "I'm sorry about that. But, well, don't try anything stupid, soldier. The best thing you can do for your family is to fight when the demons come here."

He thought I was going to try and get across—to try and save my family in a valiant rescue mission. Me and Pia against a horde of demons would have been something for the storybooks. It would also likely make us both martyrs, and I liked living too much.

It would also have meant getting closer to Atax and the others, and I'd likely try to kill him if that happened. I wasn't allowed to wear the obsidian knife earring he'd left me due to uniform regulations, but if I knew I'd be seeing him, I would definitely put it on to let him know I'd never forgive him for leaving it in the first place.

It had been a message. So now, I kept it in my pocket as a message to myself. To never trust handsome men. You would have thought I'd learned that lesson, considering fucking one had landed me in exile—even if it *had* been altruistic on my part. My mother had been grateful, at least.

But wounds festered when they were ignored. So all I said to the man in front of me was, "I won't, lieutenant. I'm not that mad."

He looked between Pia and me like he wasn't so sure. I marked him as one of the smart ones. With the handover complete, we took up our positions on the eastern part of the sandy shores of Tiger Island, where we were least likely to be attacked.

Pia and I stood with a couple of spears and our swords at our hips, a campfire before us, looking out at the crescent moon. The smell of salt in the air and the crash of the waves brought back memories.

"Remember when we sailed from there to here and we had to convince the captain that Atax and Kai weren't spirits?"

Pia grinned. "It wasn't until Atax offered to cut off the captain's head to show him how real he was that he agreed." She turned to me. "I miss them."

The hairs on the backs of my arms stood on end and I shivered despite the warm night. "I need to pee," I said faintly. "I'll be back."

"Set a shield or two," Pia warned. "We can't be too sure anymore."

"I'm setting three. I like my ass too much to expose it without protection."

Pia cackled. I didn't really need to pee, I just needed a moment to steel myself. Against what had happened. Against what was to come. Sentinel fires were lined all up and down the beach, so I wasn't worried about Pia being left alone. The girl could hold her own anyway, even without magic. I trooped up to the jungle behind our fire and pressed my face against the rough bark of a tree. My magic bubbled up within me, ravenous and agitated.

"Calm," I whispered. "I am as calm as a fae pond."

It's something my mother used to say to me as a child when my temper got the better of me. These days, I seemed to need it more than ever.

The back of my neck prickled, and I whirled around with

my spear at the ready. But there was no one there. All was dark around me, nothing moved between the bushes.

That would have been enough to placate me if not for the fact that my heart was pounding as the intense feeling of being *watched* only grew. A scent brushed past my nose, familiar and heavy. Alluring.

My instincts screamed at me to be wary.

I moved quietly, crouched as I inspected the area closest to the beach because I dared not go into the dark of the jungle alone.

Nothing moved in the quiet of the night.

Swearing internally, I made my way back to the beach and the light of the fire, that feeling on the back of my neck never ceasing its itch.

"What's wrong?" Pia asked sharply.

"I don't know," I said, glancing around. "I just have a bad feeling."

Pia growled under her breath, almost in the same way I'd heard Atax do, many times, and it set me further on edge because... I dared not let myself think that thought.

Swearing under our breaths, we scanned the ocean warily for the rest of our shift, on high alert, my adrenaline running the entire time.

WHEN WE GOT BACK TO OUR TENT AFTER OUR SHIFT, WE PUT away our things and headed to the washing tent. The area was quiet as everyone was either sleeping, on watch, or training. I finished washing up first as Pia had to wash her hair. Tentatively, I gathered my things and waited for her outside the tent, the need to guard my queen ever-present in my mind.

If there was something out there, the last thing Pia needed was to be caught butt-naked. I'd die before I let that happen. So I stood there, with my sword at my hip and my fingers twitching to burn whatever it was.

The ocean breeze brushed past my face, and with it, goosebumps erupted over me. A male voice, barely audible, muttered something I couldn't understand. I unsheathed my sword, scanning the night.

"Come here, you fuck," I muttered. I could still hear Pia rinsing her hair inside the tent, and that noise calmed me just a little.

Then, in the distance, something shifted.

I took a step forward, squinting at the midnight smoke next to the tent just ahead of me.

A man-sized shape was covered in shadow, a warrior's build, a head cocked to the side. But I would recognise even his shadow anywhere.

"Atax?" I whispered.

I was being haunted by a ghost, or perhaps a spirit of some sort, mimicking Atax—trying to trick me. Whatever it was, I did not take kindly to its presence. I stomped loudly forward.

"Begone, you fucker!" I sneered. "Or come into the light so I can blast you back into hell!"

The night was quiet, and yet still the hairs on the backs of my arms stood to attention.

Pia swore and came rushing outside, as did a few others from nearby tents. But with my momentary shift in my gaze, the thing was gone.

"What was it?" she asked. I glanced at her and then

194

groaned, because she was naked, wet hair streaming down her back, sword drawn.

"True warrior, you are," I muttered, shoving my body in front of her as a few passing soldiers gaped.

"Nothing to see here!" I called. "Stop staring, you perverts."

Grumbling, they got back into their tents.

Pia, unashamed of her nakedness, simply stared at me with those Lota-emerald eyes. They seemed to glow with their own light through the gloom. "What did you see? Spit it out, and don't lie."

I rubbed my eyes. "I'm just tired, I think."

She made a low sound of warning.

"I saw a ghost... or a spirit or something, over there." I jerked my thumb over my shoulder.

"You don't think it's one of the astral demons trying to spy?"

"Could be," I said, a dark feeling winding around me. "It... It looked familiar."

Pia, ever observant, ever aware of those around her, knew me so well that she caught on right away, body going still. After a moment, she said quietly, "We'd better tell command."

We did, and it went down about as well as a naked princess appearing stark naked outside the washing tent. Word spread fast in a place like this.

Pia got a warning, but my sighting was taken seriously, and the watch doubled. They called for a few Agnolthi's priestesses stationed here to provide more magical reinforcement as well as strengthening the quartz weapons so we could be sure they'd cut through an astral demon. We could all fight astral demons, it was part of our training as children, but they were trickier than the physical sort, able to walk through walls and solid things. Only enforced weapons could hurt them.

When we eventually got back to our tent as the dawn sun cleared the eastern sky towards Lobrathia, I froze at my bed roll.

"Pia," I said dully.

She came around to see what I was staring at, resting on my pillow as neat and as innocent as a bloody knife.

It was a black rose, its edges dusted with gold. Beside it, a tiny sketch on dirty old parchment. Three crowns and a key.

Dull realisation clanged through my mind, along with an old memory. Delicately, I sniffed the rose. Wild jungle, ocean, and pure, bestial male.

"It's him," I said thickly, snatching the parchment up. "It's fucking *him*."

23

ALTARA

The Reaper loomed above me and I had no choice but to follow the Old Ones as they fell to their knees. I sunk onto the earth, my heart shuddering and pounding under my ribs. There would be consequences for this.

A breeze swept through the clearing, and it smelled foul. No crickets chirped; even the palms stopped their gentle, skyward dance and stood as sentinels of our judgement.

"What is the meaning of this, Ashzale?" The Reaper's voice was deadly quiet. Behind him, the demons shifted, their breaths shallow and fast. They were angry that we'd taken their commander so easily. So readily.

"My mate had a blood contract to fulfil in the Carnal Fae Court, Your Imperial Highness," Zale said simply, looking up at the Reaper. His tone was purely of a soldier giving a report. "Fangar was the price. We completed the exchange. It was his life for mine."

It was then that the Reaper turned to me. A subtle shift of his head and all that malevolent weight struck me down like a boulder pressing me into the dirt. The urge to crumple was unbearable. But I gritted my teeth and bore it. I might have been on my knees, but I would *not* bow. Instead, I met his six eyes evenly.

But he said nothing and the silence became stifling.

"It has come to my attention that there are townsfolk and students from the school hiding underground." I stiffened, my breath catching in my throat. *"They need to be removed and executed. I will not have hidden rebels on my island."*

The words were out of my mouth before I could stop them. "Is this punishment for my coming here?"

The Reaper's energy bore down on me. Sweat trickled down my spine and my bones groaned, but still I refused to cower. Next to me, Zale tensed as he felt my strain down our bond.

The Reaper said, *"You will obey me, Altara Boneweaver, or suffer the consequences. I want you to know that you were responsible for the death of your people. For the young girls who hide and bide their time. For the two pixies who help them. For the children who rest in their mother's arms who thought you might still save them. I want them to know you will never come for them. I want everyone to know what you truly are."*

My blood roared in my ears and my shadows surged around me, wanting to bury me deeper from the arrows of pure terror and pain he hurled at me. "And what am I?" I hissed.

"You are just like me." He turned back to Zale. *"Ashzale. Go now. Scent them out. Take them all and tell them you did it in your wife's name."* And then he said something that sent me reeling. *"You and Raen are the only males permitted to enter Agnolthi's temple, I believe?"*

Zale, Raen, Atax and Kai stood as my blood chilled inside my heart.

"Agnolthi's temple?" Zale turned to look at me, cocking his head. The three Old Ones followed suit and then it was only four pairs of eyes waiting for my response.

"You do not need permission from her."

The sudden mental image of Zale and my brothers killing Armsmistress Vari and the girls I'd saved sent me into a deathly spiral.

There, on my knees, I imploded.

Light and shadow became a maelstrom at the centre of my being. There was no world around me anymore except the thrumming, vibrating magic that howled and roared into the ever-dark. I would not let them. I *could* not let them do this.

Then a voice that shook me like an earthquake, that singed me like lava from the inside of a volcano, raged into my mind, shoving everything aside and taking over my brain.

That female power prowled around me like a lion, her eyes wide, furious and hellbent on making me *listen*.

"The star that made you existed long before the Reaper did. And it will exist long after he is dead. The bond of starlight exists in your very soul, between the darkness of the particles that make up your bones. Do you hear me, Altara Yasani Voltanius Boneweaver? Do you mark my words, Queen of the Boneweavers?"

My heart was the bounding of a hundred tigers, my blood like the roar of a thousand lions. I understood. I understood. I understood.

My voice rang out across the clearing, strong and firm. It echoed off the trunks of the trees, off each blade of grass, off the Reaper's dark cloak. "I command you, my mate. My heart, my soul. You *will not* harm the humans on this island."

Zale's blue eyes struck me like a gong and the shock in them satisfied a part of me that was at once ancient and young.

One of his tattooed hands pressed over his left muscled pectoral and he looked upon me like he'd seen some goddess standing before him. When he spoke, his voice bore a melodic, almost ritualistic cadence. "Queen of my soul, I am yours, always yours to command."

The Reaper went still. So *still* that my hackles rose in warning. *"Ashzale may be under your command, lightning princess, but his brothers bear no soul bond with you. Go, Raen. Atax. Kai. Do as your god commands."*

Their faces were hewn from granite, their muscular bodies tense, but, silently, my brothers obeyed.

Without warning, I was gripped in a cold, vicious fist and torn from the ground.

Zale's screams echoed in my ear, but they were distant and getting further away.

A panicked tug on our bond resonated in my ears and the end of a conversation echoed through my very body. *"Your mate is no longer here to order you, Boneweaver King. Do as I command. Do not hunt her. Follow my orders and I will return her to you. Do not, and I will tear her from this Earth."*

Zale's pain struck me down our beautiful, glittering thread of starlight like a thousand splintering blows into my soul.

The scream that emerged from me, that came from a place deeper than the bases of my lungs, was pure, potent female rage that shook the night until it shattered like glass; until *I* shattered like glass and all I could see was twisted, unbridled light.

Somewhere, in the far-flung reaches of the night sky, there came a primordial reply.

24
ZALE

My mate was wrapped in the Reaper's magic and thrown into the ether, dissolving her from my vision. I cried out, my hand outstretched to reach for her, but my fingers only met air. He'd taken her. She was gone. I roared into the night.

"*Ashzale.*" The Reaper's command rang throughout my brain, his order to *stay* echoing through my being. But it was a death knell for the way it *writhed* inside of me, because the pure, molten need to find my mate violently clashed with it.

I fell to the ground as an agony I'd never felt in this lifetime hit me with the force of an obsidian axe to the lung. My tendons were tearing in two, my bones crushing—no, my very *heart* was being sliced open.

The glittering string tying me to my mate screamed, the sound mind-shattering, and it was then I realised it was actually the sound of my mate screaming down the bond. I cried out, grasping at my chest, my power lashing out.

The instinct to hunt and retrieve her was fighting against

the Reaper's orders not to, and my heart, my fucking heart, was *tearing*.

"His heart is slicing in two from the inside," came Raen's mildly surprised voice from somewhere above me.

The Reaper let out a snarl of annoyance. *"Fix it, mage."*

"Lie still, brother," Raen commanded.

Lie still? Lie fucking still? I lashed out, fully ready to tear the world apart just as soon as this pain receded and I could think properly. My power struck outwards.

"Argh!" a demon screamed, the smell of scorched skin filling the air. It must've been lightning.

I was hit across the head in a blow that should have knocked me out, but I was raging on the grass, my anger and pain too profound to fall into the unconsciousness that tried to claim me.

The clank of heavy metal sounded and something bound itself across my limbs one by one. The Reaper's magic fell on top of me so heavily that my limbs had no choice but to be pinned to the earth.

I roared, straining against them, my muscles covered in sweat, my tendons groaning.

There was more pain, this time precise and concentrated as Raen cut the skin of my chest open with one of his obsidian daggers.

"Kai?" Raen's voice was a request.

Before I could shout out, Kai sung a single sweet note and then—

My ribcage was cut open by his magic and I roared in protest.

"Sorry." Kai's voice was the distant buzzing of a bee as pressure, so much pressure that I wheezed, rained down on me. I tried to suck in air, dragging it into my lungs as my heart gave jerking thumps.

Death awaited at the edge of all things.

"My mate," I wheezed in a broken voice. "Where is Altara?"

"I am literally holding the sides of his heart together," Raen growled. "I do not know how to proceed. This should be impossible. He will die."

The ground shook beneath me and a deep groan roared around us. My laugh was the mad, rasping sound of nothing more than a monster, a broken one.

"What's happening?" Atax's voice came from somewhere far away.

Someone—a Daanav, I think—swore. "Look at the sky! Look at the fucking sky!"

I cracked my eyelids enough to see a slither of the night sky over me. The usual brilliant constellations glittered as usual except...

One of the stars glowed a brilliant, angry crimson.

I laughed maniacally again. "Altara..."

"Stop, brother," Raen growled, blocking out the night with his face. "Your heart is jiggling every time you laugh and I'm trying to hold it together." He turned away from me. "It's getting worse."

Around us, the jungle was quiet. Not even a cricket shifted in the tall grasses. Only the grating sound of my own breath filled my ears, and the irregular thud of my heart in Raen's hands.

Then, all at once, the Reaper raised his pale hand to the sky and the very world around us groaned.

A dark shadow spread overhead, its darkness heavier than

the night itself. I stared at it agape, finally going still as I realised with a cold sort of wonder what it was. At the shear, god-level power it took to cover the *entire* island in shadow. All at once, the red star wasn't visible anymore.

Somewhere to my left, Kai let out a strangled whimper.

The Reaper's face appeared next to me, looking down upon me with all six of his red eyes. Perhaps for the first time, his power shifted into something akin to uncertainty.

"Fine, Ashzale. Let us end this. You may hunt your mate, but only after you follow all my orders. Do you hear me?"

"Yes!" I gasped. "Fuck. Yes!"

The pain in my chest receded and Raen sighed as if this was all a great bother. I passed him a dry look, but he only sewed my heart together with his power, the burn of it at once comforting and irritating.

"Are you done fucking up my chest?" I asked angrily.

He smirked. "No. Kai?"

Kai's face appeared above me, his sky-blue eyes sparkling as he sang three notes over my open chest. With those notes, he slammed my rib cage back together, merging it back with the sternum.

I swore loudly as the skin, bone, and sinew sealed shut. The minutes ticked by inside my head before the Reaper waved his hand and took away the massive chains holding down my limbs. My body ached all over, my blood oozing through my veins like hot lava. I scowled as the bond between me and my mate prickled, twanging in anger.

But try as I might, I could feel nothing of my mate at the other end. Rubbing at my chest, I hissed in annoyance. This was bad. I had not done as the Reaper asked and severed my mating bond. This was his form of punishment.

Pain of all forms I could tolerate. This would just be another.

"Go, Ashzale," the Reaper commanded. *"I will be watching."*

He always was.

I bowed, grimacing at the primal burning in my gut. When I straightened, the Reaper was gone and only a few Daanavs lingered, peering at me through the jungle in the distance. I growled at them and they hastily scampered away like rats, back to whatever hole they occupied. Although…

Turning my head up to the night sky, it was now starless, cloudless and as empty as my soul. Malevolent shadows roiled above us in a dome I was sure covered every inch of the place. We'd begun the second phase of our invasion of Ellythia. The island would always be dark now, the demons able to stroll about during the day.

My next task would be easy. I needed only to hunt the humans, and most of them I'd scented before.

"To the temple," I grunted at my brothers. They nodded, observing me warily as I passed them, and they followed.

AGNOLTHI'S TEMPLE WAS DARKER THAN IT USUALLY WAS, AS IF IT were huddling into the shadows of the jungle, trying not to be noticed.

But as I laid a hand on the closed iron gate, my skin seized in a sort of spasm. I frowned, taking my hand off the gate and shaking the feeling out.

Something inside my head screamed, shouted, and banged its angry fists against my mind. For the first time in my life, I physically stumbled. Shaking my head, I looked up at the inscription over the gate.

Yasani Temple

My mate's middle name. Her mother was called Yasani, Geravie had once told me so long ago.

It was a crime among the Old Ones to enter the temple against the wishes of the high priestess. It was a law as old as the temple itself.

"What is it?" Raen asked, also looking up at the inscription.

I turned to him. "Something in my mind is…"

Raen grabbed my head and peered into my eyes. I let my mage look into me, his blue eyes going unfocused for a moment, pupils dilating. "A warning is writ there," he said, frowning.

Kai appeared over Raen's shoulder, his head cocked, Atax appeared over his other shoulder, scratching his head and making a face as if he, too, had some sort of discomfort.

"A warning?" Atax repeated.

Raen stepped back and surveyed our surroundings. "There is something at play here with these Ellythians. There is a magic protecting them. If it is of Agnolthi, none of us will be able to penetrate it."

"Their deaths have been ordered." I shook my head as ice burned inside my chest. "We must deliver."

"We cannot die in the process," Raen said. "We were not allowed to destroy ourselves, that was also an order, Reaper-given."

I sighed. "We need to get this done so I may get back to my mate. We need to hurry."

Kai rubbed his hands together, licking his lips, eyes shifting. "Tricksy tricks are needed."

Raen quirked a smile, a gleam of a thought appearing in his eyes. "Good boy. Let us move."

25

ALTARA

When I came to, I realised I must have passed out while on my knees because there I knelt in the dark…as if I'd been praying.

I blinked my eyes open, rubbing away dried tears.

There were bars around me; black, coiling metal bars that formed a dome. Heart pounding, I looked behind me, but the bottom of my cage swayed dramatically to the side as if it hung on a hinge. I grabbed onto the bars to stop from toppling over, only to see that I was suspended over the edge of a cliff. There was nothing but shadow beneath the cage, only a feeling of an intense height that made my skin crawl. To my left, it was the same. I was met only by shadows darker than the spaces between the stars. I was in the middle of *nothing*.

The thought sent me reeling, and I closed my eyes to master my breath, as my mother had taught me so many years ago.

"*We breathe through pain, Tara,*" she used to say when I practised taking on the illness of others. "*We breathe through injury,"* she'd say if I was struck during sparring. *"We breathe through sadness,"* she said when I'd broken my first bow.

So breathe I did.

When I opened my eyes, my heart was a steady metronome in my chest.

Where the fuck was I? I needed to get out. To see where Zale was.

"Magrin?" I called out, panicking.

There came no reply, no familiar brushing against my mind.

I called out again, only my voice sounded shrill and desperate. I waited.

Still nothing.

Gingerly, I turned around on my knees to avoid wobbling the cage. The cliff's edge was visible, and beyond that, extending into the darkness was absolutely nothing. I scanned my cage. There was no lock, no door to unlatch. The top and bottom were made of the same obsidian metal.

I swore softly and breathed.

The Reaper couldn't have just put me here, in this place of nothing, surely?

But he could. That is exactly the type of thing he *would* do, now that I'd shown my hand and defied him. He could have just killed me, but I had a feeling he knew that would've driven Zale rabid and he needed the King Boneweaver sane for his war. The full moon was days away.

Scanning the shadows of the mountaintop, I tried to think of something I could do to get out of this cage and onto the clifftop.

I didn't know how long I sat there for, because there was no indicator of time except the beats of my heart and the breaths I was trying to control.

209

But at some point, fiery orbs speared through the dark, catching my eye. There were just two of them, hovering in mid-air, just the right distance apart to be twins wrapped in midnight shadow. A twisted familiar feeling speared my gut, and slowly, I approached the front bars, gripping them in sweating hands.

The orbs grew bigger as the being approached me through the dark. By the time it was close enough to shoot with a bow, I could see the outline of a tall, cloaked figure.

"I admit," I called wryly, "I've forgotten your name, *organ-stealer*."

He stopped short, and though I could have thrown a dagger right into one of those flaming eyes, I did not summon any weapon.

"They call me Kraasputin," he breathed in that characteristic breathing hissing way of his. "A name that meansssss... Well, it would frighten you to tell you."

I smiled without humour. "I fear nothing, Kraasputin." A little lie never hurt anyone.

He surged towards me so fast that I lurched backward. Dark hands clutched the bars of my cage, pulling it towards the cliff, and as he pressed his face between the bars, his hood fell back and his cool demeanour disappeared like wind.

His face.

Goddess, his face.

Kraasputin was fae. His skin was smooth and fair, with ears that were curved into points, his cheekbones high, the bone structure fine—once handsome, even. But he was thin and skeletal, as if a fae male had become a wraith. A very ancient wraith.

Through a mouth with no lips, he whispered as if he

dared not ask. "Tell me one thing, Altara Boneweaver. Tell me, did he... come to you?"

I stared at him unabashedly. "Who?"

He continued to whisper. "A being, dark and terrifying. With eyessss that saw to your core? Did he come in the dark of night? Did he take soulssss with him? Did he... ask you to become just like him?"

A memory came to me, old and ragged. I'd surpassed it. Deep in the eternal forest before a black castle, as a dark queen who'd sunk into profound despair. Eyes like hooks had appeared out of nowhere.

Worse than the Reaper. Worse than anything I had ever seen, or perhaps would ever see.

"Yes," I breathed. "And then I plunged into his chest and pulled out the darkness. He..." I tilted my head, trying to bring back the unwanted memory. "Then he nodded at me and went away."

Kraasputin stared at me, silent. Barely breathing. Those flickering flames reduced to orange-red embers. Wordlessly, and hardly breathing myself, I reached out a hand. This creature was a wraith made of shadow and embers. A creature who dealt in secrets. I placed a gentle hand upon the pale, long fingers clutching my cage as if he were gripping onto them for life.

His skin was smooth but cold, and I allowed my warmth to seep into his skin.

I inhaled sharply. Those embers flickered as if they did not want to.

I removed my hand.

Kraasputin reared back from the cage, observing me as if surprised. "You did that? You... took *from* him?"

"I did." I said the words slowly, never taking my eyes off

those gentle flickers of life. "It was then that I knew I had to change. That things were not as dark as I thought. That *I* was not as dark as I thought."

He was silent, simply staring at me, poised as if in thought, his hands still clutching the cage. And then, he raised the hand that I'd touched, considering it as if it were a marvel. "At one time, I thought this world would be left to ruin, but then humans like you come along—like you and your sister, and I wonder…" The up tilt in his voice was so uncharacteristic, as if he were voicing a daydream. "I've known many queens in my time, Altaraaaa. And one day, you will be the type of queen who will look upon her court and see ssssomething good that *you* created with your mate. Wild and perfect. Furious and bright. Just like the Goddess you worship. Just like the sssstar you were born from."

I blinked at him, my chest suddenly achingly tight.

A moment of silence extended between us as we considered one another, both of us marvelling a little.

"Your sister will need help," he went on tightly. "If she wins back Lobrathia as I suspect she will, the Reaper will come for her city. It will become the seat of the battle for the human continent."

I let out a shaky breath. "Ellythia has its own battle to fight."

"Indeed." He inclined his head. "With Ellythia, he will be unstoppable. Without it… he is still a force that will not be denied. The Boneweaver Bow is what you seek. The Pentarax Guild is five miles straight ahead."

A surprising shudder ran through me as the shadows about my cage seemed to shift and, with a soft click, the metal of the bars became a door that swung open. By the time I looked back up, Kraasputin was gone, leaving only the scent of burning embers behind.

I stared at the opening for a moment, and the small gap between my cage and the cliff's edge.

The Boneweaver Bow. He'd known I needed it. Was *advising* me to get it. I couldn't help but think he'd given me two *things*, but I had only given him one. The soft touch of a debt brushed my naval, but I dared not think of that now. I needed to get out of here.

"I think I'd like a friend about now," I whispered down to my mating mark. Naina stretched out on my hand, then leapt right from my skin and into reality within my cage, her transparent blue glow an immediate comfort. She rubbed her face against my thigh and yawned. I scratched her velvet head and sighed. "Looks like we need to go to the Pentarax Guild after all, girl," I muttered, clenching a fist in determination. "Perhaps that was why they were pushing for us to go there in the first place." There was a fire in my bones now at the thought of having it. This powerful weapon that could break things. "And then we can sever this bond between Zale and the Reaper."

I climbed on her back and Naina bounded onto the cliff and into the dark.

We plunged through the shadows. Naina had steady footing on the ground, though it made my skin crawl to have us bounding into the dark. Eventually, the shadows cleared and I could see the desolate realm of the demons stretching out in all directions.

Two hours of travel later, something huge appeared on the dark horizon. A toe-curling sound hit my ears and Naina slowed her tread as I frowned at whatever evil lay ahead. A cacophony of wails, screams and unintelligible shouting filled my head like an iron helmet and I wished I could plug my ears as we made our way to the shadow before us.

It was a wall—a long wall stretching as far as the eye could see—and we were headed straight towards a solid stone gate in the centre of it. Behind it, a tower of red and black speared into the sky, glowing fires in the windows giving it a sluggish light.

The Guild of the Pentarax.

I drew my shadows around me as if they were a dense woollen cloak so that no skin showed. My vision became a little hazy as I got pulled down into that dull state of apathy where my mind was cool.

The gate was a monolith of huge black stone and set within its walls were the heads of very living demons, mouths full of incisors, gnashing, their black tongues lolling.

The two huge demon heads set at the centre of the stone gates screamed and hurled profanities in their own language as I approached, and when I finally stood before them, ran their tongues over their teeth. Movement on top of the gate caught my eye and a leathery skinned gargoyle leaned down to hiss at me. "Women are not permitted past the Screaming Gate."

An apt name. One I wouldn't forget.

My voice emerged nothing like it normally was. It was husky and rough, like sandpaper over skin and distant like a hissing, approaching snake. "*I am no woman.*"

The creature's talons clicked as he leaned down to get a better look at me. Red points of light in his eyes shone bright when he finally bared his black teeth and rasped, "True enough."

The gargoyle surveyed me and seemingly came to the

conclusion that he had better let me in. Inclining his head, the gates swung open with an eerie groan.

Red like blood and black like demon ichor, the tower of the guild of Pentarax stood like a proud and sinister king on the desolate landscape. The smell of old blood hung in the air and my nose wrinkled under my shadows.

It was not just *one* thing owed to me that lay inside that tower.

The Butcher had done the worst thing that had ever been done to my body. Had cut me open precisely in the way that would hurt the most. He'd taken something fundamental from me. My power over myself. So much so that my hands trembled at the memory, that my breath seized and the echo of my own screams resounded in my ears.

He was somewhere inside here. So were many more lethal, elite assassins, who, just like him, were capable of devastating damage.

But while my own scream roared in my ears, the sound of my *husband's* screams would forever resound in my soul. Would forever turn my blood into boiling, molten lava that demanded I fix this and lay waste to the beings who did this to us.

So I settled into the calm cold of the lethal wraith that lurked within me, climbed off Naina, and stepped through the gate.

26
PIA

Out on sentry duty over the beach with a droopy eyed Malika, I was the first to notice it.

A darkness spread across the sky over Boneweaver Island like a malevolent cloud moving at hurricane-like speeds. It spread like mould, engulfing the night sky, like oily fingers reaching, *reaching* for Ellythia.

The night watch commander gave a shout and activated the warning gong, blue sparks flashing into the dark.

Then a sour wind hit the beach, along with a wave of horrid malefic power. Malika swore as we both raised our arms to guard our faces against the onslaught.

"It's him, isn't it?" Malika cried, gulping as we both squinted up at the sky and the stars that blotted out one by one.

And then it was over us and, still reaching, heading north with the full force of that old, cruel power behind it. Even our campfires seemed to pale under the shadow.

My blood roared in my ears as chaos broke out around us; the gong resounding, the sentries kicking up the sand as they ran back to base, the commanders shouting. But Malika and I remained stock still.

I understood what this meant.

They would be on us soon.

"We need to get back to the capital, Mal," I said quietly. "We *all* do."

Amongst the chaos, a familiar force blasted through the air like the heat from a volcanic eruption. I hunched against its sheer, colossal power. There was only one Goddess with that fiery signature.

Agnolthi was the land itself. The rivers and lakes were her blood, the rich earth was her skin, every beast in Ellythia was her eyes and their song her voice.

I turned around. She stood in the lapping tide, the black ocean at her back, her silken obsidian hair whipping on her own wind. She was seated atop her golden, ferocious lion.

I had wondered when she would show herself to me.

The lion opened his mouth and let out a roar that made the sand jump and vibrate under my boots. I clenched my teeth so hard my jaw cracked, but I would not cower under that power. Under any power.

As I stood tall, she pointed at me with one fine brown tattooed finger. Her emerald eyes burned into mine.

An echo of a scream hit my ears, coming from far away, and I recognised the voice immediately.

Agnolthi stared at me and I stared at her, the shouting of my fellow soldiers fading away. The Wild Goddess' face lit up with an orange glow and the corner of her mouth quirked up in amusement at the way sweat dripped down my face at her heat, at the pounding of my heart.

Malika shouted, but I remained frozen. "Dear Goddess," my friend called from behind me. Her voice was not directed at Agnolthi, but away from us. "What the hell is that?"

It was then that I realised Agnolthi was not pointing at me, but *behind* me.

I whirled around.

27

ALTARA

The moment I passed through the Screaming Gate, the air changed, muffling the sounds of the creatures behind me. The air pressed on my skin, searched me, observed me like a living thing. It was malevolent and assessing as its fingers pressed firmly against my defences. My shadows would not yield and I merely stood there for a moment, coolly observing it back.

Who are you? It seemed to whisper.

"I have come to claim what is mine," I murmured in that cold ruthlessness of my wraith state. "If you stop me, you become my enemy. Leave me be."

The presence shifted in surprise, and after a breath, it seemed to bow. Satisfied, I stalked forwards, my head lowered like a predator, my gaze fixed on the red and black tower, my mark. My prey.

There was nothing in this universe that would stop me from claiming what I felt in my bones was my birthright.

I had been born to claim Zale as my king and husband. Therefore, I had been born to be the Boneweaver Queen, the

High Priestess of Agnolthi. This bow had been pledged to me hundreds of years before I was born and that sudden realisation shifted something in my blood.

The tower bore many windows, some that glowed with wicked red flames, some cloaked in malevolent shadow, and in more than one, there was a flash of white skin as its inhabitants observed the newcomer.

There were still twenty paces to the tower doors when a shadow skulked out from either side of the tower. They were hulking beasts with leathery midnight skin. I counted eight spindly arms that crawled like a spider's and bone white incisors that flashed as they bared them to me, their intent clear.

They hissed and scuttled towards me.

Pausing my step, I allowed my power to lash out like a hungry whip. I was full of Zale's power, as well as my own, and it might have been some of that influence that halted the beasts in place, their legs clawing uselessly as my power *pulled* at the source of their life. Power flooded into me, my magic surrounding it, gobbling it up and transforming it into golden dust that settled within my veins like liquid gold. The spidery beasts crumpled upon themselves, nothing more than a pile of flesh and bone.

I continued right past them and up the black stone steps where the giant twin doors opened of their own accord. Eyes narrowed, I walked into the dark entrance of the guild of the Pentarax.

"How did she get past the gate?" came a low, nasally voice. I turned to see two goblins, one holding a tray with a silver chalice, and both staring at me with their mouths open.

"Which way to the Boneweaver Bow?" I asked in that husky, hissing voice.

"I-It's in the centre of the tower." The goblin pointed upwards with his gnarled finger. "But no one can—"

Stone ground upon stone and the floor itself shook as the central pillar rotated in its spot, revealing a narrow, winding staircase. I made straight for it, ignoring the goblins, who turned and sprinted down separate side passages.

The stairs were steep and high as I climbed them, the muscles of my thighs and abdomen heating up. But I kept my breath steady as I wound my way around them, a bubbling in my blood confirming I was heading in the right direction.

A whisper of a song breathed down my spine, heavy and golden, silken and sharp.

It was calling out to me, I realised. An ancient magical object like that must have a voice, a kind of sentience.

The stairs ended at a second level. And now I was not alone.

Three Pentarax demons, white, tall, hulking with bare muscle, stood from their seats, their chairs scraping. They all looked alike, and it grated me to see their kind.

I stood before them, looking for another staircase to lead me to my mark.

"You're the Butcher's plaything," one said in surprise. "I recognise the smell of your magic. Come to greet your master? Have you come to die, little princess?"

Plaything.

"I have no master," I stated coldly.

He laughed cruelly and unsheathed his blade. "You came alone?" he scoffed. "Well, come here and let me see if you really bleed gold."

They never even saw the arrow coming. Black fletching bobbed up and down where the end of the arrow had lodged itself in his throat. He only had time to give me a wide-eyed grimace before he fell, his sword clattering. The other two stepped around their comrade, the dark shimmer of magic falling around them. Shields.

I let a pulse of my magic burst outwards in a wave. "I am the High Priestess of the Order of Yasani, Agnolthi's representative on Earth. The bow is rightfully mine. I have come to claim it."

"Let her go." The Pentarax on my right smirked in a way that should have made my skin crawl. "Let's see if she can lift it."

The challenge ignited my blood and that ethereal call keened as if demanding for me.

"It's that way." He jerked his chin at the wide corridor to my left.

But a single step in that direction made me cock my head. Slowly, I turned on my heel to look back at the two Pentarax standing there, watching me.

"Liar," I hissed. The song was coming from the right-hand corridor. "I think I'll go this way."

The smirk fell off both their faces as they realised they hadn't fooled me. No doubt some trap had lain in the opposite direction.

"Even if you get to it," the second snarled, thumbing his baldric lined with knives. "You'll never make it back out."

The darkness in their faces told me he was deathly serious, and I wondered exactly how many demons were currently dwelling in this place. But all I did was turn away from them and head into the dimly lit corridor that was calling for me.

Another set of narrow stone stairs allowed me access upwards, and I knew at once that I was being followed by the two demons who'd baited me. No doubt they would call for more.

On the third level, the entire long corridor was bathed in deep blue light that hurt the eyes. I allowed my shadows to make a screen to blunt the blow of that light and followed the call down the right-hand side. It was only two breaths before another Pentarax sensed me and stepped into the corridor, a bow knocked with a black arrow. He loosed it with a deftness that I appreciated, but my own arrow was flying down the corridor in the same amount of time. The two arrows met in the middle and sparks flew as they bounced off each other and fell to the stones with a clatter.

I never stopped walking as the Pentarax, though surprised, fired a second, then a third. I answered with my own, noting the adjustments he made to their flight path. My second arrow met his low—he'd aimed for my knees—and the third met his at neck height. We both shot two more arrows before he threw his bow aside, brought out an axe and charged at me.

Tutting at the disrespect he paid to what was no doubt a faithful bow, I let three daggers fly in quick succession. Hurtling towards me like a bull, he was able to dodge the first dagger, but never anticipated the second two. The first hit him in the neck, the second in the gut, and he came to a screeching halt. As he fell to his knees before me, I stepped around him and continued on.

The song brought me down the corridor, and as I walked, I knew heavy booted footsteps were gathering behind me. But it didn't matter, because at the end of this corridor, a set of double metal doors sat, glimmering with death magic.

I hurled a magic-leaden dagger at the space where the two doors met and I flung my arm up against the light and sparks that exploded outwards. Through that dagger, I pulled on the magic sealing the door shut with such rabid force that the two doors crumbled into rubble.

Suddenly, the song from the Bow became a symphony of sound, calling and keening for me. I swept forward, my skin tingling.

Although the room that lay beyond the doors was small, when I entered, the space occupied by the bow somehow became bigger, grander, a place worthy of an ancient artefact. Now, in another space completely, I paused to take it in.

It was a grand hall, rivalling any throne room I'd been in, with the ceiling curved far above me, glimmering with filigree and obsidian swirling patterns. Those markings continued all the way down all four walls and formed images of old wars fought on the backs of elephants and monsters.

The gold markings would have been unseen for the dark shroud that blanketed the hall, if not for the single object giving off bright light.

On a heavy obsidian table, laid out like a holy relic, was the biggest solid gold object I'd ever seen. Certainly larger than any long bow I'd ever come across, it seemed to take up all the space in this vast hall.

It was surrounded by shadows darker than night, in the shapes of tall men and women flanking the table. Quite visibly, they turned around to look at me and shifted to stand in a sort of guard.

Though they were not hostile figures and I sensed no oncoming attack, I would still have to pass them to get to it.

The moment was heady, and it felt like I was drunk on some carnal fae wine, my body not quite feeling like mine, my tread like I walked on air. I could have been in a dream, if it wasn't for the buzz in my veins telling me that this bow, that this moment, was *mine*.

Walking cautiously, I approached it.

Whispered murmurs surrounded me, the dark wings of their voices brushing against my eardrums. They whispered sinister things, dark things, malevolent things. Things that had no business being uttered into reality.

But these beings seemed determined to watch me, and I got the feeling that I was being assessed for my worth, for my mettle. There was curiosity there, as well as envy, I felt, and it only served to make me more determined.

I moved past them, my eyes only for the ephemeral glow of that gold.

As I reached it, I was struck by its sheer, out of this world beauty. The thing was massive, easily as tall as me, if not taller, and made from pure golden tendrils that curved into the shapes of the beasts and flora that made up the jungles of Boneweaver Island. It was a work of art, a masterpiece of craftsmanship. But not only that, it radiated a lethal, heavy presence. This was not a weapon to be used lightly.

A whispered voice sounded from my left, coming from the tall figures who would not come into the light. It was then I realised the beings who stood closest to the bow were different. No malevolence came from them, only a broad sense of power as old as time and heavy importance.

I understood I was being told to read the words on the bow. The inscriptions were not in a language I should have been able to understand. Not Lobrathian common tongue, not Ellythian nor Old Ellythian. Yet somehow, I knew its meaning clearly.

"Time and Space are no bounds for me."

I cocked my head, thinking about what that meant. Raising a brow at the figure who had whispered. I said, "An arrow loosed from this bow can... travel through—"

"Much time. Much space," it breathed. "Many have been destroyed simply by attempting to string it. To use it?" The figure shook its hooded head. "A curse. A blessing."

That should have frightened me, but instead, the bow felt *sure* before me. Felt desperate to have my touch.

"It calls for me," I said, glancing at the rest of the figures. "I believe I am the only one who can use it rightfully. Respectfully. I know what it means to be both light and dark."

I reached for it then, unable to stand it any longer. My hand was gentle and reverent as I placed it upon the centre— and found it to be as warm as skin. It hummed under my touch, the vibration tingling up my forearm, through my shoulder and right into my chest.

Something ancient spoke to me in the gleam of the bow. There was a cost to using such a weapon. There was always a cost to such power.

"You'll need all your power," Odeelia had said.

Every power and force in me gathered in my arms, my shoulders, my core, summoned by my will. It was now or never.

Placing my second hand on the bow, I hefted it up.

My wrist screamed, my arms groaned, but the bow came off the table and into my hold like it had been waiting two hundred years to do so.

"Oh you pretty, powerful thing," I cooed.

The beings around me shifted in surprise, which was a little rude, I thought, but they stepped back to give me space when a coil of golden string appeared on the obsidian glass table next to me. Grinning, I placed the weight of the entire bow into my left hand and reached for the coil. Hooking the end of the gold string at the top, I took a deep breath, brought all of my power into my spine and right arm, and bent down. My bones screamed, my marrow roared, and the blood vessels in my eyes popped.

The cost was pain.

But I was well acquainted with pain.

The bow sighed in my arms, a wispy, ancient sound, and I'll admit I teared up a little as I secured the string at its base.

I straightened.

The room was quiet around me as the bow simply gleamed.

The figures around me seemed to take a breath, and as one, they vanished.

A voice like molten lava and the crash of waves on a beach whispered around me. *"You make me proud, Altara Boneweaver."* My heart swelled to the size of the sun. *"Hurry back to your mate, for the sky itself weeps."*

As the magnificent hall collapsed into nothing but smoke around me, the sounds of shouting male voices came from a little way from the room.

Then, a deep, angry shout that promised blood. "Do not let her leave with that bow!"

28
ALTARA

The smaller room appeared back around me, but the Boneweaver Bow still remained heavy in my hands. I couldn't help but stare at it in the gloom and the need to use and do it justice was overwhelming. But I had to admit, it was not a practical thing to carry while running back through this tower.

To get out of this, I would need to be fast. And precise.

"You don't think you could go into my astral repository, do you?" I said lovingly down to it, stroking the head of the wolf close to the grip.

With a happy sigh, it faded, and I felt its weighty presence hanging alongside my other weapons, far at the back of my mind. Nodding, I stared at the closed door, where the sounds of numerous Pentarax demons came through the door.

Closing my eyes, I sent my magic out through the door and set its claws into the two closest, pulling on their power until they collapsed. Shouts sounded and more heavy boots pounded in the corridor.

"Magrin?" I called. *"I need advice."*

"We are here, Your Majesty."

Relief was a cool breeze around my shoulders.

I explained my idea, and with much glee, Magrin and the Nine appeared in a circle around me, shimmering a transparent blue. They might not be able to physically fight with me, but they could give me the information I needed.

"There's only one entrance to this room, as far as I can see," I said. "If I direct it to that wall, I should be able to get around them."

"Focus your power onto your palm," Magrin said. "Not in it, but outside of it."

I'd never externally focused my power in this way, but I had spent a long time throwing my power out into others. It wasn't too much of a stretch from that skill to this one.

It started as a glowing, golden seed that grew and grew as I poured my power into it. Rather quickly, it was the size of a watermelon and my hand strained with the sheer weight of it.

Naina got excited and leapt off the skin of my hand, hissing at the door the demons were gathered behind. The nine witches cooed when they saw her glowing form.

"A part of the king is always with you," Magrin said in wonder. "His violent energy is quite something."

"Yes, well, hopefully *this* has violent energy, too. Shall I just throw it?"

"Indeed!"

Excitedly, they all watched as I brought my hand back and flung the golden ball at the wall adjacent to the door.

Splinters flew as a low boom resounded. Shouts sounded from the demons.

"Run!" Magrin cried.

And so we did. Naina leapt through first, charging like the predator she was, incisors out. I ran after her, summoning a bow as I went. As I'd suspected, we were now in an adjacent room, a bedroom of sorts, black stones with a hard bed on the side and a collection of weapons. We made straight for the door, the nine witches hurrying after me. I flung the door open and Naina leapt through first. There was a corridor beyond, and I looked left to see a crowd of Pentarax huddling around the door to the bow room. A few of them turned to look at me, but I didn't stop to say hello and bolted the opposite way.

Two Pentarax were pelting straight towards me from the opposite direction. Naina leapt for the first while I threw a dagger at the second. He ducked in time and threw one back. I didn't dodge fast enough, and it grazed the skin of my forearm. I hissed, but it was too late to throw another dagger, and I was forced to summon a sword to meet his downward blow.

I grit my teeth against his strength, my muscles screaming.

"*Power!*" Magrin cried behind me.

"Shit!" I cried, slamming my power forcefully into his abdomen. He was sent flying backwards.

Naina was devouring her demon's throat, and I cried out for her to hurry up. Feet pounded behind us, and it wasn't until I heard the crackle of magic behind me that I realised a magical attack was being launched.

"Shield!" Magrin called out. I went to pull up a sheet of power behind me, but I'd been too slow, and the Pentarax's power hit me with the force of a blunt blow to the spine.

I screamed as I was thrown forward, crashing to the stone floor.

Naina roared.

My body spasmed in the aftershock of the attack, and at the same time, I felt Magrin and the Nine blink out of existence. I groaned, realising their presence here was tied to my magic, which was now ferociously trying to gobble up the demon magic currently incapacitating me and my muscles.

The heavy boots got closer as I lay on the stones, clutching my abdomen and groaning in pain and frustration. My protective shadows disappeared completely, allowing the world to crash into my senses in a cacophony of sight and sound.

A shout sounded from behind me as Naina leapt to attack the first Pentarax demon to reach us.

But there were too many of them, and within seconds we were surrounded. A hand roughly grabbed me by my witch's cloak and hauled me up.

I cried out, my arms not working, my legs kicking out and meeting only air. My power struggled to gobble up the magic assaulting us.

And then I was face to face with the creature straight from my nightmares.

A white, low cheekboned face and a smile that stretched old scars.

"Hello, my Altara," the Butcher purred.

Before I could say anything, his black eyes widened at something over my shoulder and he dropped me, kicking me to the side with his boot.

I slammed into the wall as a commotion rang out.

A young woman with a swinging thick black braid barged right into the melee of Pentarax demons, her sword like liquid metal flashing in the dim light, as—faster than I could even see—she struck and spun, slashed and jabbed.

Black blood spurted, and the demons cried out as they dropped to the ground.

And then fire, red-hot *angry* fire, blasted the throng as a second black-haired warrior roared in triumph and anger. Screams and the scent of burning flesh filled the air as more bodies fell.

Emerald eyes just like mine looked down on me, sprawled on the floor. Only they were shadowed with the darkness of some knowledge I could only guess at. A calloused brown hand reached down.

"Pia?" I breathed in disbelief.

"Get up, cousin." It was an order. "We need to go."

And then Malika was running up, hair in a braided bun atop her head, her beautiful face streaked with black demon blood, and a wicked, wicked grin that promised pain.

The two of them standing there before me, with their shoulders heaving, covered in sweat and the blood of our enemies, was the most beautiful sight I'd ever seen in my life. Both were dressed in the uniform of Ellythia's infantry: black tunics and pants with Xalya's axe marked on their breasts. Malika had a red stripe around both biceps, marking her as a fire-sorcerer.

They looked harder than when I'd seen them last. Their bodies were leaner, more muscled, their jaws set in determination. But there was a gleam in their eyes, too.

As if they'd been waiting their whole lives to *fight*. And fight viciously. Both of them were born warriors, but now they'd been honed into something more than lethal.

When I didn't take her outstretched hand, Pia grunted and reached down to grab me around the bicep. Naina snarled at the corridor, now full of slumped, unconscious Pentarax demons stirring back to life. Tendrils of smoke and flame came from the clothes of the demons Malika had burned.

Three of the Pentarax lurched back to their feet, including the Butcher, who, as I watched, was healing his own facial burns and an unexpected slice Pia had gotten on his chest.

Shit. How the hell were we going to get out of here without a full pursuit?

"Run," I said, finally scrambling to my feet, my legs like jelly, my head pounding. But we needed to go.

Malika took the lead and Pia came around to let me use her arm to steady myself as we rushed down the first set of stairs.

"Shields up, Tara," Pia scowled, casting a look behind us. I grunted in response and pulled on my magic once again. The golden pool inside me was only a puddle now, but to my surprise, Zale's navy-blue magic jumped in reply, and I used that to fling up a protection at both our backs. Naina hissed and nudged me from my left, urging me to hobble along faster.

"How are you guys even here?" I panted, sweating and grimacing.

"I don't know why, but Agnolthi told me to head inside this *portal*. It came out in this very corridor and we saw you. The Goddesses might not be able to help us directly, but they sure know how to use us."

I think I knew why Agnolthi was appearing to Pia, but I wasn't going to voice that just now.

"And I wasn't just going to let her go in by herself," Malika called back at us. "You look like shit. Let's hurry up. I'm not even going to ask why you're *here*." She rolled her eyes at our surroundings.

A grin spread across my face despite everything. I said

nothing about the obsidian blade in Malika's hand, but I sure as hell noticed it.

Pia laughed through her nose when she saw me looking. "Malika won't ask, but I will. Why are we here, Tara?" she asked as we rounded a corner and Malika blasted a fireball at a couple of oncoming Pentarax.

I wondered how many would be left to follow the Reaper into Ellythia. But if I could do enough damage before we left...

An idea gave me a spring in my step and I finally let go of Pia, calling on Zale's energy into my palm as I kicked up the pace. Pia raised her brows but said nothing as we sprinted down the second set of stairs.

Shouts were coming behind us and Pia barked an order to Malika, who rounded back and let us lead. The whoosh of flame sounded behind us as Malika took down our pursuers and Pia surged forward with Naina, clicking her tongue to the tiger as if they were already friends.

My cousin was fast, I realised. So incredibly fast that I didn't think I'd ever seen anyone wield a blade so swiftly that her movements were a mere blur in the air. The Pentarax never stood a chance as she slammed their swords aside and viciously gutted them, inky blood spraying.

Lucky, the uniform of Xalya's army is already black, I thought wryly.

"Come on, sloth," Malika said as she overtook me, still gaping at Pia. We headed down the final set of steps that would take us to the entrance room of the tower, and I readied my ball of blue light.

Naina pushed me from behind as my strength dwindled and I unsteadily jogged after my friends down the stairs to our exit.

Goblins shrieked in the entrance hall and scattered when they saw Malika's fireball. Three Pentarax shot a joint magical attack straight for Malika, but my friend let out a battle cry as she sent sweeping flames out right towards them, singeing their attack and everything in its path.

Malika cackled as she jumped the last set of stairs and headed outside. Some people would have said she looked mad, but I thought she looked beautiful.

Pia kicked the doors open and the three of us stumbled outside and down the steps. I gathered the last bits of my energy in my palm and steeled myself as we put as much distance between us and the guild tower as we could.

About twenty paces out, I slowed and Pia looked over her shoulder at me, a wild smile on her face as she saw what I planned and she called Malika to a stop.

A shout rang out from the tower's entrance, and I turned to see the Butcher standing inside a golden shield of *my* magic. The power he'd stolen from me he was still using. His smile was razor sharp and hungry when he called, "We will meet on the battlefield, Altara."

My name on his tongue was a different kind of torture.

In response, I hurled my blue ball of power right at him and it shot forward on its own magic.

Boom.

The last view I had of the Guild of Pentarax was of the bottom level exploding outwards into a hundred tiny pieces.

The ground shook and the tower groaned as we ran, hooting and laughing like madwomen as the entire structure collapsed behind us, and we didn't stop running until we were well past the Screaming Gate, high on adrenaline.

We were a few miles away from the site of destruction

where we stopped and fell to the ground, panting and gasping for air.

A light opened up in the air before us. A seam in the world that sparkled with a celestial glimmer.

"Oh Goddess," Malika groaned, rolling onto her side. "Let's get out of this stinking realm."

"Wait," I croaked, flinging out a hand, "I need to show you guys something first."

W e entered the glimmering tear in between the
realms, its magic brushing against my skin in a
familiar, wild sort of way.

Pia gave me a knowing look. "We need to be careful," she
said. After I'd told them about the Bow and what it meant,
they'd told me about the Reaper's shadow engulfing Ellythia.

I nodded to her as we made our way through the tunnel of
light and out to the other side. I recognised the Boneweaver
Island jungle immediately.

Malika had marched through first, determined to be Pia's
protector, and emerged on the other side, inhaling deeply
with her hands on her hips. "Ah, fresh air." Abruptly, she
pointed up ahead. "This is the giant palm tree outside of my
village! We've come out in Levu— Oh, fuck." Metal sung
through the air.

Pia and I abruptly stopped short behind her as the portal
disappeared behind us and we came to see what had made
Malika unsheathe her sword. Only one person stood in the
darkness, as if waiting for us.

It was a shock to see Ansel Voltanius.

My Uncle Ansel was a man in his prime. Or had been, when I'd last seen him before he'd left for his voyage to the southern continents. He was in his late thirties, and under the shadow of the black, starless sky, his skin was so pale it was moon-white, in stark contrast to the brown skin I'd gotten so used to seeing here in Ellythia. He was a younger version of my father, bearded, with a once-handsome face that was now riddled with scars, his eyes hollowed out, his arms skinny and malnourished. The brown tattered rags he wore must have been white at some point, and he wore no shoes.

"Uncle Ansel!" I cried, stepping forward to go to him.

But there was no happiness in his eyes, only terror as he shook his head and roared in a hoarse voice. "Tara, run!"

A black arrow hit his Achilles tendon, and he grunted, stumbling in his step but not falling. He grimaced at me, and though his voice was nothing but a whisper, I heard my uncle say, "I'm sorry."

My magic lurched, reaching out towards him and his injury, even though it was spent and weak from overuse

But a power I knew as well as my own knocked it away like an adult slapping away a child's hand. Then Zale pummelled into me, taking me to the ground and cushioning my fall with strong limbs. He pinned my arms to my body so tightly I could only just draw breath. His voice was rough when he whispered in my ear, "Be still, my mate. Obey the Reaper. Obey me."

My heart broke in two as he said it.

"The Pentarax have a very interesting story to tell, Altara Voltanius," came the Reaper's voice.

Behind me, Pia stiffened and Malika made an angry, strangled sound. Zale pulled me up to standing with him.

"Come back to me, Ashzale."

A scowl spread over my face as Zale silently obeyed the Reaper's command and returned to him. His powerful, naked back rippled in the darkness, the little light from the held torches highlighting every muscle under his skin.

It was Kai who held the flaming torch, along with Raen, who stood on the other side of the Reaper. Atax was at the end, a bow held loosely by his side as he stood acutely still. His face looked haggard next to Kai's flickering torch, and it was plain for us to see his blue eyes were fixed on Malika with predatory alertness.

Was Malika prepared to face a cold, heartless Atax? I know I certainly hadn't been.

I raised my chin and tried to make my voice firm and confident. "Let my uncle go, Reaper."

A breeze stirred the grass between us as I realised how stupid I sounded, making demands from the Reaper.

"Have you finally chosen your side, Princess?"

Zale stiffened next to his master, and the thread between us bucked and spun aggressively. As if he were trying to tell me to heel. To obey.

"I just want my uncle free. Please, let him go. Our family has suffered far too much."

"I want to hear you say it out loud. For all to hear. Answer my question, Princess. Have you chosen to side against your husband?"

All four Old Ones were staring at me now, their gazes sharp as obsidian blades. The sheer pain I felt at being across the field from them, opposing them, might have sent me to my knees. But it was Zale's face, his dark brows twitching in an *almost* display of pain that burned me to my core.

But then Pia came to stand next to me and Malika on my other side, and I was able to take a shaky breath.

"Say it, Princess. And I will free your uncle."

Hope sprung in me, new as spring, and I swallowed. "Yes. I side against you."

The golden thread screamed and strained, and I buckled, clutching my stomach as our bond wept.

"Tara," Uncle Ansel choked, and before I could have done anything, Atax was behind him, drawing his obsidian hewn sword across my uncle's neck.

The scream that tore from me made my throat bleed, and both Pia and Malika grabbed me from either side. "No!" I sobbed. "No, Atax!"

But Atax was walking away from me, and through my blurred vision, all I could see was his broad back.

"Wipe your tears," Pia's stern voice muttered in my ear. "Wipe your fucking tears, Tara. This is not over. Concentrate."

I obeyed that voice, less like my cousin's and so much like a queen's, and straightened, wiping my eyes roughly with the backs of my hands.

Kai's face was screwed up in a confused expression, and Atax was tense as he watched us, as if he couldn't decide whether to attack us or not.

But Zale and Raen were looking east through the jungle—and frowning deeply. They then looked to the Reaper, having some sort of silent conversation between the three of them. The Reaper went still, looking east as well, but not at the jungle directly to our left, but something further away.

"What is it?" Malika demanded.

Zale's gaze swivelled to mine, his frown more than displeased, his mouth a tight line, shoulders tense. He was more than angry, I knew. He was furious.

But I was angrier as my eyes flicked to my uncle on the ground, the last of my father's family. I had buried my father only weeks ago and Zale knew it. I tried to say as much in my gaze, but he met me evenly, clearly unable to care.

"It's Lobrathia," Raen said, his voice tight with displeasure. "There is lightning in Quartz City."

My anger suddenly froze on the spot.

Pia's hand gripped my wrist, her chest heaving as her emerald eyes met my own.

Lightning in Quartz.

I concentrated then, trying to use my remaining magic to *feel* further away than I could see.

"Saraya," I breathed. My sister must be taking back Quartz, our home city.

The Reaper was staring east, poised still, anger radiating from every inch of his being. My eyes flicked to Zale, standing next to the Reaper and the space that lay between them. At the black bond I could see, glowering with an evil light that had the power to destroy my friends, our home. It was now or never.

I raised my hand and *called*.

Gold flashed into reality, heavy and sure in my hands. The image of the roaring beasts, spurring me on. Kai gasped.

Zale's blue eyes flashed in recognition and I could almost feel every single muscle in his body go impossibly taut. The veins in his neck strained in realisation.

Everyone in the clearing turned to stare. Everyone, that is, except one being.

The Reaper's head was still turned east, as if he were looking and stricken by what he saw. Something in my veins prickled with heat. As if my own bloodline knew enormous power was being drawn from our family's magic. As if the High Priestess of Umali was *raging, storming* with such force that it defied even the Reaper's belief. My heart filled with hope. My sister was taking his forces down.

I had to believe that. I had to believe all was not lost here. That I had one family member left who fought for Lobrathia. Who fought for my dead father. And my dead uncle.

My muscles groaned as I took it in one hand and raised my other.

Thunder boomed ahead as Pia took out an arrow from her cloak and handed it to me.

Only then did the Reaper's head snap towards me. But everything happened in slow motion next—as if we were all under water and this moment had been marked by time as something important.

I drew the Boneweaver Bow with every ounce of my power I had left. My bones screamed in pain, and my flesh seemed to tighten over the skin of my arms. My heart pounded irregularly in my chest as the power of the bow and arrow overtook every-thing I had inside me. Tendons tore in my wrist, and in that tiny moment between my breaths, the Reaper became visible to me in a new light. Every bond that stretched out from his body became clear and open. Images flickered down those bonds, frightening and torturous and laden with evil. Some more than others. One in particular, more than the rest. One that drew me in and showed me more than the Reaper ever intended.

I screamed as I loosed the arrow.

Both the bones in my right forearm snapped. But my eyes were only on the arrow as it flew for the bond of darkness between the Reaper and Zale, the former raising a pale hand as if in an attempt to stop the blow.

But the celestial arrow found its mark.

Light exploded in a dull boom that shook the earth

beneath us. Sparks erupted and there came a roar so loud it felt like the earth itself was about to split open.

We all fell to the ground as it shook beneath us and both Pia and Malika reached for me. The three of us huddled together against the light and dark and tremors that shook the jungle.

"Zale!" I shouted, trying to see where he was, even as my ears exploded from a sound worse than a death knell. The golden thread between us screamed and shook, sending me into a blind panic. What if I had aimed wrong? What if I'd missed, or it had somehow gone awry?

The ground stabilised, and I tried to get up and run to Zale to see if he was alive, to see if there had been any consequences, but my friends held me down between them. Pia was whispering something, but I couldn't hear anything except my own sobbing and the darned ringing in my ears.

The light receded like it was being sucked away, right into the spot Zale and the Reaper had been standing, until all that was left was the darkness and stars in my vision that I tried and failed to blink away.

Across the clearing, Malika was crouched over Atax, her hand gently brushing his arm. But then, she was sprinting back to us as she said, "We need to go."

I frowned at the line of fallen male bodies. "Is he dead?!" I screamed. "Are they dead?"

But I knew the answer already. The body at the end, the heavily cloaked one, stirred.

"No. He's breathing. They're breathing," Pia said tightly. "Did it work, Tara?"

I tentatively sent out my magic as Raen rolled to his feet first, glancing at Atax and Kai before running to Zale. He squatted over his brother, fingers brushing the pulse at his neck.

My magic found Zale across the clearing and went down to his navel.

But there was only one bond that could be seen coming out of Zale. And it was as dark as night.

Raen looked up at us, and when his eyes found mine over the field, they were as cold as a midwinter's night.

"It didn't work," I said loudly. My muscles screamed, and every tendon in my arms roared in agony, those broken bones unable to heal themselves. Unconsciousness threatened to take me away. Pia and Malika hefted my boneless body between them and it ruined my soul completely as they dragged me away from Zale. My Zale—the absence of the golden thread a soul-deep wound I knew I might never recover from. I raised my right hand, only to see Naina had disappeared. "Pia!" I cried, my voice ringing out through the clearing. "It didn't work!"

The Boneweaver Bow could break bonds of the soul. And it had done just that.

"We'll get through this, Tara!" cried Malika as they ran me through the jungle and north. But I knew it was an empty promise. Everything and everyone I loved was now gone.

I let out a loud, very real heartbroken sob, right before my entire world turned dark.

When I stood, I knew that something fundamental had been affected in me. Something primitive and crucial. My skin did not feel like my own, my face did not feel like it belonged to me. My ears rang with the residual roar of the Boneweaver Bow.

The weapon of our ancestors, that my queen, my mate, had used on me.

"Brother. Are you well?" Kai bounded forward, standing on his tiptoes to peer into my eyes, so close that our chests pressed together.

Raen and Atax exchanged a look. "Zale?" Atax asked, frowning.

"There is no light in his eyes," Kai said, cocking his head. "Why do you have a corpse's eyes, brother?"

I stared at him, because what I felt defied logic. Kai was right. I shouldn't be alive. I should be rotting in hell alongside my father, being flogged by immortal demons for the rest of eternity.

Silently, Raen stepped forward to lift my left hand. It was

blank. Only smooth brown skin. My butterfly was gone. I numbly allowed him to raise the hand for everyone to see.

I knew then, with a feral certainty, that without Altara, I would never be whole again.

"My bones feel cold," I said quietly.

Kai came beside me with his torch, as if to warm me with the heat of the flames. He took my hand and tucked something in it. Though I didn't have the heart to look, I knew the sweet floral scent of a frangipani and felt the soft petals under the pads of my fingers.

Kai whined in his throat. "My head hurts."

The Reaper rose to standing with fae grace, barely making a sound in the dark. The bow had sent him crumpling down to the earth, too.

"*The Lobrathian princess was a fool to think she could wield a great weapon like that without training.*" He turned to face me. "*She did your job for you. Now, you are unbound. Now you are truly free, Ashzale.*"

Under the Reaper's dark dome this island had become hell, I realised. This was it. My punishment for every heinous and murderous thing I'd ever done in my wretched life.

"Indeed," I said quietly, looking at my right hand.

The Reaper plucked on the bond between us, solid and black and whole. I turned to my master. "I will bring the forces here to the ships. We will prepare to move in four days hence. As you command." I bowed.

His approval was a balm down the bond just before he vanished. Likely to deal with the threat in Quartz City, where my sister-in-law was causing trouble.

"Let's go, brother," Raen said, eyes glinting with eagerness. "There is much to do."

I glanced at Atax, who was rubbing at his jaw. His eyes

met mine, and he opened his mouth like he wanted to say something, but pressed his lips together as if he thought better of it. He shoved his hands into his pockets and frowned.

Dully, I led the way into the jungle.

It was a mere ten-minute walk to Levu village, five in our beast forms. I tried to focus on the grass beneath my feet, the warm night air brushing past my fur, the smell of the ripe mangoes growing outside the village entrance, but I could not. My mind slipped each time, wanting to think about the person missing from my side. The person whose scent should be in my nose, on my skin, beneath my hands.

My brothers, sensing my discomfort, huddled around me as we padded into Levu. Kai licked the side of my face and I let him, Raen rubbing his panther's side against mine. Atax growled softly, and I knew he was missing someone, too.

Something prickled at the side of my awareness and I changed back into my human form. The village was quiet, the air tangy with the blood and sweat of the people who lived under the demons now.

Two temples flanked the entrance of the village. On the right was the temple of the Mother. On the left, the temple of the Father.

Lisanthi's temple held the record of my birth story. The same temple that a princess with obsidian hair and eyes of emerald green had sought refuge from the battering rain on Ellythia's Night. Where she'd read in Lisanthi's records the origins of her soul.

But it was the thing sitting like a tiny guard at Lisanthi's temple entrance that gave me pause. The creature, barely the length of my palm, with a bulky head made of a conch shell and long, spindly limbs made of fragments of crushed shells.

His body had once been off-white, but was now charred, as if it had survived being burnt.

I shifted into human form. "Wobbles?" For some reason, my voice broke, and I scratched at my throat.

"Wobbles," confirmed the creature, pushing itself up to standing.

Kai let out a laugh and jumped forward with the intention of examining Wobbles, but my hand flung out to stop him short. I stared at my own hand in wonder. I had not meant to stop my brother.

"Confusion," Wobbles said quietly, stepping forward and ambling down the short steps. He stood on the dirt before me and held out his hand, a small flat mother-of-pearl piece—a movement made into a question.

I gave him a stiff nod, and he loped over the earth in that dilapidated, unsteady way of his, before hoisting himself up my leg, inch by inch. I did not help him and it seemed an age before he clambered up to my shoulder, settling himself to sit there as if he'd never left. His weight was familiar and something inside me broke a little more.

Swallowing as Wobbles patted the side of my neck, I turned to look at my brothers. Something in Raen's eyes made me stare at him.

"We gather the demons," he reminded me. "The warships should be done by now."

I nodded, before changing back into my tiger's form, bounding into Levu village, and roaring into the night as Wobbles held on for dear life.

A summoning for the demons.

War was coming for Ellythia, and we were ready.

31

ALTARA

Unconscious, I dreamed of what I'd seen when I'd drawn the Boneweaver Bow.

There were many bonds between the Reaper and the beings in all three realms. Bonds made between him and the demon kings, bonds between him and the fae kings, and a bond, that I guessed had belonged to his mate, a tattered and broken thing, rotten and dead, flying in the wind, the edges frayed as if it had been violently, ruthlessly slashed.

But one bond had caught my attention because it had been mildly familiar, an energy I'd felt before, in the bedroom of my dying grandmother back in the Lotus Palace. A bond between mother and daughter, so it had been then.

And now it was a bond between the Reaper and a human girl.

Compelled by the moth-eaten silk rope, I allowed myself to fall into one of its many holes.

Rahana was young in this memory, her face smooth and unlined, her hair long and silken, perhaps barely any older than the last memory I'd seen her in—the day my mother declared she was abdicating her throne and leaving to marry the Lobrathian king, as advised by the holy Mother Jacaranda tree.

She was weeping out in a back garden, where the sunlight danced in the golden jewels that had been set down her braid, and the roses around her perfumed the air. But Rahana was on her knees, leaning over a stone garden bench and crying into the sleeves of her finery, shaking with the force of her emotion.

A figure approached on gentle feet, dressed in a princely short-sleeved shirt and fine pants, a sword by his side. Pia's father, Uncle Tuskus, was much younger, only in his mid-twenties.

"Raha," he sighed, crouching down next to her. "It's alright. We'll talk to her. Aunt Parsha said—"

"It'll never be alright, you idiot!" Rahana cried. "I've been shamed! In front of my entire court and family, my mother shames me. Nothing will be the same, and it's all Yasani's fault. I'm alone here, can't you see?"

Pia's father reached out a hand to touch Rahana's shoulder, but the moment he did, she hissed like a snake and violently shoved him back.

"Rahana!" he exclaimed. "Control yourself!"

"Why couldn't *she* control herself?" Rahana spat. "Yasani got to do exactly what she wanted. Why can't I?"

"Because she was doing what she thought was right," he sighed. "She was being selfless."

Rahana gaped at her betrothed. "How dare you say that! How is leaving us and stealing the Temari Blade selfless? Mother is in such a *rage* no one can speak with her. She threw me out at first try and declared me worthless."

"She's taking her anger out on you and that's not fair," Tuskus admitted gently. "She doesn't mean what she says."

"She does." Rahana wiped her eyes, smearing kohl. "She's going to reinstate herself as queen and leave me to rot here in shame. She could have at least pretended to make me queen for appearance's sake!"

"You know it doesn't work that way. The Goddesses must ordain—"

"Leave me, you useless man."

"I know you don't mean that," Tuskus said quietly, but I could hear the hurt in his voice. "I know you don't." But he left her there, just as she'd wished.

My heart broke for my Uncle Tuskus, but also for Rahana, because I recognised that fire, that rage at an injustice. At the shame she felt at the betrayal of Yasani's leaving. It might have been a perfectly normal, accepted response had she not done what she did next.

Rahana stayed in the garden well into the twilight, refusing the servants who came to woo her to an evening meal, refusing the advice of the captain of Xalya's guard, who demanded she return, and finally, refusing the gentle word of her father, my grandfather, who bore an obsidian sword at his side and worry for his daughter.

Late into the night, she stewed there, cutting her finger on a thorn once, then twice. At the third time, Xalya's guard, keeping vigil at a respectful distance, did not notice the foul presence that swept around Princess Rahana like the embrace of a stranger at midnight.

But Rahana did. Because a Lota princess could not ritualistically spill her blood at midnight without someone noticing.

And without the Sword of Temari protecting Ellythia, I realised, *anything* could have gotten in. And there had been those who had been waiting for years for Ellythia's defences to open just a slither.

I recognised the voice in the air and the non-corporeal shadow that lurked just before Rahana.

"There is rage here," the Reaper whispered, inhaling as if scenting something delicious. *"And pain."* And then more quietly, *"And despair."*

I'd known it before he said it. Known that look of despair. That hopeless, rageless blank stare. Like a desert that did not end. Like she was drowning in a sea with no surface in sight. Like she stood before an oncoming enemy and lowered her sword.

I'd found Zale in the midst of my despair... or Zale had found me in my dark castle.

But the Reaper had come to save Rahana, and she'd taken his malevolent hand. She'd chosen malice over compassion. Evil over hope.

"Yes," Rahana said, wiping her eyes on her sleeve.

"You wish to be on the throne of Ellythia?" The tone was thoughtful.

Rahana swallowed, her eyes glistening under the gentle yellow quartz-light. I could see the thoughts running through her mind. For her whole life, she'd loved her sister and fully expected Yasani to reign as queen, with her as a supportive sister. But where Yasani's betrayal had soured her heart, her mother's public disapproval had withered it completely. She had never wanted to be queen before, but now...

"Yes." A firm set to her mouth, making her lips thin. "I do."

"I can make you Queen of Ellythia, Rahana Cheshni Lota. But it will be at a time of my choosing. In the manner of my choosing. That is the price."

"Fine. Yes." Rahana nodded. There was no joy in her face. No smile on her mouth. Only grim determination.

A quick movement from the shadows made my eyes go wide.

Rahana's gasp was soft but sharp, and when she pulled down the neckline of her dress, my blood ran cold. Between her breasts now lay a black mark. Three pairs of black dots set beneath each other. The Reaper's symbol.

"You'd better hold up your part of the deal," Rahana said fiercely.

There was only a cold laugh as the Reaper left.

But I understood why she'd done it. I, too, had been in the bottom of that black sea, swimming listlessly.

And my mother had left Ellythia vulnerable. In more ways than one, I also felt responsible for that. But Rahana had given the Reaper direct access to the Lota bloodline. She alone was responsible for the demise of her mother, even though Cheshni fought the Reaper's magic til the bitter end. It was just lucky that Pia had no magic to allow the Reaper's influence on her, otherwise she, too, might have succumbed to it like our grandmother did.

To my surprise, Rahana began crying again. This time, her sobs wracked her lean frame, and she allowed Xalya's guard to rush to her. But this time, she clung onto the commander.

The sound slithered up my spine in the worst way as Rahana's cry made me grit my teeth in anger.

Because, through her own selfishness, she'd betrayed her queendom.

32

ALTARA

When I woke up, the sea gently rocked beneath me, the breeze stirring strands of hair off my face as someone pressed a wet cloth to my forehead.

I sat up so quickly that Pia only dived backwards just in time.

"Oh," I said, rubbing my face. "Sorry, I thought…"

But I'd make a mistake, of course, because the last time Zale had pressed a wet cloth to my forehead, it had been a little rough and awkward, not the gentle touch of my cousin.

My cousin, and one of the last living direct family members I had.

Uncle Ansel was dead, and I hadn't even gotten to say a word to him. Not a hello or goodbye. I wondered if he'd even known about my father's death, if news of it had gotten to him and the other slaves. He had looked so unwell, so gaunt, that I couldn't help but think the life he'd lived immediately before he'd died had been little more than torture.

"Are you alright?" Pia asked in a quiet voice.

Her tone made me look up. There were others on the boat

with us. Xalya's soldiers, five of them, trying not to look at me.

"How—"

"Malika sent out an alert, and they came over to get us." Pia looked over her shoulder. "Commander Charad, please meet the High Priestess of Agnolthi, Queen Altara Voltanius Boneweaver."

My brain reeled under the Reaper's starless sky as a broad senior member of Xalya's army crouched down next to me, the silver markings on his shoulders glinting under the tiny quartz crystals glowing blue on his wrists. He was handsome, despite a broken nose and his high cheekbones gave him a masculine beauty I was sure the ladies ran after.

"Greetings, Your Highness," Charad said quietly, his brown eyes assessing me. I'm sure I looked a right mess. And then I remembered my bow arm had been broken. I looked down, flexing.

"Your magic was depleted using the Bow," Pia murmured. "Luckily, our Commander can heal."

"Thank you," I said, checking my power and finding that the embers were already replenishing into a low flicker. I'd taken a lot of Zale's power when we'd had sex, and then again from the Pentarax demons when I'd taken some of them out, but causing the two explosions and then using the Bow had used up my last reserves.

"They'll be coming for us now, Commander," I said, accepting a canteen from Malika. "When is the half-moon?"

"Four days," Charad said dully, looking up where the moon might have been.

"They'll be at Lota City in four days then."

Charad exchanged a look with the soldiers behind him.

E.P. BALI

"It's good to have you back, High Priestess. We need all the help we can get."

"Are you sure?" I said darkly. "They don't all think I've defected?"

"Some will," he said. "And some might think you were a double agent. I've known a few high priestesses in my time, and they never fail us. Our Goddesses always choose wisely." He gave me a small smile and straightened, giving instructions to prepare to set anchor.

I took the cloth from Pia and wiped my face, grunting at the pain I felt in my muscles and tendons. My left hand was bare except for my obsidian and pearl wedding ring.

The tears came hard and fast then, and I buried my face in my hands, trying to pull myself together and failing abysmally. There was an emptiness inside me. A coldness like a graveyard clutched at my heart, threatening to consume me.

The sobs wracked my shoulders, and I tried to stifle the sounds, but there was nothing for it. I only felt devastation.

"Oh, Tara." Pia's arms came around me and I felt Malika's fiery scent on my other side, her arms coming around the both of us.

"I can't do this," I whispered. "I can't—"

"You did all you could," Pia whispered, holding me to her chest with iron-strong arms. "You did the best you could. It was a good plan. It was just… hard."

I sobbed even harder, because that emptiness in the depths of me only felt worse by the second.

"Shh," Pia said softly. "We'll be okay, Tara. You have us. You have your sister fighting in Lobrathia. Take heart in that. Take heart in… something right now. We need to survive."

Did I even want to survive this?

"Tara," Malika said sternly. "Use those shadows you put

around yourself. Use them to blunt the blow, perhaps? For Zale."

For Zale, she said. I needed to survive to see him again. To say sorry, to tell Raen, Atax and Kai I was sorry.

Descent was my only option. Cold, apathetic descent into my shadows. Into that killing calm. I drew the cloak around me and the shadows were only too happy to obey, to be of use and shield me from myself.

I could do this for Lobrathia and Saraya. For Ellythia and Pia, Malika and Rani. The pain receded and left stasis in its wake.

"I'm okay," I said in that quiet, husky voice the shadows caused. A few of the soldiers stiffened when they heard it and I didn't blame them. "But my power needs to recover. That doesn't happen often to me."

"It's not every day one uses the Boneweaver Bow," Pia said darkly.

"Pia would offer to power share," Malika said with an effortlessly casual voice, "but well, you know, she almost killed someone doing that."

I spluttered on my canteen and Pia just stared at Malika.

"Since she's my cousin and all, *you* could offer to fuck Tara," Pia deadpanned, "but I doubt Zale would approve."

Malika and Pia stared at each other for two breaths before they both burst out laughing.

I gaped at them both, but Pia just shrugged and Malika gave me a lopsided grin. "Sometimes it's best to laugh, otherwise you'd spend all your time crying, Tara."

Rubbing at my tired eyes, I said, "My mother used to call it the healers' black laugh."

Pia gave me a sober look. "Our grandmother used to call it that."

E.P. BALI

Looking down at my hands, the knowledge that both Zale and I had contributed to her death weighed heavily on me. A stone off my chest I might never be able to remove. I said quietly, "I'm sorry I wasn't at the funeral. I'm sorry for everything."

"The way I see it," Pia said, "you saved her. You have nothing to apologise for. Nor does Zale."

My head snapped up to look at her.

"It was too much of a coincidence," she said gently, her eyes glowing. "The timing of her death— a clean cut to the heart, and the Reaper's appearance only moments later? No doubt he'd planned it all along, to use Zale like this."

"And the others." My eyes flicked to Malika.

"Atax will never forgive himself for killing your uncle," Malika said, her eyes following a coil of my shadow.

"I know," I said dully. "I do not blame him. It's the Reapers actions. It always has been."

We sat there for a moment, the three of us catching our breaths in the dark, trying to come to terms with what had happened.

That emptiness in me that would never be filled was a cavern of ugly sorrow. I locked it away, deep, deep down inside of me. Never to be seen again, if I could help it.

"How go the preparations for battle?" I asked.

"Good." Pia shrugged. "We've trained. Collected power. Agnolthi's temple will be happy to see you again. They seemed a little... listless after you left."

I shook my head. "They were doing fine before I came along."

"They need a leader," Pia said gently. "The other high priestesses will need you too." For what, though, her eyes only hinted at.

"And you?" I asked. "Your mother?"

"Has been self-crowned," she said, glancing at Malika. "No Goddesses appeared."

"And I think we all know why," Malika muttered.

Pia hissed a warning at her, emerald eyes darting about the soldiers in the barge.

"No," I said in a low voice. "Malika is right. Listen…" I pulled Pia closer. "I saw something."

Pia nodded at Malika and a bubble of something dark settled around us. A shield, muffling our voices.

"When I held the Boneweaver Bow along with the arrow, I could see all the bonds the Reaper made with other people. The ones between him and Zale and the other Old Ones, but also the demon kings across the realms, even the dark fae kings. But one of them seemed familiar to me because I'd seen a bond similar to that before, when I was with Queen Cheshni in her room before her death. Grandmother had a bond with my mother, but also a bond with Rahana." Pia's spine straightened upon hearing me mention her mother. I took a deep breath, because this very thing had been weighing on my mind for some time now. "I saw a bond between the Reaper and Aunt Rahana." Pia's mouth tightened. "When I looked into it. I saw the deal she and the Reaper made."

Malika swore under her breath. "I asked Keshmi what she thought had happened to Queen Cheshni in the first place. But she had no clue."

Malika was astute. It didn't surprise me that she'd asked the question. So I explained what I'd seen in the bond between the Reaper and Rahana Lota. Pia's court training rendered her face expressionless, but a tiny press at the corner of her mouth told me she was furious at her mother.

It was a betrayal of a new kind.

Perhaps in a way, Rahana felt it was a betrayal she had a right to. What she was owed after my mother left Ellythia to have me and Saraya.

"My mother was wrong to remove the Temari Blade," I murmured to Pia, needing her to understand that I did not take that action lightly.

But Pia shook her head. "She needed to protect you from any astral demons that would have come to take your power. They do that to newborn babies. Steal their magical seed. I'm sure they've been doing it to Lobrathians for a long time. That's why none of the high priestesses were surprised a Lobrathian girl was chosen as Umali's high priestess. I'm sure Umali had her killing the demons in her homeland."

The knowledge struck me in the gut, and if it were not for the shadows keeping me cold and calm, I might have thrown something overboard in anger. So that possibly explained why magic had died in Lobrathia.

"It's alright," Pia said. "Honestly, I'd rather have our two high priestesses than the protection of the sword."

I stared at my cousin, but she just shrugged. "Everything would be different if either of you weren't here. The demons would still have Quartz, and Zale would have started his reign of terror a lot sooner. It'd be more of a mess than it is now."

She was right. And I hoped she was right about Saraya taking back Quartz, too.

WHEN WE ARRIVED AT THE TIGER ISLAND OUTPOST, WE PASSED A herd of zekar grazing through a trough of fruit. Pia had explained to me that the zekar only needed to be asked to serve in Ellythia's military, and they came and went as they pleased as independent agents. Sensing the oncoming invasion, they'd presented themselves at the outpost. Xalya's general herself had spoken to the zekar population on Lota Island and explained to them about the oncoming invasion. Most of them were already under regular employment with the military.

"Can you spare three zekar?" I murmured to Commander Charad. "I need to get back to the temple as soon as possible." I indicated to Pia with my eyes. "With Pia Lota." I bore into his eyes with unspoken meaning. Charad's back straightened and his eyes met mine with understanding. He nodded.

Three days later Pia, Malika, and I arrived at the harbour with three naughty zekar, who'd given us attitude the entire way, but rode so fast we'd had no time to complain.

"Magrin?" I called into the night as we boarded the ship to Lota City.

"Your Majesty, what is wrong? There is a foul scent in the air."

"What do you know of war? Of battle? How can I help Ellythia survive the Reaper?"

"There is much." I could feel her savage grin. *"You know this is our speciality."*

33
RANI

"Go quietly into the night," I muttered. "May you be punished for your crime and have the wisdom to do better in the next life." Tucking the end of the cloth wrap under the body, I finished my binding of the latest corpse. Priest Gunnar, an elderly White Widower with a long silver beard, hoisted the end of the gurney and I grabbed the wooden bars at the top end.

We carried the young Lord Camar Larfaro to his final bed, a wooden pyre by the bank of the river Lisanthi. It was a funeral befitting a dishonoured household, with no one in attendance other than his immediate family and two others.

His parents, the Lord and Lady Larfaro and Camar's young sister, waited before the pyre. All three had eyes as dry as bone and faces hardened into granite. Both lord and lady had declared to fight in the coming battle to earn back the respect of their household. Their daughter would go into hiding in the palace with the other children of the city, and take up her parents' mantle if they died.

But, next to them, stood a barely restrained prince-consort, Tuskus Lota and Prince Paalus, similarly leashing his anger. It was a surprise to see them both here, and yet, not.

It had been Camar's mother who'd executed her son after he confessed, and his father who'd held him down, as was their right, in a ceremony conducted before their entire household at Larfaro estate and a representative Cholnayak priestess who'd publicly condemned him and his crimes. The formal notice had gone out the same day and then they'd brought his body here, to the swamp for cremation.

We set the body on the pyre and stood back to allow the family a moment, but Lord Larfaro merely took the torch from the priest and tossed it on the body.

Ellythian law was fair and just. Those who did wrong were punished. As Camar was. As I would be.

The flames licked high into the afternoon sky and I couldn't help but look at little Lady Larfaro, barely eight, clutching the hilt of the sturdy sword at her belt, her mouth set as if determined not to cry. But despite her efforts, a tear slipped down her tiny, round face and her lower lip wobbled.

She would have made a fine sister-in-law for Pia.

As I watched, Paalus took the young lady's hand in his own and she swallowed and gripped it back tightly.

A shrill cry high above made us all look at the sky. My blood ran cold as I saw the King of the Owls, his golden plumage catching the high sun so much like Zale's eagle form. But the cry was a warning knell that rang out over the city and we all immediately saw why. In the south, a shadow loomed and spread, moving towards us.

Without another word, the Larfaros gave the good priest and I a nod, and immediately left for their battalion in

Agnolthi's sector to receive their instructions. Pia's father and brother climbed into the royal carriage to make back for the palace.

"Go," the Priest Gunnar said. "Watch. Bring back news."

ELLYTHIANS WERE NOT QUIET PEOPLE, BUT EVERY MAN, WOMAN and child held their breath as we collectively stood on ramparts, balconies, street corners, and roofs as we watched the Reaper's black power spreading across the sky. It was like a celestial, evil monster gobbling up the pure, bright blue.

I stood just outside the entrance to the swamp, where I'd been spending every day caring for Ellythia's unwell criminals, along with the senior White Widowers. We were the only ones given leave not to train in the defensive lines, but once the battle began, it would be our job to retrieve and care for any injured brought in. And in a melee situation, that could be anyone from a high priestess and the members of seniority in the nobility down to the youngest acolyte.

But I was the only one of three acolytes who wore the pin of Cholnayak's high priestess. Othar had given me the silver scythe to set on my cowl as a sign that I worked for her directly. It was this pin that granted me access to anywhere a high priestess was granted. That meant I could go *anywhere* I wanted, unasked, unchecked.

It meant a lot that Othar trusted me with this task, because it meant she understood me completely. My need to serve. To win back my honour.

My eyes were drawn to the Lotus Palace, where some nobility were gathered. But Rahana Lota stood on the queen's balcony alone, looking up with dull eyes at the steadying darkness taking over the island she claimed to rule. Any other queen might have stood with her attendants, or her family. Cheshni had never been seen without one of her family members, usually Rahana herself, or with her sister, Parsha Lota.

But Rahana Lota always seemed to be alone these days.

We'd known the darkness was coming as the wing-brothers had heralded its arrival. First, alerting the queen, and then the rest of the city. Calling out in deep booming voices that we should not be alarmed and to stay alert.

Attack would be nigh, but not immediate.

The wing-brothers flew all over the city now, verbalising messages between sectors and the palace. They were reliable and quick and rather friendly, I thought.

It was one of them who'd come to me at sunset last week and told me that Pia and Malika were leaving south.

I wondered if they were okay, if they were watching the darkness spread from Tiger Island. The wing-brother giving me the message had his feathers ruffled a little, and I'd known before he'd even spoken that Malika had commandeered him from some other business with senior staff.

But as day turned into night and that fell shadow gathered over Lota Island, I climbed down from my vantage point and stilled, sensing the air with the thing that lay waiting under my skin.

Some tendril of power had become known to me. The high priestess Othar had taught me to notice such tendrils. To seek them out and follow their path, because the spell we were constructing required us to fill it up with such power. Dark, malicious, sad power.

I took a few steps forward before I felt pulled northward—

to the palace.

The streets were slowly emptying as the patrolling Xalya's soldiers were making sure everyone was heading indoors.

I hopped into an empty, horseless carriage and instructed it to take me to the main entrance. Xalya's soldiers noted me and said nothing as they patrolled the streets, and when I reached the front of the Lotus Palace, I strode up the golden steps with the dark power guiding me.

Inside, I wove through the halls, the various soldiers seeing my face and shiny pin and giving me a nod before allowing me to pass. To my surprise, I rounded a corner into the queen's private suites and found myself in front of four guards standing before a double set of doors.

"Jolly afternoon, lieutenant," I said, forcing a smile. "I am required inside that room."

"This is a Priestess Moot." She frowned, looking me up and down. "What is your business?"

"I am with the honourable Othar Dhumvar," I said solemnly, gesturing to my pin. "She has requested me." A small lie, but it worked more often than not. Whatever I needed was in there, and Othar would know that straight away.

She exchanged a glance with the guard next to her, but stood aside. "Just be quiet or she'll have all our heads."

I didn't bother asking who *she* was. I slipped through the crack they opened for me and padded inside. This room must be the queen's main council chambers and there was a small round table set in the middle.

Except today, it was a war council.

Everyone was clothed in the defensive armour of their order, each high priestess and flanking priestesses armed to the teeth with swords and knives. Two giant owls, including the king, Lightfeather, were perched on the balcony off to the right-hand side, listening intently. The owls themselves both had plate armour on the underside of their wings, and their chests had spelled helmets, shiny with orange quartz for communication.

The senior priests and priestesses from the other orders frowned at me and I felt their disapproving eyes on my back as I silently rounded the table and came to stand behind Othar and the two senior priestesses flanking her.

All three ignored me completely.

I had to fight the strong urge to move to the head of the high table, where the source of the dark tendril was violently pulling my body forward.

Because at the head of the high table sat the queen.

"The Queen Altara Voltanius Boneweaver sails to Lota Island as we speak," reported Lightfeather, his regal voice easily booming around the chamber.

My heart lifted at the thought of seeing Altara again. But the room was silent, and I flicked my eyes towards the senior priestess of Agnolthi, who stood behind the empty chair meant for their leader, my friend. Both their mouths twitched as if they didn't quite know what to say.

"Well," said Queen Rahana sharply, turning to Ellythia's general, who was flanked by one of her male commanders and the previous general, Lady Reeta, in her wheeled chair. "She will not be welcome when she arrives. Arrest her on sight."

I had to suppress a sigh, not understanding how our queen could not read her high priestesses very well. Each one of them bore momentary flickers of annoyance on their faces.

They knew what I did. That Altara, that Agnolthi, repre-sented *both* the light and the dark. That she might be one our most valuable assets in this war. And that she might be the only one who would understand why I was going to do what I needed to. For Ellythia, and for myself.

34
ALTARA

As our ship carefully picked its way into Lota Harbour, I stared at the fleet of quartz-reinforced armoured warships with their catapult towers sitting as waiting monsters in the gloom. All was dark in the harbour, save for tiny quartz lights floating on the water that showed the captain the way to the dock. Under the Reaper's bubble, I realised, we wouldn't even be able to see the enemy coming by ship.

But this is where the battle would be fought. This is where the enemy would try to take Ellythia.

I frowned at the shadows, wondering how Ellythia's general planned to get around that particular problem.

I got my answer immediately

Giant spotlights made with powerful yellow quartz set on huge siege towers beamed light down onto the water. We all groaned and covered our eyes until they adjusted to the harshness.

"What's that?" Malika asked sharply.

"The harbour guard," said the captain, his eyes flicking to me.

Standing at the dock were a line of armed, black-clothed soldiers, but it was not their weapons I was looking at, but the tourmaline shackles their captain held.

Pia was at my side in an instant. "Get below, Tara."

I cocked my head, considering my options. If I could incapacitate them, it might—

"Right now," she growled, so fiercely that I stared at her. "*Please*, cousin."

It was the reminder that we were family that did it. Without another word, I whirled on my heel and headed below deck.

"There's no point," the captain said dryly. "They'll board and get her." I glanced at him sharply and he bowed and hastily said, "Apologies, Your Highness."

"No need. I know how this looks."

The sound of large, flapping wings came to my ear and a gust of wind made me whirl around again.

"Whole-Feather," I said, raising a hand in greeting. "Well met, sir."

The gigantic tawny owl settled on the side of the ship, armour glinting under the quartz. He cocked his head as he peered at me with his huge eyes, no doubt his nocturnal sight giving him a perfect view of me and my shadows.

"Your Majesty." He bowed. The sailors shifted at his use of my queenly honorific. "We are offering counsel and assistance to the Ellythian crown," he said in his deep voice. "As we once did in days of old."

"That is kind of you," I said politely, hoping he wouldn't ask where Zale was. But the owl's eyes flicked down to my naval, then back again, and I think he knew right away something was amiss.

"But we have always been our *own* court," he said slowly. "And we have always been friends with the Boneweaver King." His eyes indicated the harbour. "I would advise Your Majesty to conceal yourself before you go ashore. They plan on arresting you on sight. You will be put in the dungeon."

A slight anger pulsed through my arteries, and Malika said something awful about the queen under her breath.

"My thanks to you, Whole-Feather," I said, inclining my head.

"It is I who owe you my eternal thanks," he said, flexing his wings in indication of the time I'd healed his broken wing. He lowered his voice, and I stepped closer to hear him better. "I will be your servant for the duration of this war. My first message comes from the high priestess of Cholnayak. She will be pleased to see you at her private residences for a secret Priestess Moot."

My heart filled with as much relief as was possible under my shadows. So Othar Dhumvar was on my side. I'd always known she was an astute woman.

"Then I will make my way there," I said to Pia.

"We'll have to report to our barracks commander," she said, gesturing to Malika. Her eyes were assessing on me. "Will you be alright?"

Allowing my power to envelop me so I could take on my surroundings, I said in a voice that sounded hollow even to me, "Always, cousin."

The moment the gangplank went down, Xalya's soldiers stormed the deck, but Whole-Feather murmured to me, and upon his back, we flew right over the harbour and straight to Cholnayak's district to the west of the palace. A bald, lanky figure in all white caught my eye, looking up at us from a tiny courtyard.

"Whole-Feather," I said, leaning down low. "I see a friend."

"Rani Umasri was at the priestess meeting," he said as he wheeled lower and lower, preparing to land. "She is favoured by the high priestess of Cholnayak."

"Favoured?" I repeated faintly as my eyes found Rani's confused brown ones in the gloom. As soon as we got within jumping distance of the ground, I eased back my invisibility.

Rani's face contorted in something akin to pain, and as Whole-Feather landed and I jumped off his back, my friend let out a choked sob.

Then she was running to me, and before I could say anything, Rani was a battering ram, knocking into me and wrapping her arms around my body in a fierce hug that stole the breath from my lungs.

"Oh, Altara!" she breathed. "Dear Goddess, where have you been?"

"Don't even ask," I said dully, amazed she was not afraid of my beshadowed form. "It's been awful, Rani. Truly awful."

She pulled away, her brows creasing as she held me at arm's length to look down my body. "Something isn't right." She picked up my hand and examined the coiling shadows cloaking my skin, not afraid at all. "This is your power, isn't it? Masking you, somehow."

"It protects me from pain," I said in a low voice.

A shiver went through her at the breathy hiss of my voice. "Goddess help us all. But come, Othar Dhumvar is waiting for you."

"It's not a trap, is it?" I waved at Whole-Feather, who bowed and I followed Rani into the quaint three-story building behind the temple proper. It was white and decorated with white ceramic flowers, curling like vines all the way up the facade.

"I don't think so. They appreciate what you did for Queen Cheshni. They...know that dark things are afoot. That darker things are ahead." She glanced at me and there was some meaning in her eyes that I could not decipher. She was trying to tell me something.

A series of winding corridors took us to a drawing room. Rani knocked on the double wooden doors and they opened immediately.

A senior priestess of Cholnayak blanched when she saw me, her eyes flicking up to Agnolthi's mark on my forehead. She bowed low and stood aside before letting me in.

Rani followed me closely as I entered the room. Inside, seated at a round table, were the five other high priestesses, all dressed for war.

Xalya's high priestess, Bhaivari, I remembered, stiffened as I entered, her hand unconsciously going to the axe at her belt.

But it was Lisanthi's high priestess who spoke first. "Dear Goddess," she breathed. "What in the Mother's name happened to you?"

"A nightmare, High Priestess," I replied frankly. "All might be lost for me. But all is not lost for Ellythia."

The room was quiet before she said, "Please, call me Falja. We may as well be on a first name basis if we are to plot and scheme." She cast a dry smile around the room.

Luana's high priestess, dressed in black plate armour lined with pink, and her hair braided to her head in a crown, rushed over to me and kissed me on both cheeks. She smiled briefly, her pretty face strained a little. "You must call me by my first name, too. It is Saarika."

"Tara," I said softly.

Saarika searched my eyes, and found something that made the corners of her mouth turn down. "Oh," she said softly. "Oh dear, indeed." She patted me on the back twice before standing at my side to look at the others.

Cherimani's high priestess ran forward next. A cherub-faced young woman in her early twenties, her hair also tightly braided and in silver chain-mail with multiple daggers along a baldric at her hip.

"My name is Jaya," she said, her eyes glistening as she looked me up and down. "I... I am sorry, Tara."

I stiffly nodded. At the last priestess meeting, they'd told me they were able to see the bond between Zale and I. No doubt they could now see that it was gone. I scratched the place on the back of my right hand where Naina used to sleep.

Cholnayak's high priestess groaned as she took her seat at the table. "Goddess, Tara, I've never seen a person look worse." I looked at her coolly and she shook her head. "As sorry as I am for your loss, I appreciate your"—she waved her hand at my person, indicating my shadows, no doubt—"ability to disassociate. I wondered how you dealt with what happened to you before. It serves you now, at least."

I inclined my head as everyone turned to Bhairavi, her muscular arms tensing as her lips tightened under my gaze. Behind her, sat a middle-aged woman in a wheelchair, scanning me. As I watched, her eyes began to glow with blue swirling light. She had some gift of sight then, and if I wasn't under my cloaking shadows, I would have been offended.

But detached, I understood that she wanted to see what the high priestesses were talking about.

"And you, General?" I asked flatly. "What is your opinion of my supposed defection?"

Bhairavi's dark eyes were cold on me, and her words knife-sharp. "Your husband leads our enemy, High Priestess."

"All that means," I said, absently rubbing my naval, "is that I had direct access to our enemy's plans. I've seen their troops. Their weapons. I have been privy to their strategy. All that is in my head is now available to you."

The group seemed to take a collective breath, and I turned to look at the two purple-robed priestesses of Agnolthi in the corner, who'd been watching the entire exchange with bated breath.

When they sensed my attention, they rushed forward and bowed, taking my hands and kissing them, apparently not concerned about the shadows.

"Esha. Mahi." The first was my priestess of teaching. The latter, my battle mage. Both would be instructing my troops during battle.

"We are only thankful our high priestess has returned," Mahi said, eyes lighting up. "Now we are ready for battle."

"Is..." Esha swallowed. "Is it true about the Bow?"

I nodded once. "Let us sit, and I will tell you what I know."

We sat around the table, our senior priestesses taking up their spots behind us, many of them taking notes on pads of parchment.

"One thing must be clear," Mahi said, to my surprise. The other high priestesses fixed her with surprised looks. "In this room, our high priestess will be Altara. But out there, she is

E.P. BALI

the Queen Boneweaver, and will be addressed as Your Majesty."

A slight kick to the gut was all that I felt as it was said. Not because of her respect for me, but the fact that in my eyes, I did not feel like a queen of anything right now that the tether to the king was broken.

"Of course," huffed Bhairavi. "We know exactly who she is."

"Was there a coronation?" Jaya asked softly, almost sadly.

"Ashzale placed a diadem of his own making upon my head," was all I said. They nodded in acceptance and I stilled for three breaths to prepare myself. "They will come with full force on the half-moon," I said. "They come not to kill, but to capture. This is our only advantage."

The room shifted. "They do not want to kill us?" Jaya said. As she moved, her chain-mail shimmered.

"They want to make slaves," I said bluntly. "They want to collect a force with which to take over the Continent. With Ellythian mages, *he* will have the best chance. But know that the demons enjoy killing, and will likely do so if it's easier for them. They will get excited in the melee."

But this did not surprise the older high priestesses.

Bhairavi jerked her chin at me. "What else?"

So I told them about what I'd seen and about everything Zale and Raen had spoken about while I was in their company. There were warships off the coast of Boneweaver Island, massive vessels that would carry hundreds of infantrymen with quartz-enforced weapons. They had beasts as well as Pentarax demons, or what was left of them after their tower's destruction.

And then I told them of the Boneweaver Bow, how I'd taken it, how Pia had been summoned by Agnolthi to help me, and what I most of all needed them to know—that Pia had been seeing all the Goddesses.

Othar barked a dark laugh and exchanged a look with Falja, who shrugged her red shoulders as if to say 'I told you'.

Bhairavi nodded. "We have been making the appropriate preparations for Pia. When the time is right, we will show our hand."

"There is one problem that I think we already knew," I said, and then told them of the memory I'd seen in the Reaper's bond with Rahana.

"Your presence here must be kept a secret," Othar said. "Rahana might be Priestess Prime right now, but we have been making our own preparations in light of what happened with Cheshni. May she rest in peace."

"We know it was the King Boneweaver who did it," Bhairavi said softly. "It was an obsidian blade that went clean through. Swift, but a murder none the less."

"He apologised to me as best he could," I said. "But I told him that this is war and more will die before the end."

"It was a mercy killing," Othar spat. "Nothing less. I do not care for the Reaper's views. We are prepared. We have what we need."

I wondered if that was true. Even after they told me of their plans.

At the end of the meeting, my magic sparked to life by the swirling blue in the eyes of the woman Bhairavi called Reeta. She had been Xalya's general before an incident maimed her. My magic had time to heal on the trip here, but I could have used a pick-me-up.

"Lady Reeta," I said, my voice piercing through the murmuring. "May I have your permission to heal your injury?"

Every eye in the room turned to me, and Bhairavi raised her brows.

"No healer has been able to fix my injury. Not even Lady Falja," Reeta said with a small line between her brows. She wasn't quite sure of what I was trying to do.

I glanced at Falja, who gave me a forlorn sort of nod. I shrugged. "My power is telling me otherwise."

Reeta stared at me, and after a breath, nodded. "Can't hurt to try."

Well, it *would* hurt me. But I'd faced worse and more.

She'd started to wheel towards me when my magic eagerly whipped out, fast as an arrow. Lady Reeta hunched forward with an *oof* as my power surged through her body, reaching for her spine and spinal cord. It tunnelled down the soft nerve structure, right to the end of her tailbone. The injury had been relatively low, and my power merged the damaged pieces of the nerves together. Tiny lightning sparked from my fingertips as electricity began to shoot through the healed portions of her spinal cord, the bone around them rearranging a fraction where it had originally been crushed.

My power then funnelled the injury back to me.

I gasped, folding in upon myself as a portion of my spinal bones crushed, a small shard piercing the spinal cord. Holding the table in front of me, lightning shot through my body, and I was vaguely aware of the priestesses behind me jerking backwards. My power surged excitedly, not having dealt with nerve issues in a long time, and electricity shot through me once again, healing my spine and righting itself.

On the other side of the room, Reeta was spasming, her legs bucking as my power continued to shoot down through her legs, restoring the degenerated muscle and bone.

I let out a tiny cry as my own bones took on the tissue, then healed itself with sharp, stabbing pains. Sweating, but happy with the golden power pulsing within me, I sat back up in my chair.

Opening my eyes, I found Reeta on the floor, flushed and looking up at me as she bent her right knee.

"Well," said Bhairavi, barking a laugh from the floor where she was crouched over Reeta. "Looks like your Volta-nius blood came in use after all."

35

MALIKA

Xalya's officers stormed our ship with their faces drawn and their swords out. I scoffed when their captain stomped towards me and Pia, leaning against the railing. "She's not here," I said to the wiry older man. "And we haven't done anything except escape the Goddess-damned Reaper with our lives."

I was pissed off on a number of counts. Travelling that fast across Tiger Island on the back of a fiery zekar had me sore all over. On top of that, I'd gotten *so* close to my home village, but hadn't been able to actually find my parents to see if they were okay.

Fucking bug-eyed Reaper.

If he hadn't been right there, I would have insisted we check it out before we left. But after I heard Altara snap her arm using the Boneweaver Bow, all bets were off, and I knew we just had to get the fuck out of there.

So I'd perhaps used a bad tone as I mouthed off at the captain because he looked down his nose at me.

"That's right," I said, giving him a salute. "The Reaper almost got us. Ugly six-eyed bastard."

"We know the Boneweaver Queen is on this ship," he snapped, though I noticed he paled a little. "Where is she?"

His soldiers were jumping around below deck, turning everything asunder, no doubt, as the captain cringed on the port side.

"*Her Majesty* jumped overboard a while back," I said quickly. I didn't want Pia lying to anyone if she didn't have to. She was still my queen as far as I was concerned, and I would do all the lying and heinous shit for her. "No idea where she swam off to." I cast my eye about the water dramatically, as if I was expecting her to pop out at any moment.

He looked at Pia, who nodded and shrugged as if it weren't a big deal and we couldn't do anything about it.

"Back to your battalion," he snapped, "the both of you. We prepare for attack at any moment."

"Yes, captain."

We both saluted and left him to check the rest of the ship. The owl had left towards Cholnayak's district, and I didn't envy whatever the other high priestesses had planned for Altara. Everyone would have a dangerous task ahead of them now, and we'd all be kidding ourselves if we thought there wouldn't be heavy losses.

This weighed on my mind as I strode down the gangplank after Pia. As a part of the infantry, she'd ordinarily be put right in the middle of the melee, but I just knew Ellythia's general wouldn't do that. The high priestesses still loved her, even if they had stripped her of everything. While I didn't understand their reasoning, I was almost happy she was away from her rubbish mother. I'd also seen the way our general watched Pia with owl-like eyes. Like they expected her to explode in a shower of magic at any minute or something. I'd detected no trace of power from her, *ever*, and my queen had remained tight-lipped about the appearance of any power.

When we arrived at Xalya's sector, it was something I could only describe as orderly chaos. Everyone was awake and armed, though it was surely the middle of the day and they were all lining up at the meeting hall, our biggest space for group announcements.

"What's going on?" Pia asked a passing lieutenant as we joined the lines.

His eyes widened when he saw it was her. "Uh. The— Your mother is here to bless the soldiers."

"The queen's blessing," Pia muttered. "Right."

I looked at her in question as we joined the three lines of murmuring soldiers. The queue was a mile long, but fast-moving, and every order was in attendance; fighting clothes of black, white, purple, red, pink, orange. Pia noticeably swallowed. "The queen's blessing is given to every single soldier before a big battle," she murmured. "It unites us psychically, as a force. For the mages, it works like connective tissue. United, we're stronger."

Goosebumps erupted all over me and I shivered, seeing that Pia's skin was puckered too. This would be the first time she'd be face to face with her mother since her getting kicked out of the family.

We got a few dirty looks cast our way as the line slowly moved forward. Word must have spread about our coming back with the 'disgraced' high priestess of Agnolthi. I met those looks with my own challenging one, daring them to say something to me or Pia.

But they were smart, because they didn't.

Half an hour later, we got into the audience hall, weary and hungry because all we'd had to eat was salted meat on that blasted ship. My mood soured further when I saw the queen, dressed in gold plate armour decorated with lotuses, the queen's sword at her side as she marked each soldier's forehead with her thumb.

It was a red substance pooling in a deep bowl held by our general that she dipped her thumb into each time. *Blood*, I thought. It was her blood mixed with some other substance, likely vermillion, that made a large quantity of deep crimson liquid. My skin crawled at the thought of *her* blood on my skin.

I couldn't forget what Altara had told us about how Rahana had made a blood pact with the Reaper. I didn't realise that my fist had tightened around the hilt of Atax's blade at my hip until my knuckles cracked. Glancing over at Pia, beads of sweat dappled her forehead.

Goddess, I could kill her mother for her. Perhaps a little slip on the battlefield? An accidental tumble down her palace balcony? But no, it would take a lot more to kill a queen of Ellythia. They were the most powerful being in the queendom. And with the Reaper's magic urging her on? I shuddered to think of the kind of force she could wield.

"Steady," I murmured to *my* queen. "All will be well."

She gave me a stiff nod, her emerald eyes seeming to pale under the bright quartz light of the hall.

We were three soldiers away from the Reaper's bitch when I stepped protectively in front of Pia. Ellythia's general noticed immediately and her eyes flicked to the queen, pursing her lips ever so slightly.

283

Was that disdain for the queen my eyes saw? It lifted my heart greatly, if that's what it was.

Rahana, for her part, was cold as dead quartz as she pressed her finger to the forehead of the soldier ahead of me and murmured the ritual words.

I could barely hide my anger and determinedly gripped my sword hilt, imagining it was her throat. The major-general and commanders standing beside Ellythia's general looked me up and down as I stepped forward, their eyes stopping momentarily on Atax's obsidian blade at my hip. It had finally elongated from earring to real blade for me when we got to the Pentarax Guild and I wasn't about to let it go now.

Let them look, I thought. *Bloody let them.*

Stepping before the queen, I bowed, swallowing down bile and barely restrained my cringe when she pressed her red-dipped thumb to my forehead. She smelled like flowers with metal and the coppery scent of blood. I almost gagged and stepped away as fast as I could.

Instead of stepping off the stage and leaving as I was supposed to, I stopped before the commanders and turned to guard Pia. I wasn't going to leave her alone. Not with the Reaper's bitch standing there *touching* her with those tainted hands. The senior members of Xalya's order turned to stare at Pia as well and said nothing to me, though I'd expected some snide remark.

Together, we watched Rahana purse her cold lips, dip her thumb into the ritual bowl, and press her thumb to Pia's forehead. Pia's eyes were closed, accepting the thing for what it was. A lie. A pure, fucking lie.

She bowed professionally, her face courtier smooth, and stepped away. I let her pass ahead of me, staring down the crowd of soldiers in the queue defiantly, before I followed her.

Outside, I immediately wiped my forehead with my sleeve, grabbed Pia by the arm, and dragged her into the shadows of the building, far from anyone's earshot.

At the entrance to the building, a familiar bald head turned to look our way, and I jerked my chin at Rani.

Without a backward glance at the other White Widows, she sprinted towards us, her eyes wide.

"Come, Rani," I said when she reached us. "We want your blood, Pia."

"What?" Pia asked faintly.

"Cut your thumb and mark me. I demand it."

"No!" She looked frantically between the two of us.

"Do it, and you know why."

She stared at me, her shoulders moving with a deep breath. Then she looked at Rani, searching her eyes,

Rani breathed. "Do it, Pia. Do it because it's the right thing to do."

Without another word, Pia brought out her pocket dagger and scored her thumb, staring at it as if she'd never seen blood before.

I shook her by the arms, "Say the words. I want to hear them before I die for my queendom."

A sharp intake of breath as Pia glared at me. "You're not dying." Her voice was determined, but it shook just slightly at the end.

"*Do it*," I demanded. "You know what you mean to me. To all of us. To Altara, to Rani." I swallowed. "To Kai and Atax, too. And Geravie and Keshmi and Reshmi. To all the girls at the school. Fucking do it."

Her thumb hung mid-air. A crimson drop fell to the gravel. "It would be treason, I—"

I grabbed her thumb and pressed it to my forehand.

"Say it."

"I bless thee," she whispered, blinking rapidly as if to stay her tears. "Under my blood, be fierce. Under my blood be true. Under my blood, be joined to your brothers and sisters."

"United, we are strong," I murmured, letting go of her hand.

She stared between the two of us, those emeralds shining, and just for a moment, I thought I saw a deep flicker of something more. But in an instant, it was gone. She repeated the gesture to a quivering Rani.

"Whatever happens tomorrow," Pia said, gripping both of us by our forearms, "I'm glad to have had you as my friends. I'm glad to have known you, and to have fought alongside you."

Rani sniffed and nodded. "I love you guys."

"Where is your sword?" Pia asked her sharply.

"Uh, I left it in my room."

"We're not to be without weapons anymore, Rani." I said sternly.

"I can make my own weapons," she replied calmly. "You know that."

Yes, I supposed I did.

It was then that a deep cry sounded high above us. We all jerked violently and stared up at the Reaper's sky and saw the golden glint of the King of the Owls, wheeling powerfully above us, his dark armour almost obscuring him from all vision.

The orange quartz on his helmet cast a beam that projected his deep baritone over the city.

"Demon warships surging to Lota City. They will arrive in one turn of the earth. They are coming."

Pia, Rani and I exchanged a look.

"Let's do this," I said.

WE RETURNED TO OUR BATTALIONS TO RECEIVE OUR FINAL ORDERS and formations.

Commander Varda had decided that since I was so supremely powerful, I was going to be the sole fire mage of a siege tower on one of our warships. I told him I was pissed off and ready to explode, and he only grinned at me. My squadron, along with one other, would have the sole job of protecting me, the tower, *and* Pia—or so I'd told everyone on the squad.

The siege towers had catapults at the top, and we were to load them with naptha, a highly flammable substance mined in the deserts of Kusha Kingdom, the northernmost region of the Continent. I would light them up and my catapult partners, four sturdy men, would fire the thing. After the naptha was finished, I'd set plain boulders alight, and we'd send them careening into the enemy ships. They had a long range of almost a hundred paces.

Along with the other siege towers, it would be my job to take out enemy ships. Capsize them by burning them down and trying not to get attacked in the process. Due to the Reaper's dark cloud around the island, we would be sailing out of the harbour so we could see our mark.

We had a few mages gifted with enhanced sight, who were able to see out of the shield, as well as soldiers stationed on the tiny outer islands outside the shields. They would communicate to the field commanders, and we'd be told how to manoeuvre the catapults for best effect.

Our wind mage, a reed-thin young woman called Klotha, pushed the catapults into place onto our designated ship, *The Lady Savage*, and we practised our formation one last time.

The ships creaked under the strain of Ellythia's soldiers doing their final checks and loading up their blasting weapons with charged quartz.

It was lucky we'd been keeping a stock of charged quartz over the past few weeks, because now, without the sun, we had to use the city's magic supply to load them up. But there was enough of it to light up the night, shining in multicolours.

I'd never seen so much charged quartz in use. It almost made it feel like a party as I watched the men fire the empty catapult one last time.

"Fire!" Gallu, our squadron leader, called.

With a magnificent twang, the thing shot through the air and stopped short on its rig, sending wisps of my hair blowing. I swore under my breath as we all nodded at each other.

We had this.

Below our tower was the wind mage, the shield mage, Safra, and three foot soldiers with small magic alongside Pia. All six were armed with round magic shields, dotted with blue quartz, that would deflect small attacks if the demons managed to get ashore.

There were two catapult squadrons on ships ahead of us, and I was a bit concerned that Pia was stationed on the front lines. Our general and queen seemed to think most of this battle would be fought on open water, between the ships. So in reality, our navy was our front line.

As I climbed down the ladder of the siege tower, Gallu jerked his chin at the Reaper's shadow around the harbour.

"I don't like that. Harbour soldiers won't be able to see

anything until it comes hurtling at them. We really need that shield around the island." He looked towards the palace where the queen, no doubt, was getting a hopefully restless night's sleep. On the northern side of the harbour stood a wooden platform where tomorrow, the queen would stand and direct our wider battle movements.

Gallu wouldn't say what we were all thinking. Without the Blade of Temari, the Priestess Prime needed to summon a response to the Reaper's shield—a shield of our own to hold the enemy out.

Tomorrow, we would be relying upon her. And from the looks of the soldiers in the hall at the queen's blessing, not many of us had all that much faith that she could save us.

Was it bad that I wished the old grumpy Queen Cheshni was still here?

I t was a war chant that had not been heard in Ellythia for twenty years. And not sung by the entire Ellythian army for a hundred or more years.

From somewhere in the east, a soft treble came from Luana's flute, wielded by Saarika in her high priestess warrior's armour of deep maroon. She balanced perfectly still on the rig of the catapult on the frontmost siege tower, before the boats. Her long obsidian hair whipping in the wind of her own magic, a sword and a long whip coiled at her hip.

The singing began in the northern warships, soft in cadence, but hard in meaning. Xalya's infantry began stomping their feet along the deck. Agnolthi's infantry at the harbour added their purple-booted feet, closely followed by the White Widows in the centre, banging their spears and quartz-tipped staves, adding a booming baritone.

Lisanthi's red-swathed soldiers added a stunning soprano and a clap of their hands with each stomp.

As the high priestesses assumed their positions around the harbour, I nodded to Whole-Feather, waiting for me next to Esha and Joshi, my senior priestesses. I strode forward, my shadows dense around the armour Falja had given me. Lisanthi's sector had been responsible for armour and clothing, and this morning, she'd outfitted me in thin plate armour of such deep purple it was virtually black. It covered the important areas, namely my chest and shoulders, with matching vambraces for my wrists. I had on my witch's boots because, as we'd decided, the high priestesses would mostly take to the air.

Priestess Esha tugged on the straps of my armour to make sure it was secure before I mounted Whole-Feather's back. My faithful owl was magnificent in a black armour that covered his belly and underwings, and a helmet to protect his head.

Jaya, Cherimani's priestess, flew on a flying vehicle of her own make, a chariot shaped into a dragon like in the days of old, its glittering silver facade a match to her chain-mail, her blushing pink magic like a platform underneath the flat metal bottom. Her senior priestesses flew more dragon vehicles, just above their division on the northern bank.

As Whole-Feather took to the air, Luana's flute rang out through the dark and filled the air with resonant, latent power that skittered along my skin.

"We have but one task, Whole-Feather," I said.

"Yes, Your Majesty," he replied. "And let us do it well."

My witch's boots were secure around him as we ascended into the air, above the waiting infantry and zekar calvary.

I wore a flat piece of quartz melded to metal in my right ear. Through it, the five high priestesses could speak to one other. We would co-ordinate our forces and the weapons of the Goddesses.

Othar had something up her sleeve she kept hinting

about, but she refused to speak on it, and Bhairavi begrudgingly let it go after an hour of argument.

In my left ear, I wore a purple quartz earring, through which I would speak to my three senior priestesses. Joshi, my healing witch, I'd stationed on Pia & Malika's ship so I'd have eyes on them at all times, Esha would be at the harbour, and Mahi, my battle witch, was protected on a turtle ship, manning our magical torpedoes. We had twenty turtle ships we would sail straight into enemy lines, their hardened hulls virtually indestructible, enabling the mages inside to launch close-range attacks onto enemy vessels.

My eyes found Malika in the second line of warships, ready on her tower with four men next to a loaded catapult. She raised a hand as I passed overhead, then pointed at the base of her tower. Pia stood there, armed with two swords, her face set, her mouth a hard line. I wondered where Rani was, but I'd never asked her where she'd be stationed. No doubt Othar had her somewhere important.

Othar, for her part, sat atop an armoured owl, a staff of black and silver in her right hand, the huge white jewel in its clawed top glinting in the dark.

"Let's sail, Queen Boneweaver." Bhairavi, on the back of the King of Owls, swept past me, glowing axe in hand, double swords strapped to her back, in full black plate armour she seemed to have no trouble moving in. She and the owl king sailed right through the Reaper's black shield without so much as twitching, her axe held high in the air as she instructed the first ships to leave.

"Let's see what our enemy has for us, shall we?" I murmured to Whole-Feather.

The owl gave a sharp cry as we flew over the ships dotted with black and purple armour. Mahi raised her sword, and we sailed through the Reaper's shadows together. We were in the sour, pitch-black smoke only for a breath before we came out of it, Whole-Feather shaking the dark magic off.

When we emerged, it was as if we'd burst into the air after a long time underwater. The starry night sky was a sudden and welcome reprieve from the heavy darkness of the island, and I felt like I'd taken my first breath of fresh, cool air in days.

I cast my power out, searching the dark ocean for a sign of our enemy.

"Ahead, Your Majesty," Whole-Feather said in a voice that made me snap to attention.

I had to squint at the horizon, but when I saw it, my blood ran cold for more reasons than one. Stretching out as far as the eye could see, the horizon was lined with an obsidian band, darker than the night.

Demon ships.

Bhairavi noticed it seconds before me. "Their numbers…" her voice said in my ear. "There must be a hundred warships out there."

Even under my shadows, my stomach tightened.

It was more than I'd anticipated.

Jaya's sweet voice swore in my ear and I felt her behind me on her dragon vehicle. She nodded as she passed me and swore again when she saw our enemy on the horizon.

Somewhere on one of those ships stood Zale and my three brothers—the Reaper's generals of war. From my astral repository, I summoned a longbow. Lightning zipped past my fingers and I shivered at the need to use my power for bloodshed.

"Well," Bhairavi said, "their numbers are far greater than ours."

"By how much?" Falja asked quickly. Lisanthi's high priestess was somewhere in the middle of the infantry, waiting on a rare winged zekar mare.

"Triple. Quadruple maybe," Bhairavi said.

My earpiece was quiet as we absorbed this.

"We knew they'd come with numbers," Othar said evenly. "We prepared for this."

Not for four times as many, I thought dully. *Not for a hundred warships.* They must have been building them the entire time, I realised. But the Reaper had never instructed us to go near the ocean side of the demon kingdoms. It was clear now why. Plenty of them would be half empty cargo ships to take Ellythians back to the demon realm. But even if some of them were empty...

We'd need everything we had to fight this. Everything.

The Owl King gave a sharp cry of warning.

"There is something in the water," Whole-Feather said.

I squinted down at the same time Bhairavi and Jaya dipped to see what it was. A tiny square raft was floating on the waves just below us, half submerged.

Two bodies lay atop it.

"Down," I commanded Whole-Feather sharply. He dived.

"It could be a trap!" Bhairavi warned, following us.

Whole-Feather cautiously approached the raft and I could see the remains of dead-quartz which might have spurred on its sailing.

"Not human," Bhairavi said in surprise as Lightfeather hovered next to us.

"Daanav," I muttered.

"What does the note say?"

The two blue demons were bare from the waist up, so we

could see that carved into their skin were names. One bore "Vari" the other, "Lady Trisane."

My heart threatened to stop in my chest.

"Vari is the Armsmistress from the exile school!" Bhairavi exclaimed. "What does this mean?"

"It is a warning," I said darkly, staring at Ellythia's general and knowing everyone could hear what I said. "A threat."

She clenched her jaw and nodded once. We left the demons there.

"Your Majesty, let us begin the spell," Othar said evenly into my ear.

It was Rahana's dulcet voice in my ear next. "High Priestesses, return to me."

I nudged Whole-Feather, and we soared back over the sea and through the Reaper's smoky bubble. Bhairavi and Jaya followed on their respective mounts.

Rahana stood on the queen's platform, a ten-by-ten-foot wooden structure that overlooked the harbour from behind the siege towers. She was surrounded by the Queen's Guard, the best of Xalya's and Agnolthi's priestesses, who would ensure she was safe from attack tonight.

Othar, Falja and Saarika were already on the platform in position, ready for the unbridled magic we were about to wield.

Whole-Feather hovered above the platform as there was no space for him to land. So I hopped off with thanks and landed lightly on the wood in a crouch while he flew off to wait with the other owls. Bhairavi landed a moment later, followed by Jaya, who easily stepped from her levitating dragon.

It was then, to my surprise, that I saw Paalus Lota, standing beside the captain of the Queen's Guard. I frowned at the sight because although he was dressed in thin Ellythian plate armour like a full-grown man, he was barely twelve.

"Why is he not with the other children?" I asked sharply.

The captain's eyes flicked to Rahana, who was having a word with Othar.

"The queen commanded the prince see real war," Bhairavi said tightly, sliding past me. "And that was that."

"But not the prince-consort?" I replied.

"He guards the children," Bhairavi said quietly.

An insult to her own husband. I shouldn't have been surprised.

But surrounded by the queen's personal guard, I could barely do anything.

"Gather around," Rahana commanded, determinedly ignoring me. I wondered if she was angry at her soldiers for not successfully arresting me. Every one of her guards had turned a blind eye as we made our way onto the field this evening. Rahana's face was strained, her mouth tight, features drawn. But her shoulders were square and her gait sure as she gestured to the space around her.

We assumed our agreed formation—hand in hand, with our queen in the middle. I was at the southern end, holding Bhairavi's large, calloused hand in my own.

"Let us begin," Rahana said.

We all looked out upon the harbour where our troops were silently waiting. The air was surprisingly cool for Ellythia, thanks to the sun being blocked out.

I'd never seen Rahana do magic—except for the time we'd first met when she'd tried to, rudely, enter my mental defences. The railing of the platform was lined in quartz of all colours, but we would not need to draw on them for this spell.

The shield of the Priestess Prime had historically only been used in dire circumstances in times of war. By drawing on the power of the fighting citizens of the city, it took all the high priestesses and Queen of Ellythia—the Priestess Prime— to construct it. It was why the queen's blessing last night, to connect the soldiers, had been so crucial.

That much power was colossal.

It was an old spell, the ancient words of which I'd had to learn all of last night under Falja's and then Othar's instruction, from a crumbling, yellowed tome brought up from Chol-nayak Temple's catacombs. It had taken me all night to get the enunciation right, because any single mispronunciation could lead to disaster. As it was, I'd had to practise it in parts to avoid an accident.

Immediately, a tingle began in my fingers, where I was joined with Bhairavi. My power responded, eagerly jerking towards Ellythia's general, who shifted just a little as she felt my magic tunnelling through her.

The air around us fizzled and crackled as we chanted, our combined voices ringing out across the harbour.

Magic gathered around the island, and just in the same way that I'd had an awareness of Boneweaver Island in my own body, I now felt the entirety of Lotus Island. Each rock and tree, each animal and river, even the Lotus Palace standing proudly behind us. But it was to the edges of the island that I was drawn. To the beaches and rocky shores and, of course, the harbour we stood before. Our combined magic gathered there, piece by piece, building like a physical construction. Stone by stone, we built the wall, and it shone like a shimmering blanket in front of the Reaper's shadow. The soldiers below grinned and pointed at the beauty of it. At the strength we called, the power of the Goddesses we represented.

My body thrummed, my heart pounded, my blood sang.

But only halfway up the Reaper's shield, it all went wrong.

The glittering shield distinctly fell apart, like glass shattering in a window pane, only on a much wider scale.

We chanted louder, Bhairavi clenching my hand in a crushing grip, all of us shouting into the air. But it only made my head pound for the way it did nothing.

Bhairavi let out a slow, slow breath through her nose and abruptly dropped my hand as if disgusted by the entire process. The high priestess broke the chain to the queen, stepping away from her, almost unconsciously, as if she bore some virus we might catch. Rahana stood alone, her face red, her lotus-engraved armour glinting by the quartz light as her shoulders heaved under the strain of channelling so much magic.

The only thing that permeated the Ellythian air now was silence. Heavy and telling. An awful, awful truth.

It hadn't worked.

And the only reason why was because Rahana wasn't the true Queen of Ellythia. And this proved it. Not only to us, but to every member of our armed and magical forces, watching on with disappointment.

ZALE

O n the Lotus Sea, barely fifteen minutes from the Ellythian shores, I stood on the prow of the biggest demon warship in our fleet, filled with three hundred strong, vicious, bloodthirsty demons. The black sails caught the wind, but it was the massive clusters of Lobrathian quartz that spurred us on with rapid speed.

My three brothers stood behind me, armed and ready to kill, their bodies as tense as mine.

Raen snorted. "Their shield failed. We'll be able to sail right in."

On my shoulder, Wobbles muttered into my ear, "Excitement. Anger."

"Wait for my signal," I said coolly. "And then we destroy them all."

"Yes, brother," Raen said quietly.

Atax merely grunted, his eyes searching the ships as if he'd see someone waiting for him.

"Dead," Kai sang softly under his breath. "Dead. Dead. Dead."

Behind us, the demon warriors shifted eagerly.

"General?" said Rahana tightly.

"Your Majesty," Bhairavi said stiffly. She could barely hide her disdain.

"Set sail. Let us meet our enemy on the sea."

Bhairavi bowed and signalled to the Lightfeather wheeling above us.

Rahana finally turned to look at me. I said flatly, "May the Goddesses be with us."

She raked her eyes down my shadows, her upper lip curling. Without another word, I turned my back to her. Her guards bristled at my lack of etiquette, but in my mind, she was no longer the Ellythian queen. Whole-Feather wheeled down at the same time the King Owl did, and with a shot of lightning at my witch's boot, I exploded up into the sky. Whole-Feather hastily dipped and angled himself beneath me in accordance to my trajectory and I landed on top of him. We flew off into the sky to await Bhairavi, who'd given a surprised laugh.

"Nice trick, Boneweaver Queen," she said as she passed

us, heading for the shadow shield. "Give us more of that on the field."

Every time they called me by that title, it struck me in the chest like one of my own lightning bolts. But my smile was cold as I passed through the shadows in her wake.

"Fleet Admiral!" Bhairavi called out to the ships below, her voice amplified by orange quartz.

Below, the soldiers and sailors on the ships let out a cry. At their helm, in the first ship, was Lady Reeta, appointed a new role. She waved her sword in the air, flashing her teeth at us, swirling blue eyes bright. I grinned back. Her legs looked strong, and after a night of drills, I'd had Magrin instruct me on how to make witch's boots for her. They made her steady and a force to be reckoned with.

Her seniority got her a voice in our ear with the high priestesses. "What do you see, Admiral?" I asked into our earpiece.

"The Boneweaver King stands at the helm of a central ship. At the front are huge warships, a hundred feet long or more, four stories tall. Easily holding two to three hundred soldiers each. They're coming in hard. They'll be ready to storm us with brute force."

"Let them try," I said, summoning my sturdy bow of gold and black. Behind me, Jaya and Bhairavi summoned bows as well.

Malika and the rest of the fire mages got ready as their catapult masters loaded their equipment. We'd need to act swiftly.

"Where is the Reaper?" came Othar's voice.

"Nowhere in sight right now," Reeta replied.

"His Majesty can't see him either," Bhairavi said. If the owls couldn't see the Reaper, then where was he?

Off the back of the quartz-fuel, the enemy fleet moved swiftly, and within ten minutes, I could make out the demons standing on the decks, weapons ready, faces leering. In that moment, I was more thankful for my cold-wraith state than ever. There were too many of them to count and they were here to enslave us all.

"Shields ready!" I called to Mahi, my battle mage.

"Steady!" Bhairavi called to her senior staff. "On my mark!"

Powered shields went up around each of our advancing ships, as Agnolthi's battle mages, powered with small cauldrons of communal power at their feet, stood steady.

I knocked an arrow and filled it with lightning. Demons of all kinds stood on these ships, quartz glinting on the hulls and off their weapons.

Our enemy also had catapults.

Just as we began to see the faces on the ships—

"Fire!" Bhairavi shouted.

Malika struck her catapult with fire, and it burst into flames. The catapult masters fired at the same time the enemy did.

Both attacks glanced off their respective shields.

"Fire!" the command went up again.

Catapults rained from either side as our ships met in the ocean.

"This will be a battle of power," I muttered to Whole-Feather. "Whose shields will run out first?"

But Magrin and I had worked through ideas of how to help and I was more than ready. Bhairavi, Jaya and I fired powered arrows from our mounts, aiming at shields with the intent to rip them apart. This was my speciality.

I shot my first arrow into the frontmost warship. It struck

a bright blue shield and I *pulled*. Power filled me and my magic gobbled it up greedily. Any traces of depletion from the last few days would be gone soon enough.

Within seconds, their shield went out.

"How are they powering the shields?" Jaya asked, shooting white arrows from a pink crossbow into the starboard side of that ship. The turtle boats moved forward, ready to destroy hulls.

"Demon mages using the quartz at the back of the ships!" I called back, taking the first one out with an arrow to the temple. Jaya's archers, on their dragon vehicles, crossed the Reaper's shadow and descended upon the enemy, shooting at the soldiers after I'd destroyed their shields and their mages.

It was only a matter of time before I spotted one of my own.

Kai was visible first. With his moon-white hair like a beacon in the night, he was the easiest to see. He looked up at me with a lopsided grin, as if this war was just his entertainment, and we were performers flying for his pleasure. He clapped and waved at me. I knew the other Old Ones would be there with him, but I flew off before my eyes could move around.

A twang of something uncomfortable poked at me, but I pushed it away, and without looking, I wheeled Whole-Feather as far from him as possible and headed towards the left flank. The ships stretched out, and I needed to concentrate on getting rid of these shields.

With a renewed sort of vigour, I popped each one like a soap bubble, filling me with so much power that I vibrated. I let it go by sending more arrows onto the ships, and these arrows were so explosive that they set alight the wood immediately.

Ship after ship capsized. Demons screamed, catapults flew, fire burst into life. But it felt like I couldn't work fast enough for the sheer number of ships. Soon, I was overfull with power and high on adrenaline, wildly flailing my lightning out here and there.

Whole-Feather cautioned me twice, the smell of singed feathers filling my nose. I apologised to him, but he didn't mind, I don't think, simply focusing on dodging enemy arrows and spears.

Angrily, I blew another archer apart.

Because they had more ships, they had more catapults too. And soon, our shields began to go out and the high priestesses were forced to hover near the broken ones to deflect attacks.

I'd destroyed thirty ships by the time I saw it.

A line of ships carrying catapults on the southern flank came in from the side to enclose Lotus Island. But they bore no shields around their decks. Cocking my head, Whole-Feather glided closer. A black substance filled the bowls of the catapults, and by the time I decided to capsize this ship, a similar catapult on the northern flank fired.

Black power arced through the sky—before sailing right through the shields of an Ellythian ship. The mages and soldiers on the deck screamed, closing their eyes and flattening themselves on the deck.

"Obsidian powder!" the King of Owls roared, zooming for us. "It renders our mages useless. Protect the mages at all costs! Down the ships with those catapults!"

But we'd not been ready for magic-neutralising attacks or for this many ships. They enclosed around our fleet in a U shape, effectively cutting us off from the open sea.

Black powder rained down again. And where it missed the ships, it stayed in the air like a fine mist.

"Retreat!" Bhairavi said. "High priestesses, they have too much! Retreat!"

Whole-Feather swerved to avoid the black mist and flew us back to the harbour.

"You've done well thus far, Whole-Feather," I said, patting his neck.

As we sailed through the Reaper's shadow, Falja's voice rang out. "Wind shields! Bring out the wind mages!"

That would work for a time, I supposed, as I quickly instructed my staff to signal the wind powered sorcerers. But looking down at our soldiers, waiting for the enemy to reach our harbour, I knew a majority of this battle on sea would be fought with weapons alone now.

Whole-Feather touched down amongst my purple-robed mages. Esha, who was normally the headmistress of Agnolthi's magic school, rushed towards me. "How much obsidian powder do they have?"

"A lot," I said. "Magic shields will do nothing. Prepare for physical battle. They'll reach the harbour in minutes."

"Goddess!"

Just then, a deep boom reached our ears and the first prow of the enemy ship pierced the Reaper's shadows.

"Catapults!" Bhairavi commanded from the docks. Magical catapults were launched right into the enemy warship, but it was no use. Demons were already pouring out and diving into the water.

A second warship entered the harbour, then a third and fourth. Obsidian power blasted through the air.

"Wind mages!" I cried to my own priestesses marked with blue armbands.

Cold air blasted outward from our lines, pushing the black powder back onto the ships.

Esha handed me a round, steel shield and I flung it upwards, crouching down against any further fallout.

The soldiers and cavalry watched the powder with disbelief.

"The Reaper is here!" Jaya's voice cried in my ear.

My heart sank as a foul wind brushed across the harbour, determined and searching.

"There's too many of them!" Esha cried. "Without magic, we are done for. Done."

"No," I said firmly. "There is still one thing we can do."

A familiar golden chariot with a sickly green tinge appeared through the shadow wall. I summoned my bow.

"All high priestesses to the Reaper," Othar ordered. "Jaya, get Pia to her mother. The Reaper must not know we plan to kill the queen."

I jumped back onto Whole-Feather. "Let us occupy the Reaper, shall we?" Lightning skittered down my arms.

39
PIA

I'm not sure when I realised that my mother had to die.

It might have been when I saw she'd brought my twelve-year-old brother onto the battlefield but had left my father at the palace.

It might have been when Altara told me about her agreement with the Reaper.

Or it might have been when I saw the shield of the priestess prime had failed.

I stood on the deck of *The Lady Savage* beside the catapult Malika and our squadron were firing towards enemy ships. I saw the Reaper's dark form atop a golden chariot in the sky, flown by two feral, winged zekar stallions. Mighty and monstrous was his form, and his fleet behind him filled the sea at every angle. Demons would overcome Ellythia today.

I refused to die like this.

But as our shield deflected another catapult, I knew it wouldn't last long. The only reason we'd survived the obsidian powder was because our wind mage, Klotha was funnelling it away. Glancing up at a sweaty Malika, her face fiercely concentrated upon her task, I couldn't bear the thought of her dying here, for a queen who'd done nothing for her people but sabotage them.

I should have done something.

Demon faces leered at us through our turquoise shield, ugly faces gnashing their teeth and waving the obsidian nets they were going to use to enslave us. Another demon ship sailed past our starboard side. We were completely enclosed by enemy ships.

An explosion resounded fifty feet away making wood and water shoot into the sky. It was Altara's mages on their turtle boats, shooting magical attacks. But where one ship might go down, it was replaced by the mass coming from behind it.

They were just waiting for our shields to go down, and once they were, our decks would be overcome.

The soldiers next to me swore while they watched our ship's shield mage, Safra, grab the last of the quartz from the cauldron.

Within minutes, the quartz blinked out, and his soldiers crowded around to protect him.

A second later, the shield around the ship blinked out.

Our archers fired, their personal shields giving them some protection from enemy arrows. Behind them, we waited. The demons threw ropes and grappling hooks, which snaked around our mast. Our commander cut them down with magic, but more ropes followed by the dozens.

"Brace yourselves," Commander Varda grunted. He'd returned just in time for battle, much to his great happiness. A silver shield bubbled around him, and to my surprise, he extended his shield to cover me. Blows made to my person would bounce off now, unless we got showered with more of that obsidian powder.

"Fire at will!" Varda shouted to our archers.

Klotha mage picked up the tiny glass balls of naptha she had around her belt and shot them across the sea to opposing ships, where they promptly exploded. Agnolthi's battle priestesses called them 'grenades'.

I ducked, narrowly avoiding an enemy arrow.

A shout overhead had my head jerking up. Cherimani's high priestess flew on her dragon vehicle, pink armour and silver chain-mail reflecting the light of Malika's fire.

"You!" she pointed at me. "Get on."

"What?" I shouted.

"Wind mage, get her on here!" the high priestess shouted.

Already busy launching her attacks, Klotha did her bidding swiftly, without question. I was picked up on a violent wind and sent shooting into the air. I cut down enemy ropes as I went, but an arrow glanced off Varda's shield, luckily, still around me. I landed in the dragon vehicle with a thump, and the high priestess made a face before putting a shield of her own around me.

I couldn't stand being *cared for* like I was a helpless child.

"Are you taking me to my mother?" I asked dully, grabbing on to a hand-hold as she whipped the vehicle back towards the island with lightning speed. Arrows shot at us, but her shields easily deflected them.

"Yes," she said simply.

As soon as we got through the Reaper's shadow, the sounds of powerful magic thundered through the air, making the hair on the backs of my arms stand on end.

The Reaper was surrounded by four attacking high priestesses.

Tara's lightning sizzled the air, striking the Reaper's

chariot but glancing off his shield. The winged zekar neighed in protest, but was otherwise not injured.

None of the priestesses attacked the zekar. We didn't want our own zekar allies, who made up a majority of our cavalry, to defect on us. They were mighty but proud creatures.

Ellythia's general threw her axe right at the Reaper's chariot. Fire and sparks flew in a mighty boom, but no damage was done as the axe flew right back to the general's waiting hand. Luana's high priestess, on the back of her own owl, flicked out her whip from the other side.

On and on they fought. On and on, the Reaper deflected their attacks.

With the Reaper so thoroughly occupied, he didn't notice us as we zipped past, headed straight for the queen's platform.

Cherimani's priestess tightened her lips.

"You all planned this, didn't you?" I said accusingly.

"And?" she countered, eyes scanning the battlefield. "We all know the truth of things now, Your Highness."

"Indeed," I bit back.

"Do you understand what you have to do?" she asked, nodding to the queen's platform. "You understand about Rahana's blood alliance with the Reaper?"

My hand tightened around my sword just as my stomach fell into my nether regions. My blood *boiled* as I caught sight of my mother, standing proud on the platform, wearing the lotus insignia of our house as if she deserved it.

"Do you?" she pressed.

It was through gritted teeth that I said, "Yes."

I didn't realise it would be *me* who had to do this. For some reason, I thought the high priestesses would. Or maybe my father? Or just… someone *else*.

Only the vision of our people fighting made it hit me that I was the one who had to do this. That everyone had been telling me this for so long and I'd just not accepted it. Because I was magic-less. Because I'd been exiled.

Bracelets jangled behind us and I turned to see the Goddess Cherimani in the vehicle wearing dancing clothes of a pink bralette and skirt. She twirled and blew me a kiss.

"You see her?" the high priestess asked, glancing back with a small smile.

I nodded once, and she gave me a pointed look as if to say 'see?'

"I've been seeing them all."

"It makes sense, Your Highness."

"The shield of the Priestess Prime didn't work."

"And now you know why. Your mother was never meant to be queen, Pia. *You* were. It was always you."

I took a deep, shuddering breath to calm my churning stomach, but we were there all too quickly. My mother stood in a ring of her Queen's Guard, Captain Farah in charge, on that platform from which she was staring at the Reaper. The sight of my mother standing there in queen's armour, Matri-ka's sword at her side, the human-made crown on her head ignited a fury in me. The image Altara had described to me of my mother's betrayal roared through my brain.

Pure rage laced through my very arteries, burning as it went. Our people died because of *her*.

Not even waiting for the high priestess to land the vehicle, I placed an arm on the rail, swung my legs over, and leapt.

And landed right on mother. None of the guards inter-fered as we came crashing to the ground.

I said, in a savage voice that I'd never used with anyone ever before, "*You*."

She shoved me off and we both scrambled to standing positions, our shoulders heaving as we snarled at each other.

Around us, the Goddesses of Ellythia appeared in a circle, their power making the air static. Closest to me stood Umali, who was naked, chaos and darkness incarnate, her eyes all black, her skin dark as midnight, her hair wild and down to her waist, covering her breasts. She bared fangs dripping with blood at me. My mother's eyes widened as she took them all in for the first time.

Power made the air tremble. The queen's guards stepped away. No one would dare intervene.

I pointed a finger at Paalus, trying to get past Farah to get a look at the Goddesses. "Get him out of here." I nodded at the high priestess of Cherimani, then glared at Farah. "That's not a request."

The captain of the Queen's Guard thankfully stood aside and let Paalus get on the high priestess' vehicle.

"He should see what goes on here," Rahana snapped at me. "You have *no* right."

My reply was to unsheathe my sword. "You coward," I said with disgust and levelled my sword at her. "You worthless coward."

My mother's nostrils flared as her eyes moved around the circle of silent Goddesses, staring at us. "They want us to fight," she said in wonder.

"They want you dead," I said darkly.

Her eyes shifted back to mine and something glimmered in them. "Death came for me a long time ago, daughter." She levelled Matrika's sword at me. "Get back," she snarled to her guard. "This is between me and the heir of Ellythia."

"They already know," I said darkly. "Everyone already knows what you are."

All she could do was scowl at me.

Our two swords could not have been more different. Mine, a well-made standard issue infantry sword with a steel hilt, black leather wrapped around it and a sturdy steel blade. Matrika's sword hilt was beautifully made of gold and inlaid with emeralds; a priceless, ancient weapon of our family. But it was also a two-handed broadsword.

Speed against strength, then.

"You think you can be queen?" Rahana hissed at me. "Then let us see if you are made of queen's material then." She lunged at me, sword first.

I dodged, flicking her sword aside, and we turned. The Goddess Lisanthi was at my back now.

"I'd forgotten how fast you are," Rahana said. "Good." Then she was flying at me.

She came at me with her full power behind her down-swing, and I met her with my magic-less arms, blocking her blow with pain ricocheting up my arms. I hissed, almost dropping my sword as my mother took two steps back, assessing me. "I thought when Camar died, you'd get your magic back."

My blood stilled in my veins. "What?"

I'd given much thought to the nature of death in the past few weeks and decided that it couldn't be all that bad.

The criminals in the swamp who died just... left. With their eyes closed and their bodies lax, they left for the next thing, given a reprieve from the bodily pains they'd suffered in their mortal lives. It was a welcome ending for them.

Now, under the Lotus Sea, beneath the tumultuous fighting above, everything was quiet except for the pounding of my heart and the creaking of my boat.

I'd modified the turtle boat to be able to travel underwater. It was waterproofed with metal all around it, and then topped off with metal spikes to thwart interference. The concept was ingenious, and I was rather proud of myself for it. A boat that was completely covered was impossible to commandeer, and covered all over with metal and magic, it was almost uncapsizable.

This boat *would* capsize, in fact. Just at the right time, along with its sole occupant. Its determined captain.

The extensive shields muffled out all the sound from

outside, and it felt almost peaceful to be out here, underneath the battle. As if I were already in the netherworld, separate from the rest of things. The weapon I carried inside of my body pulsed uncomfortably. It had been a hostile parasite to carry, leeching my sense of what was good and holy. What was happy and kind. I'd fought it every step of the way until now.

I remembered the conversation the high priestess Othar and I had when she'd first brought me down into the catacombs beneath the swamp and told me about it. Her plan.

My heart had leapt. How it felt like I'd been waiting years for a chance just like this. It had felt right. It had felt true--perhaps the only true thing in my life, apart from my friends.

I remembered the weight in her voice as she asked me, "Will you do this?"

She'd glanced at me during Pia's Priestess Moot and said that Pia should be given to the Widows. She'd known to plant the seed in my mind at that precise moment. So I said, "You've always known that I will."

She nodded, those black eyes never leaving me. "To the bitter end, Rani?"

I squared my shoulders as something in my heart sealed itself back together. "To the ugly, bitter, Goddess-forsaken end, High Priestess."

My little boat made its slow way out into enemy lines.

41
ALTARA

T he Reaper was unlike any force I'd ever fought, or ever imagined fighting. He was relentless in both his defence and attack, his shields were as strong as solid gold. Us five high priestesses, Othar, Bhairavi, Falja, Saarika and I, darted around him in the air, attacking from every angle at the same time. Their priestess marks burned on their foreheads as mine did-- multicoloured symbols of their Goddess-given weapons.

But Odeelia had said he couldn't be killed, only contained, and our fighting here was only to distract him from the real battle going on at the queen's platform. I'd seen Pia zoom off in Jaya's dragon vehicle, grim-faced, her eyes darting this way and that as if looking for some answer that wasn't here.

I shot a lightning strike at the left side of the chariot at the same time Bhairavi threw a mixture of fire and water at his front, while Falja tried to suffocate his shield with a net of angry red power. The Reaper's red eyes looked in all directions at once, striking out at me and Falja at the same time with a black whip of power. Mahi, controlling our dragon vehicle, swerved just in time, and we headed towards the back of his chariot.

The forces outside of the black shadow-shield could be heard: explosions, fire sizzling, energy crackling, the shouts of demons, the screams of humans. At the harbour, our calvary defended the front lines with my mages on zekar stallions, peppering the demons with blasts of their power while the infantry wielded quartz weapons.

My glance down to the harbour made me do a double take as a familiar, white bald head caught my eye.

The Butcher jumped off a small ship and looked up at me with a smile that made cold fire plunge through my veins.

"My mark is here," I murmured into the earpiece. Without another word, I broke off from the Reaper and instructed Whole-Feather to take me down to the ground. "Take me to that Pentarax."

"I don't like the way he's looking at you, Your Majesty," he said.

I said nothing as Whole-Feather touched down, because every old wound in my skin, muscle, and sinew was also now burning with vicious fire. It was memory. It was threat.

But my priestess mark also turned hot as I lightly hopped off the vehicle, and I knew it would be the only thing visible through my shadows, a tiny defiance.

As my power rippled outwards, so did the Butcher's, a matching signature to mine as he used my own magic. The other Pentarax, demons and humans instinctively moved away from the both of us.

I approached the Butcher like a tigress stalking her prey, analysing the way his corpse-white skin stretched over the bulky muscle. Marking the way he breathed and blinked, assessing his grip on his sword. My father had raised me to be a warrior, my mother, a magic-wielder. And today I would use all of my skills to their full extent.

"Your life is mine, Butcher," I hissed.

He inhaled with a smile on his face that showed his teeth, his wide shoulders moving.

"My little Altara," he said, "all grown up." When he spread his arms, golden power that I knew like my own body gathered into two balls in his palms. "When I take you this time, princess, it will be for the last time."

It was then that I saw what hung from his belt. An obsidian collar.

My eyes slid back to his. "Queen," I said evenly. "I am the Boneweaver Queen."

He only grinned wider, and I realised my mistake too late because as his blast of my own magic hit me, my power recognised it as its own and refused to block it.

The blast hit me so hard and a scream tore through my throat. I landed hard on my back, and it drove all the air out of my lungs.

I wheezed, trying to draw air, my magic pounding and *pounding* inside my veins. My shadows flew apart leaving me bare. The Butcher stood above me, the sky behind him filled with the streaking colours of lethal magical attacks.

In his hand, he held the open obsidian collar. The triumph in his eyes made me want to vomit.

My power poured out of me, lining my body with every laceration ever made to my skin, muscle, and bone. Golden light shone through those cracks, all my old weaknesses in full view.

The Butcher's face was serene as he beheld my stiffened, supine body. "All my work on display," he said, smiling.

I couldn't move as he bent over me, my own power

pinning me flat, rendering me painfully immobile. The familiar brush of his fingers over my skin sent me into a blind, rabid rage, yet all I could do was tremble with the force of it as the Butcher fixed the obsidian band around my neck.

"Mine," he murmured, lovingly touching the collar.

Deep inside my gut, an ancient celestial band snapped into place, and a soundless, primal cry erupted from every cell in my body. A golden, glittering rope burst into my view, something thicker, stronger than before, immortally linking me to Zale.

A bond that had never been destroyed, only hidden.

Somewhere out in the harbour, there came an answering bestial roar.

42

ALTARA

THREE DAYS AGO, OUTSIDE THE GUILD OF THE PENTARAX

"Wait," I said, flinging an arm out. "I need to show you something. I….need tell you about the plan."

"What is it?" Pia asked, raising her brows.

"I came to the Pentarax Tower to get the Boneweaver Bow."

"And?" Malika said excitedly, looking me up and down as if she'd missed it on me.

Taking a steady breath, I bobbed my head just once.

My heart beat irregularly in my chest as the golden thread coming from my naval hummed a new sort of hymn. Some celestial light inside of it was speaking to me in a way it never had before. An offering in its own way.

And now the bow sat heavily in my astral repository. An ancient artifact with its own wisdom. Its own way of speaking to me. Not speaking really, more *insinuating*. The moment I'd read the inscription on that beautiful gold, it had offered me a twin to the bond's offering. I thought about what I needed to do. What I *knew* in my very soul we had to do.

I promptly turned and vomited.

"You're not pregnant, are you?" Malika said, striding forward and holding back my braid.

"No." I wiped my mouth with a shaky hand. I looked up at my friends. "It's just something Zale said that I've been thinking about. When the Reaper cursed baby Zale, three queens came together to create a key. Zale's star responded to their call and sent me."

We all looked down at the ethereal blue light of the arrow, its power heavy and potent.

"I think... I think that once again, we need three queens to finally break the Reaper's hold on him. Once and for all."

"Three queens..." Malika's brown eyes flicked between Pia and me. "An Ellythian Queen and a Boneweaver Queen."

Pia made a face, and Malika glared at her. "You've been seeing the seven Goddesses for a while now, don't deny it!" She pointed at my cousin. "You're the true heir to Ellythia and you know it!"

Pia sighed and glanced at me. I gave her an apologetic shrug. "The rest of us have accepted it."

My cousin's shoulders slumped a little. "Say I play along. We don't have a pixie queen."

"No, but will a fae queen do?" came an amused voice.

Odeelia sauntered out of the portal, magnificent in her sheer gold gown and looking about with a crinkled nose.

My stomach dropped to my feet.

"Who are you?" Malika moved protectively towards Pia.

Odeelia raised her perfectly arched brows, her amber eyes glinting. "I just said, didn't I? I am Odeelia, Queen of the Carnal Fae, at your service." She spread her arms and bowed her head dramatically.

Malika unsheathed her sword. "Tara, isn't this the bitch who tried to break your bond with Zale?"

I stared while Odeelia dragged her eyes up and down Malika's curvaceous body. "That's in the past now, pretty girl," she cooed.

Malika raised her brows at me, and I let out a weak laugh. The tension between the four of us broke immediately.

"And now," Odeelia sighed, looking at Pia with interest, "it seems I'll need to do something similar anyway."

My stomach tightened. "How did you get here?"

"The portal appeared, right outside my bedroom window. It was just lucky I wasn't *busy* at the time. And, well, I'd been expecting something, because Raen kept hinting at it, the sly beast."

Raen's 'hinting' came back to me with a vivid image that I immediately shooed out of my brain.

"Odeelia is the one who told me the Boneweaver Bow was here," I said. "I think we can trust her... with this, at least."

Odeelia straightened her shoulders as if I'd given her a great compliment. "You have it?"

"Yes," I said simply.

The three stared at me in wonder for a moment.

"Well, then." Pia turned to Odeelia. "So you'd help us?"

"I hate the Reaper." The carnal fae queen raised her delicate chin. "He's an old bore and ugly as hell. I don't want the demons defiling lands that are not theirs. Let's get rid of him."

"So how do we do this?" Pia asked. "Shoot the Reaper with the bow?"

Odeelia shook her head. "The bow can't kill a creature like him. He can only be contained. His death won't come about this way. You need to be clever."

I'd been staring inwardly at my bond for a while now,

trying to understand what it had done to the night sky. The solution it was trying to give us.

"Magrin," I said out loud. "Be with me?"

The brush of a butterfly's wings swept past my mind, and in seconds, we were surrounded by the Nine witches in their astral forms, their black cloaks swaying in the breeze as they bowed low.

Malika and Pia violently twitched.

"There is no moon here, Your Majesties," Magrin said in her deep voice, bowing to Pia and Odeelia. "This place is cursed."

"I know." My voice sounded far away. "A dark sky for dark deeds."

The witches' eyes glinted in excitement as they took in the arrow and us three queens standing before them. "We need to invent a spell," I continued. "A mirror to the one that called me forth from the stars when Zale was cursed by the Reaper. He is cursed again, this time in a worse way, along with my three brothers. We need a bigger, stronger key to break it permanently between all of them."

No breeze stirred the air around us as Magrin and I stared at each other. As the Nine witches I'd saved were coming to understand what I was asking them.

"We saw the Great Star turn red," Magrin said. "We saw it crying."

My heart clenched at that, but I nodded.

"It will hurt, Your Majesty," Magrin whispered. "It will require great pain."

For Zale, I could do this. We would have to do it for each other. He would understand. Raen would make sure they all understood.

I squared my shoulders. "Good thing pain is what I'm good at."

"Join hands," Magrin instructed.

The three of us queens held hands, making a circle that we put all our focus into. Tingling shot through my fingers and Pia gave a sharp inhale.

"I didn't think I had any magic," she said quietly.

"It's not yours," Odeelia said. "It's the joining that's doing it." Her amber eyes looked back at me. "Look inward, Boneweaver Queen. What does the Great Star say?"

It wasn't speaking to me, it was screaming. Goosebumps spread over my arms as the words came to me.

I spoke without intending to, my lips and tongue shaping the words as if something older than me, wiser than me, controlled my voice now.

> *"Twin flames. Twin souls. Twin powers.*
> *Tempest forged. Storm forged. Lightning forged.*
> *Forged anew. Forged hidden. Forged immortal."*

PIA AND ODEELIA REPEATED THE WORDS, AND WE SAID IT THREE times. A magic wind stirred our hair, power seized us, and a primal force held our hands together with a frightening strength.

A deathly calm fell. As if all the souls forged in stars had stopped breathing to listen.

"The stars are listening," Magrin whispered.

A reverent hum sounded beneath all things. A familiar power, a song on a midnight breeze, a familiarity. The golden bond between me and Zale called out in yearning.

Above us, the sky exploded and sent out a shower of sparks.

"Don't move!" Magrin warned.

So we grit our teeth and squeezed each other's hands as the blue-tinged light shot straight towards us. With a beam of light, it landed, shaking the ground beneath our boots.

When the light faded, a glowing arrow had been stuck into the ground, glowing with all the colours of a rainbow and crackling with pure power.

"It's made of starlight," Odeelia said in wonder.

I swallowed. "From my star. We called it." My stomach churned as I realised I'd have to say it out loud. "When the Reaper tore me away from Zale, the pain between us was immense. I think our bond responded somehow. And I just... knew to call it. And it sent this."

"To help you." Pia nodded. "It sent you a weapon."

The power in that arrow called out to me like a promise of vengeance. But also a promise of pain.

"For the Boneweaver Bow," Odeelia finished.

"But what will it do when it hits the Reaper?" Malika asked, frowning at the powerful weapon before us.

The answer came unwanted from my tongue. "Not the Reaper, but the bonds between Zale and I. The bow destroys bonds. With this arrow, all bonds coming from Zale will be destroyed. The Reaper's and the ones between the Reaper and my brothers, and also... the bond between Zale and I. But *this* arrow is made from the same star"—I nodded to the glowing weapon before us—"so it won't really destroy it, just separate it for a while. As our new, immortal bond regrows itself, we have to"—I took a shaky breath—"make it look like it went wrong and that I've destroyed our bond." We all went silent. "The Reaper's bond with Zale will be a forgery of the real thing. He'll never know the difference."

I just had to trust that the feeling the bond was giving me was right. That it would, in fact, grow back.

"So this way," Pia said slowly, "Zale and the Old Ones will still be commanding the Reaper's forces. And when it's time..."

"They'll defect," I confirmed. "And they'll be able to manoeuvre our enemy to *our* advantage."

"This is genius," Malika muttered.

The bond was to be deeper, stronger, but elusive to the Reaper. Hidden to all others, even to us, for a time.

Odeelia shivered. "This is powerful magic. You must be careful when you shoot."

I nodded.

"By my estimate, you'll have four days before your star-soul bond snaps back into place for all to see," Magrin said. "Be prepared."

Odeelia kissed me on both cheeks, and with one final warning, we parted.

43
ZALE

S tanding on the prow of the demon warship, Altara's pain crashed down to me, a battering ram of burning agony. From a place so far deep within me I could barely reach, a rope of pure starlight burst forth, whipping through the ether and binding me back to my wife.

My brain was going to explode. "ALTARA!" I roared.

"Finally," Kai groaned, slapping his forehead. "I was getting tired of playing evil."

Altara's power leapt and spun inside of me and my brothers, as a trap door in the back of my mind slammed open. It had protected our minds from the Reaper's probing while we pretended to still be bonded to him. I raised my left hand, and the butterfly that had been hiding near my foot, fluttered back into place on the skin at the back of my hand. I allowed myself to feel a cool trickle of—

"Relief," Wobbles whispered in my ear. And then a tiny, "Uh oh."

The pure, unadulterated rage I'd been keeping buried these past three days finally got its chance to burn through my arteries, making my blood roar in my ears. Finally. *Finally* I could go back to her.

Where. Is. My. Wife?

My power struck out.

Wet sounds came from behind me and the two warships on either side of ours as every demon soldier and commander fell dead, their visceral organs splattered all over the deck.

"I'll take that as the signal then," Atax muttered.

I leapt into the air as a man and took flight as an eagle, calling out for her, my wife, my Altara. Wobbles, used to my explosive shifting, hung on just in time.

Just before Raen shifted beneath me, he said, "Ah, it feels good to be alive, doesn't it?"

"Abandon ship!" Commander Varda called. "Abandon ship!"

As soon as Pia had left with Cherimani's high priestess, *The Lady Savage's* shield had gone down and we'd been overcome by demons. The demons stuffed quartz in their boots and began leaping across to our ship, whilst others crawled across on ropes they'd thrown with grappling hooks.

Due to fighting in such close quarters, I had to be very careful about using my fire, because every time I did, one of the Ellythians fighting next to me inevitably got singed. I was precise, but with quick-moving soldiers, accidents were bound to happen.

So I got my obsidian sword out, scampered down the catapult along with Gallu and the other men that worked my catapult with me, and began clashing fire-wreathed steel with the ugly blue and red demons that charged us.

The more we felled, the more arrived in fresh ships that never seemed to empty.

But some time into it, a whip of shining energy pummelled through the air, high above us. We all glanced up to look at it in case it was some type of attack, but it was too beautiful to be something violent.

I instantly suspected that it was Zale and Altara's bond making itself finally known, and then a distinct tiger's roar filled the space between ships and I knew for sure. Everyone flinched before surging on to attack once again.

But it wasn't until the deep *boom* sound that we all knew something was wrong.

Every demon and soldier in the harbour was stilled by a colossal force. Frozen in place, our sword arms raised, demon mouths contorted into weird positions, we felt a malevolent power sweep across the battling ships.

Guess the Reaper figured out Zale had only been pretending their black bond was still in place.

I hadn't truly realised the extent of the Reaper's power until then. How easily he seemed to capture thousands of creatures and render us all still in place. How were we going to win against *that*?

We needed a way to get the Reaper out and keep him off the island—and I hoped Pia was dealing with her mother, because where else would the high priestess of tricksters be taking her?

The Lady Savage groaned as the energy swept past us and the power holding the entire harbour captive, let up. Battle began again, and this time, the demons seemed to have a distinct edge.

It was then that Commander Varda, his eyes wild, roared. "Abandon ship!"

The demons sprung into action, ready to throw tourmaline nets to round us up. But Klotha was faster. She whirled her arms in a wide arc, collected us in a tornado of her power, and we rose up into the air. I let it take me in its spin, squeezing my eyes shut.

We were whisked right off the ship and over the sea, past the Reaper's shadow-wall and onto the Ellythian docks.

Dizzy with the spinning, we were dumped in a patch of Ellythian infantry.

But there wasn't any place in the harbour that was safe from the demons and Klotha was also weakening, the sky-blue quartz on her wrists now dead. Varda shielded us for a moment so we could get our bearings. My world tilted on its axis and I swore under my breath until everything settled.

Overhead, the Reaper was trying to leave back through his smoke dome—no doubt to get at the Old Ones—but the high priestesses wouldn't leave, engaging him in lethal attacks from all sides. He had no choice but to be caught up in their snare, constantly batting away their relentless strikes.

My look upwards cost me, because I sensed the troupe of giant demons barrelling towards us almost too late. They were nine feet of bulking, charging grey muscle covered black armour, tusks coming out of their mouths with axes in their meaty hands. Beady black eyes were pinned right on us. Two held a giant tourmaline net between them.

"Oh, fuck!" Gallu shouted from behind me.

I let my fire out at its hottest. The first row of armoured demons went down, their armour melding onto their skin, their mouths open in silent screams before a water mage doused the fire, leaving the smell of charred, rancid flesh in the air. But behind them, more demons followed on their ships, rapidly jumping onto the docks and running into the harbour with obsidian chains and collars in hand. There were too many of them and we were surrounded on all sides within moments. They knocked the infantry out and chained them with obsidian. The zekar cavalry fought as best they could on the southern bank, but the demons cut them down ruthlessly.

Blue Daanav marine demons leered down at me, spears pointed at us alongside the obsidian chains. They cackled for a moment, realising they'd caught us in a trap.

"Oh, shit," Commander Varda muttered, glancing back to see where I was. His quartz bracelets were dead.

I didn't reply, only summoned a ball of fire from my hand. "You're not taking us, demon fuckers!" I shouted.

A white Pentarax demon pushed toward the front of the group and showed me all of his sharp rows of teeth. He was clearly their captain and held up his hand, filled with an identical ball of fire to mine. "You look familiar."

Panting and biting back a swear, I eyed the number we were surrounded by. There were more even behind them. "How's your tower?" I sneered. "Oh wait, I forgot, it's rubble now."

He scowled at me. "Any last words?"

I snarled at him, but any word I was about to speak was abruptly cut off by the flap of wings as a massive, brown-skinned warrior dropped from the sky.

Power rippled and obsidian flashed as the Pentarax demon's head rolled off his shoulders, his eyes widening a fraction. Black blood sprayed so fast around us that it became a whirlwind of gore and screams.

Power swept in an arc as a wind felled every demon within a ten-pace radius. We stared open-mouthed as the two warriors completely obliterated the area in bursts of obsidian and magic.

And then everything went still as eyes like pools of a fae lagoon stared at me, the pupils dilating all the way as I watched. Those eyes *scorched* me hotter than any flame I could ever produce. His rough voice was anything but playful as Atax said, "Hello, my little firebird."

I completely lost it and screamed, "You come back from inside the Reaper's asshole after weeks and *that's* what you have to say to me?"

He gaped at me for a whole second before viciously knocking out a demon running up beside him without looking. Then his handsome face spread into a shit-eating grin. "I'm going to marry you, Malika Yashra. And there's nothing you can do about it."

"Fuck you!"

"I love you."

That stopped me in my tracks completely. I stood there staring at him, in the midst of carnage and screaming and humans and demons continuing to fight for their lives. Atax's eyes shifted over my shoulder before he flicked his fingers.

A demon screamed behind me. I'd never seen him do magic like this before. I supposed he saved it for the battlefield, preferring to kill with his hands. The amount of times he could've used the power on *me*, even in jest, but never had.

"I..." I had no idea what to say as some long-standing dam broke in me. My lip trembled.

His face softened, and he spread an arm out. His voice was gentle. "I know, firebird. Come the fuck here."

So I did. I leapt over the bodies of slaughtered demons and fallen weapons and slammed into him. My Old One caught me in his arms, grabbed my chin, and crushed his mouth against mine.

His kiss was demanding and possessive and I let him consume me, just for a moment.

"Oh fuck, firebird," he groaned against my mouth. One arm tightened around my waist and I didn't even know the tears were falling before he was brushing them away with a thumb. "I missed you so much."

Angrily slapping his chest, I pulled away. "I missed you too, don't ever mention it again, old man."

When he smiled, it wasn't a smirk, it was the most beautiful thing I'd ever seen in my entire life. Atax had a face hewn by both Xalya and Luana, in its beauty and harshness... and its ability to break into the stone shell of my heart. My stomach tightened into a knot and the words tumbled out of my mouth. "You really are so very handsome."

The smile fell off his face, his eyes widening. "What did you just say?"

I wrenched away from him and blasted a massive charging demon with my fire. My enemy scrambled away, screaming, running into his comrades behind him and burning them, too.

"Nothing!" I said angrily over my shoulder as I stomped away, still clutching that obsidian blade in my hand.

But Atax pursued me, swiping with his other obsidian blade, felling demon after demon with those powerful, battle-worn arms. "No, I heard that. Say it again!" The screams of his fallen followed me.

"We need to find Pia," I called back to him.

"Firebird—"

I whirled around so fast he almost charged right into me. My fire lashed out to my left and right, singeing demons on both sides. "When we fuck for the first time, Atax, I'll be on top."

"No, you won't!" he protested. "When we make *love*, firebird, *I'll* be in charge."

Rolling my eyes, I turned my back on him and charged towards the queen's platform, shouting over my shoulder, "I'd like to see you try!"

"What did you say?" I asked my mother sharply. Her emerald eyes flashed with a brief emotion. It almost looked like regret.

"You heard me," she said quietly, but with her chin raised. "Camar was executed by Lady Larfaro. He confessed to his crime of forcing you. Confessed that you didn't lose control, that you unleashed your power on purpose to punish him."

Something inside of me shifted, something bone-deep and weary. So weary. I suddenly found that I couldn't breathe, and I clutched at my chest like I could claw the feeling out.

Everyone knew, by Camar's own lips; the entire palace likely knew by now. I had planned for no one to know. To keep it a secret to—

"You should have told me," Rahana said darkly. "I would have—"

"Would you have listened?" I breathed, dropping my hand and straightening. The Queen's Guard stood behind the Goddesses, staring. One of them deflected a passing magical

337

attack. It glanced off her shield, the light casting us in red as my mother's face remained stony.

"I would have told you to fix it," she said. "I would have demanded you execute him by your own hand."

"I did fix it," I bit out. "Justice was served. I broke him."

"And yourself with him."

I took a breath. In the exile school, I'd thought of this a lot and even discussed it with Malika. Not Rani, because she was too sweet and it felt like a corruption to tell her. But Malika had understood why I'd done it. "Such is the way of these things, sometimes. All magic has a cost."

To the side, Cholnayak, clutching onto her mighty white staff, nodded.

My chest itched, and my bones ached. The backs of my eyes burned. Camar was dead. Properly dead. I hadn't meant to kill him. I'd wanted him to suffer. How many times had I wondered if that had made me a monster? A small part of me *did* think that, but not a soul in Ellythia would blame me for this. This was our way. Sexually forcing a woman was considered the most heinous of crimes.

But dead meant finished. Whatever we had between us, Camar's sentence had been served and it was *over*.

For the first time in three years, I suddenly felt like I could breathe again. The distinct image of a seed, buried under wet earth, now sprouting with clear silver light, came to my mind's eye. And that silver light *hummed* deep and true.

My entire body sighed, and I hefted my sword as the sounds of the battle around us hit my ears with new clarity.

I said, "While we talk, our people die. Let us finish this." Rahana squared her shoulders. "You gave blood to the Reaper. You made a deal of blood with him. You betrayed our family. You betrayed Ellythia." Her mouth set into a hard line.

A mouth that had once kissed my forehead when I'd been sick. A mouth that had spoken harsh words to me in the fighting ring. A mouth that had spoken a vile promise to the Reaper. "What you did, you cannot undo."

The corner of her mouth twitched, and she flew at me once again. This time, I was ready. This time, I met her with more than just the muscle and bones of my arms holding her powerful force at bay. Her eyes widened just before we disengaged, and I came at her with a flurry of blows that she met with her blade each time. Faster and faster I pushed her, and she grit her teeth and pushed right back.

I was concentrating so hard on my blows that I didn't see her foot coming. She swept my legs out from under me and I crashed to the ground on my back. Her sword was at my throat in seconds, and I grabbed her blade with my left hand, ignoring the slicing pain, and shoved it violently aside. She stumbled sideways as I jumped back to my feet, wiping blood off my fingers.

Her brows twitched, and I bared my teeth. She came at me again, a heavy downward stroke that should have sent me tumbling down, but I held my own despite the now slippery fingers holding my sword. I shoved her aside and rounded on her.

She aimed a kick to my abdomen, and I grabbed her boot and yanked. She went down with a cry, but promptly rolled to her feet, Matrika's blade never leaving her hand.

I came at her again, and with all my strength and speed, aimed blow after blow to her head, neck and torso. She barely held on, sweat dripping freely from her now.

We had to finish this. There was not much time before the Reaper turned his attention away from the high priestesses.

With a cry, I flicked my sword in a combination of blows

that turned the air around us silver. I was so fast that she was forced to lose her grip on her blade with a cry of disbelief.

Matrika's blade went flying through the air and I raised a hand, catching it smoothly by the hilt. Rahana fell onto her knees, emerald eyes boring into my own, her chest heaving fast as I angled her own blade at her neck. She was tired. Spent from the spell of the Priestess Prime and the battle with me.

In a burst of light, I lunged forward and split her armour and undershirt open in one slice. The edges fell open to reveal the skin between her breasts. One of the Queen's Guards behind the Goddesses gasped.

Three pairs of dots under each other. The sign of the Reaper.

"I wished it wasn't true," I breathed in dismay. But there was the evidence. There was the breach that had let the Reaper into our blood line. "You would have destroyed us."

Rahana's eyes flicked around the circle of Goddesses and she seemed to cower under the weight of their accusing stares. She couldn't help but hang her head as if in shame. She was so much smaller all of a sudden. So much weaker.

I could barely believe my eyes. This woman had once been Ellythia's spymaster, feared and respected. Perhaps pitied at one time, but one incontrovertible fact remained.

"You are not worthy, mother," I said softly. "You gave in."

Finally, her eyes shifted back to me, the green in them so dull it might not have been green at all, but grey. Next to us Lisanthi shifted. The Mother's beautiful head was shaking slowly. Disappointment. Rahana flinched as if she'd been struck, squeezing her eyes shut. When she opened them, dim resignation marked her gaze. "I am sorry, Pia. I should have protected you better. I was not a good mother. And an even worse queen."

I stilled.

She said more firmly, "You need to kill me to secure Ellythia. But know that it was my own hand that destroyed me. And let it be done with Matrika's blade. Some of us cannot return from ruination."

She wanted me to kill her with the weapon of the crown princess.

My vision blurred a little. "I loved you, even after I was exiled. Even after I returned, I had hope in my heart that you would see me and love me. That you would guess at the truth. I loved you right until the day I saw you were no longer my mother. No longer a Lota. Even then, I'd known you could never be Queen of Ellythia."

Rahana closed her eyes, a tear streaming down her right eye. Even now, she would only shed one tear for me.

"I am sorry that I did not know about Camar. I failed you. I failed Yasani. I failed your father and Paalus. I failed us all. I will die with my shame upon my shoulders." She opened her eyes and stared at me hard. "That is *mine* only to bear."

Her meaning was clear to me. She did not want me to suffer for taking her life.

My own tears fell down my sweaty cheek. A daughter's silent apology. A daughter's silent goodbye. "Then go back to the Mother and I will do what you could not, for our queendom."

Rahana nodded and closed her eyes. "Spill my blood upon this land and the Reaper's hold on us will disappear."

I steadied Matrika's blade. It felt so heavy in my hand. So certain. So lethal.

Surrounded by the seven Goddesses of Ellythia, and with

her own Queen's Guard silently watching on, I raised the heir's blade and beheaded my mother in one blow.

I fell to my knees at the same time my mother's body fell to the platform.

When I opened my eyes, the seven Goddesses still stood around me, but all I had for them was body shaking, heaving sobs as my mother's lifesblood spilled through the wooden slats of the platform and onto the Ellythian soil.

Their combined presence bore down upon me. Pressing on my being, burning a brand into my soul. They were waiting for something. And truly, so was I.

From the depths of my being, I felt it.

First, my bones shook, rattling in my frame. Power like I'd never known before erupted from my body and shot into the air as a solid beam of silver light.

And shattered the Reaper's shadow around Ellythia.

46
ZALE

Raen, Atax and Kai soared behind me and I noted Atax dropping off towards where Malika and her squadron were surrounded by more demons than they could fight.

Demon numbers were huge, but the might of Ellythia lay in its magic, and currently, they had no proper queen to wield it.

With rage flooding my veins like my own mad, feverish spell, I powered through the air, following the golden rope sizzling like starfire and lightning inside of me.

The harbour was the site of a mass melee, Ellythians and demons clashing in a mess of steel, magic and blood, both black and red.

On my left, the Reaper's head snapped towards me, noting my flight past him. But Luana's high priestess showered him with blows from a cat-o'-nine-tails whip on his other side, forcing him to direct his attack to his left and away from me. He was completely surrounded by all the high priestesses except one, shooting constant magical attacks on him from all sides. I didn't know how long they'd last, but they didn't matter right now.

I needed to find Altara.

Dodging a stray magical streak of ice, I soared over the docks, guided by our golden, celestial rope. The sight of her lying on the ground, covered in a field of her own magical shield, almost undid me. My eyes found the Butcher immediately, stumbling back to his feet twenty paces away and glowing with golden power I recognised straight away.

He must have been blown back from the blast of our bond reappearing. Tucking my wings by my sides and angling my beak downward, I shot towards the earth like a magical missile. At the last minute, I shifted and landed, shattering the stone beneath me with the force of my landing. The shock jolted Altara's supine body, and she groaned, rolling smoothly to her feet.

There were no shadows around her as she rose to stare at me. She shone with her own magic, all shadows gone to the wind, every old wound on her body visible for all to see, the cracks bursting with light as if her skin were fractured parts of the earth. My heart might have broken at the sight were it not for her eyes alight with purple-white light.

The urge to be inside of her, around her, to hold her in my arms and never let go was almost enough to send me to my knees. I needed to worship at the altar of her body, worship the Goddess that she was. Instead, what came out of my mouth in a low growl was, "I'm fairly sure I told you not to run away from me again, wife."

Her eyes flicked to Wobbles still on my shoulder before they flashed with that light. Her voice was deep and husky. "You also told me to do whatever it took, *husband*."

Shivering as her voice caressed my skin, I moved to step

towards her and her face flashed with agony as she held up a finger. We both turned to see the Butcher standing ten paces away, staring at my wife with a hunger that I wanted to cut off his face.

But he was not mine to kill, loath as I was to admit it.

As if she knew what I was thinking, Altara said, "He is *mine*, husband."

It shouldn't have given me such a euphoric rush to hear her call me that, once again, but it did. "Then I will stand vigil," I said, my voice a promise of what I'd do to her later.

Whirling around, I met the axe of a tall, crimson-skinned demon. I gestured my fingers, and he soared over the fray.

Altara summoned a sword of lightning and stepped towards the Butcher, who brought up his own sword with a snarl.

I realised then that I'd never actually seen my wife in combat before. As she struck swords with the Butcher with the full force of her magic behind her, I snuck glances. She was vicious and savage and wild, but also precise and ruthless. She looked like the Goddess Agnolthi herself, golden and dark, and in between my dispatching of the surrounding demons, my jaw went slack as I stared at her as if in some dream. A magnificent dream, where the bond between us sung a joyful melody.

My obsidian sword might not have stayed still after that, but my eyes never left my wife

47

ALTARA

A colossal blast sounded from east of the harbour, behind the front lines where the queen's platform was. Pure white light shot in a column up into the sky, piercing the Reaper's shadow like a spear. The light dissolved the shadows and the entire thing evaporated like weak mist, revealing the night-time sky overhead.

Cool air rushed back onto the island and a collective sigh of relief shuddered through every Ellythian.

The half-moon shone above us, a million stars twinkling down. A sudden smirk graced my lips as I stared at that celestial light. My eyes came back to the Butcher, whose black eyes flickered in a moment of uncertainty before I danced backwards.

"Magrin?" I called

"We are here." Magrin and the Nine appeared around us and the Butcher flinched, frowning at their presence.

"Remember when I told you not to sacrifice a beast for me ever again? Well, we need to make an exception. I need to take the magic *of this creature. He will be my first and last sacrifice to Agnolthi. How did you do it?"*

"You'll need the moon, Your Majesty." She looked up at the sky and was surprised to find it clear, showing me all her teeth as she and the Nine grinned.

"Now we have it," I said.

"Then we will need to dance."

"Nothing would please me more than to see you dance, Magrin."

Hooting a laugh, she and the Nine struck up a dance in a circle, their astral forms spinning, their arms making wide, graceful arcs.

Their song was wild and familiar in my bones, trills and shrieks that filled my heart with a savage type of joy. Zale was grinning as he fought to keep my space clear, and it made me happy to see him like that. I summoned my small cauldron and set it on the ground before me. Cutting my finger with the edge of my sword, I allowed a drop of my blood to fall into it.

"I present this sacrifice to Agnolthi," I murmured.

The cauldron filled with a red mist.

The Butcher shifted as if uncomfortable, and then, deciding that the best response was an attack, summoned a great black bow and loosed an arrow right at me. Surprised, but not alarmed, I brought up my sword and the arrow glanced off it. He shot again, and once more, I deflected and stepped sideways to run at him.

He shot again, and I dodged the third arrow. He threw the bow aside as I reached him, flinging out his hands as if to attack me with my magic again. But I was ready, and kicking both feet outward, I slid across the ground down low. Thanks to the witch's boots, my slide was smooth, and I caught him off guard, knocking his feet out from under him. He lurched to the ground, and I rolled out of his path, bounding to my feet and zapping him with lightning straight out of my fingers. He jerked as it struck him, smoke curling off his skin where it was burned.

But his wound glowed gold before the skin healed over.

"I made you into this," he panted, gesturing to my body as he heaved himself onto his feet. I froze my step forward. "It's because of me that you grew to be so strong."

"That wasn't you," I said. "I did this myself." I swept my hands down to indicate my glowing skin, my magic filling the cracks he made in me. "I'm whole. And it was a power I gave to myself." I threw a dagger at his chest and he punched it aside with ease. Okay, no weapons then.

"The tithe!" Magrin cried out in her song. "A tithe for Agnolthi." The other witches cried out in joy.

With the sound of witches dancing around us, I slammed into his body with my power, invading it so violently that his entire body momentarily went slack.

"You forgot," I hissed, gripping the great thoracic artery leading from his heart, down into his abdomen in a magical fist. "That I've been using this magic since I was two years old. *I* am its master. You would never have learnt to use it as well as me." He choked as I squeezed, his arms and legs freezing under the strain. Around me, the witches cackled with glee, their song reaching a great crescendo. "Goodbye, Butcher." I ripped out the entire massive length of the artery.

Black blood spurted from his torso as his abdomen ripped open from chest to groin in a ragged, violent line. As the Butcher collapsed, his lifesblood spilled like a waterfall onto the stone of the docks and his heart fell splat on the ground. My own power charged back for me.

It hit me both like a golden summer wind and a dark winter storm. Gasping against the onslaught, magic whirred through my being, filling me up, charging me, lighting every cell in every part of my being. It filled something deeper too, and the golden rope between Zale and I vibrated with joy.

When I opened my eyes, everything sparkled like diamonds, and Zale stood before me, a bloody warrior, two obsidian blades in his hands and a look of such reverent awe on his face that I couldn't help but run into his arms.

He caught me by the arms and held me there, his blue eyes wide. "Your skin is like diamonds," he said, brushing his thumbs over my skin. "My beautiful Altara."

I let out a breath that was half a sob.

As if suddenly realising he was touching me after so long, his eyes quickly found mine. He yanked me against his body and captured my mouth with his. My husband's mouth was feral and hard against mine, devouring me whole in desperate crushing movements.

"Never again," he growled when we came up for air. "*Never, fucking again.*"

48
PIA

Chaos reigned around me as my power viciously hummed under my skin, in my bones, shiny and new. But it hurt. Goddess it hurt. Said Goddesses disappeared once my mother was dead. The deed was done and all I could do was stare at the hands that had done it.

"We need the spell of the Priestess Prime!" a priestess of Agnolthi shouted from the edge of the platform.

"Our forces cannot hold the enemy back for much longer, Your Highness," Farah, the captain of the Queen's Guard, shouted.

"It needs all the high priestesses." I wasn't even sure what the hell I was saying. All I knew was that the Agnolthi priestess was right, but none of the high priestesses were here. They were all holding off the Reaper in his blasted chariot. It was taking all of them, from what I could see, to hold him in place, going neither forward nor backwards and thus keeping the rest of us safe.

"I don't know the plan!" I cried to them. "Where the fuck is Altara?!"

"What the hell!" Malika's voice sounded behind me and I whirled around to see Atax shoving her onto the platform, his eyes thankfully clear, returned to their usual warm blue.

"Good to see you, Tax," I said quickly. Raen and Kai were on the front lines below me, fighting in a blur of magic and obsidian blades. Raen's magic flung outwards in waves of green power so dark it was almost black. His tattoos seemed to move on his face as he cast his spells, like a graceful, precise, yet lethal dancer.

Kai, on the other hand, fought with a white flute stuck between his teeth, and oddly, I could not hear any music coming out of it, but the way my magic responded to it told me there was sound.

I squinted down at him and then noticed that the demons around him fell without being touched. That their *bones* seemed to collapse upon themselves—legs, arms and ribcages collapsed, and the demons literally crumpled onto the ground with screams. He did that over and over again until the oncoming demons had to climb over corpses to get to the two Old Ones.

"Where is Rahana— Oh." Malika abruptly shut her mouth as she saw the two Queen's Guard pulling my mother and her head off the platform to take away from me. I didn't want to look at her lifeless form, but couldn't help it. I'd killed her by my own hand. I'd reduced her to nothing, and yet her own guard pursed their lips as they took her away.

But her words had rung true before she died, Ellythia came first.

"I don't know the spell." I gritted my teeth. "I need the high priestesses. We need a moment without the Reaper to get the spell started."

"Here." Farah chucked a lump of quartz at me, and I

realised that it was the ear piece my mother had been using to communicate with the high priestesses. Without thinking too much about it, I shoved it into my ear.

"Altara?" I called into it.

"Oh, thank the Goddess!" came multiple voices as the high priestesses recognised mine.

"The queen is dead," I said dully. "And my power is back."

"Oh was that *the giant beam of silver*?" said Othar dryly.

"And now I have you lot to deal with," I said dryly back. "Where is my cousin?"

"Here!" From out of the battle, Altara appeared on the back of Zale, flying in his eagle form. It took them a few moments to get to us. Tara leapt off Zale and landed on the platform, caught between Atax and Malika, both of whom hugged her in relief. Zale landed in his human form close behind.

The Queen's Guard edged away from the Old Ones, and I shot them a glance. "They're on our side. No more words about it," I said into my earpiece. "Tell me what to do."

Othar's rough voice came through first. "We need to drive the Reaper away for a moment. Thankfully, I came prepared." She grunted as she launched another attack on the Reaper from her borrowed dragon platform. "Go, Rani," she said loudly. A beam of white light shot from Othar's staff and into the harbour.

I froze on the platform as I followed the light for this 'distraction' Rani was involved in. Honestly, I'd been happy not to have seen her on the battlefield for this long, but now I knew why. She and Othar had been scheming. The white beam struck the water and did nothing but pass right through. We stared at the water for a moment.

"There," Zale said, pointing.

A tiny metal turtle boat now bobbed to the surface, weaving between capsized ships and still-floating enemy ones. Arrows glanced off the surface, falling useless into the sea.

"What is she supposed to be doing?" Malika asked.

"No!" Altara screamed, lurching towards the railing next to me. "Goddess, no!"

"What?" I cried. Her tone made my blood run cold.

"Look." Altara's heavy golden power flared and her ability to see into bonds was somehow cast into all of our minds simultaneously.

It was then that we saw the secret Othar Dhumvar had been keeping for the last few weeks.

In a dimly lit cavern, Othar and Rani stood before a glass cube filled with something that absorbed all the light around it.

"We call it a soul-bomb," Cholnayak's high priestess said in the memory. "It is made of the energy of the souls of the damned. Their collective pain and darkness will specifically attack the darkest creatures, leaving the humans alone. It's been sitting here collecting power for years now, just waiting for an attack from someone like the Reaper.

"But now it requires someone to carry it. Someone who can bear the pain of it and keep going, keep collecting the dark power, so when the time comes, it will be enough to cause colossal damage to our enemy." She turned to Rani. "It will kill the person who bears it." My blood ran cold. "I picked you out when you arrived in Lota city, Rani Umasri. You are not an acolyte of this temple. You never were. You are Cholnayak's weapon. The one person who had the power to do what was required. Your past gives you the unique disposition to take this to fruition when no one else can. To be able to push past the possibility of eternal torment? To endure the suffering required? To know that suffering awaits you and to accept it anyway? You will go down in history as one of the women who suffered and then saved us. Will you do this?"

Rani's smile was angelic and pure. "You've always known that I will."

Othar nodded. "To the bitter end, Rani?"

Our friend said, "To the ugly, bitter, Goddess-forsaken end, High Priestess."

And then moments later, Othar was holding the black orb into the skin of Rani's abdomen and looking into her eyes. Power shimmered around them, dark and potent. "Will you bear the weight of the collective suffering of our city and then, no matter how difficult, no matter what happens, when the time is right, cast it upon the enemy? And do you consent to give your life to this task?"

Rani never hesitated. "I do."

The memory faded, and the world roared back into my ears. "No," I said. "No. No. *NO!*"

But the high priestesses were already herding the Reaper out of the docks and into the sea. Past which, I realised, the border to the previous Priestess Prime shield had been.

"Wait, who is that?" Malika cried, squinting into the dark

A slender figure had swum up Rani's boat and though her hands no doubt bled from the spikes planted all along the outside, the figure pounded on the boat's surface.

"That," Atax said quietly, "is Yulara. Rani's old betrothed."

49

RANI

G entle white light breezed into my boat and enveloped me. Othar's signal.

Just as my heart leapt into my throat and I placed a hand on my chest, something pounded on the outside of my boat. A power that was all at once familiar hit me in the core.

Green fields, daisies on a summer day. Stolen kisses under a banana tree.

I scrambled to open the hatch, though Othar had told me not to.

The face that met me in the dark ocean froze my entire body. "Yulara?" I whispered. "Am I already dead?"

"No, Rani," said the love of my life, climbing inside the boat and closing the hatch. "I followed your magic and came for you. Only for you."

I stared at her dripping form. Dressed in Xalya's soldier's uniform, her athletic frame panted as she looked at me. Yulara's bright face was flushed with strain. She'd always had the sort of beauty that stopped the heart in its tracks, but here, at the end of all things, I couldn't bear to look upon it. "You can't be here. You must go!" I shoved at her shoulder in a panic.

She didn't move an inch as I pushed at her, dark eyes burning into mine with a ferocity that made all the hairs on my body stand on end.

"I love you, Rani Umasri," she breathed. "I have always loved you. Even when my father placed a spell on me to forbid me to come to you and communicate with you. And if this"— she waved her arm to indicate the ship— "is something that you must do, then I will do it with you." Her eyes flicked down to my chest. "I sense what you carry," she whispered. "The thing that corrupts your power."

We had always been entwined in each other's magic, like our powers could not survive without each other. She, more than anyone, would know the weight of the darkness I was given to carry.

But I shook my head. "I can't let you do that. You'll die."

She raised her chin defiantly. "Then we will both die together."

We stared at each other for a moment before her face crumpled and she pulled me into her arms. "I'm sorry, my love. So, so sorry my parents kept me from you. I'm sorry I couldn't break the spell they put on me. Agnolthi's grace freed me."

"Agnolthi?" I repeated. Yulara's presence here was Goddess given then.

Yulara's skin was on mine, her presence before me overwhelming. But she had always been home for me. Undeniably, this woman was my heart, my home. And even if the truth made my veins burn in anger, I couldn't help, for the first time in a long time, feel a small, pure moment of peace.

"Just hold me, Yulara," I whispered.

"I have waited so long to do so," she whispered in my ear. "And I will never let you go again. If it is to death we must go to save Ellythia, then I am glad we go together."

I n our ears, Bhairavi called for our captains to retreat
quickly back onto Ellythian soil.

"Abandon your ships," she instructed in a too-calm voice.
"Water and wind mages, push our sailors back to shore."

The queen's platform turned into chaos.

Malika shrieked by my side. "We're not letting Rani do
this! Let me out. Let me out!" She leapt for the ladder, Atax
going after her, shouting for her to wait.

Below, Raen took flight in his giant raven form, Kai
jumping on his back. "I'm not losing another sister!" my
white-haired brother shouted back to us.

It was too far to run. "Take me to her," I said to Zale.

But my husband's face was drawn as Pia was shouting
into her earpiece. "I command you to stop this, Othar!"

"I cannot contact her," Othar replied calmly. "The signal
has been given. Rani is willing."

"She doesn't know what she's doing!" Pia roared. "I need
a flying vehicle. Right now!" Jaya didn't reply. "Get me an
owl!" Pia cried to her guards. "Someone get Rani out of

there!" The guards scrambled. But Pia was *raging* and threw herself off the platform, her silver magic spraying outwards, as, propelled by her own anger, her magic shot her through the air like a bird.

"Holy shit!" someone cried.

But I didn't have time to marvel at it.

"Zale?" I said sharply, grabbing my husband's arm.

"I cannot let you," he said tightly. "If this soul-bomb targets dark powers, Tara, it will target you. Your power is light and dark, *both*."

Realisation hit me like a cold blow to the head just as the shadows inside of me quivered in reply. "Shit." I stared back out at the harbour where our friends were hurtling towards the little steel turtle boat, Pia barely a silver streak in the sky.

The circle of the Reaper's assailants stuttered for a moment and it was all the Reaper needed to shoot right out of his chariot and after Pia.

But just as Pia, Raen and Kai reached the water's edge, Raen's wings stiffened, and he immediately plucked up Pia and swerved away from Rani's boat.

Boom.

I screamed in terror just as Zale grabbed me around the waist and turned us to cover me with his large body, his shield coming around us.

The light came first, but it was not the light of any magic I'd ever seen before. It was dark, and potent, foul as a sewage and it was reflected in every building, every tree of the city before me.

Then came the sound of the explosion, the shrieking, piercing sound of the long-suffering dark. My magic screamed in response, but Zale doubled his shield around me, his power sending out a heat wave that knocked the guards on the platform off their feet and flattened them.

The explosion that resounded throughout the air was low and lethal. A deathly cold hit us in a wave, shaking the very earth. The queen's platform shook so violently that it gave way, and with a groan, began to collapse on itself.

Zale swore and, placing one arm around my waist, threw his other arm out. The entire platform stilled in its collapse, as if a giant hand was holding it together.

"Rani!" I sobbed. Not caring that we were teetering on the brink of collapse.

He grunted, and inch by inch, the platform groaned back to a straight position.

Dark wings flapped nearby and Raen was there with a screaming Pia and Kai. Kai reached for me, tears streaking from his sky-blue eyes. I gathered him into my arms as he sobbed and he held me and tightly as Raen and Zale's magic whipped outwards, melding and joining the platform back together.

Pia screamed into the night and I turned in time to see her magic lash up and out, silver fire erupting out of her body in a storm of potent energy.

There was so much power there, so much—

Kai tilted his head back and screamed in agony. His power rang out too, and below us, the demons screamed as their bones splintered by the dozens.

My power responded to theirs, and from the depths of me and my astral trove, gold called out, a high-pitched keen.

I held my hand up without thinking, and the Boneweaver Bow flashed into existence. Raen and Zale stared at me.

I rose to my feet.

Inscribed on the Bow's surface in a language that only I could read, it said: *Time and space are no bounds for me.*

Time. They told me it was a bow that defied *time* and space.

I summoned an arrow.

Zale's eyes flashed with realisation when he saw it, and he reached for me in an instant. I turned out towards the harbour. He stood behind me, with his hands over mine, and together, we drew the Boneweaver Bow.

Together, we *pulled* on the collective powers of our friends. We took Kai's power to protect their bones, Pia's power to protect their flesh, and Malika's power over fire; collected it, combined it, and drew it into the arrow.

The golden arrow shook so violently with all that power, it took all of Zale's and my strength to hold the weapon steady and draw it back far enough. Our bones groaned. I grit my teeth against the onslaught of bodily pain.

Time, I said silently. *Go back in time just a minute to protect her.* And with Zale's gentle reassurance in my ear, his hard body steady behind me, I looked at the mass of debris in the water and we let the arrow fly.

We both grunted against the pain as, with impossible speed, the arrow flew over the battlefield, leaving a low boom in its wake.

Time itself seemed to slow as light and sparks erupted when it struck something on the sea, though I felt sick to think if there wasn't anything left for it to actually strike. There would have been nothing left of either young woman.

The world seemed to warp in that area, a square of space distorted to our eyes. Then objects were flying, zipping back together, converging, twisting until Rani's silver turtle boat sat shiny and smooth in the water, bobbing on the swells as if it had never been blasted apart.

I let out a sob.

"Did it work?" Pia breathed, coming to hold my trembling hand, her shoulders heaving as she panted from the strain of her magic. Kai sniffed as he came to stand next to her.

"Go find our sisters," Zale murmured to Raen, never taking his arms from around me.

Raen burst into his raven form and, once again, Kai jumped atop his back. Together, they shot towards the harbour, Kai calling out Rani's name.

"Where's the Reaper?" Atax asked.

"Sent tumbling over the sea as planned," came Other's voice in my ear. "The explosion pulled him right out. We are coming."

Sure enough, on our southern flank, over our army re-starting their fight on the battlefield, the four priestesses soared towards us on their various mounts.

They were covered in blood and sweat, their faces shiny and drawn but their forehead symbols shone as beacons in the dark.

Jaya arrived first, on her dragon machine, holding her arm as if it were dislocated. Grimacing, she tugged on her arm and shoved at it. We all distinctly heard it snap back into its socket. Falja stumbled onto the platform next, covered in her own blood. Pia went over to her immediately, placing her hand on her wet abdomen, the puncture hole of some magical attack gaping open.

Silver light shone, and the high priestess of Lisanthi stared at Pia as her wound sealed back up.

"Your magic—"

"Finally back, yes," Pia said stiffly, turning to Othar

Dhumvar, who was stepping off the staff she'd been flying on. "How could you, Othar?" Pia hissed.

Saarika landed with a grimace, sticking her finger in her ear and wiggling it. "None of us knew, Your Majesty," she said. "Othar hid her plan from all of us."

"Rani was a consenting adult. And I also knew," Othar said firmly, her eyes out on the harbour where Raen and Kai had just landed beside the turtle boat, "that there would be a chance that the high priestess of Agnolthi would know how to use her bow." She turned to look at me.

But I was shaking. With adrenaline, terror, and rage. "You couldn't have known that I'd manage to get it. Rani wanted to give her life for us." Zale somehow sent the Boneweaver Bow back to my astral trove, his arms encircling my waist protectively. "And you enabled her. *Told* her to do it."

Othar denied nothing. "I know that redemption can be a dark path." Her eyes shifted to the still-wet stain of Rahana's Lota's lifesblood on the platform. "And some only find it in Cholnayak's arms."

Zale let out a low growl behind me. "Be that as it may, the Reaper will return. This war is still here."

Everyone suddenly straightened.

"Start the spell," Pia said savagely. "Whether Rani is alive or not, I will deal with her later."

Everyone took one look at her face, the way her shoulders were set like a predator's, the way her entire body glimmered with silver rage, and we all moved back into our positions.

The high priestesses gathered around me, the sounds of the battlefield filling my ears, the sounds of Ellythians struggling and dying making the magic inside of me surge and light up my fingertips. Despite the Reaper leaving, the demons were still docking at our harbour and rowing in with their long boats. They were determined, vicious creatures, intent on their dominance and enslavement of us.

"I never did the queen's blessing," I said quickly. "How am I supposed to gather the power of the people? It'll never work." On top of that, my returned powers were roiling about in my gut, wild and agitated. While it felt familiar, it also felt new. I wasn't even sure if I had that much control over it.

"No," Bhairavi said with a ruthless smile. "But I made sure your mark was on every soldier in Xalya's guard. Every time you served food, every boot you polished, every sword you sharpened, your mark has been on them all this entire time. They ate food made by *your* hand. They wore shoes polished by *you*. They use weapons sharpened by *you*."

364

They'd been planning this longer than I could have imagined.

Othar said, "It was just luck that your magic went cold and the Reaper couldn't access it to corrupt you. We made sure you were sent away, so you'd be out of his eye completely. That way, when it was time, you could come back in and he'd never think of trying to come for you until it was too late." As I stared at her, Othar took out an aged roll of parchment from her cloak. "You'll need to memorise this."

"What, *now*?" Malika exclaimed, gesturing to the battle still raging.

But I snatched up the parchment, still not forgiving Othar for the soul-bomb. "We have no choice. Teach me," I commanded.

"We need to drive as many demons out as possible," Bhairavi said quietly, her sharp eyes out on the harbour. "They've made it into the city. If we put up the shield, they'll all be stuck in here with us anyway."

My stomach sank. There were warriors and mages in the city, but not enough compared to the demons still pouring in and going out with the collared Ellythians.

But I couldn't go out there. I needed to learn the enunciation of the words of the spell. While I had been learning the old language of the Ellythians since I was a child in preparation for my one-day queen hood, it was still a new spell for me. The others no doubt had weeks to learn it.

"Go out there," Altara said to Zale and Atax, as we all tried not to look at the way Raen and Kai were flying back to us, two figures limp in Kai's arms.

Relief poured through me. But Rani and Yulara would still die if we couldn't protect the city. And we'd *all* die if the Reaper returned.

Altara pushed at Zale's broad shoulder. "You need to go help the city's people. We need all the fighters out there. Leave the Queen's Guard and Malika here."

He touched her cheek with a finger. "I love you, Altara,"

She placed a hand over his and said, "I love you, Zale. Now go, before it's too late."

I locked eyes with Zale as he scanned us on the platform and nodded my thanks to him. He nodded back.

He knew as well as I did what these numbers looked like. What we could see of the carnage on the platform. How the demons were putting obsidian collars on as many Ellythians as possible and shoving them back into ships. We were losing this.

I began to sound out the ancient written words before me.

My skin itched as I leapt off the platform and thudded to the ground, making for the city with Atax close behind me. The front lines were completely lost, but we *could* hold our back line in the city and make sure Ellythia's vulnerable population were saved.

"Resignation," Wobbles muttered as he hung on with all his might. "Fear."

But it was not myself that I was afraid for.

Even if they got the queen's shield up, Lota Island was overrun with demons, and we had our work cut out for us as we slashed and shot with our magic as we went. The fact that Atax was using magic at all proved how dire the situation was as he loathed to waste the feeling of a kill.

While the high priestesses had been concentrating on keeping the Reaper occupied, they'd not been able to keep the front lines secure. It had been the lesser of the two evils at the time.

Altara's face was drawn with worry, as all their faces were. While Pia tried to concentrate on her spell, the others were looking over the battlefield and behind them to where the enemy was sprinting towards the palace. Towards where, I guessed, they were hiding the children and elderly.

But the demons were not only moving towards the palace. They were moving *back* towards their ships, collared Ellythians in tow, most unconscious, many injured.

While Raen had been responsible for sabotaging the stores of obsidian power, I'd spent time disabling the warships we'd arrived in, ensuring the demons wouldn't be able to leave. They'd make it to their ships but would find the massive people-carriers leaking from their hulls and their quartz stores gone. They'd be stuck in Ellythian waters until we could figure out how to get the humans back.

We just didn't have the numbers to do it. Not save the city *and* get back its people.

How did a city recover from something like this?

They were all tired—the high priestesses, the mages, the infantry, the cavalry.

And the Reaper would be back in no time at all, with Rani's blast likely only knocking him out for a short while.

As we jumped on three sprinting demons and gutted them, Atax gave me a look that said he was thinking the same thing about the losing battle. But then his eyes snapped to the south, scanning the horizon. His pupils dilated.

I didn't look to see who it was, because I knew the magic coming from the south all too well.

Blasting into my eagle form, I left Atax to his own devices and soared into the sky with Wobbles, hurtling back the way we'd come to the harbour.

A horn sounded on the wind, sweet, lilting and... completely inappropriate for war.

Three golden ships appeared behind the demon warships.

They were beautiful, jewelled, glittering under the stars, quartz lights shining in beams of multicolours. They flew a golden flag of two fae in carnal embrace.

How Odeelia had gotten those ships in time was beyond me.

The fae queen was covered in gold armour from head to foot, her golden crown upon her curls as she stood at the prow of the central ship, a strange steel device sitting before her. She grinned and waved at me like a proud child waving to a parent.

"Look, Ashzale! I came!" she said. "And here—"

She grabbed the steel device by two tea-pot handles on the sides and pulled back on it. Potent magic shot out of it in a concentrated blue stream, hitting the enemy ships before her. The three-hundred-foot demon warship exploded in a crash of wood and water. I swerved out of the way of the debris.

"I call it a death ray!" she called happily to me, wiggling her hips as she shot it again. The warship next to it exploded, too.

Golden archers rose up behind her, soaring into the sky on wings made of golden bird feathers and fae magic. I didn't want to know where they'd gotten the feathers from and I wouldn't ask.

But they worked. Because as I wheeled around to soar back to the city, the fae archers and warriors with swords all kept up with me. Odeelia, now held between two of her flying warriors and her own magic, levitated her death ray as she flew, sequentially shooting the demon ships.

As I sailed past Rani's steel boat, I grimaced, knowing what we'd done to her in-laws. But I could hardly care about it now as I led the fifty strong carnal fae to shower their magic onto the demons assaulting and capturing the Ellythians.

Their power might have been delicate and gold, but it was still lethal.

With Odeelia holding the frontmost line and systematically destroying the demon ships, I was satisfied that we wouldn't lose any of the Ellythians to slavery.

"Zale!" Odeelia shouted after she eviscerated a line of fifty demons at the harbour. "Look!" She pointed at a fifty-foot boat sailing into the harbour, covered in Boneweaver magic.

If I'd had a mouth, I would have grinned. Instead, I let out a sharp cry that had my court looking up at me. Wobbles muttered something on my back but I already knew what this emotion was.

It was my court. Mine and Altara's court.

I hurtled towards the ship like a spear, flinging my wings out at the last moment and landing as a man before my people.

I was met by wide blue eyes and muscled brown bodies of over fifty Old Ones. Beasts made into men and women. Powerful warriors. *My* warriors.

They stared at me in wonder. One of them caught my eye.

"Cousin," I said to Ulanna Boneweaver. "It's been a while." I summoned the egg-sized ruby and handed it back to her. Three days ago, Malika had dropped it into Atax's pocket and he'd given it to me. The next day, I'd summoned my court from the Eternal Forest, having no idea if they could make it on time but trusting they would do their best.

Ulanna's blue eyes glistened as she took back the ruby she'd given Altara from the hood of her cobra's hood. "My king," she said, falling to one knee. The rest of them followed suit.

From behind me, a potent magic swept across the harbour and the sound of six voices resounded across the wind.

The spell of the Priestess Prime.

"We will help the Lotus Court," I said calmly. "We will secure the palace and city and then we return to destroy the rest of the demons. Let my reign over the Old Ones begin with an act of kindness and honour. Rise. Fight with me."

They stood up. Ulanna grinned savagely as she eyed the demons pouring over the harbour. "With pleasure, Your Majesty."

"There will be black blood in our teeth tonight!" her mate, Ulfas Boneweaver, cried, promptly shifting into his gigantic cobra form and leaping onto land.

The demons screamed as the rest of my beasts followed.

O ur combined recitation of the ancient spell strummed a lively tune inside my body. *This* time, I stood next to Bhairavi and my power pummelled into her, down the line, as Pia recited the words through gritted teeth. I had to hand it to her, although one of her guards had to go on his knees to hold the parchment up for her to read from, her pronunciation was perfect, and as we repeated the words together, a glimmering light began to show in the distance.

The air filled with a static energy that made the demons look up at our platform and targeted attacks began coming for us, arrows and throwing daggers charged with quartz. Priestesses of Agnolthi held our last reserves of quartz to maintain the shield around our platform, deflecting the attacks.

As we watched, glimmering magic like rainbow-hewn glass drew up from the soil and into the sky, creeping upwards, slowly but steadily.

It was working.

Our guards were looking south and exclaiming. Sparing a

glance in that direction, golden armoured figures zipped through the sky, shooting beams of power over the demons as if they'd been made to kill. My heart lifted as I recognised Odeelia being carried through the air by her people as she wielded some weapon that was taking out fifty demons at a time.

We were all drenched with sweat as our powers combined with the power of the Ellythian people.

I could feel it in the same way I could feel Boneweaver Island thrumming through me, I could feel the people of Lota Island, every soldier and mage, their essences combining to power this shield with such a strength that I struggled to maintain the concentration to keep my mind sane.

Raen and Kai slowly approached in the sky with the two bodies draped across Kai's lap. But I swallowed my panic down and put all my rage, anger and turmoil into the shield that was manifesting before my eyes as those two bodies flew steadily towards us, Odeelia's guards flanking them to ward against enemy arrows.

Both bodies were whole, but limp and ashen. We watched as the commander of the Queen's Guard ordered the shields down for Raen to pass through. The Old One's raven form glided smoothly over our heads and behind us, where Pia and I turned to look at a sobbing Kai holding an unresponsive Rani to his chest. I could not see any signs of life as two of my healers rushed over to her and Yulara, similarly not showing any movement.

Pia and I locked eyes. Our faces crumpled at the same time.

Our spell faltered as we all stumbled over the words of the spell, but the shield around Lota Island remained strong where it had stopped halfway up the sky.

"Rani!" Kai cried. His cry broke my heart all over again, and I squeezed my eyes shut against the onslaught of pain in my chest, the way it felt like my heart was bleeding. Bhairavi squeezed my hand until the feeling went out of it, her way of comforting me, or maintaining contact, I wasn't sure.

Behind me, my healers murmured in low voices and I felt them stepping away from Rani and Yulara. Kai's broken wail made a line of demons on the battlefield crumple to the earth, their bones shattered. My tears fell, my shoulders wracking as I sobbed out the words to the spell.

The Boneweaver Bow might have put their bodies back together, but it had not brought them back to life. It did not have that power.

Rani was dead. Rani was dead. Rani and Yulara were both dead.

"Concentrate, high priestesses!" Raen's deep voice came from behind me. "For Ellythia! For those who still live and depend on you. Don't let Rani's sacrifice be in vain."

For Ellythia. For Rani.

I squeezed the tears from my eyes and aggressively sniffed them away as Pia and I took back up the spell, loudly in the night, until we were shouting the words. *Screaming* them so that our throats turned raw, so this pain was for something.

The glass shield inched further overhead, the sides from the other ends of the island creeping towards each other in a clear dome in the night sky.

My priestess mark burned, my bones burned from the intensity the magic demanded, and my brain felt like it was on fire.

For Pia. For Malika. For Kai and Raen and Atax. For my

brothers and sisters, we screamed our spell over the battlefield.

With a low boom that shook our platform, the pieces of the shield met high above us and we were thrust away from each other, silver power sparking.

The demons below us only pressed our forces harder. I turned to go to Rani, but Bhairavi's hand was on my shoulder, Saarika's hand on Pia's.

"And now," panted Ellythia's General, her eyes hard on mine, "we must fight. We mourn our dead later."

She was right. We still had an entire horde of demons in our city.

The ground shook as Pia closed her eyes and screamed.

But it was not a cry of pain. It was a cry of pure, focused *rage*.

Pia then met my eyes and wiped her own emerald greens. We set our shoulders and did what Lota women did. We fought for our family.

Pia, somehow still with power left, propelled herself over the platform railing and directly into the fray with her silver magic. Her guards all shouted in alarm and hastened down the ladder to follow her.

Bhairavi summoned Xalya's axe and climbed back upon the waiting Lightfeather, the others taking back up their vehicles and mounts.

"Come on, cousin!" Pia roared from below, viciously swiping at the neck of a demon with Matrika's golden sword, blood splattering her face. She flicked her fingers at me and both Malika and I were scooped up and tossed into the air. I landed on the battlefield next to Malika, in a crash of my own lightning, my power excited to dance.

Kai and Raen landed protectively around us, their obsidian blades flashing so fast they were a blur.

"For Ellythia!" Pia cried.

The Ellythians around us roared as they fought.

We fought back-to-back, my cousin, Malika and I, my lightning flashing along my sword, eviscerating any demon it met and deflecting any magical attack. Pia's silver power exploded outwards with such force that her immediate area cleared of enemies for ten paces every time she used it. Her guards were forced to back away and assist the other soldiers, just as I suspected Pia had intended. Malika's fire burst out of her hands, sending the demons screaming.

In the distance, Odeelia's forces bade the Ellythians give them a free path to blast the demons trying to run.

They were trying to run back to the harbour, but Pia's shields did not let them leave. Trapped, they screamed under the weapons of the carnal fae.

It was then that I saw two tigers leap into the fray, quickly followed by an entire pack of wolves and a flock of eagles.

"Old Ones!" Kai's grief-hoarse voice cried. He waved at them and a lion roared in reply.

My mouth dropped open as a massive cobra I recognised whipped her huge, muscular tail, flinging several demons through the air, only to be caught in the jaws of excited wolves.

Pia laughed maniacally. "Help!" she cried, viciously swiping a massive demon warrior across the abdomen. "Everyone's come to help us!"

Then Zale came bursting out behind the Old Ones in his human form, his sword lashing out, Atax behind him, searching the battlefield.

A fireball hit a Daanav square in the face, its light telling

Atax where Malika was. Our lion grinned as he fought his way to us.

"The palace is secure!" Zale shouted to Pia. "We've driven them all back here."

"Thank you, King Boneweaver!" Pia called back, saluting with her sword.

Zale didn't even get to reply because it was then that a sharp screech struck our eardrums like a nail on glass.

It felt like the entire battlefield stopped to look at the glass shield. The Reaper, on his chariot, was coasting outside the shield, one finger pointed at the shimmering glass. The screeching sounded again and we all, demons included, covered our ears, grimacing against the pain.

"The fucker is trying to break it!" Malika's voice echoed around the harbour.

But it didn't work. No mark was made on the shield, not even a crack.

The Reaper wheeled his chariot back, and in the distance, a sickly green ball of light appeared, quickly growing to the size of his chariot. We collectively cringed as he flung it directly at our shield.

The green light skittered off harmlessly, dripping down like water off the back of a seal.

Pia's laugh was a sweet, savage melody in my ears.

The Ellythians cheered, and the battle picked up once again.

Between the three combined forces, the demon's numbers grew smaller, until they dwindled and we picked them off like berries on a bush, such that Odeelia and the Old Ones were over enthusiastic and fighting over kills.

Eventually, fae, humans, and Old Ones stalked around the harbour, hunting demons who'd resorted to hiding. Pia and I stood ten paces apart, panting, covered in blood, just looking at the quieting battlefield and the injured being collected by the White Widows and my own purple-robed acolytes. Malika and Atax picked their way over to us, similarly covered in gore and bickering quietly.

A cool, sweet wind brushed past me, but it did not smell of the battle.

Zale appeared at my side, covered in black blood. "Step back, my love." He nodded to indicate Pia.

I raised my brows but did as he asked.

It was then I felt it, a rumble deep in the earth, a primal groaning of the island.

The air became charged with colossal, other-worldly power. Between one breath and the next, the seven Goddesses of Ellythia all appeared in a semi circle around Pia.

Umali, with lightning crackling around her naked, midnight skin, charged with the chaotic energy of rage. Agnolthi stood in her dark robes, her eyes flicking to me and back to Pia. Luana's seductive smirk graced her shapely lips, the thin gauze of her gown leaving nothing to the imagination. Somewhere behind me, Odeelia gasped.

Lisanthi stood next to Luana, the Mother in her robes of red, her now belly swollen with budding life. Cherimani's long curling locks bounced as she did, the trickster goddess grinning, her bangles chiming as she clapped. Xalya stood with her bloody axe, her silver armour shining with its own power. Lastly, Cholnayak stood, the keeper of the end of all things, her crone's form hunched, silver hair glimmering, staff thumping the earth; once, twice, three times.

The other high priestesses gathered behind me, and this time, because everyone could see the seven Goddesses, the Ellythians began to make their way over to them, some openly sobbing at the sight of the celestial beings in our presence.

Pia stood in the middle of them all, a bloodied warrior, a dripping sword clutched in a strong fist by her side. Blood and dirt streaked her face, her arms glistening with the sweat of her exertion.

In a flash of light, a stunning crown of gold lotuses and diamonds appeared on her dark hair.

It was Lisanthi that said in a resonant alto that could be heard from the northern mountains of Lotus Island to the southern beaches of Tiger Island, *"Pia Rahana Lota, Keeper of Matrika's sword, liberator of Ellythia, blood-forged, death-forged, exile-forged we dub thee, Priestess Prime. Queen of Ellythia. Do you accept your title?"*

Pia took a breath through her nose and gave them a single, weary nod.

The high priestesses except me all dropped to their knees. "The Queen of Ellythia," we murmured.

Every man and woman on the battlefield dropped to their knees. Zale and I bowed our heads.

Umali spoke last, in a voice like an immortal storm. *"You are worthy of your people."*

Pia's eyes lit up the night before she turned to Cholnayak and, with a look of intense, glaring disdain, shoved a finger towards the queen's platform where Rani and Yulara's bodies still lay. Some silent words seem to pass between them, Pia never taking her lethal glare off the crone Goddess.

And then Cholnayak dipped her head once and the seven Goddesses vanished in a wind of wild, but soft magic.

A deep groan sounded from the queen's platform and Pia, Malika, Kai and I promptly sprinted for Rani.

As we all ran up to the platform, we found Rani and Yulara, lying on their backs, their eyes closed, but their cheeks pink, their chests rising and falling with full and steady breaths.

"Goddess!" Malika cried, falling on top of Rani while Pia tried to assess them. I let my magic out into them—but it found nothing to heal, their bodies seemingly whole except for the fact that they would not wake. Neither responded to Malika's shaking, or Pia's prodding, seemingly unconscious, but otherwise well.

"Look," Kai said, on his knees, reaching over to brush at something between the two women.

They were holding hands. Well, *clenching* hands would have been more accurate for the way that it was impossible to separate the grip they had on each other. "Yulara's imprisonment spell is gone," Kai said, glancing up at me. "I saw it when we first met them. I knew her father had done it."

I explained how Yulara and I had met while Raen levitated both young women so we could get them to the palace.

Neither stirred as Raen moved them and neither would let each other go.

"So that's why you maimed them," Malika said softly, patting Rani's cheek gently as she soared in front of us.

"They deserved it," Kai said, quietly. "Everyone deserves the freedom to love who they please."

As Malika and Raen took the two young women up to the safety of the palace, Atax approached me and the grief in his eyes almost sent me to my knees. He dropped before me, taking my hand as my own tears spilled over, knowing what he was about to say.

"My queen," he said, pressing my hand to his forehead. "I am—I can't—You must never forgive me for what I did."

I blinked as I glanced at Zale, his own face drawn, his fists clenched. I bent before Atax, putting my arms around his neck, pressing my forehead to his temple.

"I forgive you Atax," I said. "How could I not forgive my brother for doing something he was not in control of. It was not you, I know that." A dampness on my shoulder made me lean back and swipe my thumbs across both of his cheeks. I kissed him on the forehead. "I am sorry for what the Reaper made you do." I looked up at my husband, who watched me with his face fallen. "What he made all of you do. We will rebuild. We'll do better." I stood and brought Atax up with me. Kai surged forward, sniffing ferociously and I brought him too, into my arms and kissed him on his moon-white hair. "All will be well, Kai."

Zale watched me comfort his brothers, his blue eyes glistening as he took a deep breath and exhaled slowly.

When Wobbles whispered from Zale's shoulder, we all heard it. "Love. Hope."

WE SPENT THE NEXT TWO DAYS CLEANING UP THE BATTLEFIELD, healing the injured, and burning demon bodies. Both the carnal fae and the Old Ones remained to help, though bickering inevitably ensued between the two groups and the Ellythians, especially when some of the Old Ones couldn't let go of the old habit of eating the demons. Odeelia declared it uncouth, yet her eyes glittered every time any of my court passed her by, sighing dramatically. The Ellythians were in part horrified and mesmerised by both foreign courts, and it was only a matter of time before they were all slapping each other on the back and laughing, or in some cases, crying together.

War had made friends of us all.

I think my Old Ones were just happy to be out of the Eternal Forest and out in the world above, doing something meaningful. Our court was also happy to see Zale and I together with them as family once again. Ulanna aggressively hugged me when we first reunited, promising she would keep a firm eye on everyone and stop them from getting into too much trouble.

When I confronted Zale about the two carved up bodies he'd sent us on the life raft, he sheepishly rubbed the back of the neck in a very un-kingly manner. But it was Kai who enthusiastically explained it to me. "We were trying to get around the Reaper's command, my queen. So I found two demons and tortured them until they thought they were the humans from the school." He bounced on the balls of his feet, very proud of himself. "When I asked them who they were, they told us, and we killed them. Thus," he waved his hand, "we followed our orders."

I smiled wryly. It was a very round-a-bout way of doing it, but it got the job done, I supposed.

We sent an owl to tell Armsmisstress Vari and Lady Trisana back on Boneweaver Island about what had happened, and I was sure more than a few of them would want to travel back here. Zale sent a few of our court as well, because there could still be demons lurking about.

Pia was Queen of Ellythia and it felt like the most right thing in the world. She assumed the role like something deep inside of her had been waiting to do it. Aunt Parsha embraced Pia when we returned to the palace, and upon seeing the Goddess-given crown on her head, Pia's father and brother broke down crying.

They knew what it meant instantly. Perhaps Uncle Tuskus most of all, had known for a long time.

Everyone in the palace accepted it, especially since most of the Ellythians had been present on the battlefield when the Goddesses had come.

It didn't take long for Pia to take us all aside to discuss the Reaper's next move. As much as we'd had a victory here on Lota Island, this war was not over yet.

"Word has come from His Majesty," Pia said, nodding to the owl king as we sat down at her queen's council chambers. Malika, Atax, Kai and Raen also joined us, along with Bhairavi, Othar, the Owl King, Whole-Feather, Aunt Parsha, Uncle Tuskus and Paalus.

Lightfeather, sitting on the balcony rail beside Whole-Feather, fluffed his wings. "The wind whispered of a victory," he said in his deep voice. "Saraya Yasani Voltanius, High

Priestess of Umali, has successfully taken back Lobrathia as queen, using only seven of her warrior midwives."

Tears sprung into my eyes.

"Only seven warriors?" choked Uncle Tuskus.

"You've never met one of Umali's high priestesses," Aunt Parsha said wryly. "I'm not entirely surprised. Nor do I envy the chaos she no doubt reigned upon the demons. We could feel it from here."

Zale, Pia, and I exchanged a glance. We'd also felt Saraya's lightning coming from Quartz that eventful night.

Malika thumped a fist on the table. "What a thing to see that! Like the stories from the old days." She elbowed Atax next to her as if to indicate that he knew about said 'old days'.

"What will happen next, Zale?" Pia asked evenly. "What had you planned?"

"He'll attempt Quartz again," Zale said, glancing at me. "He won't admit he's lost Ellythia to anyone, and he'll head back there to secure the Quartz Quarry. It's the seat of his power over the continent, and he was awfully interested in my sister-in-law from the way he spoke about her. It was almost as if he had a personal vendetta against her. He'll head there with his dark fae forces and every demon he's got. He'll only be able to take the rest of the continent once he has that."

I'd known this was coming, but my stomach still clenched at the thought of another battle.

"Dark fae forces?" Pia repeated. "Goddess, I've forgotten they were on his side. So they'll have fae magic at their side, too."

"My sister was supposed to marry Prince Daxian of the Black Court Fae before she found her mate. No doubt he has a vendetta against her too," I said.

But Lightfeather was clearing his throat. "The Reaper has

killed all the Dark Fae kings," he said sombrely. "He has the princes taking over rule now as means of control."

"He killed *all* their fathers?" Malika breathed. "Won't that make them hate him?"

"Their allegiance is uncertain," Lightfeather said. "Time will tell."

"Whichever way they go," Zale said, "Quartz still has a large host to contend with. What we brought with us to Ellythia was only a fraction of his demonic forces. The Reaper has many demon courts on his side." He paused and took my hand in a tight grip that made my heart clench for him. "My brothers and I are responsible, in part, for the darkness that has spread over this Earth. Altara and I have decided that we will be taking our court to fight in Quartz. We still have the ship Odeelia loaned us."

My heart pounded at the thought of another bloody battle, but it also swelled at the way Zale was ready to help my sister.

Pia nodded slowly before rubbing her eyes. She looked tired, and in more ways than one. "You'll take an Ellythian company with you," she said easily. "There'll be more than a few interested soldiers, I'm sure."

"You think so?" I asked, scooting to the edge of my seat, my hands tightening on the edge of the table. "They've fought so hard already. We couldn't ask—"

"You can," Aunt Parsha said firmly. "If the Reaper takes Quartz, he'll eventually try for Ellythia again, in time. The smart thing to do is to end it there. And to do that, you need power." She clenched her fist on the table, her lined face glowing. "It would be nice to see something outside of Ellythia. If I was in my youth, I would put my own name down."

"Me too," said Paalus excitedly, "If I was older."

Pia grinned at him. "Well, if this all goes well, I'm sure we'll be travelling freely between Ellythia and Lobrathia."

We sat in silence for a moment because never in Ellythia's history had there been fully open travel between the two places. Pia grinned at us all. "Time for a change, don't you think?"

My heart lifted as I grinned back at my cousin, and Zale squeezed my hand from under the table. "I believe it is."

If this all went well, the Lotus, Boneweaver and Lobrathian seats would be joined in a truce the likes of which had never been seen. Not even in the old times. Was it too much to hope for?

"It sounds too good to be true," Bhairavi said stiffly. "The battle fought in Quartz will be on land. It'll be worse than what we saw here."

She was right.

"And we have yet to find a way to capture the Reaper," I said, glancing at Othar and then Raen. "I have every available priestess of my order searching through the catacomb library."

"Mine too," said Othar. "It's only a matter of time before we find something."

"You should send word to Saraya," Pia said, nodding to the owls. "Give her a little boost of morale? I'm sure she's been as stressed as we have."

"Whole-Feather," I said quickly, "send word to my sister. Tell her we are coming. She won't like that, but tell her nothing else."

"At once, Your Majesty," Whole-Feather bowed and leapt off the railing, his tawny wings catching the sunlight--a sun that Pia had brought back to Ellythia.

Uncle Tuskus said, "We need to—"

"What?" Pia said loudly into the queen's earpiece she always kept on now.

I raised my brows at Bhairavi, who raised her own back at me. We both went to reach into our pockets for our own priestess earpieces, but Pia waved her hand and rose from her seat.

"There's a Traveller from… somewhere." She frowned at Aunt Parsha. "Jaya is babbling excitedly and I can't understand. But she said for us all to come quickly."

ALTARA

"*Traveller?*" Parsha asked, hauling herself up. "Dear Goddess, I haven't seen one of those in years! Quick, everyone, before he pops off elsewhere!"

"What do you mean *Traveller*, when you say it like that?" Malika said as we all hurried out of the council chamber, Pia in the lead.

"Pops off elsewhere?" Paalus said excitedly. "A Traveller is a person who can travel between worlds, Lady Malika!"

Kai let out a whoop and set off at a full sprint down the corridor, Paalus running after him as Malika grumbled about 'not being a lady'.

Pia just laughed, breaking into a jog herself.

When we all got to the entrance hall, the Queen's Guard had their swords angled on a young man a little older than me. The first thing I noticed was the mild smile he had on his handsome, tanned face as the guards scowled at him. His skin was paler than any of us with Ellythian blood, and even if it weren't for his skin, it was quite obvious that he couldn't possibly be from here.

Jaya, swathed in a sheer pink cloak, clapped her hands when she saw us. "Come see, come see!"

"He is definitely a Traveller," Aunt Parsha said, her eyes alert on the young man. "But it is always wise to be wary of Travellers—they always know things the rest of us do not."

When we stopped before the guards, Pia impatiently waved them away and they parted so we could see him properly. He was a little shorter than my Old Ones, six feet at least, with long mahogany hair that brushed the collar of an unusual thick black jacket-- definitely not suited to Ellythia's perpetual summer climate. His legs were covered with a thick black material I'd never seen before, and he had sturdy black boots with silver buckles. As unusual as his clothes were, my magic was responding to his strange power—it was at once foreign and sort of flighty. Like a fledgling bird that had just learned how to use its wings. At the same time, his eyes flicked about the hall in a very observant way and the flirtatious lopsided grin he bore told me he had, at one time, been a troublemaker, and perhaps finally started to grow out of it.

"You're a Traveller?" Pia asked curiously in Ellythian, stepping forward to stare at him with her head cocked. Her glittering sword was at her side—as it always was, and though her features were stunning, the muscle on her body and the way she carried herself told everyone that she knew how to fight. Not that any of *us* needed reminding.

The young man's dark brows shot up as he beheld the Queen of Ellythia, no doubt taking those details in, and when he spoke, it was in the common tongue we spoke on the continent, only with a strange accent. "Yeah, I'm a Traveller, and I've come from Chrysalis. That's supposed to be a reputable place that you guys know about, according to this pretty young lady."

Jaya clasped her hands and blushed when she was indicated by him. He spoke with such a casual, carefree manner—as if he didn't have ten warriors with their swords angled at him, not to mention Zale and my brothers glowering at him.

Malika seemed to take this all in offence because she hissed, "You are addressing the Queen of Ellythia, young man!"

"Ah, of course, Your Majesty." The Traveller quickly swept a gallant bow with a confidence that suggested he'd done it before. "Sorry, we don't really have those where I come from."

Perhaps not—he just thought fast on his feet.

We all exchanged a silent look.

"Chrysalis School?" Pia asked, switching to an accented common tongue. "Where they teach magic to adults? And how can you understand Ellythian?"

"That's the one. Nice people over there." He nodded with a faint smile as if he were at a garden party talking among friends and I couldn't help but relax a little. "Travellers can understand all languages, but speaking is a little harder."

But Kai clearly couldn't help it any longer. He bounded forward and grabbed the young man's hand, bringing it to his nose for sniffing. "What's your name? You smell funny."

"I'm trying a new aftershave." The Traveller rubbed his clean-shaven jaw as if he was embarrassed. "My name's Hugh. Hugh Carter."

"What is after-shave?" Kai asked.

Hugh watched him with amusement. "It's a thing you put on your skin... well, after you shave."

"That's funny, I just rub dirt on."

I hid a smile.

"Yeah," Hugh Carter said, as if he didn't find that odd.

"Well, I'm here to speak to the High Priestess of Ag-nol-thee. Is that how you say it?"

"What do you want with my wife?" Zale stepped forward a little threateningly. His common tongue was accented, but he pronounced it well, and it only made him sexier.

Hugh blanched a little at Zale's glower, but as Kai shoved his hands down Hugh's pant pockets, he didn't protest. Kai pulled out a tiny yellow packet and held it up to sniff it.

"Professor Clementine Eyesmith sent me to speak to her," said Hugh, eyes shifting between Kai and Zale warily. But I saw him note Wobbles on Zale's shoulder, and his eyes lit up as if he were delighted.

"Eyesmith!" Grandmother Parsha said, stepping forward. "Boy, the princess from the Court of Light is alive?"

"Yes, ma'am. As batshit crazy as ever, but we call her *professor*, not princess."

A strange turn of phrase, but I pocketed that thought.

"The Court of Light?" Pia said, frowning. "That's the abandoned court in the Solar Fae Realm, correct, Grandmother?"

"Yes, the royal family fled after pledging their daughter, Clementine, to the Reaper as his mate to try and temper his power when he got out of hand."

Zale grabbed my hand possessively as I said, "Wait, Zale, you told me the Reaper killed his mate?"

"That's what we were told," Zale growled, as if the thought of such a thing angered him.

"He's had a few mates, our Reaper," Parsha said, not taking her eyes off Hugh Carter. "He killed the first and rejected his second when he eventually found her. That's the story we heard, anyway."

"Sounds like something he'd do," I murmured. Turning

back to Hugh Carter, I said, "So this Princess Clementine Eyesmith sent you for what, exactly? I am the High Priestess of Agnolthi."

The young man straightened his spine as the attention came back to him. "She was summoned by the Princess Saraya and told them about this thing called the Darkmaul Dagger. That's the weapon they're going to make to contain the Reaper, since he can't be killed. But she said that if you guys are going to capture him successfully, you'll need a second weapon. He'll see it coming otherwise."

"What type of weapon?" I asked, though I thought I already knew.

"She called it Agnolthi's Bow. An arrow shot into the eyes ought to do it." My stomach flopped at the thought of using the power of the bow again. Hugh continued, "Into all of his eyes. Apparently, he has six. That's to stop him from seeing out so you can dagger him." Hugh mimed stabbing himself in the gut.

I nodded slowly. "I understand, Hugh Carter. Thank you."

Kai, who had been steadily unloading Hugh's pockets and holding random things up to the light this entire time, said, "What's this?"

Hugh reached for the green oblong-shaped tube. "That's my lighter. Oh, you can have that one, if you like." He took back the 'lighter', and let Kai have the yellow packet. "It's chewing gum. Freshens your breath. Don't swallow it though, it'll stay in your stomach for seven years otherwise." Kai cocked his head as he began excitedly opening the yellow packet. "Anyway, I think that was all Professor Clementine had to say."

"What does she want in exchange for this information?" Pia asked suspiciously. "What does she stand to gain?"

"She wants him dead, doesn't she?" Hugh said quietly, a distant look in his eye. "These dark beings, we want them all dead. For the good of mankind."

"And beast-kind," Kai said around the white lolly he was now chewing on.

"Yeah." Hugh put his hands in his pockets. "And we were hoping if *we* needed anything later on… that you would assist us with information and whatnot."

Pia nodded. "Of course, we would return the favour. I would like to visit Chrysalis School one day myself."

Hugh grinned, looking Pia up and down a little flirtatiously. "Yeah, it's a cool place. You should definitely come."

"Cool…" Malika narrowed her eyes at Hugh.

He smiled at Malika too, until Atax began softly growling. Hugh cleared his throat and took a flat tin carefully out of the inside of his jacket. "This is Jupiter. He's a dragonfly asleep inside. You can use him to send a message to me in case you need anything. Just open it and he'll wake up. They can travel between worlds, just like me." He stepped forward and handed the tin to Pia, casually ignoring the way Malika, Atax, and Kai closed around him as he did so. "Your Majesty," Hugh finished.

Pia took the tin. "Thank you, Hugh Carter. We appreciate the information."

"If that's all, I'm off then. Bye." Hugh waved a hand, and right before our eyes, he disappeared from existence.

Paalus gasped loudly, and Kai laughed in amusement.

"Goddess," Malika said, making wide eyes at me.

"Quartz," Raen said suddenly. We all turned to stare at him, but he was looking at me. "Your arrow needs to be made of quartz. It's the only material you can infuse enough power into for the plan to work."

A bubbling sort of excitement struck me. "I've never shot an arrow made of quartz before. Zale can make it, can't you, husband?"

The corner of Zale's mouth lifted. "I would make you an arrow made of the moon if I could." I grinned at him under my eyelashes as Kai began talking loudly about his new 'chewing gum'.

"Let's check the stores," Pia said. "My grandmother was hiding all sorts of things down there."

After the excitement of the Travellers' exit died down, we went under the palace. It turned out that there was indeed an entire underground chamber full of the precious types of quartz the Lotus Palace had been importing from Lobrathia over the centuries. We took Bhairavi with us, naturally the weapons expert, and we all combed through the shelves until Zale pointed at a set of dark blue crystals with a sheen of gold. "That'll work best with our combined powers," he said. It did sort of have the colouring of his power and the gold in it called to me.

We took a large chunk of it, and for the rest of the day, Zale chipped at it with one of Raen's obsidian daggers, mixed with his own power.

"It needs to have enough power to be able to split itself into six," he said as he worked. "As much faith as I have in your power to shoot, I'd rather you not draw the Boneweaver Bow six times."

In truth, I had been wondering how many bones I'd have to break to manage six draws, so it was just lucky that one of us had the wits to think of making the arrow split itself. When I told Zale as much, he smirked over the blue quartz.

"I got the idea from the time you came to get me from

Odeelia's court. You were so angry that you summoned three bows to hover in the air, ready to strike her all at once."

"That'll be one to tell the grandchildren," Raen said with a grin.

Zale went still. When he raised his head to look at me, his blue eyes were like the sea on a summer's night. "When this is over, Altara Boneweaver, I'm going to *fill* you with my children." He spoke with such an intensity that it made both me and Raen blush.

56

ALTARA

In the nights between the Battle of the Harbour, as it was now being called, and our departure to Quartz, Zale and I spent most of the time in a rabid sort of lovemaking. My husband was virtually insatiable in his lust, and so was I, in the way we clung to and moved against each other's bodies. When he was inside me, we exchanged magic, sometimes vigorously and sometimes slowly and carefully, with Zale leaving no doubt in my mind that he loved me. I made sure I returned the gesture, with his groans and soft murmurs in my ear only spurring me on until we were sweaty and spent *and* full of each other's magic.

"I'm never leaving your side again," he murmured, half asleep, against my hair on the night before we left. "That's including the battle in Lobrathia."

"Yes. Yes, I know," I murmured sleepily, brushing his arm up and down until his breathing settled and I knew he was asleep, even though his arms tightened around me. And I thought that, with his scent in my nose, and his arms around me, this feeling of being eternally safe was something I could get used to.

But there was still a war to win, and so the next day, we silently got dressed and went to meet the others in Rani's room, which had become an unofficial meeting point for us in the mornings. Although our friend and her love had not yet awoken, we still wanted to include them in everything. In my eyes, Yulara had redeemed herself by dying for Rani, because no doubt Rani had tried to stop her from joining her on her 'mission'. Malika had never left Rani's side, and she had taken to sleeping on a pallet on the floor in their room. She and Atax were getting more and more unbearable by the day. This morning, we arrived to find Atax saying, "Good morning, Lady Malika." He reached to touch her hand, but Malika turned her nose up at him.

"Oh, so it's *Lady Malika* now?" She glared daggers at him.

"Would you two just fuck already?" Pia's exasperated voice came from behind me.

Kai choked on his coconut water.

"Finally, someone said it!" I agreed, grabbing onto Zale's forearm and batting my eyelashes at him. He brushed my cheek. "It's working *wonders* for us."

"Yes, Zale is far less volatile these past two days," Pia agreed. "Malika, as your queen, I order you to bed Atax by the time you return to Ellythia, or I will tell the harbour guard to arrest you on sight."

Malika whipped around and gaped at Pia.

"Don't worry, we'll make sure of it," I said. "Everyone ready to leave? I don't want to miss it."

"You'll make it on time, according to Whole-Feather," Pia said. "All the charged quartz has been loaded. And apparently some of the Old Ones are swimming in?"

"There are a few Boneweavers in our court who don't mind their shark forms," Zale confirmed. To our surprise, we found Wobbles hoisting his shell-body over Rani and sitting himself between the two women. He crossed his legs over each other and reclined back on the pillow as if to settle in

"Wobbles help," he squeaked, nodding at Zale.

My husband was smiling softly. "I think they'll need him more than me for a little while."

"Well then," Pia said, taking in a deep breath, "none of you *dare* die over there. We've been through enough as it is." She indicated to Rani and Yulara.

I grabbed Pia and hugged her. "We'll do our best."

Soft growls from behind me were confirmation from Zale and my brothers.

We headed down to the harbour, armed and ready to meet the two large ships that would carry the volunteering Ellythians and the entire court of the Old Ones. To my surprise, we had a big host of a hundred Ellythians helping us, all led by Lady Reeta, with her swirling blue eyes and now sturdy legs.

"I've had enough of being restrained," she said ruefully, in response to my raised brows. "I'll be happy to adventure out of Ellythia and see what the Continent is like."

When we'd asked Malika if she wanted to come, she'd only said, "Are you kidding?" and began packing a bag. Malika had hardly left the village Levu, on Boneweaver Island, and her zest for travel had been awakened during the trip to Lota Island. Ellythians in general did not leave their queendom, so more than a few soldiers jumped at the chance, weary as they were.

The Old Ones of our court, on the other hand, had been stuck in the Eternal Forest for so long they were also keen to see the Continent. I also thought that some of them were curious about the kingdom that I, their queen, had come from.

After a little thought, it was decided that Ulanna Boneweaver would stay behind on Boneweaver Island as Zale's representative.

With quartz speeding us along, Lady Reeta estimated it would take us a single day to reach Quartz Harbour. It might very well ruin the boats, she warned, but Zale insisted the Reaper would act swiftly.

The zekar refused to come, stating they'd had enough of war, so the Ellythians brought a company of horses, since I'd mentioned it would be a bit of travel between the harbour and Quartz city itself. We boarded our ships, loading on the provisions as we went. There was a large party to see us off, including my fellow high priestesses. There were priestesses from my temple as well, taking a quick break from the recovery and healing efforts. Mahi, my battle priestess, offered me a bundle wrapped in black cloth.

"We found these in our stores before battle," she said, opening the bundle. "But we didn't know what half of them did, so we didn't want to use them. Esha did some research and said that *this* one"—she pointed to an odd arrow with the head of a crescent moon, instead of a shaft—"is an astral arrow. It can go through solid things as well as strike astral demons. The warrior midwives fight against them in Lobrathia, so we thought it would be of use. You can load all of them with magic."

"Thank you, Mahi," I said. "Zale and I will experiment with them on the trip over. I'm sure they will come into use."

We said our goodbyes, and with the high priestesses blessing us, and Jaya playing her flute to bid us a safe journey,

Lady Reeta activated our quartz and we sped out of the swelling waves of Lota Harbour.

To Quartz, I thought, looking at the horizon. We were going back to the place I'd called home for eighteen years.

As if he knew I'd had some nostalgic thought, Zale came and encircled my waist from behind, kissing my neck. Now, I thought, looking around at Kai, Atax, Raen and Malika exploring the ship in front of me, my home was with Zale. It could *only* be with Zale and the Old Ones.

That thought made me a little sad as we sailed over the rough sea. Perhaps it even felt like a little betrayal to Saraya. She also had her own husband by now, and if she had claimed Quartz as her own kingdom to rule, then surely she would accept that I, too, had claimed Zale and Boneweaver Island with him?

"I can't wait to see my sister again," I said to Zale. "It's been months. We only got that glimpse of her power down in the demon realm."

"I couldn't imagine being away from my brothers that long," he replied. "But I admit I am curious about my brother-in-law."

"Me too," I said. "In that, he's the brother of the man she was *supposed* to marry. What a scandal that would have been in the fae courts for my rule-abiding, law-loving sister! I thought you forcing me to marry you was scandalous enough."

"And I'll never apologise for it."

I smiled softly as I thought of Saraya. "There's something I need to tell you about my sister, Zale." I turned in the circle of his arms. "Glacine hurt her. She... hurt the both of us. With me, she took me to the Butcher that one time, but with Saraya..." I swallowed. The pain of it had never really left me. "Saraya tried to hide it from me, but I knew that Glacine used to whip her." I stared at Zale's chest, my throat tight. "We could never *do* anything about it. We were only young, and she was the queen, with so much power. After our mother died, we were vulnerable. It went on for years."

"That's why you tried to kill her that day in the demon realm," Zale said softly, his thumbs making small, soothing circles at my back.

"Yes, but…" I looked up at him. "I know Saraya will want to do it. Especially now that Glacine betrayed our father."

"We will help her do it, then," Zale said. "We'll help destroy the people who did this to our family."

"Our family," I repeated softly, plucking at a thread on his shirt.

He kissed the top of my head. "*Our* family."

I wished my mother could have met him. I wished my father could have met Zale and my brothers. My mother would have *loved* Pia and Malika and Rani like her own. In this war, we fought not only for the living, but for the memory of the dead, too.

WE WERE ABOUT AN HOUR FROM SHORE, AND IT WAS WELL INTO the night, when Whole-Feather, who'd been scouting ahead, let out a low warning hoot high above us. We cleared a portion of the deck for him to land.

"The wind speaks of dark magic," he said seriously, his eyes glistening orbs by the quartz-lamps. "And the demons are on the march to Quartz."

A chill ran down my spine and I gripped Zale's hand tightly. "And my sister?"

"Out with her army on the front lines," he replied smoothly, fluffing his wings a little. "She is a fierce queen, Your Majesty."

I grinned without humour. "She's better with a sword than I am," I said to the ship in general. "And what about the fae forces?"

"Most have defected from the Reaper and are fighting with the humans." The entire ship let out a collective sigh of relief. "Although," Whole-Feather continued, "their forces look smaller than the last time I'd seen them. And they are led by the fae princes turned kings. It seems they were not happy about the Reaper executing their fathers."

"They'll provide some magical coverage," Zale said, nodding. "This is good news."

As Whole-Feather took back to the air, Zale turned to me. "You and I will need to focus on the Reaper," he said. "If they have created the dagger to contain him, as the Traveller said, then we will need to work together with Saraya to trap him."

"Right," I said, taking a deep breath and flexing my bow arm. "I hope they're ready."

We were twenty minutes from shore when Whole-Feather silently landed on our ship again. "Demon ships headed to Quartz Harbour," he said quickly. "Just as you said, Your Majesty." He bowed to Zale. "Ten vessels."

"Thank you, Whole-Feather," Zale said calmly. "That's about how many I expected, considering the losses in Ellythia. They'll have no obsidian powder left. It should be easy to take them out."

Zale had told us about how they'd planned to take Lobrathia both from the water and from land. It was a smart move, to attack from both sides, but the demons were not expecting *us* to take them out from behind.

He nodded to the designated team we'd assigned to the task. Raen took Malika and Atax on his back as a huge raven, while a couple of other Old Ones took shark forms to destroy their hulls from the undersides.

Zale was getting antsy, and while we hadn't planned on it, I gave him a pointed look and summoned my bow. His face brightened before he burst into his eagle form.

"Get on, wife," he said.

I waved at Kai, who pouted in return, as I climbed onto Zale's back. "See you on land, my little flower," I said to him.

He beamed at us and, as we took flight into the night, Kai ran along the deck, following us until he couldn't any more. I turned back to look out over the ocean. In the distance, I saw land. My stomach clenched with old recognition.

Lobrathia.

My heart soared to see Quartz Harbour again. How much had changed since I'd last lain eyes on those buildings? But all was not as it was when I'd left, with a bustling and busy harbour. Now, all was quiet and dark.

But I didn't have time to think on it because the demon ships were already ablaze when we reached them, with Malika hooting with laughter as she rained fire upon them from the middle. I began on their left flank, Zale wheeling me into position while I filled arrows with lightning and shot them at demon mages first, shattering any shields and then shooting the decks with lightning that set the ships burning within minutes. I was practised, having done this a hundred times at the battle of Lotus Harbour.

"A beautiful sight, my love," Zale said in approval.

"Why thank you, husband. And look, Malika and Atax seem to finally be cooperating."

Atax held Malika tightly around her waist while Raen wheeled them strategically over the ships. Malika, on the other hand, was cackling madly, with the wind in her hair and throwing red hot fireballs down onto the enemy. Both were laughing, and I swore Atax gave Malika a sneaky kiss on the neck.

Within minutes, the water was ablaze, and we had to direct our own two ships to sail around them right into the silent Quartz Harbour.

"This land is cold," Zale said, shivering a little under me as we flew into Lobrathia and waited for our host to lay anchor. Behind us, some Old Ones were swimming ashore, while others were rowing to land with the Ellythians and the horses. If the battle had already started, they wanted to arrive together to make an impact—and Zale had always been one for a dramatic entrance.

I smiled wryly as the cold air hit my bare arms, not covered by armour. "It sure brings back memories of Saraya and I shivering during dawn training. At least the warmth in Ellythia makes it easier to get up in the morning."

"I don't envy you that." He paused. "I smell battle and blood up ahead… and magic. A lot of it."

My stomach buzzed with anticipation and fear as our forces assembled at the harbour, with the Old Ones taking on their beast forms, snarling and ready for battle. No doubt they scented the blood in the air just like Zale. In the lead was Raen in his panther form, Atax in his black lion form, and Kai as a leopard with moon-white fur that practically glowed in the night. Behind them, Lady Reeta assembled the Ellythian cavalry.

Zale dived, and I was just able to turn my surprised scream into a war cry as he swooped in front of our host and soared up again.

Our court roared, the sound skittering up my arms and making me grit my teeth. Then we were off towards Quartz at a rapid speed, the horses and beasts racing each other in the wake of Zale's powerful flapping wings.

Zale, seemingly catching a bloodlust from the wind, dived again.

"Hold on," was all he growled as his eagle body changed beneath me and morphed into something completely new. Black and gold patterned fur covered a huge muscular body that was something between a lion and bear, with a massive throat, and I could just make out a mouth full of fangs.

"Goddess, what are you?" I asked, gripping his short fur and keeping low against the wind as his powerful muscles flexed and elongated beneath me.

"A beast made for war. Be alert, my mate."

It was the sound that I heard first; the roaring, screaming sound of hundreds or thousands of bodies on a battlefield, combined with the dull scream that lethal magic made as it sailed through the air and the dull boom of it hitting its mark. The hairs on my arms stood on end as we pummelled towards the huge stone gates of Quartz City.

Something eighteen years old in me sighed as I laid eyes upon the city I'd grown up in, the backs of my eyes pricking… until I saw the battlefield on the city's eastern side. Then anger fuelled me, and my magic demanded to be released. My fists clenched around Zale's fur as lightning skittered over my arms.

"My sister, Zale. I need to find her and her mate."

Someone at the city gates called out as we came up, but it was two broad-shouldered warriors standing with the bearing of kings in front of the city gates and poised for battle, that drew us up short. They were not men, but *fae*.

Both had an aura of danger, tanned skin, and pointed ears. I recognised prince, now King Daxian in his battle armour straight away because I had met him at Saraya's engagement. Except now, he was missing one eye, a black eyepatch covering the empty socket. He looked far older since the last time I'd met him, with a hard stare I usually saw in veteran warriors.

But the fae on our left bore a dark and powerful magic that made Zale tense under me as we came to a stop before them. His two eyes were a fascinating all-black, sparkling with red and blue lights that might have been mesmerising if not for the fact that his stance screamed *lethal predator*. In one hand, he held a long white bone that made my magic pound against my ribs excitedly. Though it was white and clean, it oozed a concentrated, dark magic.

Could that be the Darkmaul Dagger Hugh Carter had mentioned?

Raen led our host onto the battlefield, a pale Daxian staring at them as they ran past, but the black-eyed fae continued to stare at us.

Something in his face told me he recognised me, while I most definitely remembered *him* from the way he'd come late to Saraya's engagement. He seemed to struggle with something for a moment before clearing his throat and saying, "Altara Voltanius?"

Dear Goddess, his voice was a low, guttural, barely human sound I'd often heard from Zale. I knew at once he suffered

407

from Zale's same I'm-barely-human-half-the-time affliction. Saraya and I would have much to talk about.

"You are my brother-in-law." I grinned into his sparkly black eyes. "Drakus Silverhand!"

He pointed to my right hand where my mating mark sat. "Is that—"

"There will be much to discuss later," I said quickly. Goddess, he was too observant and *already* playing older brother. "Because—" I raised a hand and summoned the Boneweaver Bow, which arrived in a flash of heavy, striking gold. Both fae flinched at the sight of it, and rightfully so. "We have work to do, Drakus Silverhand."

Drakus nodded, his body coiled and tense as if ready for action. "My mate has been taken by the Reaper."

The way he called my sister "my mate" made me want to jump up and down with joy, though now was not the time. But shit. It was happening.

"If he has her, we need to act fast," Zale warned.

"Lead the way, brother-in-law—" I turned to Daxian, unable to help but feel that he'd been slighted by the whole Drake and Saraya business, and bowed where I sat. "And, Your Majesty."

Daxian's one eye glimmered, but he said nothing as he swiftly bowed back. Drakus promptly turned and sprinted through the city gates at an impossible speed.

"He is half-god, according to Lightwing," Zale said, leaping into a chase. *"And I fully believe that now."*

I waved up at the city gates as we went through, catching a cheer from the line of female archers standing there before Zale sped into the city, Daxian not far behind us.

My magic jolted and keened inside of me, fully aware of the battle going on outside the gates, but also with the familiarity of the city. These streets I'd walked, the cold, damp sort of smell. It was quieter than I'd ever seen the place, like a ghost of its real self. Oddly, I recognised Saraya's magic too, permeating the air like a real, living thing. Patches of it called out to me from the crevices in the walls, from inside houses and apartments, from the wood and stone itself. I supposed she'd worked in the city her entire life, and now, with my own advanced magic, I could see her everywhere. They were bonds she had between the women she'd saved and healed in pregnancy and birth.

"Your sister's magic is powerful," Zale said. *"Umali's high priestess is written all over here."*

We passed two young women patrolling the street, who, to my surprise, had deep brown skin, and were holding glowing swords. Zale said, *"Ellythians, Tara. Holding astral swords."*

Surprise riffled through me before I remembered something.

"Remember when we were down in the demon realm and they told us my sister ruined the palace and saved some of the slaves? Could there have been Ellythians in those slaves my sister brought back?"

"They bear her mark," he said. *"Looks like she anointed them warrior midwives."*

I wanted to cry and scream with joy at the thought that my sister was building her own temple with priestesses here. But I didn't get to think about it too much before Quartz palace came into view, and what I saw on the palace ramparts made my entire body twitch violently.

"Dear Goddess!" I exclaimed. "What is that?"

Z ale swore under his breath as he came to a stop beside Drakus. Our family's lightning power was on full display in its most chaotic form—a dome of white-hot energy swirling and crackling with lethal lightning. I knew it was Saraya's by the feel of it in the air, on my skin and around us.

"It's Saraya's power," Drakus confirmed tightly. "She's made a shield. What do you know of her Ellythian powers?"

I stared at him because this was clearly Lobrathian power on display.

"It's buried in the wounds of her back," he said. "Glacine and the Reaper knew before us."

"Glacine must have known that when she'd spent years torturing my sister," I said to Zale. Her power was buried in her wounds? Holy Mother.

"I've seen this happen before," Zale said. *"The damage inflicted upon her must have made her hide herself all those years ago. It's sort of the opposite of what my father did to us. Where our powers came out, hers were buried deep."*

"Like the shadows I used to protect myself." Something dark

and oily twisted in me as I realised my sister was having a crisis exemplified by her own magic.

Drake said, "She's been trying to unlock her power to its full potential to be able to use the Sword of Temari properly. So far, she has been unsuccessful."

A flash of agony came across my brother-in-law's face, as if the thought of Saraya in pain was unforgivable. It was then that I knew for sure that he loved her.

But what he was saying made sense to me. Far too much sense.

"Can you tune into her?" I asked, thinking about how Zale had reached out to me when I'd been out of reach to everyone else, even myself. "Her mental gate must be in protection mode if she's summoned a shield like *that*."

Daxian and Saraya's Ellythian warriors joined us as Drakus looked up at Saraya, his power reaching out to her.

"She's powerful," Zale said, impressed. *"I've never seen anything like it. No wonder the Reaper was fascinated by her."*

My heart swelled with pride for my sister, but it was useless if we couldn't help her.

Daxian came up next to Drake and tapped his eyepatch. "I can see through it. She's on her knees, there's a little human baby in her arms. Her eyes are shut. I don't even think she knows what she's doing. The Reaper is trying to get through it."

Anger coursed through me at hearing that the Reaper had involved a baby in this. Of course Saraya would prioritise protecting a baby over everything else.

"Your stepmother is also up there," Zale said. *"With his chariot."* He hesitated, as if he wanted to say something more, but had decided against it.

Drake's fist tightened around the bone in his hand, and I eyed it for the power it was giving off.

"She feels stuck," Drake said, confused. "Why would she feel stuck in there?"

An Ellythian stepped up next to us. Somehow, she looked familiar. But she was looking up at Saraya's ball of lightning. "I think she's exhausted her power using the shield. That's an incredible amount of magic she's using now."

"She needs more juice," I said, nodding at the Ellythian woman. "She needs to free herself and release that power. But she needs *more*." I looked at Drakus, knowing he'd probably try and give her his power like Zale would. "But it can't be anyone else's power. It has to be hers."

I looked over at the city behind us. "It's almost as if Saraya's power is etched all over the city. I'd never noticed it before."

"She's an Ellythian midwife," another Ellythian woman, small and slender, said. "I saw it when we first came in and knew straight away. We put a little of ourselves into each patient we heal. She's saved so many of the city's women that a little of her exists everywhere."

That made me want to cry, and I felt Zale's reassuring tug down the bond.

"Can we draw it out? Give it back to her?" Drake asked.

A thought struck me and I summoned the astral arrow, one of the many arrows my priestess Mahi had given me. Its silver upturned crescent moon, Umali's symbol, I remembered, glinted under Saraya's lightning. "I have an astral arrow that shoots through space. If I can draw out the magic, I can collect it into the arrow and shoot it into her. That'll give her the boost she needs to get out of her own wounds."

Zale growled in approval and the plan suddenly came together.

The slender Ellythian woman clapped excitedly. "We need to gather the city's women, then! All of them!"

"Run door to door," Drake commanded. "Tell the mothers of the city their queen needs their help."

"There won't be many in the houses," the first Ellythian woman said. "They're all on the battlements."

Drake and the Ellythians left, leaving Zale and I to watch my sister kneeling in the swirl of her own power. My poor sister had been through as much pain as I had this past year. She'd found her mate, been taken captive by demons and escaped, razing a demon kingdom to the ground. She'd taken Quartz back as queen, and now she was fighting for her life here. I said as much to Zale.

"I'd almost expect no less, knowing the women of your family. Speaking of, that taller Ellythian woman is a relative of yours."

"Really?"

"She seems to take after Aunt Parsha. Perhaps one of her grandchildren."

"Whichever it is, a reunion needs to wait until we deal with this."

"Agreed."

THE FIRST WOMAN TO RETURN WAS AGATHA, SARAYA'S CITY midwife mentor. She reminded me of Geravie in that old timer's no-nonsense slap-you-across-the-head if you mucked up attitude. She jerked her chin at me and said, "So you've come back in the nick of time, have you?"

"Yes, Agatha, I have. Meet my husband." I patted Zale's neck.

Agatha raised a brow. "Well, if you'll tell me where I can get one of those, I'll forgive you for leaving."

I grinned as Zale said, *"Tell her there's plenty on the battlefield."*

"I'll do no such thing. She won't be able to concentrate otherwise."

They gathered the women quickly, with some of them sprinting down the cobblestones, eager to help. Carefully, I stood on Zale's back to get a better view of them all, my witch's boots keeping me stable.

Somebody cried out my name, recognising me, and it got loud very quickly. Zale let out a growl, which made everyone snap their mouths shut.

"I'm back to help!" I cried in what I hoped was a reassuring voice. "Up there"—I pointed to Saraya's glowing orb of light—"Saraya fights a battle with the demon emperor. But she can't do this alone."

I gestured to them. "Gather in a circle." Obediently, they did, and we eventually had a massive circle of women in front of me, standing side by side. "Each of you Saraya has ever healed or helped with her magic in pregnancy or birth holds a tiny little part of her power inside of you. I want you to release it now, into this." I held up the astral arrow. "All you have to do is think about her. Think about the time she helped you or your daughter or someone you know. Hold that thought in your mind like a prayer. Hold tight and I will gather it. Can you do that?"

"Yes!" a young woman, pushing to the front, a baby on her hip. "The Reaper has taken my little girl! I'll do anything to help Saraya kill him!"

"Yeah!" the crowd of women cried.

My heart fell in dismay at the thought of the Reaper going

after human children. The creature knew no bounds. We needed to be rid of him as soon as possible.

"Alright then. Hold hands with your neighbour and let's do this. Let's help my sister."

As the women did as instructed, some of them closing their eyes, I held the crescent moon arrow between my palms and closed my eyes. My magic leapt to attention, keen to finally be used, and soared out of me. In this instance, none of the humans before me had magic, so I had to give a little nudge to look further and search deeper. The bonds between these women and my sister stretched out before me, a hundred ephemeral and glittering threads. Some were bonds laced with pain and discomfort, because no doubt, at the time of their healing, there had been something painful going on. But I tugged on those little memories, those accents of purple light, and they came willingly, as the women producing them were willingly giving them up. One by one, my magic reeled them in, and I sent them into my arrow. The metal began to vibrate in my hands, slowly at first, and then fiercely, until it took my own magic to contain the wild, concentrated power of the powerful memories. Only when every last ounce of magic was collected did I then give my magic permission to stop drawing from the women of the city. The entire time, Drakus watched on intently, his entire body tense, his face stone. I felt for him then. No doubt it was difficult to watch your mate in so much pain.

"He's showing great restraint," Zale remarked in my head. *"His body is telling me he wants to tear this place apart to get to her."*

I summoned the Boneweaver Bow, and it arrived heavy in my arms. People behind me gasped as I carefully knocked the astral arrow. Steadily, I drew it back, my arms straining, my tendons groaning. *For Saraya,* I said silently to the bow. *Deliver the power of the women to Saraya and let her have the strength to come out of this.*

Zale said quietly, *"Steady, my love. I am so proud of you."*

His gentle words somehow eased the pain of the burden of drawing back the bow. *Zale was proud of me.* That thing alone meant more than the sun. That he was here, by my side, helping my sister and our home city, our entire court in tow. *For our family.* A little tear fell from my eye as I closed them shut, then with a steady exhale, loosed the arrow.

Carried on that powerful magic, we all watched as its glowing light soared right up to the palace roof and over the ramparts, until it sailed smoothly into Saraya's defences. Her own magic had recognised it as familiar and accepted it. I loosed a breath from my lungs in relief as I felt it strike true.

Now it was Saraya's job to work with it.

I jumped off Zale's back and went to my brother-in-law to say as much, but Drake was staring at the bow as if he'd been struck by it himself.

"Altara," he said in that low rasp that made every woman in the area involuntarily stare at him. "Do you think you can do that one more time, but for someone else?"

"I suppose so," I replied, trying to study his face because his demeanour had changed completely. "What's wrong, Drakus?"

He took a deep breath that moved his shoulders. Now I was worried. He said, "I'm not sure if you know this, so I am sorry if it comes as a shock to you, but it was your stepmother who killed your mother and caused your father's disease. She used poison, both times."

The world suddenly narrowed down to Drakus' face. My

blood roared in my ears as my shadows leapt out of me to try and protect me from this pain.

But no. *This* I wanted to feel. *This* I wanted to seep into my bones and remember forever.

I clutched onto Zale's fur so hard it must have hurt him, but my mate did nothing but say, *"We will kill her, Altara, and display her head outside for all to see. She will regret the day she ever came into your family."* He let out a low, rumbling growl that rattled my bones.

It was his bloodthirsty words that centred me, and his sound that grounded me.

When I spoke, my voice was a hiss. "She needs to die, and painfully."

"I agree," Drakus said. "I took the poison from your father before he died." He gestured to a faint blue swirling magic I could now see in his neck. "I think I'd like to return it to her before Saraya slits her throat."

I had to take a deep breath to control the pure rage speeding through my blood. "Right." I nodded. "And you want me to shoot it into her?"

"Can it be done?"

My grin was vicious. "Let's do it, brother."

As I tucked a new arrow into my astral repository, we watched power flare up on the palace battlements. Someone let out a shout as a wave of power hit us with crackling heat.

Daxian muttered next to Drakus, "It's working."

And then Saraya's dome of lightning simply blinked out.

Drakus was in the air in an instant, flying on wings made of shadows. I barely had the chance to register them before Zale burst into an eagle form of black and gold. Leaping on top of him, we were shooting after our brother-in-law and above the palace roof within seconds.

A figure I was sure was my sister was getting up from the ground, a sparkling, powerful blade in her hand, with a hilt of deep blue and gold.

"The Temari Blade," Zale said with awe. "I'd know its power anywhere."

Opposite her was Reaper in his fae illusory form, a tall, broad-shouldered male. But the fucker was extending his hand towards my sister.

418

"My lady," the Reaper said. "Will you join us?"

Over my dead body! At the same time Zale swore, Drakus gave an animalistic snarl and fell towards Saraya with the look of a beast going to claim his wife.

Zale gave a sharp cry of warning and said to me, *"Dear Goddess, is that our Saraya?"*

I couldn't even reply as I beheld my sister—or the being she had become. I'd seen the Goddess Umali at Pia's coronation and Saraya looked much the same. Her skin skittered with blue-white lightning all the way around, her power making the air around us fizz dangerously. Her eyes were a solid glowing blue that made me shiver at their intensity. I couldn't deny that her power scared me a little. It was like Umali's; dangerous, chaotic, unhinged, and lethal.

But as soon as the Reaper saw all of us, he attempted to shoot away to his chariot where, to my chagrin, Glacine was waiting. And the wretched woman was dressed for battle in thin plate armour.

Except the Reaper had underestimated Saraya.

My sister was a blur as she made for the Reaper like an insanely fast predator and viciously grabbed him around the back of the neck with one of her hands. His body seized as her lightning struck through him, going stiff as a board, and then vibrated on the spot, his handsome fae-self dissolving, leaving the black cloaked, six-eyed form to come through. His true, ugly form.

But the Reaper was not to be outdone. Equally fast, he swung around, his fist pummelling towards Saraya's jaw. The punch struck her—but Saraya merely remained in place, unmoved, unaffected.

I choked in part hurrah, part horror.

Drakus was snarling, but Saraya was smiling as she held

onto his neck firmly and Zale was about to say something to me when my sister—my dear, sweet, law-abiding sister—reached for one of the Reaper's eyes and with her fingers, and plucked it out.

The Reaper's magic flared out, hitting us in a wave of fury and pain, but Saraya merely pushed him away from her as if he were an irritation. The Reaper stumbled back, hunched and clutching his face, his magic lashing out.

Zale's shield went up around us just in time, and I would've cried out to Drakus, but he was already reaching for Saraya, and she wrapped them both in a shield of lightning, which easily deflected the Reaper's green magic.

"Now!" Zale commanded.

We all responded, moving into action to attack the Reaper at the same time. Saraya let out a stream of lightning so powerful it lifted her up into the air, alongside Drakus, who flew up on his own shadow-wings. I fired arrows of hot lightning directly at him, one after the other, never stopping the stream. If this was going to work, the attack needed to be combined and brutal. And Goddess, the feeling of Saraya's and my power working together was a glorious feeling I could never forget—we'd never used our magic in unison like this before.

The Voltanius sisters, avenging our parents. My magic rose up, eager to fight, and I knew light was glittering all over me as my priestess mark burned. Zale veered this way and that so I could shoot the Reaper on all sides, and quite quickly, the smell of something rotting filled the air, the creature himself falling onto his knees under our barrage of lightning.

"He's weak. Tara, the arrow!" Zale cried into my mind.

I summoned the blue quartz arrow in my right hand and

exchanged my regular bow for the Boneweaver Bow in the other. With a cry, I deftly filled it with one last burst of magic and shot it true. Saraya stopped her assault when she saw it, and the arrow flew straight at the Reaper, split into six glimmering quartz arrows filled with the combined power of Zale and I, and thudded firmly into each one of his six eye sockets with a sick crunch.

"He won't be able to see now!" I cried, hoping they understood my meaning.

Zale let out a piercing cry that hurt my ears, and below us, the Reaper screamed, his ear sockets bleeding black blood. Drake understood immediately, and both he and my sister shot downwards. Drakus darted behind the Reaper's hunched body and snapped that white bone in half on his knee, tossing a piece to Saraya, who now stood in front of the Reaper.

As one, they shoved both pieces of bone into his torso.

In a fascinated horror, we all watched the Reaper fold into himself, the two pieces of bone working together to suck his body into it. There was binding magic in there so powerful that Zale and I both shuddered under its force. Then all that was left was one heavy black bone, made whole again, and it fell onto the palace roof with a sick, heavy thud that made me want to vomit and laugh at the same time.

Saraya looked to Drakus, who rushed towards her, aggressively crushing his mouth against hers.

And then I saw Glacine, trying to run away. I summoned my third special arrow of the night, the one filled with the poison Glacine had used to slowly poison my father.

I shot it right into her wretched arm. She went down with a cry.

"Get her," I hissed.

But Zale had already tucked his wings in and dived. Deftly, I leapt on top of Glacine and wrenched her horrible form against my body, shoving her onto her knees.

Saraya and Drake turned to stare at us as Zale guarded my back.

It was then that I saw the chariot with the two severed heads sitting on spikes. My father. Uncle Ansel. My heart twisted. I wrenched Glacine's neck *hard*, ready to snap it. Ready to kill this woman in the most painful way I knew how.

"Look at what I found, Sara!" I said viciously, holding Glacine's chin in one hand, her neck in the other. "Say the word, and I'll break her neck."

"No." Saraya's voice was deep and husky, somewhat like mine when I went under my shadows and her electric blue eyes flashed dangerously. "She is mine. She has been mine from the start. Let her up. I will fight her properly."

Breathing hard, I nodded, stepping away from the woman we'd called our stepmother. I'd known Saraya would want to be the one to do it, just like how Pia had to be the one to kill her mother. There was a right way to do things, and this was it.

Glacine stumbled to her feet, pathetic and panting as she stared daggers at my sister. She attempted a fighting stance.

"Look," Saraya said, turning and baring her back. Her white shirt was shredded, and through it, we could see smooth brown skin, no sign of any scars from her whippings. "I am free of you now. Whatever you did to me is long gone. After this, none of us will ever remember you."

I grunted in agreement while Drakus looked at Saraya as if she were the sun warming his face. Behind him, I could see the baby the Reaper had kidnapped, being cajoled by two small creatures, one black, one rainbow coloured, only as big as kittens. They stood protectively around the baby, shielding her from what was about to happen.

Saraya smiled at Glacine, but it was cruel and powerful, and her words held the cadence of deep meaning. "There is a special place in hell for those who take advantage of the kindness of others."

My heart sank because I knew my sister had suffered immeasurably while I'd been away. She'd suffered her whole life. But what happened next filled me with violent satisfaction.

Glacine hurled red, angry magic at Saraya, but before I could do anything, it just skittered off my sister's lightning-laced skin like it was too weak to do anything. Like it was weak, and pathetic. I grinned triumphantly.

"Now, you'll pay for what you did to my family," Saraya hissed. "Now, you'll go to hell where you belong. Now, you *lose*." Saraya summoned that beautiful shining magical blade and in one lethal, vicious swipe slashed it across Glacine's throat.

I sighed in relief as our stepmother crashed to the stone, her red blood spilling. Glacine choked on her own blood before she went limp, forever. Saraya lifted her head towards the stars as Glacine's blood continued to spurt mortally out of her body. "Father, Mother, I've fulfilled my vow."

And so had I.

"The stars are always watching," Zale said softly to me.

"I love you, Sister," I managed to choke out. "And I'm so glad to see you today." I hoped she understood my meaning. I hoped she understood what I'd been through to get here, and what I also knew *she'd* been through to be able to land the killing blow to Glacine. To the Reaper as well.

Saraya turned those lightning eyes onto me. "Altara, my heart, we make our parents proud today."

I wanted to dance and cry and kiss everyone. It was done. And we'd done it together. We *had* made our parents proud. That was all I ever wanted. "I know they are both watching."

With power pulsing dangerously between the both of us, the time for hugs would come later. Now, we were violently charged. Now, we were going to end this war. Saraya turned to check on the baby being guarded by the small kitten-like creatures.

"That creature was covering the baby's eyes," I said. "And the black one was covering its ears."

"*Clever cubs,*" Zale said affectionately, eyeing the tiny creatures.

The baby's mother crashed through the door that led to the castle, followed by Daxian and some of the Ellythian women. Saraya rushed to collect the baby and take it to her.

I turned to Zale and kissed him on his beak. "*You did well, my love,*" he said, nuzzling me.

"There is still a horde to kill," I heard Drakus say darkly.

With a flash, I summoned the Boneweaver Bow and everyone turned to look at us.

Saraya said with a slightly scary smile that delighted me, "Then let us destroy them." I turned away to let my sister and her husband have a moment while I looked out at the city and inhaled the night air.

The wind held the tang of blood. And demon stench.

Saraya suddenly cried, "Then catch me!" She promptly took a run up and leapt off the palace roof. I gasped, but the static energy of her power was so strong that it carried her on its own accord. Even so, Drakus didn't hesitate to leap after her, catching her in the air and refusing to let her go.

"She really is Umali's high priestess," I said out loud, remembering the frightening naked Goddess at Pia's coronation.

"She and Pia will get along nicely," Zale mused.

"I think you and Drakus will, too," I replied as I climbed back on him.

"Why ever would you say that?" he asked innocently as he, too, leapt off the roof to chase them.

With Altara secure on my back, we followed Saraya and Drake onto the battlefield and got our first look at the Reaper's forces.

As I expected, this was easily four times the size of what we had dealt with at the harbour on Lota Island. Demons, humans, and dark fae fought over a broad stretch of land, with the demon armies extending back as far as I could see.

Though I'd never been to Quartz City, the Reaper and I had gone over maps to strategise the best way of conducting battle. His demon generals had done their best to replicate our plan without me, and with the sheer numbers of demons from courts all over the subterranean realm, it was a bloody battle that the humans were losing. The magic of the dark fae was keeping the enemy at bay, but even they could see they were fighting a losing battle.

But everything changed when the four of us hit the field, combined with the *new* oncoming army. And I didn't mean the Old Ones.

Fresh-faced fae with coloured wings were flying over the

field, shooting magical arrows that tore apart dozens at a time.

"Who are they?" Tara asked me, impressed as she shot arrows of lightning, while Saraya was blasting pure lightning over the demons straight from her hands. *"They have actual wings!"*

"Sky court fae," I said. The only reason I knew was because being on the westernmost aspect of the solar fae realm, my father used to trade with those whom Kai used to call 'the pretty fae with butterfly wings'.

Drake dropped Saraya, and she flew on the charge of her own lightning once again.

"The Reaper is dead!" Her voice rang over the battlefield, cutting through the shrieks and screams. "Your battle is lost. The Reaper is dead!"

The Lobrathians and fae let out cheers.

Saraya and Drake became a force on the battlefield, my sister-in-law's lightning lashing out across enemy lines like a divine sword, cleaving through hundreds, charring their bodies and leaving them a mess of smoking rubble.

It was then the demons on the back lines began to run. The combined forces of the Old Ones, with the fresh magic of the Ellythians and Altara's and Saraya's aerial lightning attacks, we made savage work of the numbers. Raen, Atax and Kai tore apart demons with relish and I longed to join them.

My brother-in-law, for his part, kept one eye on his wife, and the other he kept on the demons whose hearts he ripped out with his bare hands.

"A man after my own heart," I said to Altara as I pointed him out, tearing into a particularly large grey-muscled demon with tusks.

"*Very funny,*" she said, not at all amused, and shot a demon general mounted on a reptilian beast, right between the eyes, his entire head exploding for emphasis.

The battle died down within the hour after that, and eventually, I descended to land next to Raen, who was healing an Ellythian warrior with a head wound.

Atax and Malika had already set about scouring the battlefield for the injured, and Altara rushed to a row of injured Lobrathians being laid down outside a white tent set up by dark fae lords. Kai skipped up to her, dutifully keeping watch for his queen.

I shifted back into my human form and found Drakus Silverhand watching me from beside a fallen fae. He drew a sheet over the warrior's head and rose. His black eyes were fixed on my face, the lights in them blinking rapidly in an assessing way. He prowled over to me, and I let him take my measure as a man. I watched him take in my tattoos, my eyes, my long black hair, and—Altara would be proud—I *had* summoned pants on to meet my brother-in-law for the first time.

Then he was standing before me, a hair shorter than my own tall height, but he made a formidable presence, nonetheless. He was tanned, but not as brown as me, with fine fae features, including the pointy ears and fine bone structure. He was built like a warrior—the type I'd be wary to fight—and I could see the top of a black tattoo peeking out from where his black shirt opened at his chest. Although he looked fae to any normal eye, if the all-black eyes didn't give it away, my instincts screamed at me to see that he was a lot more dangerous than that. No doubt that was the half-god part coming out. All in all, I thought we'd probably get along nicely.

To my surprise, he stuck his hand out, and in his low rasp, said, "Thank you for coming to help us."

I stared at him for a heartbeat before I took his calloused hand and shook it. "Anything for family, brother," I said.

His brows raised a little. "So you *are* Altara's mate?" He glanced down at my left hand where my black butterfly mating mark sat.

Allowing myself to smile a little as we glanced over at my wife tirelessly healing her countrymen, I said proudly, "She bears my mating mark and my wedding ring."

He gave a small nod. "Sara won't be happy she missed the wedding."

"Tara isn't happy she missed yours."

"Considering it was in the demon realm and by force, I'm glad she *wasn't* there."

"I forced Tara to marry me, as well."

Drakus stilled, trying to gauge my meaning, but I shrugged good-naturedly. "She's happy about being the Boneweaver Queen, otherwise she would've killed me by now."

He let out a breath. "If she's anything like Sara, then I'm sure—did you say *Boneweaver*?"

"I am King Ashzale Boneweaver. They call us the Old Ones in Ellythia."

Drakus' brows knitted together as he swore under his breath. "They call me Prince Drake Voltanius now," he said softly, as if it were still new. "So the legends are true. Dear Goddess, I thought I'd never see the day." He ran his hand through his dark brown hair and turned to look at the beasts of my court, amongst the humans and fae, comforting the injured and helping with their magic. Raen was talking to a fae with long blond hair—well, *flirting* would be more accurate.

Malika was busy setting fire to a pile of demon carcasses, while Atax wouldn't leave her side. "My brother"—I pointed to them—"is new to having a woman, look how he fusses over her." On cue, Malika promptly slapped Atax's hand off her shoulder.

Drake laughed under his breath. "I can't talk, I'm still learning how not to get beaten up myself."

"What are you two old ladies gossiping about?" Altara's voice from our other side made us both jump. "Husband, I need your help."

"At once, my queen," I said quickly, inclining my head to Drake—who was now smiling in amusement—and letting Altara drag me away to assist with the healing queue.

A LITTLE WHILE LATER, WE HEADED BACK TOWARDS THE PALACE with the other senior members of the Lobrathian and allying courts. The Darkmaul Dagger—which turned out to have been made of one of Drake's actual forearm bones—was given to an Obsidian court mage who was going to take it off-realm completely for safekeeping. Honestly, I was happy it wasn't going to be anywhere near us, and I think everyone felt the same.

The Reaper was gone—for good. And it would, perhaps, go down as one of the happiest days of my life, after my memories of Altara took first, second, and third place. Raen, Kai, Atax, and Malika all sighed with relief as the room emptied and it was just the two Voltanius sisters, Drake, his two brothers, my own brothers, and Malika. Queen Saraya Voltanius looked at us over Altara's shoulder. She looked so much like my wife, for they were only a year apart in birth, except she was slightly taller, her hair curly, and her green eyes harsher, more assessing, in that way older sisters were. Her static, furious power reminded me, in every moment, that she was High Priestess of Umali, Goddess of Rage.

"Saraya," Altara said slowly, "and everyone, I'd like you to meet my husband, King Ashzale Boneweaver, who also happens to be my star-born mate."

I stepped forward and bowed as a king would do to a queen. "Your Majesty."

Saraya's jaw went slack as she took in the black tiger mating mark on her sister's hand, then showed her own mating mark on her right hand—a black, twisted tree.

Altara yelped in excitement, brushing her fingers over her sister's skin and grinning. Saraya looked between my wife and me, her eyes lined with silver. "Your husband?" she repeated in a hushed voice. Drake came to stand beside her for support, I think, because it was something I would have done. Saraya asked, "How did you get married so quickly?"

Altara's cheeks turned pink. "The circumstances were a little unusual. I was actually married to two— Uh, maybe we can talk about that later."

"Your Majesties," said Malika, pushing past Atax and bowing low next to me. "I bring word from your cousin, Queen Pia Lota of Ellythia."

"*Queen* Pia?" Saraya said, blanching. "Whatever happened to our Grandmother Cheshni?"

Altara and Malika exchanged a look, and Saraya sighed, rubbing her eyes. "Come, sit down and let's eat. You must tell us everything, and"—she looked around me to my brothers—

"it looks like I have more brothers now than I ever imagined. You look hungry."

If I didn't like her before, I did now.

"Ooh," Kai said, bounding forward to get on one knee and kiss Saraya's hand. "I love you already."

One of the small fae creatures on the dinner table next to Saraya leapt for Kai, who immediately caught her. The rainbow-coloured creature, with its wide opalescent eyes, licked his nose, and after a thought, Kai deftly licked her back, making her squeal.

Altara and Saraya both laughed at the same time, light and tinkling. The combined sound was at once a balm that unravelled something deep in the centre of my gut. Almost every muscle in my body relaxed.

Drake and I exchanged a look, and he grinned at me.

Altara and Zale told Queen Saraya and Prince Drakus the story of what had happened when Altara had run away to Boneweaver Island so many months ago, punctuated with commentary from me and the Old Ones. The new Queen of Lobrathia was as sharp-eyed as any warrior I'd met in Ellythia, and only an idiot wouldn't see that she'd been bred to become a queen. I'd expected nothing less from someone who was Pia's cousin and Altara's older sister. Even exhausted, her emerald eyes were keen and questions astute. More than once, her mouth tightened—at Altara's mention of being taken by the Butcher and then again at the ordeal at Queen Odeelia's court in the Eternal Forest, and then again when Altara revealed her idea of tricking the Reaper. Prince Drakus was the strangest thing of all to me, because he wasn't like any fae or beast I'd ever met before. He sat so still at the table that I was doubtful he was even breathing at all, but I could tell he was always attuned to the movements of his queen wife.

Atax sat next to me, incessantly filling my plate with food

and insisting he be near me at all times. In truth, I loved his presence. Here in this foreign kingdom, with its cold wind and the lingering stench of the battlefield, I found myself leaning into him more and more.

Sometimes, I even wanted to tell him that, but I settled for batting his hands away instead. I didn't even know *how* to be nice to him. Sometimes Raen would nod at me encouragingly, as if he knew I wanted to try something different. Damn mage. He saw everything. Kai didn't help either, randomly giving me little smiles that made me want to pat his head.

What was I turning into? Some sappy-eyed maiden? I couldn't bear the thought. I was a battle-hardened warrior who'd rained fire not once, but *thrice* now, in battle, I couldn't afford to be smiling and batting my eyelids at Atax.

But towards the end of Altara's story, she turned to Zale and there was this look in her eye that made my heart do funny things. A soft glimmer of something pure and light that made the backs of my eyes burn. Then Zale—damn him too—reached up and brushed his thumb over Altara's cheek.

I'd been seeing displays like that from them recently and the movement was so tender, so honest, that I found my hand creeping towards Atax like a vine looking for the sun. I thought my lion might have been falling asleep by this stage because we'd been here for a while, and the battle adrenaline was dissolving, making my own eyes droopy. So I assumed—or was hoping—that he might not notice me dropping my cold hand onto his massive one.

But damn it, he did.

He turned his palm over and I kept my eyes on Altara, who was relaying Pia's coronation now, determined to let this *hand thing* be something that only half happened in my imagination. I let my hand rest in his palm and his fingers curled around, engulfing my hand completely like a lion who'd gotten his teeth around prey.

But it was warm, so fucking warm, and something stirred low and deep in my stomach.

Finally, Queen Saraya noticed my droopy eyes and kindly told us there were plenty of spare rooms in the eastern wing if we didn't mind a little dust. So off we went. But the lion shaped into a man next to me wouldn't let go of my blasted hand.

I let him drag me along, because I was tired, having used up almost all of my power burning up demons, as Altara led us to rooms where we could bathe and sleep.

It wasn't until Atax and I were alone in a quiet bedroom that I suddenly became wide awake. He let go of my hand and drew the thick curtains shut. I lit a few candles for light, my stomach tightening with every second that passed by.

"I'm too tired to bathe," I said defiantly, standing with my legs apart, as if poised for battle.

"Okay," he said simply. Then he promptly stalked back around the bed, past me, and pulled the door open. He said over his shoulder, "Sleep well, firebird." *And then left.*

I was left in the dark, gaping at the shut door, with only the burning between my legs for company.

So I did end up bathing, angrily scrubbing demon blood off my skin and then shoving my hand between my legs to relieve myself of the severe and consuming heat that was tingling though my lower stomach. The nerve of that beast! It was supposed to calm me down, but two rounds later, I was still burning for eyes like a fae lagoon and large, veined hands that engulfed my own.

Except now I was also furious.

Dressed in a clean nightgown someone had left for me, I

yanked open my bedroom door and realised we'd been put in a suite of adjoining rooms. I'd been in a sort of mad, heat-filled daze as Atax had led me here and hadn't noticed my surroundings all that well. But now, all four doors were closed, and I knew Altara had taken Zale back to her bedroom, so these rooms must've been only for me and the Old Ones. Closing my eyes, I cast my magical awareness out to find the arrogant lion I was looking for. In the room across from mine, a dark energy, sleek like a panther, promptly sat up to acknowledge my presence. Before I could mentally retreat out of Raen's room, a shadowy finger pointed me to the door next to my own, as if to say, *"He's in there."*

Blushing furiously, I mentally sped out of Raen's room and physically stomped to the room next to mine, not even bothering to knock and flinging open the door.

Atax was fast asleep on his stomach. I couldn't help but stare at him in that moment. The sheet stopped at his lower back, showing me the smooth plane of his naked skin, the rippling muscles that the full moon, pouring in from the open window, cast in silver. Tender heat soared through my entire being, pooling in my core... before I realised that his broad back had stopped expanding with breath.

"Wake up," I demanded, not even sure what I was going to do yet.

He didn't even open his eyes. "What do you want, fire-bird?" But his voice was husky and deep, hitting me right between the legs. I flinched as my womanhood gave a sala-cious, delicious throb.

Atax's eyes flew open, and he sat up so quickly that I took a step backward.

"What?" I said, more sharply than I meant to.

"Are you going to follow your queen's orders or not?"

Atax said aggressively, running a hand through his loose black hair.

The nerve! "What orders? To spread my legs for you?" I said, rolling my eyes at him as if that's the last thing I wanted. I turned away with every intention of going back to my room because this had been a stupid idea and I was letting my clitoris rule me.

"*Firebird,*" he growled. I froze. "*Look at me.*" Something in his voice made me damn well turn. Something that didn't hit me in the clitoris at all—but right in my chest. Atax's eyes burned scorch marks into my skin. I bit my lip, suddenly unable to think properly. He stood, slowly, with all the feline grace of a king lion. His voice was low and dangerous. "You'll be following my orders by the time this is done, little firebird."

Holy Mother Goddess, my stomach did funny things at his words, at the bestial, intense gaze. The promise in it. All I could do was toss my head and tear my eyes off my Old One, though it was half-hearted.

"Uh-uh." He was on me in an instant, hands on my waist, holding me firmly in place. "You don't get to turn away from me anymore." His face was inches from mine and there was a retort on my tongue, but it died with what he said next.

"I meant what I said on the battlefield at Lota Island, firebird. I don't *want* you. I need you like I need air. I couldn't fucking breathe for those two weeks I couldn't be with you. Hearing you calling me Grandpa even though I fucking hate it, I loved it because it was coming from *your* mouth, with *your* fire, with *your* glare." He took a breath, his fingers burning at my waist and I couldn't help but notice the shadows under his eyes, the weariness that clung to him like a spiderweb. When he continued, his voice was a little broken. "I love it when you cuss at me. I love it when you stare daggers at me. I love it when you push me away. And I couldn't stop thinking about how much I should have told you that I loved you before I was forced to leave you. There is nothing that will be able to take away the regret I had in that moment when the Reaper took me over. It's something I'll remember for the rest of my life. That *desperation*—"

I shut him up by covering his mouth with mine, because I couldn't bear it anymore. The fire between my legs, in my heart, at the backs of my eyes needed this. Atax's mouth softened against mine. We melted into each other and it felt like the relief of sitting down after a long day. To surrender into him felt like I'd been holding my breath this entire time and now finally… I got to exhale.

We kissed like we'd never kissed anyone else before. Atax's mouth was possessive and demanding on mine, desperate in a way that I'd never, not in my wildest dreams, thought was possible. My own mouth responded in turn, my hands reaching up to grasp at the broad plain of his shoulders, his neck, his surprisingly soft hair, the scruff on his jaw. He crushed my body to his and I could feel every muscle of his chest and hard stomach pressing against mine.

It was too much. And not enough.

"Atax," I gasped, breaking off the kiss.

But it was like he couldn't bear to take his lips off me, because he licked and sucked down my neck like my skin was water and he was dying of thirst. "Ah fuck, Malika, you feel like heaven."

His kisses on my neck shot straight to the space between my legs, rivulets of pleasure driving up through my core. With his arms around me, I felt safe.

I didn't know that safety could feel like this. That it could feel this good. Unbidden, a tear escaped my eye and my chest let out a shuddering breath.

"Malika," Atax whispered my name in a way he never had before. I tried to hide my face as he came up from my shoulder, but he tilted my chin up with a finger and kissed both my cheeks. "What's wrong?"

"Nothing," I said, letting him wipe my tears with his big thumbs.

Gently, I took one of his hands and led him back to the bed, hitching my nightgown up and climbing on. As he lay down behind me, I pushed him onto his back and climbed on top of him in a straddle. His hands came to rest on my upper thighs and I pulled my nightgown over my head, leaving me completely bare.

Atax's breath stuttered, his pupils dilating as I stared into them. Abruptly, he sat up, cupping my cheeks and pressing his forehead against mine. "Firebird," he whispered.

"Grandpa," I whispered back.

He laughed under his breath, running his hands down my back. "Will you let me make love to you now, my beautiful, precious firebird?"

My stomach flopped, trying to register that he was calling me those… things. He thought me *precious*.

"I want you to keep my sword." He touched the obsidian earring dangling on my own ear, a twin to the one on his own ear.

All I could do was inhale a shaky breath and try to stay the tears that threatened to consume me. My throat tightened and I knew I couldn't reply in words.

I ran my finger over his full bottom lip, enjoying his roughness, his hardness against me. His arousal was impressive where I sat, and I ground my hips against him as a test.

Atax groaned, his hands tightening on me. "This is torture, firebird."

I brushed my lips against his. "Good."

"Cruel woman." His abs tensed and I got only a second's warning before he flipped me onto the bed and pinned me with his hips.

A giggle escaped from my lips before I pressed them together. He kissed my mouth lightly. "Don't do that," he whispered. "Let me see you laugh." He ground himself against my clit, that shooting pleasure centre almost driving me wild. "Let me see you moan. Let me see all of you. Because I want all of it, firebird. I want every inch of you. Grumpy and mean or not. I want to love *all* of you."

His words made a tear slip from me again, and I blinked rapidly against the foreign feelings inside of me. "I want—" I swallowed and inhaled carefully, saying something that I'd never said to anyone before. Never thought I *would* say to anyone. "I want all of you too, Atax." He stilled over me, his blue eyes widening slightly as he stared.

I traced my fingers down his sides until I reached his pants. I hooked my fingers into them and tugged. Only then did he swallow and pull them off. I opened for him, and slipped a hand down to palm his manhood. He was big, his girth filling my palm as I slid my fingers up his shaft. I bit my lip at the anticipation of him and rubbed his broad crown against my entrance. I let him feel how wet I was. That I was ready now.

He inhaled sharply, his eyes closing for a moment before he buried his face in my neck and groaned, low and deep. I positioned him and he sank into me slowly. I moaned at the stretch, at the feel of him—a man of his size, a beast of his savagery—being so very gentle with me. Because it was Atax, lethal and arrogant but gentle and focused. Always focused on me.

Any sex I'd had before was furious, vicious fucking. No one had ever entered me so slowly, so adoringly like this, and it felt like a salve to a wound deep inside my bones. Inch by inch, Atax stretched me open until he filled me completely. My moan turned into a whimper as my lion kissed me deeply, moving inside of me with slow, languid movements.

"I've waited so long to have you, firebird," he whispered against my mouth. "You made me wait so fucking long."

I gasped, knowing it was true as I held onto his huge arms, then his face as he kissed me again. His tongue moved against mine and I moaned into his mouth, tendrils of sweet pleasure twining upwards from my centre, through my spine. He kissed along my jaw, along the line of my neck so gently, so adoringly.

"Let me look after you," he whispered. "Let me take care of you, firebird." And then he wrapped his arms around me and drove into me, deeply, firmly, but always lovingly. The pressure built up until I was dizzy and crying out, gripping onto his hard body for dear life. And Atax held me throughout it all, deep sounds of pleasure rumbling through his chest, sounds that hit me in my core.

"Atax!" I cried. And it was like the sun was bursting through my head. Tears sprung from my eyes as I came with a mind-blowing ferocity, my chest opening up, my fingernails digging into his shoulders.

"Malika," he groaned, before crying out and emptying himself into me. His seed was hot, his gaze no longer entirely human as we both breathed hard and stared at each other in an intense sort of wonder that I couldn't help but believe was not of this earth.

I really did feel like a bird, soaring high on the waves of our mutual pleasure, our closeness.

"Again," I whispered.

"Anything for you," Atax whispered.

I would do anything for him, I realised. I would set fire to armies, kill for him, hurt anyone who came against us. As Atax began to move inside me again, already hard as stone, those beautiful eyes told me he would do the same for me.

If this was what love was, then I wanted more of it.

We made love long into the night.

ALTARA

The next day, our work continued. Last night, for the first time ever, Zale and I fell asleep in each other's arms almost immediately. He woke me up with his mouth between my legs, his wicked tongue licking and sucking until I was screaming his name, pulling his hair, and he was grinning with a look in his eye that could only be called joy. It was after that, that he turned to suspiciously look about my room and asked who else I'd brought in here. I silenced him by throwing him onto the bed and practically swallowing his manhood. There was nothing better than listening to his rumbling groans as I licked up and down his massive length, the muscles in his spectacular abs tensing until he came in hot bursts in my mouth. He watched with his tiger's eyes as I swallowed each burst, his hips doing small, involuntary thrusts. When it was over, I smacked my lips and grinned at him, to which he lunged at me, threw me down on my bed and fucked me senseless.

Our powers twined around each other, gold and navy blue, our bond humming as Zale filled me with his power.

And when I screamed as I came, I bit down on his neck to avoid waking everyone up, but Zale loved that, coming immediately, somehow still able to spill seed into me.

Later that morning, after Zale insisted on washing me and my hair, we joined Saraya, Drake, the Old Ones, and Drake's two brothers outside. The blonde with long hair, so graceful I was sure he was a dancer, was introduced to me as Lysander. He kissed my hand with a smile that lingered. Zale let out a low growl, but Lysander's blue eyes only dilated in delight. His second brother-in-arms was Slade, a hulking dark-haired fae with scars on his neck, who'd made it clear he'd claimed Blythe, one of Saraya's closest maids that we'd grown up with. She was a gorgeous young woman with a great sword arm and inky dark hair. She made eyes at me like she had a story to tell me later.

Drake's nostrils flared as he passed me by, and inwardly, I cringed.

"He can probably scent what we did this morning," I said darkly through our bond.

"Don't worry, they did the same," Zale said, completely unabashedly. Drake suddenly grinned at Zale and I scoffed, grabbing Saraya's arm and tugging her away from the men, beckoning to Blythe and Malika—who, I was most happy to notice, was walking a little gingerly.

"They're going to be awful together," I said to Saraya, jerking my head at our two husbands talking quietly to one another.

"You think so?" She grinned at me. "Just don't let Drake pull a deck of cards out."

Blythe snorted as we made our way to the healing tents to do our rounds and see what else needed to be done.

Jerali Jones, our palace armsmaster, who had no equal

with a blade, was supervising the first tent, and I dragged Zale forward, because I wanted Zale to meet them.

"Altara." Jerali strode towards us as we entered, grey eyes lighting up. "We need to talk about your new lightning arrows. I want to see them at work."

"No hi or hello or nothing!" I said loudly. "Just wants to see my sparkly weapons!"

Jerali grinned and pulled me into their chest. "I knew you'd be fine, you naughty thing. Probably been throwing arrows all about in Ellythia, eh?"

Zale was behind me in a heartbeat, towering over the both of us. "You are Jerali Jones."

To my surprise, Jerali went a little pale. "Yes, Your Majesty," they said quietly, bowing. "I recognise you from your painting in the Daanav palace. I was born there."

I gaped at my old armsmaster. "What? When? Why did you never tell us!"

Saraya laughed darkly at my elbow. "I wouldn't have known either, if it weren't for our capture of Kraasputin."

Jerali nodded, grey eyes serious. "My mother was pregnant when she was taken, I believe. I was the only one to escape the kingdom, to my knowledge. Queen Yasani found me as she sailed on her ship and took me under her wing."

"No wonder you fight so well," Zale said. "I saw you on the battlefield. They train the children ruthlessly, the Daanavs."

Jerali nodded, as I was still gaping at her. "I hadn't intended on telling anyone. But Kraasputin trades in information, and we had nothing else to give in exchange for knowledge about how to use the Temari Blade. So I told him about the Daanav Kingdom."

I glanced at Zale, frowning. "But the Kraasputin already

knew about the Daanav Kingdom," I said. "Not that long after I arrived on Boneweaver Island, he told me he gave Fangar's cock back after I took it from him."

Jerali frowned, because they didn't know about my power to take organs from people yet, so I quickly filled them in.

"He already knew," Saraya said in wonder. "Kraasputin swapped information for something he already knew. Why would he do that?"

"He was a little easy to catch, if I'm honest," Jerali said, looking disturbed. "I wonder if..."

"He let you catch him?" Drake finished.

Jerali nodded.

I swore under my breath. "He's a complicated creature," I said, looking up at Zale. "He helped me escape from the cage the Reaper put me in and told me the location of the Pentarax tower. He was fae once, right?"

"He was the first king of the fae," Saraya said quietly. "Fern the First, he was called." The Old Ones looked at Saraya sharply. This was news to everyone, then. "We are both Niyati."

I'd learnt this world only yesterday, when Saraya told me that she and Drake were creatures bound in *destiny*. That a Niyati was a being who created a crucial turning point in the world. They were often destructive, which is why when they were born, their mate was also created to help control their power. Two sides of a coin.

"But why help us?" Zale asked.

My eyes fell to my sister's naval, where a number of bonds emerged, but one of them stood out, tentative but glistening.

"Because," I said, squinting at that thread, "that means

there is still something unfinished between us. I see the thread from you, well enough. I also owe him a debt."

"What in the seven Goddesses does he want from *us*?" Saraya threw her hands up in the air and everyone in the vicinity flinched as if lightning was going to come out at any moment. No one was going to forget the way she razed the battlefield.

I laughed darkly. "There's only one way to find out."

THAT EVENING, ON SARAYA'S OFFICE BALCONY, WE SUMMONED Whole-Feather, who'd been hanging around Quartz in case we needed him, and asked if he could find the Kraasputin. After a slightly uneasy bow, he said he could, and Zale and Drake insisted we follow him.

Saraya and I exchanged a look, but both males were adamant.

"See?" I said. "They're no good together."

"You're right," Saraya said loudly. "They'll need to be separated soon."

I ignored the smack Drake gave to my sister's ass as Zale burst into his eagle form. Drake let out a—if I'm honest—slightly mad cackle as he leapt onto the balcony railing. Whole-Feather beat his wings and leapt into the sky as I climbed onto Zale's back. Saraya let out a laugh as Drake grabbed her and they fell off the railing together, only for Drake to soar back up into the twilight sky on shadowy wings, with Saraya held underneath him, her arms outstretched as she was flying, too. There was a grin on my face as Zale let out a cry and we leapt into the air after them.

Below us, the citizens of Lobrathia laughed and waved at us. We spotted Malika and Atax waving where they stood with the Old Ones and fae in the city, helping with repairing a house destroyed by the demons.

A lot of Lobrathia had been desecrated by the demons during their brief rule, and the Old Ones and Ellythians were more than glad to help before we were to leave next week. We had our own kingdoms to rebuild, after all.

It did not take Whole-Feather long to find Kraasputin. He began his descent into the southern area of the forest that stretched out at the edge of Quartz.

"I suppose he wanted to be near in case anything interesting happened," Zale said wryly to me.

My feelings about Kraasputin were mixed, and I'd told Saraya, Drake, and Zale what he'd said to me in the demon realm. There was a kindness in him, and Saraya agreed with me.

We landed in a clearing in the darkness, with only Saraya's purple quartz bracelets lighting up our faces. Zale changed back into his human form.

"Where is he?" Saraya said, casting her eye about suspiciously.

Whole-Feather let out a low hoot, jerking his beak up ahead, and both Drake and Zale crowded around both of us sisters.

He arrived in a whoosh of black and burning coals, and just for a moment, he looked like the Reaper, making me startle. But those burning orange flames for eyes were something the Reaper never had.

Saraya flinched, but then said calmly, "Hello, Fern."

He visibly shivered at hearing his old name. I said, "Sir, the game is up. We know you wanted us to owe you something. I see the unfinished bonds."

"Clever queensssss," Kraasputin said in his deathly hiss,

but his tone was not unkind. "Sistersssss reunited." He turned to me. "You have the Boneweaver Bow, I hear?"

"Thanks to you," I said evenly. "Yes, I retrieved it."

Those flames licked in their sockets.

"My one wish," he said, "is that, at a time of my choosing, one day, when I ask for it, that you will end me." The clearing was silent as a cool breeze slipped past us and we registered his words. The first king of the fae was asking us to take his life.

"Why?" I breathed, but I thought I knew the answer already.

"I have been alive long enough," he whispered. "Too long. Weary are my bones. My mind. My soul. I will be ready soon."

"You helped us," Saraya said wryly, "when you could have caused more trouble."

"I am not an evil creature," he hissed softly. "Not purely, in any case. I remember being good and wise. Not all was lost to the void." He turned to me with those burning orbs and I shivered as I knew his meaning. Not a bad creature. Not a bad person. Twisted. Sometimes cruel. Capable of bad things. But capable of good things too.

"A Niyati can only be killed by another Niyati," Saraya said. "But we don't have another Darkmaul Dagger."

"Indeed, Your Highnessss. The dagger is for containing only, not killing. The Green Reaper is a being tied to others, that is why his death wasn't an option. But I am tied to no one. You will not need a dagger. That is why we also need both the Temari Blade and the Boneweaver Bow. To be certain. The weapons of Agnolthi and Umali assure me. It will also keep my Tyaag safe." He inclined his head to Drake and

449

something passed between them until my brother-in-law nodded back.

I let out a long exhale, as did Saraya.

"And you are sure about this?" I asked. "This is all you want?"

"I have had long to think about it. And long to plan your debt to me to secure it. I wish to be put out of my misery."

"I can respect that," Zale said suddenly. "And I'm only two hundred years old."

The laugh that burst from me made me cover my mouth. "I can respect it too, King Fern." I curtseyed. "When you are ready, I will be there."

Saraya smiled at me. "As will I, Your Majesty."

Kraasputin seemed to sigh with relief, his shoulders moving just a little. Then he bowed. "My thanks."

"If you are not asking for our wives to do it tonight, will you sit with us?" Zale asked smoothly. A small campfire suddenly began from a bunch of dry sticks and three logs rolled themselves to form a circle around it. "We are kings and queens, after all. It would do us some good to speak." Zale smiled down at me and I returned it. Whole-Feather sidled up to the fire, settling down between the logs to warm his wings.

Kraasputin looked at Zale intently for a moment. "Indeed?"

Zale shrugged one shoulder. "I'm sure there are many things I could tell you about what I learned with the Reaper. For interest's sake. And... if you are going to die, someone should know your story."

"A good idea," Drake said, taking Saraya's hand and pulling her over to sit on one of the logs.

"For interest's sake," Kraasputin repeated carefully, before slowly making his way to a log.

Zale and I sat down opposite Saraya and Drake.

After a moment, Kraasputin began speaking, and for the next hour, the five of us sat, riveted.

There was a low, groaning sound, and I abruptly realised it was coming from my own throat. I squeezed my eyes, then blinked them slowly open to find the world was blurry. I was lying down on something soft, but it did nothing for the burning, world shattering pain in every bone of my body. My thoughts scrambled, memories and visions and dreams melding together in a whirlwind. I tried to separate them, tried to make sense of what I'd seen. *Where* I'd been. A deep sense in my gut of something *more*.

"Confusion!" came a squeak. "Pain."

"She's waking up!" came a female voice. "Oh Goddess, they're both waking up!"

"You stupid, stupid girl!" came an elderly woman's voice, choked up.

"Now, is that any way to speak to someone who's just woken up from the dead?" came a third familiar voice.

"I can't say I recommend it," Yulara muttered from next to me.

Awareness zapped me like one of Altara's lightning bolts, and I sat up so fast my muscles screamed and my head spun. But I ignored it all to look down at the person next to me. The person whose hand I held. Yulara's face—a face made by the Goddesses themselves—was squinting back at me. I looked down at our entwined hands and Yulara gave me a squeeze.

But then I saw something that made me gasp out loud. "Goddess!" My voice was a broken croak, but I couldn't care less as I raised our joined hands to look at the back of mine, and then the back of hers.

The black ink was not earthly in origin, *could not be*, for the perfect, intricate way it marked the back of our hands. My right, her left.

Identical marks. A scythe, wrapped in daises.

Yulara smiled weakly at me. "Rani. My Rani," she whispered.

This woman had died for me. With me. We'd been to a place that had been *more* than this place. A place I'd never forget. And now...

To my surprise, Wobbles, Zale's small companion made of shells glued together, stumbled forward and placed his tiny hand on ours. "Love." He said, looking up at me.

I finally looked around the room we were in. Plush curtains, luxurious rugs, stone floors, golden walls. This was Lota Palace. And standing in front of me was Pia, her emerald green eyes bright and filled with tears.

"Pia?" I whispered.

She smiled, nodding and reaching out to hug me around the neck. Matrika's sword was at her side.

"We won?" I whispered in disbelief. So it had worked? *Had* it worked? "We won?" I asked.

E.P. BALI

Pia straightened and my eyes passed to Geravie, dabbing her eyes in a chair by the window, but standing opposite her, with her hand pressed against her mouth and tears streaming from her eyes, was a woman I'd not seen in four years.

"Mother?" It was a broken, choking sound that I barely recognised as my own.

"We won, Rani," my mother whispered. "Because of you, the Reaper was sent out of Lota Island, only to be vanquished by Queen Altara and Queen Saraya in Lobrathia. It... It's over. *All* over." Her eyes flicked to Pia, and so did mine.

My best friend was staring evenly at my mother, her hands crossed over her chest. "Rani and Yulara will be ladies of *my* court," she said firmly. "Yulara's family will have to work to win back my good graces after the dark magic they used, and so will you for your lack of intervention."

To my startled surprise, my mother curtseyed deeply. "Yes, Your Majesty. We are determined to do that."

Pia—Queen Pia, oh how my heart swelled—looked down at me and her arms fell to her sides, the smile reappearing on her face. She nodded to where I still held Yulara's hand. "They appeared not long after you came back to life."

"But how?" I asked in disbelief.

"We are mates," Yulara whispered. "Our union is ordained by the heavens, Rani. As we always knew." I swallowed thickly at what I saw in Yulara's eyes. They were shadowed, haunted, an awareness of things that we were never supposed to know. I knew my own eyes reflected that same shadow. But we were back here. Amongst our friends. To live our lives again. A decision Pia had made. A command to Cholnayak to return us. Yulara's eyes shifted to Pia's and I only saw gratitude in them. I turned to look at my friend, my

454

queen and my heart swelled. She'd given us another chance at this.

"The stars are always watching," Geravie said in a low voice. "And apparently, so is the Queen of Ellythia."

Pia gave Yulara and me the most brilliant smile.

EPILOGUE: ZALE

FOUR WEEKS LATER

The night was bright on Boneweaver Island, and the beach was stunning under the full moon and all the stars. The Great Star burned a solid white, once again, over the island, and watching *my* Altara's face as she looked up at it made my heart fill to bursting.

"Are you ready?" my wife asked me, her ever-watchful emeralds on my face.

I dragged my own eyes down her perfect, luscious form. She was dressed in the traditional gown of the High Priestess of Agnolthi made by the town seamstresses off a pattern for Boneweaver Queens the island monsters had dug up in my family castle. It was a deep plum gown that hugged her curves like a silken glove, the plunging neckline showing the space between her breasts and the long chain of diamonds I'd gifted her from the solar fae realm. There was a dainty star sat the end of it, right between her breasts.

I leaned down and brushed my lips against it. "Wife, I've been ready since the first day I dragged you onto this beach to marry me."

Altara shivered as I straightened. She placed her callused hands on either side of my face and planted a sweet kiss on my lips.

With Saraya's and Pia's coronations behind us, and Palace Boneweaver about halfway finished, it only seemed right for our coronation to be held. We had attended Saraya and Drake's coronation a few weeks ago, and then came back to Boneweaver Island to begin planning for our new lives with our court.

With the help of the island monsters, we'd set about rebuilding Boneweaver Palace and repairing any damage to the island towns that had been caused by the demons. We'd travelled to each town and village to personally offer the residents a place in our kingdom, or if they wished, to find their fortunes on Tiger or Lota Island as part of the Ellythian queendom.

Most chose to stay. Having spent many generations here already, they considered it their home. Armsmistress Vari and Lady Trisane also chose to stay and run the school, which would no longer be a place of exile, but a school where any girl who wanted to learn magic or fighting could come and be taught by the best. Raen was building another school for males, so that eventually, when our children grew up, they would have a place where both Old Ones and Ellythians studied and played together.

Tonight was not just about Altara and me, it was about all of us. As I grasped her hand and we walked out of the jungle path, down the sand to the quartz altar together, we walked past our gathered friends and family.

Our bond thrummed as I felt Altara's emotions soar with joy. Everyone who could come from town had come, along with our court of Old Ones. My cousin Ulanna and her mate,

Ulfas. Odeelia and a few members of her court stood next to them, the carnal fae queen modest in a gown of green and gold, her crown sparkling under the moon. To my surprise, she wept as we passed, nodding in encouragement and dabbing a handkerchief to her eye.

On Altara's side, her Nine witches were present in their astral forms, as well as Armsmistress Vari, Lady Trisane and the girls Altara saved from the school, who were openly crying too. Geravie, the priestesses Reshmi and Keshmi, held the two pixies, Leela and Trouble, the light surrounding them making them look like golden orbs. Altara's senior priestesses were also present, Mahi, Esha and Joshi. Next to them were Malika, our Queen Pia, Uncle Tuskus, and Paalus. Rani and Yulara held hands next to them, with Wobbles on Rani's shoulder, his conch shell head resting against her neck. The two young women now always had a distant and knowing look in their eyes that told me they'd seen things mortals were not meant to see, during their brief deaths. They hadn't parted since they had woken up, and had continued to serve in Cholnayak's temple as volunteers, not Widows. Rani's hair was growing strong, now curling about her young, but too-old eyes.

At the head of Altara's side stood Saraya and Drake, my sister-in-law's Lota-green eyes shining as she held Drake's hand. Fluffy, the black fae creature, sat on his shoulder, while Opal, the rainbow coloured one, sat on Saraya's, their mouths slightly parted in wonder.

On my right, up close to the altar, was Raen and Atax, who was holding Kai's hand as he wiped his eyes, his upper lip trembling. His hair had been braided by Malika, and it looked beautiful with a tiny frangipani tucked in the side. Malika and Atax were were now our ambassadors and together, they travelled between Ellythia and Boneweaver Island conveying news and negotiating trade contracts. It was the best sort of role for them and they enjoyed the travel alone together.

Altara and I came to a halt before the quartz altar.

"Lucky you wore clothes for this," she said snidely.

Indeed, both of us *should* have been naked, but practically everyone except Odeelia begged me to forgo the rule. I looked down at myself, smirking. The pants were a fine black cotton and the shirt and a short-sleeved obsidian silk embroidered with purple and gold beasts and a full moon. It was perhaps the finest thing I'd ever worn, though I loved the way Altara looked at me when I showed up in it more than wearing the thing itself.

As we waited for the moon to reach its peak in the sky, I closed my eyes and felt the entirety of Boneweaver Island under my feet. A few tigers had come to watch the coronation, as well as some zekar and the island monsters, all hidden in the depths of the jungle so that only the hairs on the backs of the arms knew they were really standing there. The fae lagoon just south of here had an octopus exploring its tunnel from the ocean, and in Taraka town, a baby wailed for his parents. His father went to him, after kissing his pregnant wife on the brow at the kitchen table.

A little pang of longing struck me in that moment, and perhaps I was unprepared for it because I opened my eyes to find them a little damp as I looked at my wife.

"I want to fill your belly with cubs," I said out loud.

Drake let out a sound that was half a snort, half choked laugh, while Saraya elbowed him. Raen just smirked.

"Hurry up and make us uncles!" Atax whisper-yelled at me. Our family around us sniggered.

My wife only turned her emerald eyes to me and smiled a secret smile. Agnolthi's mark on her forehead suddenly lit up pink.

Geravie let out a sharp "*shhh*" as the quartz altar lit up before us and a sweet, celestial wind stirred our hair.

The earth groaned under us and began to tremble. We all dropped to our knees as behind the altar, Agnolthi appeared on the back of her lion steed, framed by the swelling, midnight ocean.

Her lion let out a mighty roar, sharp canines flashing white. I felt extremely compelled to shift and return the gesture, but I refrained, gritting my teeth and returning his amber-eyed stare.

The townsfolk began weeping behind us.

Agnolthi was magnificent—so much like my Altara—with her leaf-green eyes, cascading inky black hair, golden skin, and long black trailing gown. Her lips were painted a deep crimson and black tattoos lined her face and fingers. In one hand, she held an arrow, in the other, a small black cauldron. With celestial grace, she slid off her lion and strode so lightly across the sand to the altar that she appeared to skim the ground. Altara's hand found mine, and she squeezed it reassuringly.

Agnolthi smiled down at us, her voice resounding in all of our minds, in that way of Goddesses. "*Under the stars we make a king tonight. Under the moon we make a queen. Bring forth the crown.*"

Behind us, Ulanna leapt to her feet and carefully brought my crown to the altar and placed it there with a deep bow. Agnolthi lifted the obsidian glass and gold crown, smiling as she weighed it in her hands. It had been made by my court, down in the active volcano we called The Womb off the western coast of Boneweaver Island. A Boneweaver king's crown-making was a ritual event where his court mined the obsidian, then beat and forged it with their combined magic. It was an approval, a blessing, a wish.

"*This crown was made with loving hands, Ashzale Boneweaver,*" Agnolthi said. "*Your beasts have seen you and marked you as theirs. Marked you as worthy.*" She held up the crown for everyone to see. "*And now I mark you as worthy. I anoint you, King Ashzale Boneweaver, High Priest of Agnolthi, Starborn, cursed-born, curse-free. Stand.*"

As I rose, my crown landed heavy on my head, Agnolthi's power bearing down on me. "*May you rule wisely. May you rule fairly.*"

"I will," I promised.

"*Bring forth the queen's crown.*"

While the king's crown was forged by his people, the Boneweaver Queen's crown was forged by her king. While I'd given Altara a temporary diadem down in Odeelia's court, her official crown had been made by me, alone in the fires of The Womb. For hours I toiled in there, magicking the perfect obsidian glass, tipped with pearls. It was fierce and proud, beautiful and regal, just like her. I summoned it in a flash of light and laid it upon the altar. The light of the quartz illuminated it perfectly, as I'd planned, showing the tiny pinpoints of light that looked like stars, sparkling all the way through its surface. It glittered like her skin when she sank into her full power.

Altara gasped next to me, still on her knees, and Agnolthi gave an approving smile.

"*This crown was made by your king husband, your starborn mate, Altara Yasani Voltanius. You have proven yourself worthy. The beasts and birds and the island itself have deemed you worthy of your crown. Your title.*" She took the crown and held it up, and I heard Saraya and Geravie crying quietly. "*I anoint you Queen Altara Yasani Voltanius Boneweaver, High Priestess of Agnolthi, star forged, storm forged, lightning forged. Curse-breaker, bond-breaker, wielder of the Boneweaver Bow. Rise.*"

Altara stood next to me, the Bow appearing in her hands, its golden light illuminating her face as her crown appeared on her dark hair. She laid the Bow on the altar as Agnolthi ran her hands lovingly along the surface. "*I bless this Bow, this celestial weapon. May it serve you well.*"

Altara took back her bow, hefting it easily despite its considerable weight.

"*Turn and greet your people and beasts as their king and queen.*"

The ground shook as we turned and we knew Agnolthi had gone. I took Altara's hand and several mighty roars from the jungle shook the sand under our feet. Excited, our Old Ones burst into their beast forms and let out roars, howls, and cries themselves. I grinned at them all as our humans cheered and clapped.

Altara caught my eye and quirked a dark brow.

Traditionally, a Boneweaver king took his queen in front of his court. But when Altara had mentioned it, I had wryly shaken my head and said that times had moved on, and I didn't think any of my brothers would appreciate that at all.

I wasn't my father, and Altara agreed.

So I took her hand as she returned the Bow into her astral repository, and our friends parted for us as we walked through them and down the beach, cheering in our wake. My hand tightened around Altara's, my heart pounding, the grin on my face starting to hurt my cheeks. We kicked off our shoes and walked through the warm tide until the sounds of our friends and their partying were but a whisper in the wind. We didn't speak, out loud or through our bond, as we walked, our fingers twined tightly around each other's. The sound of the ocean—*our* ocean—was a melody that made my heart sing, where it thudded red and true and *all* hers.

Altara sighed as she looked upon the moon, a soft smile on her lips. I stopped there, just to look at her, the perfect planes of her nose and her jaw as the moonlight worshipped her features. Her eyelashes were pretty fans across her cheeks, her lips plump and inviting. I couldn't help but move even closer towards her and she instinctively turned to me, her eyes still closed.

"Zale," she breathed. Her voice alone held the power to send my blood roaring. I brushed my lips against one of her cheeks and then the other, my fingers under the soft skin of her jaw. She smiled, and I kissed her lips. "My king."

My cock woke up in my pants. "My queen," I whispered against her mouth.

"Take me amongst the waves." To my delight, she pulled away from me, her eyes blinking open, and she stalked into the water, her fingers unlacing the ties at her back. I watched her for a moment. My goddess of a wife, as her gown slipped slowly down her shoulders, her back, the soft curve of her hips, down her full thighs, and into the tide. She looked at me over her shoulder, a mischievous smile a call to the beast inside of me.

"I'm coming," I said hastily, suddenly realising I'd been staring and not moving. Ripping off my shirt, I tossed it to the sand. I pulled down my pants and made my way to her, completely naked with only the stars to bear witness.

My arms came around to caress her stomach as she pulled her hair to one side to allow me to kiss the soft skin of her neck. She melted into me, our bodies softening into each other as the water swelled around our ankles. And then she turned, her fingertips brushing up my arms until they came around my neck, leaving fire in their wake. She jumped up, and I caught her around her backside in time for her to kiss me fully. Me entire body burned as I kissed my wife deeply, my tongue caressing hers, my hunger for her growing until I was a rumbling, growling mess, and she was moaning and writhing against my manhood.

I dropped to the brushing tide, laying her on the wet sand; the water surging around us only to retreat as I devoured her mouth, her neck, her breasts. Those beautiful nipples were peaked in the night and I feasted on them, forcing her to make delicious sounds of pleasure. It spurred me on, licking and sucking her precious skin, lower and lower until her sweet pussy was in my mouth, my hands lifting her ass up to meet my tongue away from the water. Her heady taste, her powerful scent, was enough to drive me mad, but I wouldn't have her until she screamed for me—and she did. With her hands on her breasts, she gave into my tongue as I flicked her nub, calling out my name in a way that made me rock hard and ready. Only then did I leap up and sheathe myself in her wet heat, completely and all at once. She moaned, deep in her throat, calling out my name again. But I was beyond words now, the beast in me completely entranced by his mate's scent and sound, her delicious warmth, the perfect flush of her skin.

"Take me, Zale," she moaned, holding onto me as if she wanted my entire body inside of hers. "Oh Goddess, take me."

"Tell me you are mine," I managed to get out between deep, powerful thrusts.

"I'm yours. Oh Goddess, I'm yours. Who else's would I be?"

I slammed into her like the beast I was, grunting with each thrust, growling, and hoping that she understood how obsessed I was with her, how much she meant to me, not just her body but her entire being, her very soul. Our bond sang and screamed with pleasure, humming a sacred, golden tune older than time.

Roaring, I drove myself into her until I was dizzy, but my cock wanted more, my bond wanted *more*. Her magic poured into me and I poured myself into her mixing with one another until even I couldn't tell which was which and who was who. With my nose full of her precious scent, I thrust her legs over my shoulders and stilled. She opened her eyes, those emeralds were pure, joyous, *light*.

"My mate," I growled reverently, brushing my knuckles down her cheek. And then I said the words that Boneweaver males had been saying, asking of their mates since the dawn of time. "Will you do me the honour of having my cubs? Will you bear my seed with your power, with your body?"

She shivered and her perfect lips smiled. "Can you scent that I'm ovulating?"

I rubbed my nose against her calf and rumbled my assent. Her smell was sweet and alluring, a signal to me, a hope.

Altara cleared her throat and sighed with satisfaction. "Ashzale?" I stared down at her intently, every cell in my body poised with infinite concentration. I did not breathe. Then her eyes bore into mine and she said with a savage sort of seriousness. "*Breed me, husband. Give me your seed. Come in me.*" Her power flared. "It would be an honour to bear your cubs with my power. With my body."

I could have roared into the night for the desire and satisfaction that poured through me. My magic pummelled down my stomach and my balls were suddenly heavy and aching with pure *rabid* need that could only be satisfied by this woman.

I rutted into my wife.

Deeply, powerfully, wanting to give her everything, all of me, all of what I had in this body. My hips were frenzied as they thrust, her cries desperate and pleading, and just when I thought I was about to lose control, I came into her so hard that when I roared, the birds and beasts fled from the nearby jungle.

Altara screamed my name, her fingernails digging into my arms as she cried out how much she loved me, over and over, and I tried to tell her without words, with my hips and magic alone, that I loved her more than life, more than anything that existed. My magic soared into her and her power met mine glowing with brilliant force. Deep within her sacred place they combined in a dance as old as the stars.

When we made our way down from the high of release, I lay on the sand with her head on my chest, my cock still in her heat, looking up at the sea of stars above us and the sea of water around us. Everything was perfect.

"This heart," she murmured, tracing the skin of my chest with her gentle finger. "This heart is good, Zale."

I placed my hand on hers and swallowed. "Even if it's not," I said into her sweet-smelling hair. "You'll be here to tell me. To keep me in line."

I could feel her smile along my chest. "And you have to keep *me* in line."

My arms tightened around her. "Never. You doing whatever you want is so much fun to watch." Her scent was heaven in my nose, ambrosial, like a divine flower made just for me and—

My magic reared its head, the beast in me freezing, listening, scenting.

"Tara?" my voice was hoarse.

"Yes?" she said playfully.

"Is— Is that…"

She sat up and looked down at me, biting her lip. Gods, she was beautiful, framed by the heavens, with me still inside of her. Tugging on my hand, she laid it on her lower stomach, just above the dark curls of her hair. "Do you feel it?" Her eyes were lined with silver until they were overfilled, and two tears streamed down her cheeks. "It's only early. We'll have to watch it take root together but the magic has…"

New magic pooled deep within her, my hand heating up as it felt *it*. It wasn't Altara's power I was feeling, but something completely new. Something borne of our combined powers. It was as blue and as pure as the summer sky.

My heart—my old, red beating heart—tried to leap out of its ribcage. I sat up and kissed my wife square on her lips, almost wishing Wobbles was here to define the maelstrom of emotions in my heart. But I only needed my precious Tara. I whispered her name in reverence, because that was the only acceptable thing to say. To worship at the feet of this woman who'd already given me so much and was about to give me more. I needed to be worthy of it; I needed to make sure she was safe and plump with food and pink-cheeked with happiness, and our palace was not even ready—

"You're not going to get all beastly, are you?" she said, placing a hand over mine where it still felt her stomach.

"Oh," I said, shaking my head and marvelling at this new, miraculous kind of magic and the way it was lacing with hers. This feeling of being whole, complete. Of being in love with this woman and the life we would lead together. The lives we would bring into this world together. "You thought I was beastly before?" I let out a low, dark laugh. "You have no idea."

EPILOGUE: ALTARA

Deep in Blossom Court of the Solar Fae Realm lay the garden of the great Mother Jacaranda, where new kings and queens came to get words of wisdom for their reign.

It was here that my mother received the prophecy that would change everything by giving her the choice to go to Quartz to have her daughters, or to stay in Ellythia.

My mother had made the most difficult choice of her life, and because of it, the realms of our great Earth were joined by peace.

Drake and Saraya had come with their guard, Slade and Lysander, while Kai, Atax and Malika had come to escort me and Zale. In her hands, Malika held the long parchment which made up the United Realms Treaty, which the rulers of all the kingdoms—human, fae and beast—had signed. We were going to build a new world where there could be free movement and trade between the Human Realm, the Dark Fae Realm, Solar Fae Realm, Ellythia and Boneweaver Island. There was still a lot to rebuild, but we were well on our way.

Saraya walked out of the curling golden gates and towards the waiting Drake. She smiled reassuringly at me as she passed, looking positively queenly in purple, the sunlight catching on her quartz crown. I breathed a small sigh of relief seeing that smile, and brushed a hand over my lower belly.

I had been watching the tiny seed inside me grow every day, and sure enough, its signature had grown such that Zale estimated, by the time we returned to our court, the Old Ones would be able to scent my pregnancy. He claimed that all hell would break loose—with joy—as this was the first Boneweaver child in centuries. Drake had known right away, cocking his head when we'd first arrived here and a small smile on my face was all the confirmation he needed to grin at me, the stars in his all-black eyes turning a brilliant gold for a brief moment.

And then Zale was prowling towards me across the verdant grass, like he always prowled at me, with that tiger's lope. His blue eyes were as clear as the tropical sea on a summer's day and just as warm. "Ready?" he asked, taking my hand. He was magnificent in the obsidian crown our beasts had given him, along with black pants and a black coat.

I wore full regalia as well, a deep pink gown and black sash, my obsidian and pearl tiara and my hair long and loose.

"Ready," I confirmed.

We walked through the golden gates, the glittering metal depicting the first king and queen of the fae. The immortal jacaranda trees lining the stone path were in perpetual bloom, their blossoms a stunning violet and purple explosion. A cool breeze rustled their leaves as we passed, as if they spoke to one another of secret and mysterious things only trees knew. They carried a sweet, fresh scent to my nose that reminded me of new spring, picnics in the shade, and swimming in sapphire blue lakes.

As our bond buzzed under my giddy energy, Zale made a contented sound at the back of his throat and sent an impression down our golden rope that suggested we'd be swimming naked in a fae lake before the day was up. I chuckled softly under my breath, still in disbelief that *this* was my life now.

At the end of the path stood the mighty Mother Jacaranda, the Queen of Trees, her ancient form reaching high into the sky with the biggest branches I'd ever seen. Her trunk was a rich brown, her adorning blossoms every shade of purple imaginable, a crown of her own making.

My mother had stood on this spot once, had heard of the fate of her potential daughters. She'd made a decision here and the weight of that bore down on my shoulders.

A voice like the old dark places between roots came to my mental ear. *"Who approaches?"*

Zale squeezed my hand and said evenly, "I am King Ashzale Boneweaver, High Priest of Agnolthi, and this is my wife, Queen Altara Yasani Voltanius Boneweaver, High Priestess of Agnolthi."

"Star-born, storm-forged," she replied, her flowers rustling. *"Let us see what omens are whispered on the winds of time and space."*

It was a warm, magical wind that swept around us, searching, questioning, finding. Goosebumps erupted all over my arms, and the golden bond between us hummed contentedly. A second bond now lay between us, a pure-white bond of creation and I couldn't wait to watch it grow.

When her voice came next, it was warm like summer rain. *"The stars speak. The stars have spoken. The stars are always watching, King and Queen Boneweaver. They tell me of great deeds, of great duty, of great love."* She shivered all the way up to her highest leaves, and I practically quivered with anticipation. Zale glanced at me, his lips twitching. Whatever she had to say, we would deal with, together. *"They tell me they plan to send you many star-seeds, should you request it."* A breath. *"Maybe too many."*

I stilled on the spot, then managed to raise my brows up at Zale. His shoulders were shaking with silent laughter.

"She means..." I said in disbelief, looking down at my lower stomach where magic now danced in dense blue light.

"Yes." He chuckled, his eyes glistening.

I turned back to the Mother Jacaranda. "Is that it?"

Her voice was melodious with humour. *"You will reign with the stars at your back, Queen Boneweaver, have no doubt about it."*

Zale bowed deeply, his hand over his heart, and I curt-seyed, low. "Our thanks," he murmured, throwing me a smirk.

We made our way back out of the garden and through the golden gates where Zale promptly leaned down and buried his face in my neck, inhaling like he wanted to get drunk on my scent, the tickle of his breath giving me butterflies. I would never hear the end of this, I was positive. No doubt all Zale heard was permission to have as many cubs as possible.

"Permission to fuck as much as possible, you mean," he said down the golden rope.

"You awful beast!" I slapped him on the chest in false admonishment, then I grinned. *"We would have done that anyway."*

When we broke apart, I rested my cheek on his chest and looked at my sister and her husband. The way Drake dotingly looked at Saraya was something out of this world. Something more than the grass and the trees and the wind. Something sacred.

As if he knew what I was thinking, Zale murmured into my mind, *"What do you see when you look at them?"*

I swallowed thickly. *"The same thing I see when I look at you, when I look at my brothers."* I turned my face up towards his and he tucked a strand of hair behind my ear. *"Something deeper than love, if that's possible,"* I said. *"His heart beats for her. His entire being orbits her as the Earth orbits the sun."*

Zale smiled. *"And he will orbit around her until the end of time. Just as I will for you. Perhaps the four of us will sit upon the star that made us and laugh at the antics of our grandchildren."*

My heart swelled to the size of the giant trees around us. I felt Saraya's eyes on mine and turned to look at her. Her head was tilted against Drake's shoulder in the most endearing way, her eyes glimmering emerald gems under the fae sun.

"You look so happy, Tara," she said softly.

I sent my magic outwards to her, a small, beckoning invitation. Her brows rose a little at the request, but her magic swept towards me, an evening tide brushing against my insides, the gentle midwife checking me over.

When she reached my womb, her mouth fell open and her hand came to her lips. The backs of my eyes were aflame as I nodded in confirmation. Saraya's crescent moon priestess mark burned brightly, her eyes spilling with tears as she rushed at me with a sudden sob. When we wrapped our arms around each other, she smelled like flowers and the power of a latent storm.

"We have everything we could ever want, little sister" she whispered into my ear. "Our parents would be so proud of us. Of us and the family we've made. Of what we overcame to get here and what is to come."

I sniffed. "I wish they could've met our husbands. And our children."

Next to us, Drake slung his arm around Zale, murmuring his congratulations.

Saraya kissed the top of my head and leaned her forehead against mine. Our priestess marks burned against each other. Two fires that could never be put out. "One day we'll meet again," she said softly. "And when we do, they will tell us that they were watching the entire time."

The End

of

The Archer Princess Trilogy

Thank you for coming with me on this epic saga about the Voltanius sisters!

If you enjoyed this novel, pretty please leave a review at the retailer of purchase, it helps me make a living out of my work.

Signing up to my mailing list means that you get first peek at everything I produce, including book covers, new releases, exclusive excerpts and bonus material that I don't post anywhere else.

Check it out at www.ektaabali.com

If you love Zale and his brothers and want more male leads just like him (and perhaps even more villainous) you'll love Scythe, Savage, Xander & co in Her Vicious Beasts, my MFMMMM Contemporary Fantasy WhyChoose Shifter Romance. Read the prequel free is this anthology.

If you'd like to find more about Hugh and Chrysalis School, take a look at my Upper YA series: The Travellers

ACKNOWLEDGMENTS

Phew! I can't believe this series has come to an end. That was six books, around 600k words, written in about 14 months.

When I first wrote the Warrior Midwife, I never actually intended to write Archer Princess. But around the beginning of writing Warrior Queen, I knew it was needed and am SO happy with the way this saga has turned out. At the beginning of 2022, I would never have guessed that *this* would be the result. But it could never have happened without the help of a whole group of people that I will be eternally grateful for.

Thank you to my parents for putting up with me and dodgy writerly moods—my tears and frustrations. Thank you for the cupcakes each release and for supporting me in not only becoming a midwife but also starting an independent publishing business.

Carly was the first person I contacted to make my covers and I knew from the start that they were going to be something special. These covers just kept getting better and better, with all the little details you included, everything came out perfectly. Thank you.

This final book was edited by Maxine, Sheree and Carrie. Thank you for your tireless efforts, your keen fae eyes and for generally hyping me up and giving me all your real-time reactions. I'll treasure those always.

Finally, thank you to everyone who has taken the time to read this entire series. It's been a journey we've had together with Saraya, Drake, Altara and Zale. Sometimes it's a little scary to me how real they are, and if their stories touched you, I am glad for it. They'll always be there, living their lives in Quartz and Boneweaver Island and whenever you want to visit them, make sure you say hello for me.

ABOUT THE AUTHOR

Ektaa P. Bali was born in Fiji and spent most of her life in Melbourne, Australia.

After graduating Killester College in 2008, she studied nursing and midwifery at Deakin University, going on to spend eight years as a midwife in various hospitals.

She published her first novel in 2020, the beginning of a middle grade fantasy series, before going on to pursue her true passion: Young & New Adult Fantasy.

She currently lives in Brisbane, Australia.

facebook.com/ektaabaliauthor
instagram.com/ektaabaliauthor
youtube.com/ektaabali

ALSO BY E.P. BALI

New Adult Fantasy

The Ellythian Princesses:

#1 The Warrior Midwife

#2 The Warrior Priestess

#3 The Warrior Queen

#1 The Archer Princess

#2 The Archer Witch

#3 The Archer Queen

Her Vicious Beasts:

#0 The Beginning Prequel

#1 Her Feral Beasts

#2 Her Rabid Beasts

#3 Her Tortured Beasts

#4 Her Psycho Beasts

#5 Her Monstrous Beasts

Upper YA Dark Fantasy

The Travellers:

#1 The Chrysalis Key

#2 The Allure of Power

#3 The Wings of Darkness